MAGICAL MOONLIGHT

She opened her eyes to find they were in a sheltered glade on the far side of the lake. Lacy ferns and shrubs grew all around them. Moonlight shimmered in ribbons of silver on the face of the water. "It's beautiful."

"You are," he said, his voice thick.

"Thank you."

"Kathy…"

Just her name, yet she heard a hundred and twenty-five years of loneliness, of yearning, in his voice.

He slid his knuckles over her cheek. His thumb traced the outline of her lips, and then he kissed her.

Magic. It could only be magic, the rush of emotion that swelled up within her heart and soul. He was so gentle, so tender, she knew somehow that he was as awed by what was happening between them as she was.

Other *Leisure* and *Love Spell* books by
Madeline Baker:

WARRIOR'S LADY
LOVE FOREVERMORE
LOVE IN THE WIND
FEATHER IN THE WIND
CHASE THE WIND
THE ANGEL & THE OUTLAW
LAKOTA RENEGADE
APACHE RUNAWAY
BENEATH A MIDNIGHT MOON
CHEYENNE SURRENDER
WARRIOR'S LADY
THE SPIRIT PATH
MIDNIGHT FIRE
COMANCHE FLAME
PRAIRIE HEAT
A WHISPER IN THE WIND
FORBIDDEN FIRES
LACEY'S WAY
FIRST LOVE, WILD LOVE
RENEGADE HEART
RECKLESS DESIRE
RECKLESS LOVE
RECKLESS HEART

Under A Prairie Moon

Madeline Baker

LEISURE BOOKS   NEW YORK CITY

In memory of Eddie Little Sky,
who was my first "crush" and the inspiration
for all my dark handsome heroes.

A LEISURE BOOK®

June 1998

Published by

Dorchester Publishing Co., Inc.
276 Fifth Avenue
New York, NY 10001

ISBN 0-8439-4372-6

The name "Leisure Books" and the stylized "L" with design are trademarks of Dorchester Publishing Co., Inc.

Printed in the United States of America.

Prologue

A lynch mob was an ugly thing. Dalton Crowkiller stared down at the handful of men who surrounded him, his heart pounding like a runaway locomotive, his throat desert dry, his palms damp. He shifted in the saddle, feeling the rough edge of the noose tighten around his neck.

The big bay beneath him stamped restlessly. In moments, someone would give the horse a sharp slap on the rump and there would be nothing between him and death but a few feet of rope.

He swallowed the bile that rose in his throat as he tried to imagine what those last moments would be like. If he was lucky, the drop would break his neck and his dying would be quick and merciful. If not . . .

He shook the gruesome image from his mind as his gaze shifted to the woman standing in the distance. The breeze stirred the hem of her long white nightgown and ruffled the collar of the blue silk robe she wore over it. Her hair, the reddish-brown of autumn leaves, tumbled over her shoulders. She was staring back at him, her eyes wide and scared and guilt-ridden.

His gaze imprisoned hers. If she had the nerve, she could save him. She was the only one who could.

Come on, he thought, *come on . . .* He stared at her, willing her to find the courage to say the words that would free him. *Damn you, I don't deserve this. . . .*

She took a half-step forward, her expression uncertain. Hope flared in his heart. Flared and died when she turned and ran up to the house, leaving him to face his fate alone. . . .

Chapter One

Montana, 1998

With a sigh, Katherine Marie Conley wiped the tears from her eyes. Crying wouldn't help. Nothing would help. Wayne was gone. Her old life was gone, and it was time, past time, to accept it and get on with a new life.

Filled with determination, she turned away from the pretty, slow-moving stream and looked up at the house that was now her home. It stood on a small grassy rise, a rambling two-story ranch house that had once been the showplace of three counties. A wide cement driveway led up to the veranda, which ran the length of the front of the house and wrapped around the southeast corner where the kitchen was located. A creaky old rocker stood in one corner of the porch.

The property was hers now, hers to do with as she pleased. It was a shame the Conleys had let the place get so run-down. The paint, once white, was now a dirty gray. There was a hole in the attic roof big enough to drop a cow through, which was sure to mean a heck of a leak when it rained. One of the upstairs windows was broken. The barn was in even worse shape.

The house had been in Wayne's family for almost a hundred and twenty-five years. Since he was the oldest son, it had been passed on to him when his grandfather passed away, and now it was hers. Of course, it had been remodeled several times in the course of the last century. The outhouse and washtub had been replaced with modern plumbing; electricity had done away with candles and tallow lamps. Sadly, no one in Wayne's family had chosen to live here for the last twenty or twenty-five years.

The house hadn't been left empty all that time. Wayne's family had rented it out to hunters or to city people looking for a rustic getaway, but no one had stayed longer than a few days at a time. Wayne had told her that everyone who ever stayed at the ranch claimed to have heard strange noises in the night, or to have seen lights flickering in the barn. Things disappeared. An item left in the living room would mysteriously turn up in the kitchen. Keys were lost. Wayne had dismissed the tales as nonsense.

To Kathy's knowledge, no one had stayed in the house for the last four or five years. It had taken her two days just to sweep out the cobwebs and make a dent in the dust.

Kathy sighed. She didn't believe in ghosts or goblins or things that went bump in the night. She didn't believe in aliens or monsters. She wasn't afraid of the dark. And she certainly wasn't afraid of an old house, even if it was supposed to be haunted.

She wasn't afraid of hard work, either. She was, in fact, looking forward to it. Fixing up the old place would give her something to do, something to think about besides Wayne and how empty her life was without him. They had never come here together. Except for the fact that it had belonged to Wayne, there were no shared memories of the two of them in this place. If she was lucky, she would work so hard during the day that she would be too exhausted at night to do more than eat, bathe, and fall into bed.

Dusting off the seat of her jeans, she started walking up the narrow dirt path that led to the back porch, imagining how it would look when flowers replaced the tangled mass of weeds and sticker bushes that lined both sides of the path.

She felt a rush of cold air as she neared a huge old oak. Once, when he was telling her about the property, Wayne had mentioned this tree. It had been a hanging tree, he'd said. According to legend, the last man to have been hanged there had put a curse on the ranch. Kathy didn't believe in curses, either, but according to legend, every Conley who had tried to make a go of the place from that time to this had failed. The cattle had been sold, and then, acre by acre, the land had been sold off, until all that remained in the family was the house and the five acres

11

that surrounded it. Five acres where there had once
been thousands.

Another gust of cool air brushed her cheek; she
glanced up at the leaves of the tree, but no wind
moved among the branches. The air was quiet and
still. She felt a sudden sense of unease slither down
her spine. She thought of the movie she had watched
the night before, remembering how the hero had remarked that cold air was a sure sign of a restless
spirit.

She was turning away from the tree when she saw
what looked like a body hanging from one of the
branches. With a gasp, she took a step backward, her
hand pressed to her throat. And then she laughed. It
was just a drifting shadow.

Chiding herself for letting her imagination run
wild, Kathy turned away from the hanging tree. She
didn't believe in ghosts, she reminded herself, but this
would certainly be the perfect spot for a haunting if
what Wayne had said about the tree was true.

Shaking her head at such nonsense, she walked
briskly up the path. She would finish unpacking this
afternoon; tomorrow she would decide which pieces
of the old furniture she would keep, and then call the
Salvation Army to come and haul the rest away. If
she started painting on Monday, she could have the
downstairs done by the weekend. It would take
weeks, perhaps months, to fix the place up. But it
didn't matter. If there was one thing she had plenty
of, it was time.

Time. She thought of all the bumper stickers she
had seen. So many books, so little time. So many

men, so little time. So much chocolate, so little time. . . .

She smiled as she wiped away the last of her tears. A hot fudge sundae was just what the doctor ordered.

The sound of a woman crying roused him from a deep, dreamless sleep. How long had he been drifting this time, he wondered, floating weightless, mindless, at the edge of eternity?

He watched the woman wipe away her tears and knew, at last, what hell was. It was being able to see a woman and not touch her; hear the soft sound of her weeping, and not be able to comfort her. He had always been a sucker for a woman's tears; this one had wept as though her heart were breaking, and there was nothing he could do about it. Nothing at all.

He stared up at the hanging tree and wondered when it would end.

Pressing a hand to her aching back, Kathy dropped the roller into the pan and admired the newly painted walls of the downstairs bedroom. She had picked a soft shade of blue called Mysterious, and it had done wonders to brighten up the room. She had painted the adjoining bathroom the same color.

She sat down on the rusty old bed she had dragged into the center of the floor. It was one of the few pieces of furniture she was keeping, at least for the time being. Head cocked to one side, she mentally redecorated the room. First on the list was a new bed. A blue print spread and dust ruffle for the bed. White curtains, or maybe vertical blinds for the two windows. Maybe a cute little white wicker desk and chair for one corner. A white ceiling fan. She had already ordered new carpeting; a rich dark blue, it would be delivered in a few days.

Rising, she gathered up the paint roller and pan and carried them out to the service porch, then went back and rolled up the plastic sheeting she had used to cover the floor. Tomorrow she would paint the living room, Wednesday the kitchen, Thursday the library, Friday the dining room. Next week she would start on the second floor.

After cleaning up the mess in the bedroom, she went into the bathroom and turned on the water in the tub. A long soak in a hot bubble bath was just what she needed to soothe the ache from her weary muscles. Climbing up and down a stepladder had strained leg muscles she didn't even know she had.

She added some scented bubble bath to the water, then stretched her back and shoulders. She didn't think she had ever worked so hard in her whole life as she had in the last few days, but it had been worth it. She needed the distraction, the sense of accomplishment.

Slipping out of her paint-splattered clothes, she pinned up her hair, then stepped into the tub, sighing as the deliciously hot water closed over her. *Ah,* she thought, her eyelids fluttering down, *heaven.*

He stood in the doorway, staring at the woman reclining in the tub. Once, he would have felt guilty for spying on a woman while she was bathing, but no more. He had few diversions these days, and he took his pleasure when and where he could find it.

Before, troubled by her tears, he had not paid much attention to the woman's appearance. Now, he noticed that her skin was the color of warm honey. Her hair was a dark reddish-brown and slightly curly. Her eyebrows were delicately arched; her nose was small and turned up a little at the end. Her lips were a pale, pale pink.

His gaze moved over her softly rounded shoulders, his hands itching to reach out and touch her skin. How long had it been since he had touched living flesh, since he had caressed a woman? He clenched his hands into tight fists, his gaze sliding lower. She was covered in frothy bubbles from her shoulders down, but he had no trouble imagining the rest. Full breasts, a trim waist, long, shapely legs. She was tall and slender and auburn-haired, reminding him all too vividly of the woman who had literally been the death of him.

Kathy sat up with a start, her gaze darting toward the hallway. She crossed her arms over her breasts, shivering, as a draft of cold air whispered over her skin. She could have sworn she had seen a man standing in the doorway. A big man dressed in black from head to foot.

Grabbing a towel, she stepped out of the tub and tiptoed to the door. She glanced up and down the hallway, but there was no one there.

Blowing out a sigh of disgust, she padded into the bedroom and put on her nightgown. Deciding to spend the night in the living room to escape the smell of the new paint, she grabbed a pillow and a couple of blankets from the bed. She spread the covers on the floor, plumped the pillow, then slid under the covers and closed her eyes. The first thing she intended to buy was a new bed. She hadn't kept the king-sized bed she had shared with Wayne, or slept in it again after he died. She just couldn't.

A new bed. A new life. Tears filled her eyes. She didn't want a new life; she would have given anything to have her old one back.

He wandered through the house. He hadn't been inside for a while . . . he didn't know how long it had been. Time no longer had any meaning for him, but the house was as he remembered it—large rooms with oak trim around the doors, vaulted ceilings, a huge stone fireplace in the parlor, three bedrooms upstairs.

He wandered into the kitchen. The Conley family had made a lot of changes in the last hundred years. The old iron cook stove was gone, and in its place stood a shiny white stove with silver knobs and a black door that reflected everything in the room, except him. The old ice box was gone, too, and a new gleaming white one with black handles stood in its place. There were a couple of odd-looking contraptions on the counter that the woman had brought with her. The counter top was new, too. Once made of rough wood, it was now made of small square shiny tiles.

He walked back down the corridor until he came to the parlor. The woman was sleeping on the floor. In his time, it had been unheard of for a woman to live alone, especially a young and beautiful woman like this one.

Moving closer, he saw that she had been crying again. What was it that caused her such grief? he wondered. And why was she here, living in the house of the man who had killed him?

Chapter Two

Kathy woke with a sigh. A glance at the clock on the windowsill showed it was after nine. She jackknifed into a sitting position, thinking she had overslept, frowning because she hadn't made breakfast for Wayne or kissed him good-bye, and then she remembered that Wayne was gone. She wasn't in their cozy Chicago apartment; she was in the wilds of Montana.

She sat there for a long moment, fighting the urge to cry, and then, with a strangled sob, she huddled under the covers and let the tears flow. How long would it take, she wondered, how long until she didn't think of him every minute of every day, until the hurt and the emptiness went away? He had been gone for almost a year. Everyone she knew had assured her that, in time, the pain would grow less, but no one had said just how much time it would take.

She cried until her throat ached, and then she sat up and gave herself a good scolding.

"You're not the only woman to have lost her husband, you know. You had six wonderful years with a wonderful man. A lot of women never have that. You have a place to live, a comfortable bank account, your health . . ."

And she would have given it all up to spend one more day with Wayne, to tell him she loved him one more time. Love . . . she was never going to love anyone again. It was too painful.

She dressed quickly, then went into the kitchen, where she rummaged around in the cupboards for something to eat.

Deciding on a bowl of cereal and a glass of orange juice, she grabbed a bowl, a spoon, the milk and the juice, then sat down at the kitchen table, wishing again that they'd had children. The fact that they didn't was all her fault. Wayne had wanted to have kids right away, but she had wanted to wait. She had just got a promotion at work. His computer business was just getting off the ground, and she had wanted to wait until it was solid, until they had a sizable nest egg, before she quit her job to become Susie Homemaker. She hadn't been keen on the idea of having kids, but when they did, she intended to stay home to raise them. Her mother had worked, and she had hated it.

Now Wayne was gone, and she was alone. Well, not really alone. Wayne's mother and younger sister were there if she needed them. Her parents lived in Northern California, but they were still only a phone call away. She had three brothers and a sister and a half-dozen nieces and nephews and yet, for all the family she had scattered over the country, she still felt alone.

"Good grief, Katherine Marie Conley," she muttered irritably, "snap out of it!"

She hated this side of herself. She had always prided herself on being a strong, independent woman, had always been so sure she could handle whatever trials came her way. She didn't cry at movies, didn't melt at the sight of big-eyed babies or furry kittens, had always considered herself a sensible woman, but Wayne's death had turned her life and everything she believed in upside down.

Wayne. He had been a wonderful man, caring, supportive, sensitive. He had been the one who cried at sad movies and went gaga over babies and kittens.

She finished her cereal, rinsed the bowl and put it in the dishwasher, along with her glass and spoon.

It was time to stop feeling sorry for herself and get to work. The living room wouldn't paint itself.

Later that night, after a quick dinner and a leisurely bath, Kathy sat cross-legged on a quilt on the floor in the middle of the living room, a cup of hot tea cradled in her hands. A fire blazed in the fireplace, the flames throwing shadows on the freshly painted, cream-colored walls. Country music played on the radio.

The dark blue carpet she had picked out would look wonderful in here, she thought. She would hang vertical blinds at the windows. Use lots of plants. Buy a new mantle for the fireplace, something in light oak.

Yesterday, she had called the Salvation Army to come and pick up the furniture that had been left in the house, deciding she would start from scratch. The only things she had kept were the bed she was sleeping in, the table and chairs in the kitchen, and a well-preserved four-drawer oak dresser with an oval mirror that she had found in one of the bedrooms upstairs.

Without carpets, drapes or furniture, sounds echoed off the walls. It was sort of eerie, living in a house with practically no furniture. Maybe she should keep it that way, she mused as she looked around. There was nothing to dust, nothing to vacuum.

She blew out a sigh, wondering why all the country songs seemed so sad, wondering if she would ever smile again.

Feeling melancholy, she stared out the front window. Tomorrow, she would find some sheets and cover the windows. Staring at the glass with the darkness behind it gave her the creeps. It was like looking into black, empty eyes.

Her new carpet was coming the next day. While the men laid the rug, she would paint the kitchen. She had picked out a nice cheerful yellow, not too bright . . . She went suddenly still, her breath catching in her throat, as something moved out in the shadows, something that looked like the silhouette of a tall man.

Scrambling to her feet, she ran to make sure the front door was locked, then ran into the kitchen to check the back door. Heart pounding as if she had just done ten miles on her treadmill, she hurried down the hall to the bedroom. Delving in her suitcase, she grabbed the gun she had bought before leaving Chicago.

"Don't panic." She took a deep breath. "Don't panic." She knew how to use the gun; she had taken lessons at the firing range back home.

Taking slow, deep breaths, she stood with her back to the wall, the gun aimed at the floor. When she was calm again, she walked through the house, then went into the living room, flipped on the porch light, and looked out the front window.

There was no one there.

"Of course there's no one there. It was just your imagination." She laughed, a soft shaky laugh. Of course, that was all it was.

But that night she slept with all the lights on, and the gun beneath her pillow.

He stood beside the old brass bed, staring down at her. She had seen him, he was sure of it. There was no other explanation for the way she had behaved. In one hundred and twenty-five years, no one had ever been able to see him. No one. Everyone who had stayed in the house had sensed his presence. He had made sure of that. For the last quarter of a century or so, it had been his only amusement, scaring the hell out of the people who came here. He had enjoyed it immensely. After all, if he was going to be a ghost, he figured he might as well act like one.

But she had seen him.

It made him feel whole again, alive again.

*   *   *

Kathy finished rinsing the pale yellow paint from the roller, covered the pan and roller with a dish towel, then stretched the kinks out of her back. Casting a critical eye over what she had just done, she nodded with satisfaction. Grabbing a soda out of the fridge, she kicked off her shoes and walked through the house, enjoying the feel of the new carpet beneath her bare feet. There was nothing like new carpeting, she mused. It turned the old house into a home.

Changing out of her paint-spattered sweats and into a pair of shorts and a halter top, she went outside and sat down on the back steps, gazing out over the land. Her land. She had always thought it was silly for people to fight over a particular stretch of ground. Dirt was dirt. But there was something about this place that called to her, that gave her a sense of peace, of belonging. It was a good feeling. Maybe it wasn't the land at all that people fought and died for, but that sense of belonging.

After a few minutes, she got up and walked around the house. She would have to hire someone to paint the outside and repair the roof, or maybe she would give it a try herself. How hard could it be? She would definitely have to get someone to repair the barn, though, but that could wait until later.

Tossing the empty can onto the back porch, she walked down the path to the stream. She wanted to refinish the cupboards in the kitchen, too, and replace all the doors in the house. The kitchen and bathrooms could use some new linoleum, and maybe new faucets. She needed to buy some grass seed, and flowers, and maybe some fruit trees. The list seemed endless.

When she reached the stream, she waded into the shallow water. It felt wonderfully cool. Impulsively, she sat down in the middle of the stream and closed her eyes. *If only Wayne could see me now*, she thought. *Wayne* . . .

She had so many regrets. . . . She wished she had told Wayne she loved him more often, that they'd had children, that she had spent more time doing things with Wayne and less time worrying about her job.

She had always heard that the road to hell was paved with regrets. Now she believed it.

Opening her eyes, she stared up at the hanging tree. She wondered how many men had breathed their last dangling from the end of a rope on that very tree. No doubt they'd had regrets aplenty. . . .

She gasped as an image wavered before her eyes. It wasn't a shadow this time, she was sure of it. But if it wasn't a trick of the light, what had it been? A chill ran down her spine. For a moment there, she thought she had seen a body dangling from a rope. That was impossible, of course, and yet she had seen it so clearly—a tall man with jet-black hair long enough to brush his shoulders. His skin had been dark, too, his left cheek bisected by a thin white scar. He had worn a pair of black pants, a black shirt and boots. But it was his eyes that had held her attention. Black eyes filled with hate and rage.

Shaken by what she had seen, or thought she had seen, she stood up. Stepping out of the water, she sat down on the grass and let the sun bake her dry.

And then she felt it again, that draft of cool air she had felt before.

Feeling foolish for being frightened by a chill, and yet unable to stay there a moment longer, she scrambled to her feet and ran up to the house, yelping when she stepped on a sticker.

With a sigh, she stopped running and plucked the burr from her foot. What on earth was the matter with her? Running like the devil himself was at her heels. Of course the air was growing cool. The sun was setting.

Chiding herself for letting her imagination run away with her, she walked the rest of the way to the house, proud of herself because she didn't look back once.

Kathy glanced around the kitchen. Someone had been there. She was sure of it. She had left a box of cereal on the kitchen table this morning with the top securely closed. Now it was on the sink. Open.

Filled with trepidation, she tiptoed through the rest of the downstairs. Except for the kitchen table and chairs and the bed, there was no furniture in the house, nothing for an intruder to hide behind.

She peered into the bathroom, then made her way to the bedroom. Nothing. Grabbing her gun from beneath the pillow, she went to the staircase. She put one hand on the bannister, took a deep breath and slowly climbed the steps, grimacing as the old wood creaked beneath her feet.

All the bedrooms were empty. She was about to go back downstairs when she felt it again, that brush of cool air against her skin. Maybe the place really was haunted. This wasn't the first time she had put something down only to come back and find it wasn't where it should be. She had left her hairbrush in the bathroom last night, only to find it on the kitchen table this morning.

She shivered as another breath of cold air whispered over her skin. Very slowly, her heart pounding, she turned around, and then blew out a sigh of relief. Ghosts, indeed! The draft had come through the broken window in the bedroom across the hall.

With a sigh of relief, she went downstairs to fix dinner.

Chapter Three

He stalked the dark shadows of the land, remembering, always remembering, the life that had been stolen from him. Rage and the need for vengeance rode him with whip and spurs; the fact that he was helpless to exact the revenge he desired filled him with bitter frustration.

His hand brushed his thigh, reaching for a gun that was no longer there. He craved the taste of a cigarette, yearned for the smooth warmth of a shot of whiskey. He missed the acrid stink of smoky saloons, the throaty laughter of his favorite soiled dove, the smell of cheap perfume that had clung to her dusky skin.

He loosed a vile string of obscenities as he walked down to the stream. No matter how he tried to stay away from this one place of all places, he was inevitably drawn back here.

Blowing out a sigh, he rested one shoulder against the rough bark of the hanging tree. How many times had he relived that last night? A hundred times? A thousand? Even now, he could vividly remember the bitter taste of fear in his mouth as Whitey Blair dropped the noose around his neck. Mounted on a skittish bay gelding, hands tightly tied behind his back, Dalton had stared down at the men gathered nearby, his stomach churning, his teeth clenched.

Dirty Injun.

You'll never rape another white woman.

Rape! That was a laugh. She'd been used more often than a two-bit whore. But no one had believed him. He'd been a stranger, a half-breed gunfighter who sold his iron to the highest bidder.

He had stared at Lydia, waiting, praying that she would find the courage to tell her husband the truth. She had stared back at him, her eyes wide and scared, and then she had turned and run into the house, taking his last hope with her.

The Triple Bar C cowhands had stepped back, torches held high, as Russell Conley strode forward.

"Got any last words?"

Dalton shook his head.

Conley grunted. "If you know any prayers, now's the time to say 'em."

"You're hanging an innocent man."

"And you're wasting our time."

Dalton thought of arguing further, of demanding

that Conley ask Lydia outright just what had happened in the barn, and how they got there in the first place, but he knew it would be a waste of breath. Conley would never believe him, never accept the word of a half-breed hired gun over that of his own wife.

"Go on, then, get it over with, Conley. But you'd better bury me deep because I swear to you, I won't rest until I've proven my innocence. My ghost will haunt you until the day you die, and my blood will curse this ground."

"You through?" Conley held a quirt in his hands. He tapped it lightly against his palm.

Knowing he was seconds away from death, Dalton stared out over the heads of the cowboys, gazing at the distant mountains. He'd lived a hard, fast life, and most of the things that were said of him were true, and maybe he deserved to go to hell, but he didn't deserve to die like this, hanged for something he didn't do.

"Wakan Tanka, unshimalam ye oyate . . ." Great Spirit, have mercy on me . . .

From the corner of his eye, he saw Conley raise the quirt, heard the cowhands draw a collective breath as the quirt came whistling down on the bay's hindquarters. . . .

Dalton shuddered at the memory. He could still remember the almost light-headed feeling of fear that had taken hold of him, still hear the sharp crack of the leather smacking against the bay's rump, the gasp of the Triple Bar C cowhands as the horse bolted, leaving him dangling in the air, gasping for breath. . . .

Dalton swore a vile oath. Damn, but hanging had been a bad way to go.

The dishes were done; she had taken her nightly bubble bath and locked up the house.

Wrapped in a warm robe, Kathy went into the living room and sat down in front of the fireplace, staring at the flames. A country ballad played on the radio, but it was still too quiet. There had always been noise in Chicago. Car alarms, sirens, the sound of traffic on the street, the hum of the air conditioner in the summer. Maybe tomorrow, instead of painting the library, she would go shopping for a stereo and see what the town had to offer in the way of furniture.

Feeling bored and restless, she went upstairs. Wandering from room to room, she visualized how each one would look when it was painted and decorated. She ran her hand over the top of the dresser in the largest bedroom. She loved the look and feel of the old wood and decided to do the whole upstairs, and maybe the downstairs as well, in antique oak.

The dresser was on casters and she moved it across the floor, deciding it would look better on the far wall. It was rolling pretty well when one of the wheels suddenly stopped turning. The dresser came to a sudden halt. Kathy yelped in surprise as the bottom drawer fell out, landing with a thump on the floor. It was then that she noticed the small notebook jammed in a crack in the back of the drawer between the bottom and the side.

Curious, she pried it free. The leather cover was stiff, brittle with age. Opening it carefully, she scanned the first page.

The words *My Diary, The Year of Our Lord, 1873* were written in faded, flowing script, and below that she read the name *Lydia Camille Winston Conley.*

Kathy stared at the words, her heart suddenly beating fast as she sat down on the floor and turned the page. Lydia wrote sporadically. The first few entries were about how much Lydia hated living on the ranch, how she longed to go back to Philadelphia, how she wished she'd had the nerve to defy her father and marry the man she loved instead of the man who had dragged her away from her friends and family to "this dismal uncivilized wilderness inhabited by smelly cows and coarse men."

Kathy turned the page, but the next one, and the next, were blank. Frowning, she flipped through the pages, wondering why Lydia had stopped writing, and then she came to an entry dated February 20th.

A day I will never forget. It was cold and gray, with the promise of rain. Went to town with Russell. It would have been an unremarkable trip except it was the first time I saw him. He was standing on the boardwalk as we drove by. A man, clad all in black. He stared at me as we passed by, and I knew, at that moment, that he was going to change my life.

March 5th.
Carmen and Whitey were going to town today
to pick up the mail, and I went with them. As I
had hoped, he was there. He was sitting on the
boardwalk in front of one of those smelly sa-
loons, his black hat pulled low over his eyes, one
booted foot resting on the rail. He is the most
frightening, handsome man I have ever seen. His
name is Dalton Crowkiller. Rowdy said he is half
Sioux Indian.

He tilted his hat back and looked up at me for
a long moment before he removed his foot from
the railing. "Excuse me, ma'am," he said.

I nodded, unable to speak past the lump in my
throat. His voice was low and soft and deep. But
it was his eyes that left me speechless. Black
eyes, the blackest I have ever seen. They looked
at me as if he knew everything I was thinking. It
was most disconcerting. And exciting.

March 22nd.
Asked Russell to take me into town this morn-
ing. Rarely have I seen him look so surprised.
Of course, since I have never before asked him
to take me anywhere except back to Philadel-
phia, I guess his reaction was to be expected. It
was just after noon when we arrived in town, if
a place as dirty and dismal as Saul's Crossing
can indeed be called a town. Told Russell I
wished to look for dress goods at the mercantile
and did not want him hovering over me. He
looked disappointed, but went off to the livery to
do whatever it is the men do there.

He was sitting on the boardwalk in front of the saloon next to the mercantile. My heart was pounding as I slowly crossed the street. Thought I would faint when he looked up at me through those dark, mysterious eyes. And then he smiled at me.

There are no words to describe the effect that look had upon me.

Kathy sat back, grinning. It was like reading a Wild West soap opera. She had seen a photograph of Lydia Conley once, taken before the woman went insane. She had looked every inch a lady, from the top of her well-coiffed head to the tips of her high-button shoes. No one, looking at that innocent, heart-shaped face, would ever have suspected her of cheating on her husband.

''Proves you just never know,'' she murmured, and turned the page.

April 1st.

There was a dance at the schoolhouse to-night. Dressed with care in the new silk and lace gown I ordered from New York. Russell said I was beautiful, but I did not need him to tell me that.

Everyone in town seemed to be at the dance. It is not surprising, since there are so few enter-tainments in this forsaken place. Knew the mo-ment I stepped into the building that the one man I wanted to see was not there.

Because it was expected, I danced with every man who asked me, from fat old Horace Miller to pimple-faced Billy Watkins. Russell beamed, pleased that I was the belle of the ball, such as it was. The town ladies glowered at me. It is obvious they are jealous, the old cats, as if I cared.

It was about ten o'clock when Rufus Overfeld came striding toward me. He is short and fat, with bushy white whiskers that reach to his chest. Not caring that it was quite rude, I turned and fled.

It was wonderfully cool outside after the stuffy heat of the schoolhouse and I walked into the shadows, anxious to be alone and more disappointed than I cared to admit that he was not there.

And then I heard a voice, a voice I knew was his. "Don't you know better than to go off alone?"

Could hardly speak, hardly think, as he materialized out of the darkness.

"It's not safe out here," he said. "All kinds of wild critters roam the darkness."

"Are you one of them?" The words were supposed to sound teasing, coy, but I only sounded frightened. He is like no other man I have ever met.

"The wildest of the bunch." His voice was low, dangerous, exciting. He was dressed all in black again, from his hat to his boots. His eyes glittered like polished ebony in the moonlight. "What are you doing out here?"

Some of my self-confidence reasserted itself.

He was just a man, after all, and I knew how to handle men. "What do you think?"

He laughed softly. "I think you're trouble."

"Are you afraid of trouble?"

He laughed again, the sound soft and husky. "Honey, I'm not afraid of anything."

"Prove it."

"Oh, I aim to," he drawled. And before I could think to say ah, yes, or no, he drew me up against him and kissed me and I knew in that moment that I'd been looking for this man my whole life.

Felt light-headed and dizzy when he let me go.

"You'd better get back before you're missed," he said, his voice husky.

"When will I see you again?"

"I don't think that's a good idea."

"Don't you want to?"

"Want's got nothing to do with it. You're a married woman, and I've never been one to ride in another man's saddle."

His words angered me. No man had ever refused me before, yet this man, this half-breed, had turned me down. It was a humiliation unlike any I had ever known and I vowed that, somehow, someday, I would find a way to get even.

Kathy shook her head. Lydia Conley had certainly been full of herself. Rich and spoiled, she had probably never been denied anything she wanted. It must have been quite a shock, having a man tell her no.

April 5th.

Something is troubling Russell, something to do with water rights. Overheard him talking to the foreman, telling them to double the night guards. Jack said he had heard that Burkhart was bringing in a hired gun, and Russell laughed and said maybe he had better hire Crowkiller to even things out. Jack laughed then and said he'd heard that Crowkiller could—I am quoting him here—draw quicker than you could spit and holler howdy. Cowboys are nothing if not colorful in their descriptions.

Dalton Crowkiller is a gunfighter! I could not believe my ears. And yet I should not have been surprised. One has only to look into those black eyes to know he is capable of anything, even murder. And to think I flirted with him.

April 17th.

Impossible as it seems, Russell has hired that man! When I asked why, he told me not to worry my pretty little head about it. Men! Sometimes they are so aggravating. As if I cannot figure it out for myself. Some of our cattle have been poisoned. Two of our cowboys have been shot at. Crowkiller is obviously here to put a stop to such goings on. The thought makes my skin crawl.

April 18th.

He has invaded my home. He takes his meals with us, rather than with the hired hands. He sleeps in the downstairs bedroom. Every time I look at him, I feel the sting of his rejection. And always, in the back of my mind, is the knowledge that I offered myself to him, and he refused. He watches me constantly, his eyes hot. I should hate him. I do hate him, and yet I have never known anyone like him. He scares me, and yet I think of him constantly.

May 1st.

His eyes follow me whenever I am in the room. His very presence is a constant torment. I wonder that no one else is aware of the vibrant attraction between us. The very air seems to hum when we are in the same room. His image haunts my every waking thought. I dream of him every night, dreams that leave me feeling weak and helpless and yearning for his touch.

May 12th.

I saw him practicing with his gun today. He is a deadly shot. Almost faster than the eye could follow, he drew his gun and fired six times, hitting the six bottles he had placed on the corral fence. Greased lightning, one of the men said. I can only agree. Watching him draw and fire filled me with a strange excitement. I wonder how many men he has killed. He moves as stealthily as a cat.

June 30th.

Asked Russell to take me into town today, but he said he was too busy. I pouted, and he said he would find someone to take me. Almost fainted when Dalton brought the carriage around. My heart was pounding wildly as he helped me onto the seat, then vaulted up beside me.

Have never been so aware of any man as I am of him. When we are not together, I think of him constantly. When he is near, my whole being seems to come alive.

He lifted the reins and clucked to the horse, his every movement fluid. The silence between us was thick enough to cut. I could think of nothing to say, so I stared straight ahead, acutely aware of his thigh brushing my skirt, his shoulder bumping against mine when we hit a rut in the road.

Never did the ride to town seem so long.

"Where to?" he asked.

"The . . . the millinery shop, please," I said, hardly able to speak.

He reined the horse to a halt in front of the shop. I watched his hands, big brown hands, loop the reins around the brake. He vaulted to the ground, then came to help me out of the carriage, and I felt those hands at my waist.

"How long will you be?" he asked.

"I don't know. An hour?"

He nodded. "I'll meet you here in an hour, then."

He looked down at me, a faint smile on his lips. *"The store's that way,"* he said.

Embarrassed to be caught staring, I turned away as quickly as I could. In my haste to get away from him, I tripped on my hem and would have fallen if he had not caught me. He held me for a long moment, a knowing look in his eye. Oh, but I hate that man! I hate the way he makes me feel.

Later, on the way home, he stopped beneath a shady tree and without a word, he pulled me into his arms and kissed me. *"Is that what you've been wanting?"* he asked, looking smug.

And I slapped him. Slapped him as hard as I could.

He looked at me a moment, one brow raised, and then he laughed out loud. Laughed! At me!

"Take me home," I said, furious that my voice was shaky, that he had laughed at me, that I wanted more than just one kiss.

"Yes, ma'am," he replied insolently.

The ride home seemed to take forever. I hope I never see him again.

Dalton didn't come to dinner tonight. Later, I overheard Russell and the foreman talking. Apparently Dalton is *"taking care of business,"* whatever that may be.

Kathy stretched a kink out of her back. There was little doubt in her mind about the kind of business Crowkiller had been taking care of. Poor Lydia. How awful it must have been for her to be hopelessly smitten with a man she so clearly considered inferior. He must have been a terribly sexy man. That, combined with his bad reputation, would have been a powerful lure to a genteel woman born and bred in Philadelphia.

What was it about bad boys that women found so attractive?

With a shake of her head, she turned the page.

July 2nd.

The sheriff stopped by this afternoon. It seems there was a killing out at the Burkhart Ranch last night. Russell sent me to my room while the sheriff spoke to Dalton, claiming the discussion was not meant for a lady's ears! Of course, I did not remain in my room. Could not hear everything that was said, but the sheriff accused Dalton of killing one of Mr. Burkhart's cowboys and accused Russell of hiring him to do it. Russell denied everything. Dalton told the sheriff to come back when he could prove it. Barely made it back up the stairs before the sheriff came storming out of the parlor, his face beet-red.

July 4th.

Celebration in town today. Russell insisted we go. It was such a bore. Only the thought of perhaps seeing Dalton alone persuaded me to accompany Russell. Cannot believe the foolishness that ensued. Pie-eating contests, shooting contests, wrestling matches. Men. Do they never

*grow up? Cannot imagine Dalton indulging in
such silliness.*

*There was a dance that night, a repeat of the
one held in the spring. At last, when I had given
up all hope, Dalton arrived. He came to speak
to Russell and when they had finished, I laid my
hand on Dalton's arm and asked him to dance
with me. I almost laughed at his chagrin, for
there was no way he could refuse me. I half expected him to say he did not know how, but, with
a slightly exaggerated bow, he led me onto the
dance floor. He dances divinely, or perhaps it is
only being in his arms that makes it seem divine.
He did not speak, but no words were necessary.
His heat engulfed me. It was over too soon, and
he was leading me back to Russell. His eyes held
mine for a long moment, and then he left. I did
not see him again that night.*

July 8th.

*Dalton has been gone these past four days.
Dare not inquire as to his whereabouts.*

*Am getting quite good at eavesdropping! Rus-
sell and the foreman spent an hour in Russell's
study tonight. Russell shut the door and locked
it, making it very hard to hear what they were
talking about. Overheard Jack mention Dalton's
name more than once, along with the fact that
there would not be any more trouble with Burkhart, at least for the time being.*

July 10th.

He has returned! Saw him tonight at dinner.

There is something different about him, though I do not know what it is. Something about the look in his eyes. He seems harder, colder, than before.

July 18th.

He has been back for over a week, and I have not had a chance to see him alone, though why I should want to, after the horrid way he treated me the last time, is quite beyond me. He is a most annoying man!

July 27th.

At last, I saw Dalton alone. Russell had gone to bed, but I could not sleep. Deciding to take some air, I went out on the front porch, and he was there. For a moment, we looked at each other, neither speaking. The tension between us has been building for weeks. He wants me. I know he does. His eyes moved over me, hotter than the summer breeze. He would not refuse me this time, he could not. I have never wanted anyone the way I want this silent stranger. I would do anything to have him. I do not care what he has done or who he is.

Could not think of anything to say, but it did not matter. There was no need to speak. I knew what he wanted, what I wanted. He stood there, watching me out of those enigmatic black eyes as I walked toward him. My heart was pounding, my whole body aching for his touch as I slid my arms around his neck and pressed myself against him. He swore as his arms went around me, holding me tightly against him, and I knew I had won. I could feel his hands on my back, burning my skin, burning my soul. I wanted him, had to have him. Taking him by the hand, I led him into the barn. And still we did not speak.

He lit one of the lamps, then stood there, hands clenched, watching me from hooded eyes. I put my arms around him and kissed him, and he kissed me back. It was a harsh kiss. There was nothing of gentleness in it. It was everything I wanted, everything I needed. No other man has ever made me feel like this, hot and cold and shivery all at the same time.

We fell back on the straw in one of the stalls. He kissed me until I was breathless, until I writhed beneath him. I tore off his shirt, eager to feel his skin against mine.

He swore under his breath as he lifted my gown. With a shock, I realized he was cursing me, but I did not care. I had wanted him for weeks and now I meant to have him.

And then, abruptly, he let me go. I stared up at him, impaled by his eyes. Eyes filled with hatred and self-loathing. "Damn you," he muttered.

"What is it?" I asked, panicked by the thought that he had changed his mind.

"I can't do this," he said, and stood up.

"Wait." I grabbed his arm, but he pulled away, and I realized he was going to leave me. I think I must have gone a little crazy. "If you

*walk out that door, I shall make you regret it for
the rest of your life."* It was an empty threat,
and sounded foolish even to me.

"I'm already regretting it." He put on his
shirt as he turned to leave, and I screamed at
him. Screamed with all the rage and pent-up
frustration I felt at that moment, screamed because I was married to a man I did not love,
screamed because I had let this stranger humil-
iate me a second time.

He stood there, staring down at me through
those impenetrable black eyes, and I knew I had
to get rid of him, knew I could not endure the
agony of seeing him every day, of knowing that
I had tried to seduce him and he had rejected
me, not once, but twice.

Through a crack in the barn door, I saw a
light come on in the house. Fear churned in
my stomach as I realized that Russell must
have awakened and found me gone. And in
that moment, I knew how I would get my revenge. I was not sure how I would explain my
presence in the barn in my nightclothes at this
time of night, but there was no time to worry
about it. I ripped my gown down the front and
mussed my hair, and then I screamed again, as
loudly as I could.

Dalton looked at me, comprehension dawning
in his hell-black eyes. *"Damn you!"*

He turned on his heel and had taken several
steps toward the door when it burst open. Russell
stood there, his rifle cocked and ready. For a

moment, I thought Dalton might try to draw his weapon, but then two of the cowboys appeared, hastily tucking in their shirttails.

"What the hell's going on here?" Russell demanded.

I crossed my arms over my bared breasts and sat up, sobbing hysterically. No words were necessary.

"Get his gun," Russell said. Taking off his shirt, he handed it to me. "Cover yourself."

Dalton stood staring at me, his whole body rigid with anger, as Rowdy Lawson took his Colt.

"Whitey, get a rope."

Cowering in the stall, I watched as they tied Dalton between two posts. He was looking at me, his face devoid of expression. I shrank back against the inside of the stall, oblivious to everything but the accusation in those unforgiving eyes.

And then I heard a sharp crack. Dalton flinched, and I realized that Russell had stripped off Dalton's shirt and was whipping him.

Knowing I should put a stop to this before it went any further, I stood up. "Russell, wait!"

He did not look at me. "You should watch this," he said. "You'll sleep better knowing your honor has been avenged."

"No . . . no, I cannot."

"You will." He looked at me then, and I wondered if he knew, if he had known all along.

I waited for Dalton to say something in his

45

own defense, but he said nothing. This confused me. Surely he was not going to take the blame to spare me. And then I realized that he knew Russell would not listen to him.

Russell raised his arm, and the whip came whistling down across Dalton's back. Again and again and again. I can see it so clearly, even now. His whole body was taut, every muscle clearly defined. Sweat poured from his body, mingling with the blood running down his back and shoulders. His hands were clenched into tight fists, the knuckles white with the strain. And all the while he looked at me.

I flinched with every stroke of the lash. I had not meant for this to happen. I had only wanted Russell to send him away so I would never have to look into those eyes again.

Again and again the lash cut into Dalton's flesh. My stomach churned from the sight of so much blood and torn flesh. I waited for him to scream in pain, to faint, to accuse me of trying to seduce him. But he remained mute, his face a mask of agony.

After what seemed like hours, Russell came to me. His face and chest were splattered with blood. He didn't say a word as he took me by the arm and led me outside. I longed to tell him the truth, to confess my guilt, but I could not form the words.

Russell spent the entire night in my bed that night, the first time he had done so since our wedding. Now, as I write this, he is sleeping soundly, and I realize that, even though he has never said the words, he loves me, and that I have done him a terrible wrong. I vow I shall never betray my husband again, and pray that Dalton will find it in his heart to forgive me for my cowardice.

July 28th.

Dalton Crowkiller is dead. Russell woke me early this morning and made me go to the hanging. He wouldn't even allow me time to dress. He said he knew I would want to be there to see the man who had attacked me get his just due. I shall never forget the look in Dalton's eyes as he waited for me to tell Russell the truth. Coward that I am, I could not say the words that would have saved him, nor could I watch. Surely my soul will be damned for all eternity for what I have done.

July 31st.

He is here! Oh, Lord, help me, Dalton is here. I saw him tonight, standing at the foot of my bed, his black eyes filled with rage and accusation. I begged him to forgive me, but he said nothing, only stood there, staring at me through burning black eyes.

September 4th.

Should never have written all this down. What if Russell finds it? Will have to hide it someplace where he will never look. Should burn it, but

*cannot bring myself to do so. It is all I have left
of Dalton.*

September 5th.
   *His image haunts me. I cannot escape him. I
see his face everywhere I look, see him everywhere I go, staring at me through dark, haunted
eyes. What can I do, what can I say, that will
put his soul, and mine, to rest?*

Chapter Four

Kathy sat back, stunned by what she had read. It explained so much, she thought. No wonder the woman had gone mad. No wonder people believed the land was cursed. And maybe it was. A year after Dalton's death, Lydia had given birth to a son and then gone quietly insane. The next year, a drought had wiped out most of the Conleys' cattle herd. The following year, a fire had destroyed the barn and part of the house.

Kathy stood up, stretching the kinks out of her back. She had never believed in curses, yet bad luck had dogged the Triple Bar C Ranch, just as Dalton Crowkiller had promised.

With a yawn, she glanced at her watch, surprised to see that it was after midnight.

Rising, she put the diary in the top dresser drawer,

then went downstairs to fix a cup of hot chocolate. She was almost through painting the downstairs. She would tackle the library tomorrow, the dining room on Friday. Saturday, she would drive into town and look for furniture. The first thing on her list would be a new bed. The old one she was sleeping in looked quaint, but the mattress was soft and lumpy and smelled musty.

Sitting down at the kitchen table, she began to make a list:

1. New bedroom set, sheets, bedspread, curtains, pillow, ceiling fan
2. Living room set—oak/blue print
3. Bookstore—look for Ashley's latest novel
4. Buy groceries. Don't forget toothpaste.
5. Rugs & shower curtain, for bathroom

She looked over her list. Filling it would take up most of the day. But that was good. She liked being busy. When it was quiet, like now, she had too much time to think of things she didn't want to think about.

Finishing the last of her hot chocolate, she put her cup in the sink. As she was turning away from the counter, a movement outside drew her eye. She leaned forward for a better look, then gasped as what she had thought was a shadow coalesced into the shape of a man.

Curtains, she thought. *I've got to get some curtains for the windows.* Mesmerized, she stood there, staring at the dark silhouette. It was the same man, she thought frantically, the same man she had seen before. She was sure of it.

As though feeling her gaze, he turned toward her. She couldn't see his face in the darkness, but she could feel his gaze seeking her out, knew he could see her clearly with the kitchen light behind her.

She backed away from the window as he started toward the house. With a cry, she ran into the bedroom and grabbed the gun from beneath her pillow.

"You won't need that."

She whirled around, then screamed when she saw him standing in the doorway. How had he gotten into the house so fast? Why hadn't she heard the back door open?

"Who are you?" she demanded. "What are you doing here?"

"If I told you, you probably wouldn't believe me."

Kathy clutched the gun tighter, hoping it would give her some much-needed confidence.

"I know how to use this," she warned, annoyed because her voice was shaking almost as badly as her hands.

"Yeah." He laughed softly. "I can see that."

He wasn't the least bit afraid of her. And not only was he *not* afraid, he had the unmitigated gall to laugh. Out loud! She held the gun in both hands, the way she had been taught, but she couldn't seem to stop trembling. Her gaze moved over him. Tall and lean, he was dressed all in black. Long black hair fell past his shoulders. A thin white scar bisected his left cheek. No, it couldn't be . . .

He rested one shoulder negligently against the doorjamb. "You gonna use that thing?" he drawled, his dark eyes filled with wry amusement.

"If I have to."

He lifted one brow. "You ever killed a man?"

"Of course."

He laughed again, a deep, rich, masculine sound that made her toes curl. "Now, why don't I believe you?"

She lifted her chin. "All right, maybe I've never killed anyone." She took a deep breath, some of her panic ebbing. "But there's a first time for everything."

"True enough. I admire your grit, ma'am."

"Thank you," she said, and then blushed. Why was she thanking this intruder! "Don't move," she said. "I'm going to call the police."

"I wouldn't, if I were you."

"I'm sure you wouldn't." Transferring the gun to her right hand, she reached for the phone. It was an old rotary one, surely an antique. She'd have to remember to buy a new one when she went to town. She glanced away from the intruder just long enough to dial the Operator.

When she looked up again, he was gone.

"Operator. May I help you?"

"What? Oh, no, thank you."

Replacing the receiver, the gun still clutched in her fist, she went to the doorway and glanced up and down the hallway. He was nowhere to be seen.

Shoulders sagging, she went to check the back door. It was locked, as was the front door. So, how had he gotten in? Returning to her bedroom, she sat down on the bed and slid the revolver back under her pillow.

It was him. It had to be him.

Dalton Crowkiller.

In the morning, sitting at the kitchen table with the sun pouring in the window, the happenings of the night before seemed like a bad dream. She didn't believe in ghosts. But if he wasn't the ghost of Dalton Crowkiller, who was he? How had he gotten into the house so quickly last night, and left without making a sound, without opening a window or unlocking a door?

Brow furrowed, she stared out the window, the cup of coffee in her hands slowly going cold.

"Smells good."

She jerked around, coffee spilling over the edge of the cup to splash on her hand and over the table. "You!"

He was standing in the kitchen doorway, looking much the same as he had the night before. She stared at him, noticing that there was a faint shimmer around his form that she hadn't been aware of last night; other than that, he looked whole, solid. Real. Handsome as sin, with his dark eyes and roguish smile.

"Sorry. I didn't mean to scare you."

"No?" She put the mug down, wiped her hand on her robe, then folded her hands in her lap to keep them from shaking. "I thought that's what ghosts did."

He smiled faintly. "Guess it comes with the territory."

"I don't believe in ghosts."

"I never did, either."

"You don't look like a ghost."

He lifted one hand, studying it as if he had never seen it before, and then shrugged.

"You're him, aren't you?" she murmured in disbelief. "Dalton Crowkiller."

He nodded. "You've heard of me?"

She stared up at him, her heart racing. He was every bit as devastating as Lydia had claimed. "What do you want?"

He laughed softly, bitterly. "Lots of things. A cup of that coffee. A cigarette. My life back."

"What are you going to do to me?"

"Do to you?" He studied her thoughtfully for a moment, his brow furrowed. "Is that why you think I'm here, do you some kind of harm?"

"I don't know. I've never met a ghost before."

"Well, that makes us even. I've never been a ghost before."

"I don't believe I'm having this conversation."

He grinned at her, a totally disarming expression that made him look younger, more vulnerable. "Me, either. I can't remember the last time I talked to anyone."

"Why me?"

"Because you can see me." He shook his head. "No one else has."

"Except Lydia." According to the woman's diary, she had seen his ghost, and it had driven her insane. Kathy was beginning to understand why. She was feeling a little crazy herself.

54

His eyes went hard and cold, and his whole being went still. "What do you know about her?"

"I found her diary."

He frowned a moment. "A diary? She kept a diary? Where is it?"

"In the dresser. Upstairs."

She blinked, and he was gone. She sat there for several minutes, too frightened to move. She wanted to believe she had imagined the whole thing, or that she had fallen asleep for a few minutes and dreamed it. People didn't see ghosts in the light of day, did they?

She was trying to gather enough courage to go upstairs when he appeared in the kitchen again, Lydia Conley's diary in his hand.

He dropped the book on the table in front of her. "What does it say?"

"You can read it for yourself."

"No," he said tersely, "I can't."

"You can't read?"

"Only what little my ma taught me. By the time I figure out all those words, you'll be as old as I am."

Reaching for the book, Kathy opened it and began to read, acutely aware of the tall man who paced the floor beside her, his expression hard, as he listened to Lydia's account of what had happened.

With a sigh, Kathy closed the book. "Is it true, what she says here?"

"Most of it."

"So Russell Conley really did hang an innocent man."

"Innocent of raping his wife, anyway."

"Were you really a . . . gunslinger?"

He nodded. "Yeah, and a damn good one, too."
He laughed. "I always thought some young gun
would take me out. I never thought I'd get hanged
for rape. Shit, I never took a woman by force in my
life." He swore softly. "Rape! I could have had her
a thousand times."

"I can't believe she let them hang you for something you didn't do."

"Just proves that you didn't know her."

"I saw a picture of her once." The photograph she
had seen had been in old-fashioned sepia tones. Lydia
had been sitting on a straight-backed chair, looking
directly into the camera, her expression solemn. Apparently people hadn't believed in smiling for the
camera in those days. "She was very beautiful."

"So's a mountain lion. But you don't want to take
one to bed."

She couldn't help it, she laughed, the sound dying
in her throat as he reached toward her. Instinctively,
she drew back.

His hand curled into a fist, and then he lowered his
arm. "Afraid of me?"

She wanted to deny it, but something in his eyes
compelled her to tell him the truth. "Yes. You can't
be real."

Dalton blew out a sigh and turned away from her.
She was lovely, warm and alive, and he had a desperate urge to touch her, to feel living flesh, to see if
he *could* touch her. In times past, he had tried to touch
those who had stayed in the house, but to no avail.
He knew they sensed his nearness. He had heard them

speak in hushed voices of feeling "something" in the room, a "presence," a whisper of cold air. But this woman saw him. Could he then touch her, and be touched in return?

"So, what do you want from me?" she asked.

He blew out a deep breath, then turned to face her once more. "Your name?"

"Kathy. Kathy Conley."

"Conley."

She heard the hatred in his voice, the bitterness. "I was married to Russell Conley's great-great-grandson."

"Was?"

"He died recently."

He grunted softly. "Is that why you cry?"

"Yes."

"What happened to him?"

"He was killed in a car accident."

Dalton nodded. He knew what cars were. Loud, smelly conveyances that had replaced the horse and buggy. He had even ridden in one once, for a short while. If he'd been alive at the time, it would likely have scared him to death.

"How long have you been a widow?"

It was an ugly word, she thought. "Ten months, two weeks, three days."

"My condolences."

"Thank you." Needing something to do, she stood up and poured herself another cup of coffee. *I must be hallucinating,* she thought. *This can't be happening.*

She sat down, the mug cradled in her hands. He sat

down across from her, closed his eyes, and inhaled deeply. She recalled that he'd said he would like a cup. "Do you want some coffee?" she asked.

He opened his eyes, his gaze intense. "More than you can imagine." He raked a hand through his hair, obviously agitated. "But I can't drink it."

"What's it like, being a ghost?"

"It's like being in limbo. I can see people, but until you came along, they all looked right through me."

"Have you really been haunting this place for a hundred and twenty-five years?"

He looked stunned. "Has it been that long?"

"Yes. I guess time doesn't mean anything to you, does it?"

"Not really." He had no concept of time anymore. Hours, days, they meant nothing to him now.

"Why are you still here? Why haven't you gone on to whatever it is that lies beyond the grave?"

"I'm not sure, but I think, when I damned Conley, I damned myself as well." He snorted softly. "Hell, I never thought anything would come of it. Who can think clearly when he's got a rope around his neck?" He massaged his throat. "Hell of a way to go, hanging."

Kathy nodded. "Is there a heaven, and a hell?"

"I don't know about heaven," he muttered, "but I sure feel like I'm in hell."

She sipped her coffee, her mind whirling as she tried to recall everything she had ever heard about ghosts. Weren't they supposed to be people with unresolved pasts, people who thought they had left unfinished business?

"Maybe if you removed the curse, your soul would go to . . . to wherever it's supposed to go."

He grinned wryly. "Kind of late, don't you think? Conley's long gone."

"Well, that's true, but his heirs are still alive. Wayne's—" She swallowed hard. "Wayne's mother is still living."

"What are you suggesting? That I go to his old lady and say I'm sorry?" He slammed his palms down on the table. "Even if I wanted to, I can't leave this place."

"What do you mean?"

"I mean I can't leave the county. I've tried. Lord knows I've tried. But every time I try to put this place behind me, it's like I hit a stone wall."

"That's weird." She frowned. "Maybe Janet could come here."

"Why? She wouldn't be able to see me, or hear me."

"It probably wouldn't do any good, anyway. She doesn't own this place anymore. Wayne's grandfather left it to him."

"And now it belongs to you."

Kathy nodded.

"So you think if I tell you I'm sorry, I'll be zapped into eternity?"

"How should I know? But it's worth a try."

Dalton's gaze moved over her. She was an incredibly pretty woman, with her curly auburn hair and suntanned skin. She had brown eyes, large and dark, like those of a doe. Guileless eyes that revealed her every thought, her every emotion. What if she was

59

right? What if he told her he was sorry and that somehow ended the curse? What then? He hadn't lived the kind of life that merited a trip to the pearly gates. And he was in no itching hurry to find out firsthand whether hell was a real place or just an empty threat.

Kathy cocked her head, waiting, wondering what was going on behind those fathomless black eyes.

He leaned forward, so close that she could feel the coolness surrounding him. "Can I touch you?"

She blinked at him. "What?"

"Can I touch you?"

"I don't know," she replied, her voice shaky. "Can you?"

He stood up and rounded the table. She watched his every move, her brown eyes wide, filled with apprehension, as he lifted his hand and laid his palm against her cheek.

"Soft," he murmured. "So soft. And warm."

Kathy shivered. His palm was cold against her skin.

"I won't hurt you," he said, mistaking her trembling for fear. "Can you feel my hand?"

She nodded, her heart in her throat. "It's cold."

"Is it?"

His fingers slid up into her hair and she shivered again, but for an entirely different reason this time. His touch was gentle, tender, almost erotic. He was looking at her, staring at her as if he had never seen a woman before.

"I'd forgotten," he murmured, "forgotten how soft a woman's hair is. And how good it smells." He lowered his head and took a deep breath. "Your hair smells like"—he smiled at her—"like peaches."

Her mouth was suddenly dry, her heart beating wildly as he dragged his knuckles over her cheek. She drew in a ragged breath as his thumb traced the outline of her lips.

"So soft," he whispered.

He couldn't be a ghost. Ghosts didn't have substance, did they? But she could feel his hands moving over her face and in her hair, the calluses on his palms when he cupped her cheek again.

"Damn." Abruptly, he drew his hand away and backed up a step.

She stared up at him, breathless and confused by the feelings he aroused in her. "Mr. Crowkiller—"

"Dalton," he said, his voice low and husky. "Call me Dalton."

"Dalton."

He looked down at her for a long moment, his eyes hot, his hands clenched at his sides and then, muttering something she didn't understand, he vanished from her sight.

Kathy stared at the place where he had been, her skin still tingling from the touch of his hand.

"Damn is right."

Feeling the need to get out of the house, she went into town that afternoon. Saul's Crossing was a small town located about fifteen miles from the ranch. Originally, it had been nothing more than a few shops, a general store and a couple of saloons, which had been patronized by the local cowboys. Now, it was more of a tourist trap. Many of the original buildings had been restored. Still, for all that it was only a few blocks long, it had an amazing variety of small shops and a few large department stores, including a Sears and a Wal-Mart.

She parked her car at one end of town, deciding to explore from one end of the shopping district to the other.

It was a pretty day, warm but not hot. She passed Norton's Hay and Feed, which was one of the town's original buildings. In addition to selling hay, they also rented horses, several of which were standing head to tail in the shade, idly swishing flies. She passed the Square Deal Saloon, which had been restored and turned into a family restaurant.

She found several of the items on her list in Kirby's General Store: shower curtain, new towels, sheets, a lovely pale blue-and-white print bedspread with matching curtains for the bedroom, a couple of blue throw rugs for the bathroom.

Across the street, she saw a bowling alley, a movie theater, and a small Hallmark store. She grinned when she saw a horse tethered to a hitch-rack in front of the video store.

She found a bedroom set, a sofa and love seat, an oak coffee table and matching side table in Lawson's Furniture Emporium, established, according to the sign over the cash register, in 1871.

She pointed at the sign as the clerk rang up her purchases. "You've been in business a long time," she remarked.

"Yes, ma'am. My family were some of the original settlers." He smiled at her. "I'm John Lawson. Would you like this delivered?"

"Yes, please. To the Triple Bar C."

He blinked at her, then checked the name on her Visa card again. "You're not related to *the* Conley family, are you?"

"Yes, I am."

He whistled softly. "And you're staying out at the ranch?" He shook his head.

"Yes, why?"

He grinned, somewhat sheepishly. "Well, folks hereabouts claim it's haunted."

"Yes, I've heard that, too. How soon can I expect this stuff to be delivered?"

"I'm afraid I won't be able to get it out to you before Saturday. Our delivery truck's in the shop for repairs."

"Saturday will be fine, thank you."

"I remember my great-granddaddy talking about what happened out at the old Conley place the night before the hanging. His daddy was there."

Kathy slipped her credit card and credit slip into her wallet. "Really?" she asked. "What did he say?"

He leaned back against the counter, arms folded over his chest. He was a handsome young man, of medium height, with dark blond hair and brown eyes.

"Well, near as I can recall, it happened the year before my great-great-granddaddy—his name was Rowdy Lawson—opened the store here in town. He was just a young man then, in his early twenties, working as a cowhand for Russell Conley. He never forgot that night. He wrote all about it in the letters he wrote to my great-great-grandmother."

Kathy's heart was pounding so loud, she was sure

63

Lawson could hear it. "What did he say?"

"Near as I can recall, he said Crowkiller claimed he was innocent, but of course, no one believed him. Aside from being a hired gun, he was a half-breed, you know. Couldn't be trusted. My great-great-granddaddy said everybody knew he'd cause trouble sooner or later."

"I read somewhere that he was innocent."

Lawson snorted. "I don't know where you could have read a thing like that. No, he was guilty, all right. My great-great-granddaddy said he was always watching Lydia Conley. I think Rowdy had a bit of a crush on her himself."

"Well, I can't blame him. Judging from the picture I saw, she was a very pretty woman."

"I've got an old photograph of her here somewhere. Hang on a minute." Lawson rummaged through his desk, then pulled out a cigar box. "This belonged to my great-great-granddaddy. He kept a picture of Lydia. My great-grandmother said he kept it because it made her mother jealous. Here." He thrust a faded photograph into Kathy's hand. "You look a lot like her."

Kathy studied the picture. Lydia didn't look so prim and proper in this picture. Her hair was down, curling over her shoulders, and she was smiling, as if she had a secret.

"I don't see much of a resemblance," Kathy remarked.

"No?" Lawson stood behind her, peering over her shoulder. "I do."

"Well, if you say so." She placed the photograph

on the counter. "Thank you for everything." She shifted the strap of her handbag on her shoulder and picked up her packages. "I really need to be getting home."

"Nice meeting you, Miss Conley."

Mrs. she almost said, but then let it go. He might ask about her husband, and she really didn't want to talk about Wayne, didn't want to explain she was a widow. "Thank you. What time shall I expect you on Saturday?"

"Noon?"

"Fine. Thanks again."

She thought about Dalton Crowkiller on the ride home. What had he been doing for the last hundred and twenty-five years? What was it like, to be a ghost? Why, except for Lydia, was she the only one who could see him? She had always had a secret yearning to write a book. What would he think about letting her write the story of his life? Even if it was never published, it would give her something to do to pass the time at night.

She pulled into the driveway and switched off the ignition. She sat in the car for a minute, looking at the house, her resident ghost momentarily forgotten. As soon as she got the inside painted, she'd get started on the outside. White, with dark blue trim. Or maybe a deep forest green with white shutters. She glanced at the barn, wondering if maybe she should have someone come out and demolish the thing and start from scratch. Of course, she didn't really need a barn, although it was a great place for storage. There were about fifteen boxes of stuff in there that she hadn't gone through yet. She had a feeling that she didn't need most of it.

With a sigh, she got out of the car, opened the trunk, and started removing her packages.

"Here, let me help you."

Startled by his voice at her elbow, she jerked upright, her packages tumbling to the ground. She yelped as she hit her head on the lid of the trunk. "Stop sneaking up on me like that!"

He looked at her, one brow arched in wry amusement. "Want me to shout 'boo' next time?"

She glared at him, one hand rubbing her head. "Just what I need," she muttered, "a comic gunfighter."

She closed the trunk while he picked up her packages. Side by side, they walked up the path to the porch steps. She held the door open for him.

"Where do you want these?" he asked.

"In my bedroom."

He lifted one brow; then, stifling whatever he had been about to say, he turned and walked down the hall toward her room.

She was in the kitchen, mixing a pitcher of lemonade, when she sensed his presence behind her.

"So," he asked, "how were things in town?"

"Fine, I guess."

"I reckon the place has changed some since I was there last."

"No doubt." She dropped some ice cubes into a glass and filled it with lemonade. "Did you know a young man named Lawson when you worked for Conley?''

"Rowdy Lawson?"

"That's the one. He was one of Russell Conley's cowboys.''

"Yeah, I remember him. Skinny kid, always mooning around after Lydia.''

"Really?" She sat down on one of the chairs. "I met his great-great-grandson in town today. He runs a furniture store.''

Dalton grunted. "Guess some things haven't changed." He hesitated a moment. "You look a little like her, you know—like Lydia.''

"Do I? That's what Mr. Lawson said. He showed me her picture. I didn't see any resemblance.''

"It's your eyes," Dalton said quietly, "and the color of your hair.''

"Oh.''

Silence stretched between them. It made her uncomfortable.

"I was thinking . . . that is, how would you feel if I were to write your life story?''

He pulled a chair from the table, turned it around, and sat down, his arms crossed over the back. "Why would you want to do that?''

"I don't know. I thought it might be interesting." She shrugged. "It was just an idea.''

"A book about me?" He grinned. "You mean like those dime novels Buntline churned out? Sure, why not? Maybe you can make me famous, like Hickock and Earp.''

"Maybe. I read somewhere that Ned Buntline

made something like twenty-thousand dollars a year on those dime novels." She took a sip of her lemonade.

"That's a pile of money."

Kathy nodded. "I did a report on him in high school. He was quite a character. Ran away from home when he was only ten or eleven and became a cabin boy on a freighter. When he grew up, he was quite a ladies' man. Married eight women."

Dalton whistled. "Eight women. When did he find the time to write?"

Kathy grinned at him. "That's what I wondered." She took a sip of her drink. "Tell me, what's it like, being a ghost?"

"I don't know how to describe it. Like being invisible, I guess. It was boring as hell before you got here. No one could see me, or hear me. Sometimes I'd break things or move things, just to prove I existed."

"Like that box of cereal the other day?"

"Yeah. I got a kick out of scaring the folks who stayed here."

"Did you really appear to Lydia?"

His expression went dark. "Yeah." He grunted softly. "I'm not the one who drove her crazy, though. It was her own guilty conscience."

Kathy tilted her head to one side. "Did you see her again, after she died?"

"At the funeral. It was quite a shindig." He snorted softly. "Fit for a queen. Everyone in town showed up."

"No, I mean—well, did you ever see her spirit or her ghost or whatever?"

"No. Far as I know, I'm the only ghost in these parts."

"I hope so."

He grinned at her. "I think you could take on an army of ghosts."

"No, thanks, one is enough. What have you been doing all these years?"

"Doing?" He shook his head, his expression thoughtful. "I just sort of . . . drift."

"Drift?"

"I don't know how to explain it. Kind of like being in hibernation."

"That's really weird."

"Yeah, you could say that." He glanced around the kitchen, thinking of all the changes he had seen on the ranch. Indoor plumbing and electric lights. Shiny iceboxes that didn't use ice to keep things cold, but made ice, instead. "You got one of those television sets?"

"A TV? Yes, why?" It was in the barn, along with her computer and fax machine. She hadn't brought it, or her entertainment center, in yet, wanting to wait until she was done painting before she set things up.

"The last of the Conleys to live here, they had one. It was . . . interesting."

"You watched TV?"

"Nothing else to do."

"What was your favorite show?"

"*Star Trek*."

The thought of him perched on a chair somewhere,

watching Captain Kirk and Mr. Spock travel through the galaxy on their five-year mission to seek out new life forms made her laugh, and once she started, she couldn't seem to stop. And then, without quite knowing how, her laughter turned to tears.

"Kathy?" Dalton looked at her, puzzled and distressed by her tears. "Kathy, don't cry."

She took a deep breath. "*Star Trek*," she said, sobbing. "It was Wayne's favorite show."

"Shit." He stared at her for a moment, watching her shoulders shake, listening to her heart-wrenching sobs, and when he couldn't take it anymore, he did the only thing he could think of. He drew her into his arms and held her close, one hand awkwardly patting her back. "Go on, honey," he drawled softly, "cry it all out."

She burrowed into his arms, her face buried in the hollow of his shoulder, and cried until she was dry and empty inside.

"I miss him so much," she murmured, her voice muffled against his shirt.

He didn't know what to say to that, so he didn't say anything, just held her tighter. They stood that way for a long time, his arms around her. She smelled like fresh peaches. Her hair tickled his skin, her body was soft against his, warm where he was cold. An emotion, a need he had thought long dead, stirred to life within him, awakening feelings no ghost should be having.

Knowing it was wrong, he brushed his lips across the top of her head. Lord, it had been over a century since he'd held a woman in his arms. Her nearness jolted him, her femininity calling to everything male within him.

He knew the exact moment when she realized what he was thinking. Her breath caught in her throat, and she went suddenly still in his arms.

Muttering an oath, he loosened his hold on her. "I'm sorry."

She looked up at him, her eyes filled with surprise, her cheeks flushed.

"I—" Kathy drew in a deep breath, not knowing what to say. She knew when a man was aroused, knew desire when she saw it. But . . . "I didn't know ghosts could—that is, that they ever—" Her cheeks felt hot and she knew she was blushing furiously.

"Me, either." He released her and took a step backward. "Damn."

"I think—" She ran her tongue over lips gone dry. "I think I'll start dinner."

Flustered, she turned away to pick up her lemonade. When she turned around again, Dalton was gone.

Chapter Five

A long string of vile oaths trailed behind Dalton as he walked along the stream. Why the hell did she have to come here? He had been resigned to his lot in life—or death—until she showed up on the scene. He woke from time to time, but mostly, he had just drifted through a thick gray fog, unaffected by the passage of time, by the changes taking place in the world.

Pausing, he picked up a rock and skipped it across the water. One, two, three, four . . . She smelled like sun-ripened peaches. Her hair was thick and soft, so soft. And her skin . . . smooth and soft and warm, so warm.

Damn! A man who'd been dead for a hundred and twenty-five years shouldn't be thinking like this, feeling like this. He was as randy as a young stud, ready to mount the first mare who crossed his path.

He stared into the water, wondering if a good soak would cool him off.

Kathy . . . even her name was soft. He closed his eyes, only to be tormented by the memory of how she had looked in the bathtub that first night, her cheeks rosy, her hair piled atop her head, her body clad in nothing but bubbles.

He opened his eyes and looked back at the house, wondering if it was too late to scare her away.

Kathy was nervous and on edge all evening, waiting, wondering what she would say when she saw him again.

Every time the house creaked, she looked up, expecting to see him, which was silly, since he never made a sound.

She went into the bedroom after dinner and sorted through the things she had bought that day.

Going into the bathroom, she spread the rug on the floor, put the new towels on the shelf, and hung one over the rack near the sink. She put up the new shower curtain, as well.

She had bought a matching curtain for the window over the tub, and she went off in search of a hammer to put up the new rod.

Returning to the bathroom, she stood on the tub, one foot on either side. She was humming softly as she hammered the first nail in place and reached for the second. And then her foot slipped. With a shriek, she felt herself falling. In an instant, she imagined herself landing in the tub. What would she break? An arm? A leg?

But she never hit the tub. Strong arms caught her, held her safe.

"You damn fool. What are you trying to do, break your neck?"

She stared up into his eyes, beautiful black eyes fringed with short, thick lashes. "Hi, Dalton."

"Hi, Dalton!" He cocked one brow. "That's all you've got to say?"

Rescued from certain injury, she felt a bubble of hysterical laughter rise in her throat. It took all her self-control to keep it bottled up.

"Thank you," she said, as sober as a judge.

He glared at her. "Damn fool woman, trying to do a man's work."

She felt her temper start to rise. "Excuse me?"

"You heard me."

"Listen, you male, macho jerk..." The words died in her throat as a slow smile curved his lips.

"Macho jerk?"

"You don't even know what it means, do you?" she asked smugly.

"I'm not an idiot. I may not know what the words mean, but there's no mistaking that tone of voice."

"You can put me down now."

"Maybe I don't want to."

Her heartbeat accelerated. "Don't you?"

He shook his head. "You feel real good right where you are."

"Do I?" She felt warm all over. Hardly aware of

what she was doing, she slid her arms up around his neck.

"Kathy."

She felt his muscles flex as he held her tighter. This close, she noticed there was a faint white scar at his hairline. "I think you'd better put me down."

He hesitated a moment, then did as she asked; her body slid against his as he lowered her to the floor.

Flustered, she bent down to pick up the hammer.

"Here," he said, "let me do that."

"I can do it."

He lifted one brow.

"Well, I can!"

"I know." With a wry grin, he took the hammer from her hand.

She would have argued further, but she rather enjoyed watching him, watching the play of muscles beneath his shirt as he hammered the last three nails in place.

"Anything else?" he asked.

"No, I don't think so."

Dalton put the hammer on the sink, then rested one shoulder against the door jamb while she threaded the narrow white rod into the slit in the top of the curtain.

She was getting ready to climb on the edge of the tub again when he took the curtain from her hand. "I'll do it."

With a *humph* of annoyance, she crossed her arms over her chest. Had the men in his time really thought women so helpless? Of course, it was easy for him to put the rod in place. He didn't have to stand on the edge of the tub. He didn't have to stand on anything.

Madeline Baker

He just sort of floated upward. How could he be so solid, yet defy the laws of gravity? She had always thought ghosts were ethereal creatures, without substance. But there was nothing intangible about Dalton. He was as solid as a rock.

"Anything else you want me to do?" he asked.

"I didn't *ask* you to do that."

He glanced around the room. Bathrooms were a relatively new invention, certainly a big improvement over the old outhouses. "I always had a hankering for my own place."

"You never had a home?"

"Not really. Never stayed in one place long enough to sink any roots."

"Let's go to the kitchen," Kathy suggested. "I want to get something to drink, and then maybe we can get to work on that book."

"Sure." He followed her into the kitchen, admiring the fit of her Levi's, the alluring sway of her hips. Women hadn't worn pants in his day. It was an innovation he rather liked.

Kathy pulled a root beer out of the fridge, then sat down at the table. "Let's see, I guess we should start at the beginning. Where were you born?"

Dalton settled into the chair across from her. "Near the Little Big Horn."

She picked up a pencil and began writing on the scratch pad she had used to make her grocery list. "When?"

"In the summer of 1844."

She looked up at him. She knew he'd been born over a hundred years ago, but somehow it hadn't seemed real until now. 1844. She shook her head. "Who were your parents?"

"My father was a Lakota medicine man. My mother was a white woman. She'd been taken in a raid by the Cheyenne. My father bought her for three ponies and a buffalo robe."

It sounded like a Movie of the Week. "What were their names?"

"The ponies?"

She looked up, and he burst out laughing.

"No, silly, the names of your parents."

"My father was Night Caller. The Lakota called my mother Star Singer but her *wasichu* name was Julianna Dalton."

"How did you get to be a gunfighter?"

Dalton shook his head. "I don't know. It wasn't anything I planned. It just sort of happened."

"Well?"

"Well what?"

"Tell me how it happened."

He sat back in the chair, legs stretched out in front of him, arms folded over his chest. "I guess it all started when I was about fourteen. Some traders came through our village, and I traded some beaver pelts for an old Hawken."

"Hawken?"

"It's a rifle made by Sam Hawken and his brother. Anyway, I got to be a pretty good shot with that gun. Later, I got hold of a pistol. I liked the way it felt in my hand. I was going on fifteen when my father was killed in a raid against the Crow. My mother decided she wanted to go back to her own people. I didn't want to go with her, but I couldn't let her go alone. I bid my grandparents good-bye, promising to return as soon as possible, but I never did."

"Was your mother happy, living with the Indians?"

"Not at first, but she'd pretty much resigned herself to it by the time I came along. She told me once she hated my father until the day I was born." He looked away, his expression suddenly distant, melancholy. "She said she couldn't hate him any more after that. Said the love she felt for me kinda spilled over onto him."

Kathy looked up. "Go on."

"I can't imagine why anyone would be interested in all this."

"I'm interested."

He lifted one brow, then shrugged. "My mother was from Boston, and that's where we went. It was like nothing I'd ever seen before. Men in tight suits and women bound up in layers and layers of clothing and big hats. Lots of buildings and smoke. I'd heard people say Lakota villages smelled bad, but the streets of Boston smelled a lot worse. People stared at us. Looking back, I guess I can't blame them. You didn't see many people parading around in buckskins.

"We went to my mother's house. Her people didn't live there anymore, and no one knew where they had gone. I knew then and there that I'd never make it back to the Lakota, knew that I couldn't go off and leave my mother alone in a strange land.

"I sold my Hawken for twenty-two dollars and we used the money to pay for a room. My mother bought a second-hand dress and a pair of shoes and after several days, she found a job working as a house-keeper for some rich family, name of Worthingham. They gave me a job, too. Let me look after their horses. My mother slept in the house, and I slept in a room over the stable. I hated it, at first anyway. But they paid me good, and I liked working with their horses. As time went by, I got to liking city life pretty well. I didn't have any expenses, and I acquired a taste for fine whiskey and expensive cigars.''

''Did your mother ever find out where her family had gone?''

''No. We'd been with the Worthinghams about two years when their butler asked my mother to marry him, and she said yes. I left the Worthinghams a few months later. There were big things happening in the West, and I had a yearning to be a part of them. During my years with the Worthinghams, I'd bought myself a new Colt .44. When I wasn't busy, I prac-ticed shooting at targets and quick-drawing my gun.''

He paused to give Kathy time to catch up. He stud-ied her bent head, noting the beauty of her profile, the way her hair fell over her shoulders to frame her face.

''Okay, go on.''

''I didn't have much to do with people in Boston, and those I did associate with accepted me for what I was. Nobody cared much that I was a half-breed. As soon as I left Boston, all that changed. Seemed nobody had a good thing to say about Indians.''

''I'd think it would be just the opposite,'' Kathy said.

79

Dalton shook his head. "People in Boston read about the Indian wars, but the news didn't really mean anything to them. They were too far away from it all. It was different out West. Decent white folks were suspicious of me because I was half Indian."

"I guess that makes sense," Kathy decided. It was a lot easier to be tolerant of people when you weren't directly involved with them. "So, what happened next?"

"I was in a saloon in Virginia City when a man started giving me a bad time, calling me names. He was a little drunk, and so was I. Next thing I knew, he was drawing on me." Dalton shrugged. "When the smoke cleared, he was dead. People came up to me then and started slapping me on the back, congratulating me for killing him. Seemed the man I'd killed had been a well-known gunslinger name of Hager Whittaker, and now that he was dead, his rep was mine.

"It didn't mean much to me at first except free drinks and—" He looked at Kathy, then grunted softly. It had meant free women, too, but he didn't think she would appreciate that. "Not too many days later, a friend of the deceased came after me."

"And you were faster."

"Yeah. For a while there, seemed like there wasn't a day went by that I wasn't defending that reputation. I don't know if people finally decided to give up, or if I'd gunned them all down, but things quieted after I shot Stu Cassidy. Then I started getting offers."

"Offers?"

"Yeah, you know. People started offering to pay for my gun."

"Oh. Have you killed very many men?"

"More than my share, I reckon."

"Did you ever go back to your father's people?"

He blew out a sigh, remembering the promise he had made to his father. "No, I never did. I regret that. I always aimed to but—" He shrugged. "Just never found the time."

Kathy put her pencil down and stretched her back and shoulders. "I guess that's enough for tonight." She yawned. "Do you ever get tired?"

"No, just bored out of my mind." He smiled at her. "You don't know how glad I am that you're here."

"Yes, well . . ." She felt her cheeks grow hot as he continued to look at her, his dark eyes filled with admiration, and desire. "I think I'll get ready for bed. Good night."

"Good night."

She stood up, acutely aware of his gaze on her back as she walked away.

In her bedroom, she closed and locked the door, then thought how foolish it was to try to lock out a ghost. No doubt he could walk through the walls if he was of a mind to.

She went through her nightly routine, washing off her makeup, brushing her hair, flossing her teeth, and all the while thinking of what he had told her, wondering how many men he had killed. She had never known anyone who had taken a human life.

She shivered as she crawled under the covers. *Gun-*

fighter. It always seemed kind of romantic in the movies, all those old Hollywood films about Wyatt Earp and Frank and Jesse James and Billy the Kid.

Have you killed many men? she had asked, and he'd replied, *More than my share, I reckon.*

She tried to rationalize it, tried to tell herself that times had been different then, but the fact remained, ghost or no ghost, he was a killer, and he was living in her house.

She started painting the library early Friday morning, the same shade of cream she had used in the living room, and all the while she thought about Dalton Crowkiller, about the questions she would ask him that night, like what it had felt like to kill a man, and why he had never married and settled down.

It didn't take long to paint the library; one wall was mostly windows, two had floor-to-ceiling bookshelves. She thought of all the books packed in boxes in the barn, along with all her knickknacks, and knew the shelves wouldn't be empty for long.

She took a break for an early lunch, then went to work in the dining room. She would have to find a table, she thought, and maybe a hutch, one of those big, glass-fronted things, sort of like the one her grandmother had had.

She kept waiting for Dalton to appear and when he didn't, she wondered where he was. How did a ghost spend his days? He had said he didn't get tired, didn't eat, didn't sleep. What *did* he do?

*　　*　　*

Dalton stood in the doorway, watching Kathy. She was wearing a pair of paint-stained blue jeans and a green T-shirt. Her hair was pulled back in a ponytail that swayed back and forth as she moved. She had a nice figure, all soft and round. And she was alive, so alive. She seemed to glow, and he knew, without knowing how he knew, that it was because she had a good heart, a good soul. He had never known a woman like her. Growing up with the Lakota, he hadn't given much thought to girls. He had been too busy learning to be a warrior. Later, in Boston, he had kept to himself. He hadn't been an outcast, exactly. In the East, no one cared that he was a half-breed. But he had ever been aware that he was different, that his Indian blood set him apart from everyone else.

And then he had gone West. Moving from one rough town to another, he hadn't come into contact with many "ladies," but he'd met a lot of soiled doves. Young, old, new in the business or as hard as nails, most of them hadn't cared that he was a half-breed, hadn't cared that he hired out his gun, so long as he had an itch to scratch and the cash in his pocket to pay for it.

And then he had met Lydia Conley. He lifted one hand to his throat. It seemed fitting somehow that a so-called lady would be his downfall. Lady! She had been a bigger whore than any light-skirt he had ever met.

His gaze moved over Kathy as she climbed down the ladder. Kathy . . . now, she was a lady through and through.

She paused at the foot of the ladder, her gaze on the doorway. "Dalton?"

How had she known he was there? He materialized before her, pleased to note that she didn't jump out of her skin this time. He gestured at the room. "Looks nice."

She nodded. "How do you do that?"

"Do what?"

"Make yourself visible."

"I don't know how to explain it. I just sort of think it, and it happens."

"Can you walk through walls, too?"

"Yeah, when I've a mind to."

"Oh."

He looked at her carefully. She was staring at him as if she had never seen him before. "You all right?"

"What? Oh, yes. I was just trying to imagine what it would be like to be a ghost."

"I told you. It's boring as hell."

"Well, I was going to clean up, and then go for a walk. Do you . . . do you want to come with me?"

"Best offer I've had in years," he replied.

"Okay. I'll meet you on the back porch in half an hour."

He recognized a hint when he heard one. "Half an hour," he said.

Side by side, they walked along the stream.

"This place hasn't changed much," Dalton mused aloud. "Not like the rest of the world."

"I thought you couldn't leave Saul's Crossing?"

"I can't, but I've learned about the changes

through the people who have come here over the years, and from watching the news on the television.'' He plucked a stick from the ground and rolled it back and forth between his fingers. "People talk about progress. They've replaced horses with fast automobiles. Built bigger houses. Made pictures that move and talk. But it seems to me that people are still the same.''

"I guess that's true. Maybe people never change. Maybe the human race is destined to keep making the same mistakes over and over again.'' She paused. "Would you choose the same way of life if you had it to do over again?''

"Become a hired gun, you mean?''

Kathy nodded.

"Probably. It was a good life for a man like me.''

"A man like you?''

He blew out a deep breath. "I had no money, and no hope of making any. There was no way for me to rise above what I was in Boston, the half-breed son of a housekeeper. I could have stayed there and spent the rest of my life looking after the Worthinghams' horses, or I could have gone to work on the docks, I suppose, but that wasn't for me. When we left the Lakota, I had thought to go back, but living with the whites spoiled me. I got to liking soft beds and having a full belly summer and winter.''

He tossed the stick in the water and watched the current carry it away. "It was an easy life, being a hired gun. After I killed Whittaker, there were a bunch of young guns who came to try me. I killed them all, but it wasn't murder. It was never like that.

I never shot anybody in the back. And with each killing, my reputation grew, until no one dared face me. I had to do very little work for the money I was paid. A few jobs a year—'' He shrugged. ''In Boston, I was a half-breed nobody, but in Ellsworth or Kansas City, I was Somebody. You understand what I'm trying to say?''

''Yes, I guess so.'' She hesitated a minute, then asked in a rush, ''How many men have you killed?''

''Do you really want to know?''

She nodded slowly.

''Nine.''

It was a lot, yet far fewer than she had expected.

He grinned at her. ''You look disappointed.''

''No, no, I just thought—''

''You thought it would be more. Dozens, maybe.''

She nodded.

''Not every job involved killing. I was a payroll guard for a while. Another time I escorted a banker's wife to San Francisco. Once I had a big rep, I rarely had to draw my gun.''

Kathy nodded again, wishing she had brought paper and pencil along. ''How come I can see you so clearly? I thought ghosts were—you know, invisible or transparent.''

''I don't know.'' It was a riddle he hadn't solved yet, her being able to see him when no one else could.

She touched his chest with her fingertip. ''And you're solid.''

''Being invisible is easier.''

''Is it?''

86

"Yeah. Takes a lot of energy to materialize and to stay that way."

Kathy shook her head. It was amazing, just amazing.

"You don't believe me?"

"No, I believe you. I was just wondering why I can see you, and no one else ever has, except for . . . never mind."

"Except for Lydia."

Her name sounded like a curse, the way he said it. That quickly, the easy camaraderie between them was gone. "Dalton, I'm sorry."

"Forget it." Suddenly restless, Dalton walked away from her. Lydia. He hoped she was burning in the deepest, hottest part of hell.

Chapter Six

John Lawson arrived with her furniture shortly after noon on Saturday. Dressed in a short-sleeved Western shirt, faded blue jeans, scuffed boots, and a tan Stetson, he looked as though he had just stepped off the cover of a Western magazine. In addition to her furniture, he brought her a bouquet of bright yellow daisies.

"Welcome to Saul's Crossing," he said, offering her the flowers with a flourish and a smile.

"Thank you." She glanced past his shoulder to where a tall, beefy young man clad in black jeans and a sleeveless black T-shirt stood leaning against the back of the truck. "I see you brought help."

"Yeah, that's Sonny. Actually, I'm here to help him. He could probably carry all this stuff in on his own without breaking a sweat."

Kathy checked out the other man's brawny arms and smiled. "I think you're right."

It didn't take the two men long to unload the truck. Kathy stood in the kitchen doorway, out of the way, while they carried things in. Once, feeling a brush of cool air, she glanced over her shoulder, but if Dalton was there, she couldn't see him.

"Well," John said. He took off his hat, wiping the sweat from his brow with the back of his hand. "That's everything."

"Nice meeting you, ma'am," Sonny said.

"You, too. Can I offer you something to drink? A coke, or some ice water?"

"A glass of cold water would be welcome," Sonny said.

"We'll wait out on the porch," Lawson added.

Kathy went into the kitchen and filled two tall glasses with ice water, then carried them outside.

Sonny took his and drained it in one long swallow. He wiped his mouth with the back of his hand, then handed her the glass. "Thank you, ma'am," he said politely, and ambled down the stairs.

Kathy watched him slide into the passenger side of the trunk. Lawson had been right. All that work, and Sonny wasn't even breathing hard.

"Well, I guess we'd better be going," John remarked. "We've got another delivery to make." He smiled at her as he handed her his empty glass.

"Thanks for everything," Kathy said.

"Glad to do it." John descended one step, then turned to face her. "Any chance you'll be coming into town again soon?"

"I would imagine. I've still got a lot of rooms to furnish."

"Any chance you'd go out with me next Saturday night? Say dinner and a movie? I . . . oh . . ." His voice trailed off, and Kathy saw him staring at her wedding ring. "Sorry, I didn't know you were married."

"I'm a widow," Kathy replied, wondering if the words would ever get any easier to say.

"Oh. I'm sorry. How . . . I mean, was it sudden?"

"A traffic accident. Almost a year ago."

"I'm sorry to hear that. I'm divorced myself. Listen, it's been a while since I asked a woman on a date. I don't know how long, that is . . ." He cleared his throat. "Maybe it's too soon, but . . ." He looked up at her, obviously flustered. "Is it too soon for you to be dating?"

Kathy hesitated a moment. She hadn't gone out with anyone since Wayne passed away. It was on the tip of her tongue to refuse, and then she shook her head. Maybe it was time to rejoin the land of the living. "I'd love to go out with you."

"What time shall I pick you up?"

"Why don't I meet you in town? I'd planned to drive in anyway."

Lawson smiled, revealing a dimple in his left cheek. "Great. Why don't you meet me at the store at six-thirty?"

"All right."

"See you then." Whistling softly, John descended the stairs. He slid behind the wheel and gave her a wave and a smile, then pulled out of the yard.

A date. Kathy rested her elbows on the porch rail, her chin cradled in her hands, her toe tapping nervously. She had a date.

"So, that's John Lawson."

He'd hardly startled her at all this time, she thought. No doubt she was getting used to having him creep up on her. "Yes."

"And you're going out with him."

Kathy straightened up, wondering why she felt guilty. "Yes, I am."

Dalton grunted softly. He didn't like the idea of her being with another man, but it wasn't his place to say so.

"Well," Kathy said, "I guess I'd better get busy."

He followed her into the house, stood in the living room, his shoulder braced against one wall, while she flipped on the radio, then moved into the middle of the room to survey her new furniture, her brow furrowed in thought.

When she started to push the sofa across the floor, he went to help her.

"Thanks." She glanced up, her gaze meeting his. "You don't have to do this."

He shrugged. "It's not like I've got anything better to do."

She nodded, acutely aware of the tension that hummed between them. He was the most *male* male she had ever known. He radiated more raw sexual appeal than any living man she had ever met. There was no denying the attraction she felt for him, or the fact that he stirred feelings within her that she had never thought to feel again. She wiped a hand over

91

her forehead. When he looked at her through those deep black eyes, excitement bubbled up inside her, making her feel young again, desirable.

For a moment, time seemed to stand still. On the radio, Johnny Mathis was singing, *Chances are you'll think that I'm in love with you . . .*

As though rooted to the spot, she watched Dalton walk toward her until he was close. Too close.

She licked lips gone suddenly dry.

"Dance with me?" he asked, his voice low and husky.

She blinked up at him, startled. Of all the things he might have said, this was the most unexpected. "What?"

"Dance with me. I won't step on your toes, I promise."

She was sorely tempted to laugh. The idea of waltzing around the living room with a gunfighter seemed ludicrous somehow, but a moment later she was in his arms. Her heart was pounding so loudly, she was certain he could hear it. She searched her mind for something to say to break the tension that flowed hot and sweet between them, but nothing came to mind, and she was aware of nothing but the intensity of his eyes and the welcome prison of his arm around her.

"Where did . . ." She cleared her throat. "Where did you learn to dance?"

"Boston. My mother taught me."

She nodded, unable to think of a response.

He held her for several moments after the music ended.

Kathy took a deep breath, certain she would never be the same again. Taking a step back, she ran a hand through her hair. Every nerve ending in her body was humming with desire.

Crossing the room, she switched off the radio.

"Let's try the sofa over there, against that wall," she said, in her most businesslike tone of voice.

Dalton nodded. He never should have asked her to dance, he mused ruefully, but it had been the only way he could think of to get her in his arms.

An hour later, she had the living room arranged to her satisfaction. Standing in the middle of the floor, one finger tapping her chin, she made a slow circle, thinking of what else she needed . . . a picture over the sofa . . . something Western, horses, or maybe a sunset. A tall plant for the corner, a lamp for the end table. She would put the entertainment center there, between the two front windows.

Dalton stood to one side, watching her. It annoyed the hell out of him that he couldn't seem to keep his eyes off her, that she filled his every thought. Dancing with her had been a mistake. Now that he knew how good she felt, he ached to hold her again, to run his hands over her skin, to watch her eyes grow dark with passion. Damn.

"Okay, ready to tackle the bedroom?" Kathy asked, and then could have bitten her tongue. Being in the bedroom with him didn't seem like such a good idea, but the words had been said and there was no graceful way to take them back.

Dalton nodded, glad for the distraction, and then wondered why he thought being in a bedroom with

Kathy would change the direction of his all-too-lustful thoughts.

Lawson and Sonny had put the bed frame together before they left, so all Kathy had to do was decide where she wanted it. Finally, she decided to put it catty-corner, with a nightstand on each side and the dresser against the only wall without a door or a window.

Dalton stood in the doorway while she made the bed, his gaze lingering on her shapely fanny as she smoothed the sheets. Muttering an oath, he forced himself to admire the room instead. He didn't know much about decorating, but the room looked good, feminine without being frilly. The dark blue carpet, the blue print spread, the pale blue walls . . . it looked nice, homey. His gaze rested on the double bed, imagining her there, imagining himself there, lying beside her, holding her in his arms. Damn and double damn!

"Well, that's everything," Kathy said. "Do you have anything planned for—" She broke off, blushing self-consciously.

"No," he replied with a wry grin. "I don't have anything planned. What's on your mind?"

"I thought maybe we'd do some more work on that book."

"Sure, if you want."

"I'll have to unpack my computer," Kathy mused as they left the bedroom.

"Computer?" He'd heard the word before, but had never seen one.

"It's like a typewriter."

He grunted softly.

She sat down at the kitchen table, and he took his usual seat across from her.

"Let's see, where did we leave off?" She thumbed through her notes, hoping she would be able to read them when she had time to transcribe them. "Why don't you tell me what it was like, living with the Lakota."

Dalton tipped his chair back, his expression thoughtful. "It was a good life. Hard at times, but good. The Lakota were an honorable people."

He stared past her, looking out the kitchen window. They were gone now—his parents, all the people he had grown up with. Dead and gone. He knew, from overhearing people talk and from watching television, that times had changed. People didn't ride horses anymore. Cowboys and gunfighters had gone the way of the Pony Express and high-button shoes. He had been shocked the first time he had seen a woman in shorts. Not that he hadn't liked it. She'd been a pretty, redhaired girl with gray eyes and a dimple in her chin, one of the people who had rented the house from time to time. In his day, a man had been lucky to see a woman's ankles; now women ran around practically naked, showing off their legs and just about everything else.

He looked at Kathy, wondering if she ever wore shorts.

"Dalton?"

"What? Oh, yeah."

For the next two hours, he told her about growing up with the Lakota, how his whole family—mother, father, grandparents, aunts, uncles—had all had a hand in raising him, how he had learned to ride and track and hunt, how he had learned to live off the land. He told her about his first horse raid against the Crow, and the first time he killed a man.

"That's something you never forget," he said. "The heat of battle, the blood singing in your veins, your heart pounding in your ears when it's over because you know it could just as easily have been you lying there in the dirt."

"What about all the other men you killed later, in gunfights? Do you remember them, too?"

"Every one." He saw their faces in his dreams sometimes, shadow faces that haunted him as he drifted through time and space, caught between this world and the next.

"Have you ever been shot?"

"Oh, yeah, couple times." He lifted his hand to the scar near his hairline. "Shooter by the name of Lonnie Dwyer almost got lucky over in Bodie. I've got a nasty scar on my back, too."

"Someone shot you in the back?"

He nodded. "Some low-down coward name of Rudy Phillips."

"Did you . . . ?"

"Damn straight!"

"Bodie? Isn't that in California?"

"Yeah. It was a hell of a town in my day."

"It's a ghost town now."

He laughed softly. "Figures."

"What was it like, when you were there?"

"Loud and dangerous. There were thirty mines in

operation back then, and thirty-five saloons, as I recall." He laughed softly. "And sixty brothels."

"Sixty?"

"Yeah. The saloons and the brothels were open round the clock. Hardly a day went by that there wasn't a killing in one or the other. I recollect hearing someone say the town had a man for breakfast every day. Town had three breweries. They worked round the clock, too."

Kathy shook her head, unable to imagine such a place. Sixty brothels open round the clock. She did some quick mental arithmetic. If a girl worked an eight-hour day . . . three girls per day times sixty . . . one-hundred-and-eighty girls times however many girls worked in each saloon . . . say ten girls for every saloon . . . eighteen-hundred working girls . . . could that be right?

"How long did you stay there?"

"Couple months. Some prospector hired me to watch his back to and from his mine and while he played cards. He should have hired me to keep an eye on him when he was flat on his back."

"What do you mean?"

"Saloon girl claimed he refused to pay her for services rendered and stuck a knife in his ribs. He died the next day, and I hightailed it out of there the day after."

"Where'd you go next?"

"Abilene."

"What brought you to Saul's Crossing?"

"Nothing. I was just passing through. It was a peaceful little town, and I decided to stay a while."

He grunted softly. "Biggest mistake I ever made."

"What, exactly, did Russell Conley hire you for?"

"There was bad blood brewing between him and Burkhart, the owner of the adjoining ranch. Water rights, as I recall." A smooth smile flickered over his lips. "Burkhart was making all kinds of threats, but he was all wind. As soon as he heard I was on Conley's payroll, the fight was over."

Kathy cocked her head at him. "That's all it took? Just the mention of your name?"

Dalton nodded. "Pretty impressive, huh?"

"You killed one of Burkhart's men, though, didn't you?"

"Yeah, but it didn't have anything to do with the fight between Conley and Burkhart. It was just between him and me."

"How come I never heard of you?"

"Too many other fast guns running around, I reckon. Buntline was making Hickock and Cody famous. I wasn't looking for that kind of attention." He gestured at her yellow legal pad and grinned. "Course, it doesn't matter now. You can make me as famous as you want."

Kathy grimaced. "Shoot, I'm no writer. I doubt if anyone will want to buy it even if I can figure out how to turn it into a coherent story."

"Well, if you ever get the thing published, you'll have to read it to me."

"Don't you want to learn to read?"

"What for? Doesn't seem any point in it now."

"Well, reading might help pass the time. I have a lot of books out in the barn."

He shook his head. "Time isn't the same for me as it is for you."

"What do you mean?"

"Before you came here, I wasn't really aware of time passing. I don't know how to explain it."

"Well, try."

He frowned. "It was sort of like sleeping, I guess. I'd drift off. Sometimes I'd hear voices and there'd be people here at the house and I'd come up and take a look around." He shrugged. "When they left, I just went back to . . . drifting."

"That's too weird," Kathy said. She stood up, stretching her back and shoulders, trying to imagine what it would be like to be caught between this world and the next. "I need a break."

"It's gonna rain tonight."

Kathy glanced out the window. The sky was clear and blue. "I don't think so."

Dalton nodded. "I can smell it in the air."

"Uh-huh."

He winked at her. "You'll see." He rose from the chair with effortless grace. "You gonna rebuild the barn?"

"I guess so, why?"

"Thought maybe you'd buy a couple of horses."

"Horses?"

He nodded, a faraway look in his eyes. "I had a right fine buckskin mare. I sure miss her." He slid his right hand down his thigh. "And my hardware."

Kathy shook her head. He hadn't mentioned missing any people, but he missed his horse. And his gun.

"I could rebuild the barn for you," he said suddenly.

"You?"

"Why not? I've got nothing else to do."

"I don't know. I never thought about getting a horse. I've never even been on one."

"No? Shit, I could ride before I could walk."

"Well," she said dubiously. "We'll see."

Later, after dinner, she hauled her computer into the house and set it up. It took a while, but eventually she found Dalton's name on a web site that listed little known Western historical facts.

Crowkiller, Dalton (1844–1873). Born in Dakota Territory, Crowkiller gained notoriety when he killed Hager Whittaker in a gunfight in Virginia City.

Crowkiller is believed to have gunned down more than two dozen men in cold blood in his short career as a hired gun. He was hanged in Montana July 28, 1873, for raping the wife of Russell Wayne Conley, a prominent rancher. Conley's wife, the former Lydia Camille Winston, later went insane from her ordeal at Crowkiller's hands.

"What does it say about me?"

"How do you know it's about you?"

"I may not be able to read much, but I recognize my name when I see it."

She read the entry to him, feeling her ears burn at

the volatile oaths that flew from his lips.

"Two dozen men! Where the hell did they come up with that?"

"I don't know," she replied. "Literary license, I suppose."

"Damn liars. Two dozen men in cold blood. I never shot anybody in the back, or anybody who wasn't about to shoot me."

"I believe you," Kathy said. "Calm down."

"Calm down! How would you feel if someone wrote a pack of lies about you?"

"Well, I guess I'd be upset."

"Maybe it's a good thing you're writing that book," he muttered.

"Yes, well, don't get your hopes up. I don't know that anyone will ever want to publish it."

"You'd better go close the windows."

"Why?"

He grinned at her. "It's raining."

"Is it?" She listened a moment and then she heard it, the soft whisper of rain on the roof.

"I'd better find a bucket," she said, pushing away from the table. "There's a hole the size of the Grand Canyon in one of the bedrooms."

He laughed softly. "Better find a big bucket."

"Maybe I can cover the hole with some plastic," she said, thinking of the plastic sheeting she had used to cover the floor when she painted.

She opened a drawer and rummaged around until she found the hammer and a handful of nails.

"What do you think you're doing?"

"I'm going up on the roof."

"I'll take care of it."

"I can do it."

He shook his head as he took the hammer and nails from her hand. In his day, women had been content to act like women.

"Dalton."

"Let's not argue about this, okay? That roof's gonna be slippery."

"Well . . ."

"Besides, if you break your neck, I won't have anyone to talk to."

Defeated, Kathy blew out a sigh. "I'll get the plastic."

She spread towels over the carpet to soak up the water, then put a bucket under the hole in case the plastic didn't hold. Even though she could have taken care of the leak herself, she was glad she hadn't had to climb up there. She might not be afraid of ghosts and goblins, but she was afraid of heights. She glanced up as she heard the sound of hammering, imagining Dalton up there, hair blowing in the wind. The leak wasn't quite as bad as she had made it out to be, but she was still going to have to see about getting the roof repaired or replaced.

"How's that?" he called.

"Fine." She picked up the wet towels, carried them downstairs, and dumped them in the washing machine.

A few minutes later, Dalton came in the back door.

"I'll get you a towel," she said, and then stared at him. He wasn't wet.

He grinned at her, then shrugged. "Don't ask. I

don't know why." The sun didn't warm him; the cold of winter didn't affect him; he didn't get wet when it rained.

"Well," she said, covering a yawn with her hand, "I think I'm ready for bed."

"I'll say good night then."

"Good night. Thanks for taking care of that leak for me."

He nodded, his mind filling with images of Kathy getting undressed, slipping between sweet-smelling sheets, her hair spread like dark silk over the pillow. He cleared his throat. "If you buy some shingles, I'll repair the roof."

Desire hummed between them. She had a sudden, inexplicable yearning to touch him, to run her hand over that wide, muscular chest, to press her lips to his.

"Kathy?"

"What?" She stared at him, her mind blank. What had they been talking about?

He moved toward her, and she backed up, afraid he would try to kiss her. Afraid she would let him. The roof. They had been talking about the hole in the roof. "I'll probably just have the whole thing replaced."

He crossed his arms over his chest to keep from reaching for her again. "That's probably a good idea."

"Yes. Well, good night."

"Night."

He watched her leave the room, thinking it was too bad the rain had no effect on him, because he could sure as hell use a cold shower.

Chapter Seven

The next week flew by. She painted the upstairs bedrooms—one a pale sky blue, one a darker shade of
blue, and one white.

Now, cleaning up the mess from the last one, she
wondered idly what she was going to do with three
empty rooms. One of them, the pale blue one, maybe,
could be used as a guest room, in case her parents or
her mother-in-law came to visit. She decided to set
up her computer and her fax machine in the other blue
one. And the third . . . maybe, she mused with a grin,
she could offer it to Dalton. Of course, since he didn't
sleep, he probably didn't need a bedroom.

Dalton. He continued to come and go in her life,
appearing and disappearing so frequently that it no
longer startled her. She liked his company, liked

having him around. His presence kept her from getting lonely, or bored.

He spent his days working on the barn. Sometimes it all seemed like a dream, though a very strange one at that, her inside the house, painting, and Dalton out in the barn, repairing broken-down stalls and putting new shingles on the roof. It was a good thing she didn't get any visitors. She couldn't imagine what people would think if they drove up and saw a hammer and shingles floating over the barn roof, apparently moving by themselves. As soon as he finished fixing the barn, they were going to paint it. She hadn't decided what color, probably the traditional dark red with white trim.

They worked on Dalton's life story every evening after dinner. He had led an exciting life, though not one that appealed to her. Always on the move, always looking over his shoulder, never knowing when someone would try to gun him down. He had won and lost an amazing amount of money on the turn of a card, boasted that he had once drunk Wild Bill Hickock under the table. He'd met Billy the Kid, played poker with Wyatt Earp and his brother, Morgan, traded insults with Doc Holliday.

She had brought her computer in from the barn and spent a part of each afternoon typing up her notes. She wasn't sure if the writing was any good; she doubted if anyone would even be interested in reading it, but she found it fascinating, and it gave her a sense of purpose.

She had brought in the TV, too, much to Dalton's

delight. He watched it while she cooked dinner, and she had taken to eating dinner in the living room to keep him company. A typical male, he liked to watch sports and the news, though why a ghost should be interested in either of them was beyond her.

Going into the kitchen, Kathy washed the paint from the roller and brush, glad that, for the time being at least, the painting was done. It had never been one of her favorite things to do.

She could see Dalton through the window. He was putting new hinges on the door of the barn. Though the day was hot, he didn't seem to be perspiring. She stood at the sink, everything else forgotten, as she watched the play of muscles across his broad back and shoulders. She experienced an unexpected thrill of excitement as she imagined what it would be like to slip her hand under his shirt and run her fingertips over those rippling muscles . . .

"Stop that right now," she muttered. "He doesn't even exist."

Oh, but he did. He might be dead. He might be a ghost. But he definitely existed. And his very existence was playing havoc with her emotions.

As though he sensed her watching, he turned toward the house and waved. If it had been Wayne out there, she would have taken him a glass of lemonade, but Dalton didn't eat or drink. And since she couldn't think of any other excuse to go out there, she waved, then turned away from the window. Maybe doing the laundry would take her mind off Triple Bar C's resident ghost.

*   *   *

It was Friday night, and they were watching TV, some old Western starring John Wayne and Montgomery Clift. Dalton was sitting on the sofa, long legs stretched out in front of him, one arm flung over the back of the couch.

Kathy gestured at the screen. "Did you ever go on a trail drive?"

"Me? Hell, no. Miserable, dirty work, driving cattle. Eating dust all day long." He shook his head. "It's even worse than they make it look."

"Did you ever meet a whore with a heart of gold?"

He snorted. "Honey, there ain't no such thing. I'm not sure most of them even *had* hearts."

"Really?" she asked, wondering if he was kidding.

"Oh, yeah. It was all business with those girls. They wanted their money up front, or you could forget it."

"Did you . . . ah, consort with a lot of easy women?"

Dalton shrugged. "I had my share. Of course, there were some who wouldn't have anything to do with me."

"Really?" Considering his raw good looks and sexy smile, she found that hard to believe.

"Yeah."

"But why?"

" 'Cause I'm a half-breed."

She stared at him, not understanding.

"Some whores had their limits, I guess. Indians were considered less than human. I was just one step above."

"That's ridiculous," she retorted, even though she

knew it wasn't. There was a lot of talk today about equality, but you couldn't legislate people's feelings and there was still a lot of prejudice in the world. "I'm sorry."

"Don't be. I did all right."

She could believe that. Even as a ghost, he exuded enough charm for ten men. It was hard to imagine him as a hired gun. He seemed more likely to laugh than shoot.

"I'm gonna go make some popcorn."

Dalton nodded. He watched her leave the room, admiring the way her jeans hugged her body, the sway of her hips, the fall of her hair down her back. Just looking at her made him ache. He longed to hold her, to taste her, to feel her hands running over him. He wanted to take her hot and quick, and slow and easy. He wanted . . . a harsh bark of laughter escaped his lips. Even if he could make love to her, it was doubtful she would let him. Even if she wasn't still mourning her late husband, he was a ghost! Sometimes, when he was near her, when he was hungry for her, he forgot that he wasn't alive anymore, that even though he had form and substance, he wasn't part of her world. Hell, he wasn't part of *any* world.

Frustrated with needs he couldn't fulfill, he lunged to his feet and stalked over to the window. Staring out into the darkness, he wondered if maybe he should do as she had suggested and say he was sorry for the curse he'd put on the Conley spread. Maybe a little repentance was all that was needed to end this miserable existence. Except he wasn't sorry. Damn Russell Conley. He'd had no right to string him up without a fair trial. Fair trial! That was funny. He hadn't gotten any kind of trial at all. But then, like a lot of big ranchers, old Russell had thought of himself as judge, jury and executioner, may he rot in hell.

He drew in a deep breath. Rage, anger, desire . . . they were wasted emotions in a ghost. And yet he was being consumed by them all.

He heard her footsteps in the hall and knew he couldn't be near her and not touch her.

He was gone before she entered the room.

Saturday morning dawned bright and clear. The first thing Kathy thought of when she woke was that she had a date with John Lawson. A date. That meant washing her hair, doing her nails, finding something to wear . . . A date. She hadn't been on a date with anyone but Wayne for over seven years. She doubted she even remembered how to act.

She lingered in bed, her thoughts wandering, until hunger drove her to the kitchen. She decided on French toast and a glass of orange juice for breakfast.

She was standing at the stove, thinking about what she was going to wear that night, when a breath of cool air told her she was no longer alone.

Glancing over her shoulder, she saw Dalton sitting at the table. "Good morning."

He grunted softly. "Morning."

"Where'd you disappear to last night?"

He shrugged, then crossed his arms over his chest. "Nowhere."

"Well, you weren't in the living room when I got back."

He lifted a brow. "Miss me, did you?"

She started to deny it, then looked away. She had missed him. Why couldn't she admit it? She turned the bread in the pan, glad to have an excuse to look away from his probing gaze. She spent far too much time thinking about him. It made her feel guilty. Wayne hadn't even been gone a year yet, and she was already mooning over another man. A man, hah! He wasn't even real. For all she knew, he could be nothing more than a figment of her warped imagination.

She spread butter on the French toast and let it melt, then put it on a plate and poured a glass of orange juice. There was no place to sit but at the table. Feeling suddenly shy, she sat down across from Dalton. She felt funny, eating in front of him.

She sprinkled powdered sugar over the bread and took a bite, acutely aware of Dalton Crowkiller's dark-eyed gaze.

"So," she remarked, "how are you coming with the barn?"

"Fine. Why don't you come out and take a look when you get finished there?"

"All right." She had avoided going out there. She had a hunch that, when he wasn't in the house with her, he stayed in the barn. Of course, it was just a hunch. Who knew where ghosts went? She remembered him saying he couldn't leave the county, but did he ever go into Saul's Crossing, visit other ranches in the area? For all she knew, he could be haunting every house in the neighborhood.

Dalton sat back in his chair and crossed his ankles. "I found a pretty little palomino mare for sale."

"You did? Where?"

"Over at the Holcomb ranch."

"Where's that?"

"Down the road apiece. Used to be the Burkhart place."

"Oh. You know, I'm not sure I want a horse. They're so . . . big."

"You'll like this one."

"I will?"

He raked a hand through his hair. "I wish you'd go take a look at her."

"I guess if I bought a horse, you'd be more than happy to ride it for me."

He smiled, like a little boy who'd just been caught with his hand in the cookie jar.

She put her knife, fork, and glass on her plate, then carried them to the sink. "How much are they asking for this wonder horse?"

"I don't know, but whatever it is, she's worth it."

She made a face at him. "We can go look this morning, if you want."

The Holcomb place was located about twenty miles to the east. It looked like something out of a movie, with clean white fences, a manicured lawn, two big red barns, and a long, low, ranch-style house.

Kathy glanced from side to side as she drove down the long driveway. Horses grazed in lush pastures on both sides of the roadway.

Ray Holcomb met her at the gate. He was a short,

rotund man, with wavy brown hair and dark brown eyes. He wore a dark blue work shirt, jeans, scuffed cowboy boots, and a Texas hat.

"Mrs. Conley? I'm Ray Holcomb. Welcome to the Circle H," he said, extending a hand to help her out of the car.

"Thank you."

"So, you're in the market for a horse? Well, you came to the right place. If I do say so myself, and I do often," he said with a shameless grin, "we raise some of the best riding stock in the state."

"I'm afraid I don't know much about horses."

"That's okay," he said, slapping his thigh, "I do. I picked out a few I thought might suit. They're in the barn. Ready for a look-see?"

Kathy nodded. Dalton walked a little behind her. She saw him so clearly, it was hard to believe no one else could.

The barn was enormous, and spotless. Long, narrow windows lined the walls above the stalls, providing cross ventilation and light.

"You said you didn't have any experience," Holcomb said, guiding her toward the back of the barn, "so I picked out some real gentle animals. This is Jocko." He pointed at a dark brown horse with a white mark on its forehead. "He's ten years old and trail-wise. Gentle as an old dog."

Kathy glanced at Dalton, who shook his head. "No, I don't think so. I was looking for a mare."

"A mare? Hmmm. I'd recommend a gelding, especially for a beginner. Less temperamental. However, I do have a pretty little filly for sale. She's over here.''

Kathy followed Holcomb to the other side of the barn.

"This here's Taffy Girl," Holcomb said. He ran a beefy hand along the mare's neck. "She's five years old. Good clean lines."

"That's the one," Dalton whispered.

"I'll take her."

"Don't you want to try her out first?"

"Try her out?"

"Well, sure. You wouldn't buy a car without driving it, would you?"

"No, I guess not."

"I'll saddle her up for you."

Holcomb entered the stall and threw a faded red blanket over the mare's back.

Kathy walked a few feet away, then turned and looked at Dalton. "You didn't tell me I'd have to ride her!" she hissed.

"You'll be all right."

"I've never even been on a horse!"

"Don't worry, I'll help you."

"Oh, fine."

"Here we go."

She jumped as Holcomb came up behind her, leading the mare. The horse looked bigger close up than she had in the stall.

"I've got a practice arena out back," Holcomb said.

Kathy smiled. "Great."

She followed Holcomb to the arena, her insides

churning. How had she gotten into this mess?

Holcomb opened the gate and led the mare inside, then glanced over his shoulder at Kathy. "Coming?"

She took a deep breath, then entered the arena. Holcomb helped her mount, adjusted the stirrups, and handed her the reins.

At a total loss as to what to do next, she sat there for a moment, feeling foolish. The mare blew out a breath and stamped her foot, her ears twitching back and forth. Kathy felt a whisper of cool air, and then she felt a large hand slip over hers, heard Dalton's voice whisper in her ear.

"Relax," he said. He touched his heels to the mare's sides, and she started walking.

Startled, Kathy rocked backward a little, only to be brought up short by Dalton's chest.

"Take it easy," he said again. "Try to pretend I'm not here."

"Oh, sure," she muttered, flustered by his nearness, by the touch of his callused hand over hers.

He slipped his other arm around her waist, then urged the mare into an extended trot.

"What are you doing?" she exclaimed.

"Trying her out. Stop worrying and relax. I won't let you fall."

If he told her to relax one more time, she was going to scream. Gradually, as she realized she wasn't going to fall, she began to enjoy the ride. The mare had a smooth gait, kind of like a rocking chair.

But it was the man behind her that made Kathy's heart flutter with nervous excitement. She was increasingly aware of his arm, rock-hard around her waist, of the broad chest at her back. She told herself it was ridiculous to feel the way she was feeling. He was a ghost, for goodness' sake, but she couldn't help wishing that he was real.

They circled the arena three times; then Dalton turned the mare in the opposite direction. Changing leads, he told her, and explained that a lead was determined by which leg the horse extended first in a canter. Horses were like people, he said. Some favored the right and some the left.

He reined the mare to a halt, then backed her up for several feet. "Buy her," he said.

He slid over the horse's rump and went to stand by the mare's head while Holcomb helped Kathy dismount.

"So," Holcomb said, "what do you think?"

"I'll take her. How much is she?"

"A thousand dollars."

Kathy almost choked. "A thousand dollars!"

She heard Dalton swear. "Prices sure have gone up," he muttered. "Do you have that kind of money?"

"Too much?" Holcomb asked.

"Well, it's a little more than I had planned on." Actually, the price was no problem; she had the money. She just hadn't realized horses cost so much.

Holcomb ran his hand over his jaw, his expression thoughtful. "Well, fact is, I'm kind of horse poor at the moment. I could let her go for eight hundred, but that's my rock-bottom price."

"Gee, I don't know . . ."

"I'll throw in that there saddle and bridle."

Kathy looked at the mare. She *was* a pretty thing, with her shiny golden coat, snowy mane and tail, and big brown eyes. Still, it *was* a lot of money. She was about to say she'd have to think it over when she looked at Dalton. The yearning in his eyes was her undoing.

"I'll take her, if you can deliver her to my house."

"Sure, no problem. Just tell me when and where."

"The Triple Bar C."

She was getting used to the surprised look people gave her when she told them where she lived.

"No shi . . . I mean, is that right? I didn't think anybody was living there."

"I've only been there a few weeks. Will you take a check for the horse?"

"Sure. You can pay my driver when he drops her off."

"Okay. Is tomorrow afternoon convenient?"

Holcomb nodded. "Yes, ma'am." He tipped his hat. "Nice doing business with you, Mrs. Conley."

"Thank you. Oh, wait! What do I feed her?"

"You don't know much about horses, do you?"

That was putting it mildly. "No."

"She needs hay and oats, and plenty of water. She gets a flake of hay in the morning, and again at night."

"A flake?"

Holcomb spread his hands about four inches apart. "A flake's about this wide. I'll send along a bale of hay to tide you over."

"Thanks."

"A bale should last about a week."

"A week. And where do I buy it?"

"You can get it from the feed store in town, or you can grow your own."

Kathy nodded.

"She'll be needin' shoes in about two weeks."

Kathy looked at the mare's feet and frowned. "Shoes?"

"You sure you want a horse?" Holcomb asked.

"Yes. I'm ... I'm going to take lessons." She glanced at Dalton. "And I have someone to look after her."

"Uh-huh. Well, horseshoes last a month to six weeks. You can find a shoer in the phone book. I recommend Ray Hadley. He's one of the best around."

Hay. Oats. Horseshoes. What had she gotten herself into? "Thank you, Mr. Holcomb."

"Ray."

"Ray."

"I'll walk you out."

"I can find my way. Thank you for everything."

Kathy pulled onto the highway, then scowled at Dalton. "Stop that!"

Dalton angled a glance in her direction. "Stop what?"

"Grinning."

"Oh. Sorry." He tried, but he couldn't completely wipe the smile from his face. He had always loved horses. Once, he had dreamed of raising the best horses in the territory. It was why he had started selling his gun in the first place, to get a stake to buy a place of his own.

Kathy couldn't help it. For the first time in months, she laughed out loud. Oh, and it felt so good to laugh again. It was soothing, healing.

Dalton watched her, pleased by her laughter. It made her look younger, washed some of the sadness from her eyes.

Kathy blew out a deep breath as her laughter subsided. The world looked brighter somehow. She slid a glance at Dalton as she turned onto the road that led to the ranch. "Thanks. I needed that."

"Any time."

"Maybe you could teach me to ride."

"My pleasure."

It took her a moment to recognize what she was feeling. It was hope.

Dalton paced the living room, long angry strides that carried him from one end of the room to the other. He could hear water running in the bathroom. It was Kathy, getting ready for her date with John Lawson.

He went to the window and stared out. Damn. A fire churned in his gut. Maybe he really was in hell.

He swore softly. It had been hell being so close to her today, having his arm around her as they rode around the arena, smelling the fresh, clean scent of her, feeling her hair blow across his face. He'd ached for her so bad, he was surprised he hadn't fallen off the damn horse.

He heard the water stop, and he was overcome with

a sudden urge to slip into her room. She would never know he was there. Just one look, he thought, what would it hurt? It took every ounce of his self-control to stay where he was, hands clenched into tight fists, his gaze fixed on the scene outside the window.

He heard the bedroom door open. Moments later, she was there, a vision in a pair of black pants and a red silk shirt that brought out the red highlights in her hair.

Never, in all his life, had he seen anything more beautiful, more alluring. Desire rose up within him, hotter than the fires of the unforgiving hell that surely awaited him.

A slow smile spread over Kathy's face as she read the admiration in his eyes. "Thank you," she murmured.

He nodded, incapable of speech. Silence stretched between them.

"Well." She picked up her handbag and car keys. "I've got to go. Bye."

"So long." His voice was thick, raspy.

He watched her cross the room, go out the door, down the steps. Watched the sway of her hips, clearly outlined in those slinky black pants. Watched her open the car door and slide onto the seat.

He cursed John Lawson with every vile oath he had ever heard as he watched her start the engine and drive away.

Kathy smiled at something John said as they walked down the street toward the movie theater. Dinner had been pleasant. John had asked about things out at the ranch, and she had told him she had finished painting the inside and was about to start on the exterior. He had offered to send Sonny over to help, but she declined, saying she wanted to do it herself. Over dessert and coffee, he had told her some funny stories about people he knew in town.

The theater was crowded when they arrived.

"It's always like this on Saturday night," John remarked. He waved to a couple of people as they took their seats.

Kathy drew several curious stares, mostly from women. Were they old girlfriends, Kathy wondered, or just hopefuls?

The lights went down and she settled back in her seat. She wasn't surprised when John handed her the popcorn, then slid his arm around her shoulders. It was warm and cozy, sitting there in the dark, sharing a box of popcorn. It reminded her of her high school days.

They left the theater hand-in-hand. "Would you like to go get a cup of coffee?" John asked.

"I don't think so. It's late, and I'm a little tired."

They talked about the movie as they walked to the parking lot behind the furniture store, where she had left her car.

John took her other hand in his. "I had a good time tonight," he said.

"Me, too."

"Maybe we can do it again soon?"

"Yes, I'd like that."

"Kathy . . ."

He leaned forward, waiting, letting her make the

decision. Curious, she closed her eyes and lifted her face for his kiss.

His hands squeezed hers, drawing her closer, and then she felt his lips on hers. It was a quiet kiss, warm and pleasant, like a summer day.

"Sweet," he murmured.

She smiled at him, not knowing what to say.

"Next time I'll pick you up," he said. "This doesn't seem right, letting you drive home alone."

"I'll be fine." She unlocked the car door. "Thanks, John."

"Thank you. I'll call you the first of next week, okay?"

"Okay. Good night." She slid behind the wheel.

"Good night." He leaned down and kissed her again, then closed the door.

She turned the key in the ignition and pulled out of the driveway. Glancing in the rearview mirror, she saw John standing where she had left him, watching her drive away.

With a sigh, she pulled out onto the street. She'd had a good time, and John was a nice guy, but it was Dalton Crowkiller she thought of on the ride home. What had he done all night? Probably watched TV, she thought with a grin.

Suddenly anxious to see him, she stepped on the accelerator, eager to go home, to Dalton.

He was sitting in the old, beat-up rocker on the front porch, one booted foot resting on the rail, when she pulled into the yard. She could feel him watching her as she parked the car.

"Have a good time?" he asked as she climbed the stairs.

The tone of his voice, thick with accusation, made her defensive. "Yes, I did."

He grunted. "Are you gonna see him again?"

"I guess so."

"When?"

Kathy frowned at him. "What's the matter with you? You sound like my father."

He muttered an oath as he stood up, towering over her, his dark eyes blazing. "Dammit, Kathy . . ."

She took a step backward, frightened by the intensity of his gaze. "What?"

"Nothing," he said, his voice thick. "I'm sorry." His hands clenched and unclenched at his sides. "Did he kiss you good night?"

She nodded, unable to speak for the sudden dryness in her throat.

"Like this?" he asked, and sweeping her into his arms, he captured her lips with his.

Kathy's eyelids fluttered down as a torrent of emotions flooded through her. John's kiss had been as mild as a balmy summer day. Dalton's was a storm at midnight, filled with untamed fury and passion. Her arms went around his neck and she clung to him, the only solid thing in a world filled with turbulence. One hand cupped her buttocks, drawing her closer as he deepened the kiss, his tongue sliding over her lower lip, sizzling like lightning, making her knees go weak.

She heard a soft moan and realized it had come from her own throat.

He drew back a moment, his dark eyes hot, searing

her skin, burning a path to her heart, and then he kissed her again. She melted against him, lost in the power of his touch, drugged by the aching need he aroused in her. Steeped in pleasure, mindless with desire, she pressed herself against him, felt herself sink into him, through him . . .

With a soft cry, she pulled away. "What's happening?" She stared at him in horror. "Dalton!" His form was wavering, becoming transparent, and then he was gone.

Suddenly weak, she dropped down on the rocker and buried her face in her hands. This couldn't be happening.

She couldn't be falling in love.

With a ghost.

Chapter Eight

He stood beneath the hanging tree, a being with no more substance than the wind, aching to be whole again, human again. A hundred and twenty-five years of loneliness, of solitude. Surely that was penance enough for any man.

He lifted his gaze to the heavens. "Please . . ."

He had left so much undone. He had made a promise to his father, a promise he had never kept. He had promised his mother he would see her again before the year was out. And there was a piece of land waiting for him in Wyoming. He had always intended to settle down there, build a house, raise a few horses, but somehow he had never found the time. There had always been another job, another offer. And then there was the little matter of the life that had been stolen from him. He was not yet thirty. He wanted the years that should have been his. He wanted a home and a family, a chance to refute the lies that had been told about his life, and his death.

He wanted Kathy . . . in his arms, in his bed, in his life. He wanted to know everything about her, to be a part of her world.

He wanted the impossible. Damn, he had always wanted what he couldn't have.

Kathy stood on the side veranda, her arms crossed over the rail, staring toward the stream. Where was Dalton? She hadn't seen him since the night before. Even now, she wasn't certain what had happened. One minute he had been kissing her, and the next he had vanished. He seemed so solid, so real, she had been startled by how quickly he had disappeared. What was it he had told her, that it took a lot of energy to materialize? She didn't know whether to be flattered or insulted that kissing her had burned up so much energy that he had vanished. Once, just before sleep had claimed her, she thought she had felt a breath of cool air whisper past her bed, but she couldn't be sure if it had been real or if she had just imagined it.

Dalton. Just thinking about him made her smile, filled her with girlish excitement as she anticipated seeing him again.

"You're behaving like a teenager with her first crush," she muttered, but she couldn't help it.

A rising cloud of dust caught her eye and she walked to the front of the house, shading her eyes against the bright glare of the sun.

Moments later, a truck and trailer pulled up to the veranda and a short, bowlegged man hopped out. "Mrs. Conley?"

"Yes."

"I've got your mare here. Do you want her in the barn, or the corral?"

"In the barn, I guess. I'll go write you a check."

The man touched his hat with his forefinger, climbed into the cab of the truck, and drove to the barn.

Kathy hurried into the house and grabbed her checkbook, shaking her head as she wrote out a check. Eight hundred dollars. For a horse! She must be losing her mind, she thought, probably the result of too much quiet and too much fresh air.

Going outside, she walked down to the barn. Might as well take another look at her horse.

"She's all settled, ma'am," the cowboy said. "I'll just go get your saddle out of the truck."

Kathy handed him her check. "Thanks."

The wrangler tipped his hat again, and left the barn.

Kathy stood outside the mare's stall. "Eight hundred dollars," she muttered. "I sure hope you're worth it."

The mare poked her head over the door, snuffling softly, and Kathy jumped back.

"She won't bite you."

"Dalton!" Kathy glanced over her shoulder, delighted to see him, to be able to see him.

"She just wants you to pet her." He ran his hand over the mare's nose, then scratched under her jaw. The mare extended her neck, obviously asking for more, a look of equine contentment in her dark eyes.

Hesitantly, Kathy ran her hand along the mare's neck. Her coat was soft and sleek.

"Here's your saddle, ma'am. Where do you want it?"

"Oh, I don't know—"

"In the back of the barn," Dalton said, "there's a rack."

"Over there," Kathy said, gesturing toward the rear of the barn.

"Mr. Holcomb said for you to be sure to call him if you have any trouble with the mare, or any questions."

"I will. Thank you."

"Good day to you, ma'am."

"Good-bye." Kathy watched the cowboy walk away, then whirled around to face Dalton. "I can't believe I let you talk me into buying a horse," Kathy said when they were alone again.

"You won't be sorry."

"I won't?"

"I guarantee it. We need to repair that corral. You don't want to keep her locked up in here all the time."

"If you say so." Kathy shook her head. "Now I've got to go into town and buy hay and oats. What else do I need that you didn't bother to mention?"

"A brush and a curry comb, maybe a blanket for winter, a block of salt."

Kathy glared at him. "I remember once my girl-friend asked her dad for a horse, and her dad said no.

He said it wasn't buying the horse that was expensive, it was keeping it. I think I'm beginning to understand what he meant.''

Dalton scratched Taffy Girl's ears. "It's a small price to pay," he remarked, "for the years of pleasure she'll give you."

"Yeah, right," Kathy replied skeptically.

"Come on, I'll give you your first lesson."

"Now?"

"Why not?"

She looked at Dalton, at the light shining in his eyes, and smiled. "Sure, why not?"

Dalton found an old, beat-up halter in a pile of tack, along with a dandy brush. He showed Kathy how to slip the halter in place, then led the mare out of the stall. He brushed one side of the horse, then told Kathy to do the other side.

She reached for the brush, felt a tingle, like cold electricity, when her hand touched his. Maybe it had something to do with his ghostly aura, maybe it was just the man himself, but she had never been so aware of anyone else in her whole life.

Their eyes met and held for a moment; then she took the brush from his hand and ran it tentatively over Taffy Girl's shoulder and back.

"That's right," Dalton said. "You don't have to be afraid of her. She won't bite you."

"How do you know?"

"She's too much of a lady for that." He ran his hand along the mare's neck. "Aren't you, girl?"

Kathy watched his long-fingered hand slide over

the mare's coat and wondered what that hand would feel like sliding over her skin.

Dalton looked at her over the mare's back. "Of course, it always pays to be careful. You don't want to stand directly behind any of them. When you're walking with your horse, you want to keep a good grip on the lead and stay close to her shoulder."

Kathy nodded. As her confidence grew, she found she rather liked brushing the mare. It was soothing somehow.

Dalton grinned. "There's an old saying, something about the outside of a horse being good for the inside of a man."

"It is kind of fun, I guess. I'm done. Now what?"

"We check her feet."

"Her feet?"

"All four of them. Before and after every ride, you want to check her feet."

"What am I looking for?"

"You want to check her shoes, make sure her frog is clean, that she hasn't picked up any stones—"

Kathy burst out laughing. "She has a frog?"

Dalton shook his head. He lifted Taffy's Girl's left foreleg and braced it on his thigh. "Here," he said, pointing to the inside of the hoof. "This is the frog."

"You don't expect *me* to pick up her feet, do you?" Kathy asked, alarmed.

"Darn right, but we won't worry about that today." He checked all four feet, then patted the mare on the shoulder.

"What do we do next?" Kathy asked. "Clean her ears?"

"We saddle her up."

Dalton showed her how it was done, cautioning her to be sure the blanket was flat and smooth. A wrinkle in the pad could cause sores on the horse's back. He showed her how to set the saddle and cinch it in place.

"Some horses swell up when you saddle them," Dalton warned, "so after you tighten the cinch, you want to go back and check it again before you mount up."

Cars were far less trouble, Kathy mused as she followed Dalton out of the barn. You didn't have to fill the gas tank if you weren't going anywhere, but a horse had to be fed twice a day. Tires had to be checked regularly, but not every day.

"Mind if I try her out first?" Dalton asked.

"Be my guest." Kathy stood in the shade, watching as Dalton swung effortlessly into the saddle.

He rode the mare in a wide circle—walk, trot, canter. Then reversed direction. They made a pretty picture, Kathy thought, the beautiful golden horse and the handsome, dark-haired man. Dalton rode easily, his body moving in perfect rhythm with that of the horse. He loved it, that was easy to see.

After a few minutes, he turned the mare down the long dirt road that led to the stream. With a shout, he urged the horse into a gallop.

Kathy watched them disappear amid a cloud of swirling dust, wondering if she could ever learn to ride like that.

They returned about ten minutes later. Dalton

reined the mare to a halt a few feet in front of Kathy. He was grinning from ear to ear.

"Having fun?" Kathy asked dryly.

"Oh, yeah." He reached forward and stroked the mare's neck. "She's a damn fine horse."

"Well, if she isn't, it's your fault. *You* picked her out."

"Come on," he said, swinging out of the saddle. "Your turn."

"Promise you'll catch me if I fall?"

"You won't fall. Here ya go," he said, and boosted her into the saddle. He quickly adjusted the length of the stirrups to accommodate Kathy's shorter legs, then looked up at her, one hand cupping the heel of her tennis shoe. "You got any boots?"

Kathy stared at his hand, so big and brown, gently cradling her foot. "You mean like cowboy boots? No."

"Get some."

"Why?"

"Not safe to ride in flat-heeled shoes like these. If your horse spooks, or you take a fall, your foot's likely to slide right through the stirrup. Getting hung up in a stirrup's a good way to break your neck."

"Another expense," she muttered. "You didn't tell me horseback riding was such an expensive hobby."

Dalton shrugged. "Where I come from, it wasn't a hobby."

She was tempted to stick her tongue out at him.

He handed her the reins, showed her how to hold them, how to apply pressure on the bit to make Taffy

Girl rein left or right, warning her to pull back gently on the reins when she wanted to stop.

Then, holding onto the bridle, he clucked to the mare and they began to walk forward. Kathy's first instinct was to grab for the saddle horn.

"Both hands on the reins," Dalton chided. "Try to move with her. Get the rhythm. She's got a nice, smooth walk. Don't stiffen up—just relax and let your body move with hers. That's better. She's got a soft mouth and responds quickly to the bit, so you don't want to jerk on the reins. You do, and you'll find yourself flying over her head."

"I'll never remember all this," Kathy wailed.

"Sure you will. Pretty soon you won't even have to think about it."

He walked her to the edge of the driveway, turned, and headed back. By the time the house was in sight again, Kathy felt a little more at ease.

"Okay, ride her over to the barn and back," Dalton said. "Let's see how you do on your own."

Kathy lifted the reins and clucked to the mare, and Taffy Girl moved out, smooth and steady as you please. When they reached the barn, Kathy pulled on the reins and the horse made a wide turn and started back toward the house.

Dalton was smiling when she reached the porch. "You're a natural," he remarked.

"Yeah, right," Kathy muttered, secretly pleased by his praise. "Can we go down by the stream?"

"She's your horse. I guess you can go wherever you want."

"Would you walk with me?"

"Sure."

He didn't hold the bridle this time, just walked alongside, his hands in his pockets. "If you get some lumber, I'll start on that corral."

"Okay. I'll go into town tomorrow. I need to see about having some hay delivered, too." She grinned down at him. "Looks like I'd better start thinking about trading my car in for a pickup truck. And buying myself a cowboy hat."

Dalton rested one hand on her foot. "And boots. Don't forget boots."

The warmth in his eyes flooded through her like summer sunshine. He had beautiful eyes, as dark as a midnight sky. When he smiled at her, as he was smiling now, it was hard to believe he had once been a hired gun, that he had killed almost a dozen men. That he was a ghost . . .

Taffy Girl lowered her head, reaching for a clump of grass. The movement pulled on the reins. Kathy leaned forward, one hand grabbing for the saddle horn, and the magic of the moment was broken.

Dalton blew out a sigh. Taking hold of the bridle, he started walking toward the stream.

Kathy sat back in the saddle, content to let Dalton guide the mare. It was a beautiful afternoon, warm and clear, fragrant with the scent of grass and trees and wildflowers.

When they reached the riverbank, Dalton tethered the mare to a low-hanging branch. He lifted Kathy from Taffy Girl's back and they sat down on the thick, spongy grass that grew along the edge of the water.

"I think I'm going to like horseback riding," Kathy remarked.

"I knew you would." He picked up a smooth, flat stone and skipped it across the water. *One, two, three, four* ... Her arm brushed his, and her nearness seeped into him, as warm as the sunlight shining overhead.

They sat there for a long time, not saying anything. Kathy tried not to stare at him, but it was impossible. She laughed, a silent laugh filled with amused bewilderment. Maybe she had lost her mind. Maybe he wasn't really there at all. Maybe he was just a figment of her imagination. After all, he didn't even cast a shadow. That seemed strange. If he had enough substance that she could touch him and feel his touch in return, why didn't he have a shadow? Maybe he'd lost it, she thought, like Peter Pan.

A ghost. It just wasn't possible. And even if it was, ghosts were supposed to appear in the middle of the night, moaning and dragging heavy chains and trying to scare people half to death. They weren't supposed to have impossibly broad shoulders and sexy smiles and eyes as deep and black as a midnight sky.

Impulsively, she reached out and touched his shoulder.

Dalton looked at her, a question in his eyes, and she shrugged, feeling suddenly foolish. "I can't believe you're real."

"I don't suppose I am."

"But you're here. You *are* here, aren't you? I'm not imagining this."

"That's a mighty strange question to be asking me," he said with a wry grin.

She grinned back at him. "Yeah, I suppose it is. How did you get that scar on your cheek?"

"In a knife fight."

"With who?"

"A Crow warrior. I caught him trying to steal my horse."

"Did you . . . did you kill him?"

"No."

Kathy blew out a sigh. "Well, I guess we should be getting back. I have a lot of work to do."

With a nod, Dalton rose smoothly to his feet. Offering her his hand, he helped her up.

"Thank you," she murmured. Heat washed into her cheeks as he continued to hold her hand, his dark eyes fixed on her face, making her feel suddenly self-conscious. "What's wrong?"

"Nothing." He shook his head, his hand tightening around hers. "It just feels so good to touch you."

"Does it?" Her voice sounded thick, as if it were mired in molasses.

Dalton nodded. His thumb made lazy circles on the back of her hand. His touch sizzled up her arm like heat lightning.

"Kathy . . ."

She swallowed, her gaze trapped in his. He was going to kiss her again.

Slowly, slowly, he lowered his head and brushed his lips across hers. For all that it was a gentle kiss, barely more than a whisper of touch, it reached all the way down inside her, awakening feelings she had thought buried with Wayne.

His arms went around her waist and he drew her up against him.

Kathy stiffened in his embrace, remembering the last time he had held her like this, the way he had vanished from her sight. It had frightened her, the way he faded away to nothing.

"Just let me hold you," he murmured. "You feel so good in my arms."

He held her gently, one hand lightly stroking her hair. She could feel him holding back, keeping a tight rein on his emotions, as if he, too, feared that he might suddenly disappear.

She rested her head against his shoulder and closed her eyes. A fragrant breeze ruffled her hair. The hum of insects and the purling of the water made a pleasant symphony. A soft sigh of contentment escaped her lips. He felt so solid, so real. And it felt right to be in his arms. Why did she feel so guilty, then, as if she were betraying Wayne?

"We should go."

He released her immediately, his gaze searching her face. "I'm sorry."

"No, no, it's all right. Really. I . . ." She couldn't tell him the whole truth, so she told him a part of it. "I'm just afraid you'll disappear on me again."

Dalton looked at her for a long moment, as if judging the truthfulness of her words, and then he grunted softly. "I guess I'm not the only ghost here, am I?"

"What do you mean?" Kathy asked, though she knew perfectly well what he meant.

"Never mind." He turned away. It was stupid, he thought, one dead man being jealous of another. Worse than stupid. It was pointless.

Wordlessly, he lifted her onto the mare's back. Taking up the reins, he vaulted up behind her and turned Taffy Girl toward home.

Chapter Nine

Kathy woke late Monday morning after a long, restless night. With a yawn, she slipped out of bed, padded into the kitchen and put the coffee on; then, only half awake, she went into the bathroom and took a long, hot shower.

Eyes closed, she rested her forehead against the tile and thought about the day before. Dalton had been silent and withdrawn on the ride back to the ranch.

I guess I'm not the only ghost here, am I?

She had known perfectly well what he meant, she just hadn't known how to answer him. Was it her fault if she still missed her husband, if she felt guilty for enjoying another man's company, another man's kisses? Another man! That was rich. If only it was that simple.

Leaving the shower, she dried off, dusted herself

with powder, pulled on a pair of comfy jeans, a faded T-shirt and her tennis shoes. Going into the kitchen, she poured herself a cup of coffee, added milk and sugar.

Staring out the window, she wondered where Dalton was. If he didn't sleep, what *did* he do all night long? She'd have to remember to ask him.

She poured another cup of coffee, expecting him to appear any moment, and when he didn't, she walked down to the barn, thinking to find him there.

The mare stuck her head over the stall door and whinnied softly when Kathy entered the barn. Kathy smiled; then, after a moment's hesitation, she scratched the horse between her ears.

The mare had hay and fresh water, proof that Dalton had been there earlier. So, where was he now?

Leaving the barn, she went back to the house. She made the bed, drank another cup of coffee, and then, with a sigh of resignation, she picked up her purse and her keys. If he didn't want to see her, that was fine. She didn't want to see him, either.

She tried to think of everything except Dalton on the drive to town.

Hay . . . She hoped there was only one kind. Too bad Dalton had decided to make himself scarce; she could have used his expertise.

Boots . . . Brown ones, she decided, not too expensive in case she didn't like riding as much as she thought she would. Dalton's boots were black, a little scuffed.

A hat . . . White would be her first choice, but that didn't seem practical. She didn't want black. Maybe some neutral shade, like gray. If Dalton owned a hat, she was sure his would be black, and that he would look great in it.

Darn! Even when she didn't want to think about that man, he crept into every thought.

Dalton. She didn't want to like him, didn't want to think about him, or be fascinated by him, yet she seemed to have no control over either her emotions or her thoughts where Dalton Crowkiller was concerned. Like the words to an old song, he was always on her mind. She had never known anyone like him, not just because he was a ghost—which was a major distinction in and of itself—not because he was part Indian, not even because they had been born a hundred and twenty-five years apart, but because of what he had been. A hired killer. The mere idea was fascinating and repellant at the same time.

She pulled into the parking lot behind Norton's Hay and Feed and switched off the engine, wondering, with a wry grin, how Dalton Crowkiller had ever talked her into buying a horse in the first place.

Taking a deep breath, she got out of the car and went into the store, which consisted of two parts—a small section in front where supplies were displayed and a much larger section out back that held bales of hay and straw stacked one on top of the other.

There was only one clerk, and he was busy with a customer. To pass the time, Kathy walked down the closest aisle, glancing at the goods on the shelves. There were empty plastic spray bottles, brushes and metal combs and funny looking things that resembled brushes without bristles.

She walked down the next aisle, reading the labels on cans and bottles: Neatsfoot oil. Saddle soap. Show Sheen. Repel-X. Cowboy Magic. She saw some rectangles that looked like red bricks but proved to be salt blocks.

The back wall was covered with bits, labeled with odd names like curb and snaffle and spade. She saw a display of reins, surprised to note they came in brown or black leather, or nylon in every color of the rainbow.

She saw saddles and bridles, some plain, some decorated with silver. And saddle blankets, some in solid colors, some woven in Indian designs.

"Can I help you?"

Kathy glanced over her shoulder at the clerk, who had come up behind her. "I certainly hope so. I just bought a horse, and . . ." She shrugged. "I've never owned one before. How much of this stuff"—she made a broad gesture that encompassed the multitude of items on the shelves—"do I really need?"

The clerk winked at her. "Well, I could say all of it, but mainly you need a good brush, a curry comb, a hoof pick, some fly spray, a good paste wormer—"

"She has worms!" Kathy exclaimed.

"Probably." He plucked a tube from the shelf. "This is as good as any. You need to worm her every four weeks or so, and then she needs to be tube wormed at least once a year." He grinned. "The vet does that. Horses need shots once a year, too. Influenza, encephalitis—that's sleeping sickness—and tetanus."

"Good grief," Kathy muttered. "What have I gotten myself into?"

"It's not as bad as it sounds."

"I thought all I needed was hay. And oats."

"What kind of hay do you want?"

"Kind?"

"We have alfalfa, oat, and Bermuda."

"I don't know."

"Alfalfa, then. How many bales do you want?"

Kathy shook her head. "How many do I need?"

"How many horses do you have?"

"Just one."

"Well, it depends. Do you want it delivered?"

"Yes."

"Well, if you order a ton, delivery is free. Anything less than that, and delivery is ten bucks."

"A ton!"

"It's only about sixteen bales, depending on the weight of the bales. That should last you about four months."

Kathy blew out a sigh. "Okay, give me a ton. And some oats. And whatever else you think I need."

The clerk chuckled. "Yes, ma'am."

She stood at the counter while he drew up her bill: sixteen bales of alfalfa hay, a sack of oats, dandy brush, curry comb, spray bottle, fly repellant, hoof pick, paste wormer, salt block, fly mask, day sheet . . .

"What about a saddle?"

"I've got one," she assured him quickly.

The clerk nodded. "Okay. Just checking."

She was shaking her head over the bill when she left the feed store. She dumped all of her horse's "necessities" into the trunk, then headed down the street toward the middle of town.

"Kathy! Hey, Kathy!"

Glancing over her shoulder, she saw John Lawson hurrying toward her. "Hi, John."

"Hi." He smiled broadly. "What brings you to town?"

"Shopping. I bought a horse."

"You did?"

She nodded. "It seemed like a good idea at the time." She shook her head as she took a last glance at the receipt from the feed store, then shoved it into her pocket. "Now I'm not so sure. I had no idea horses required so much stuff."

"Maybe we can go riding together sometime."

"Do you have a horse?"

"Not anymore, but I can rent one from Norton. What do you say?"

"Sounds like fun. But not until I've had a few lessons."

"Have you had lunch?"

"No."

"If you're hungry, I'm buying."

Kathy smiled. "If you're buying, I'm hungry."

Dalton stood against the hitch rail in front of the barber shop, scowling as he watched John Lawson smile at Kathy. A sharp stab of jealousy rose up within him as he watched Lawson take Kathy by the arm and lead her across the street. They were laughing companionably as they entered a small cafe.

Damn! He hated seeing her with another man,

hated thinking about her with another man. It was wrong, it was impossible, but when he looked at her, he wanted her. Wanted her in the most primal way a man could want a woman. Though he had only known her for a short time, he thought of her as his. He wanted to be with her, protect her, provide for her. He didn't want her smiling up at Lawson, or any other man.

He swore again, bemused by the whole situation. A ghost lusting after a flesh-and-blood woman. It would be funny, if it didn't hurt so damn bad.

He hadn't been to Saul's Crossing in more years than he could remember, but he hardly noticed the changes as he crossed the street and entered the cafe. Determined to torture himself, he stood near their booth, watching the two of them together, listening to the husky sound of Kathy's laughter, noting the way her eyes crinkled at the corners when she smiled, the blush that stained her cheeks when Lawson told her how pretty she was.

He itched to lean across the table and bury his fist in Lawson's face, to drag Kathy into his arms and kiss her until he had wiped the memory of Lawson and every other man she had ever known from her mind.

Damn, damn, damn! He had been a fool to follow her to town. Turning on his heel, he stormed out of the restaurant.

Kathy's head jerked up as she felt a rush of cool air.

"Is something wrong?" John asked.

"What?" Kathy drew her gaze from the front of

the cafe. She could have sworn she had seen Dalton there a moment ago. "No, nothing."

"How about some dessert? Molly makes a great blueberry pie."

"Not this time. I've got some more shopping to do."

"We're still on for this weekend, right?"

"Right."

"Good." John put enough money on the table to cover the check, then stood up and offered Kathy his hand. "I'm glad I ran into you."

"Me, too."

"I'll pick you up Saturday, about six?"

"Okay."

"Wanna walk me home?"

Kathy smiled. "Sure, cowboy."

Hand in hand, they walked across the street to the furniture store.

"Thanks for lunch," Kathy said.

"Thanks for keeping me company. I usually eat alone. This was much better." He hesitated a moment, then brushed a kiss across her cheek. "See you Saturday."

"Saturday," Kathy repeated.

Turning away, she walked down the street toward a shop that sold Western wear. As she opened the door, she felt a brush of cool air against her cheek. She whirled around, her gaze searching the sidewalk.

"Dalton?" she whispered. "Dalton, are you here?"

Shaking her head, she stepped inside the store and made her way toward the shoe department. She took a seat, told the clerk she wanted to see some moderately priced cowboy boots, and sat back in her chair.

After trying on six different pairs, she bought the first ones she had tried on, a pair of brown Justin boots with a low heel.

Tucking the box under her arm, she crossed the store and began trying on hats, surprised to find that they came in every imaginable color—red, green, black, white, gray, purple, beige—and a wide variety of styles—flat brims, wide brims, straw, felt. Hatbands also came in a wide variety, some decorated with silver, others with feathers, some just plain.

She had narrowed it down to two—a pearl gray with a plain black band and a dark beige with a braided leather hatband—when she felt a brush of cool air at her back.

"The gray one."

A shiver of excitement raced down her spine at the sound of his voice. "Dalton." She glanced over her shoulder, unaccountably pleased to see him standing behind her.

"The gray one," he said again.

"You think so?" She brushed a lock of hair from her forehead, settled the hat on her head, then turned to study herself in the mirror. She wasn't surprised to see that Dalton cast no reflection.

"It looks good," he said quietly. "I wish I could buy it for you."

His voice floated over her, soft, caressing, as intimate as a kiss.

"I'll take this one," Kathy told the saleslady.

"Very good, ma'am."

She followed the clerk to the cash register and paid for the hat.

"Thank you, ma'am. Come again."

"Thank you," Kathy murmured, and left the store, acutely conscious of Dalton at her elbow.

He didn't say a word as he followed her to the parking lot. His silence made her strangely uncomfortable.

She put her packages in the trunk, unlocked the car door, and slid behind the wheel. She felt a whisper of cool air as Dalton settled in the passenger seat. He was angry with her. She could feel it rolling off him in waves.

She pulled out of the parking lot and turned onto the highway, determined not to say anything until he did.

It was a long, quiet ride back to the ranch.

She parked near the barn, opened the trunk, and picked up the sack that held all the horse stuff she'd bought.

Dalton stood near Taffy Girl's stall, watching Kathy while she put everything away.

"Did you have a good time?" he asked at last, and there was no mistaking the underlying note of jealousy in his voice.

"Well, what do you know!" Kathy muttered sarcastically. "It speaks." She gasped as Dalton's hand closed over her arm. "Take your hand off me."

"I asked you a question!" he said, his voice a low growl.

Slowly, deliberately, she peeled his fingers from

her arm. "Yes. I had a good time. What business is it of yours?"

A look of unbearable anguish passed over his features. "None," he said hoarsely. "None at all."

"Dalton . . ."

But he was already gone.

It was after midnight and Kathy sat on the sofa, a cup of hot chocolate, forgotten, in her hand. She had tried to sleep, but every time she closed her eyes, she saw the misery in Dalton's eyes, heard the torment in his voice. How could he be jealous of her friendship with John? Why did she care?

Why, indeed? That was the question that had kept her awake for the last two hours.

"I'm sorry, Kathy."

Three words, softly spoken, yet she felt as though someone had just pulled a huge thorn from her heart. "Me, too."

As soft as a sigh, he materialized beside her on the sofa. "Maybe I shouldn't bother you anymore."

"You're not bothering me."

He smiled sadly. "Aren't I?"

"Don't leave me, Dalton. Please." She didn't stop to wonder why she needed him; she knew only that he had become important to her and she couldn't bear to think of never seeing him again.

"This isn't doing either of us any good."

"I know."

"Kathy . . ." He reached toward her, then withdrew his hand. "I . . ." He swallowed hard. "I hope you'll be happy with Lawson, or . . . or whoever else you . . . shit, don't cry.''

"I'm not," she said, and burst into tears.

Muttering an oath, he took the cup from her hand and set it on the end table. Then, knowing he was about to make the second biggest mistake of his life, he drew her gently into his arms and tucked her head beneath his chin. And she went to him willingly, burrowing against him, her arms wrapping tightly around his waist. He couldn't help noticing that her body fit against his perfectly.

"Kathy, ah, Kathy, don't cry, darlin'. Please don't cry."

"I can't help it," she wailed softly. "I can't lose you, too."

"You won't." With a hand that trembled, he stroked her hair. "I'll stay as long as you want me."

"You promise?"

"I promise," he said, and wondered what right he had to make such a vow.

She sighed, and then relaxed in his arms. A moment later, she was asleep.

And Dalton Crowkiller, half-breed drifter and hired gun, admitted he was in more trouble now than he had ever been when he was alive. He had been in lust before, many times, but this was the first time in his life—he grinned ruefully—or his death, that he had been in love.

Chapter Ten

Kathy woke in her bed the next morning with a smile on her face and no memory of how she had gotten from the living room into the bedroom. But she had a clear memory of being held in Dalton Crowkiller's strong arms, of falling asleep wrapped within the warmth and security of his embrace. Of feeling utterly at peace for the first time since Wayne had passed away.

Dalton. In spite of everything, she was falling in love with him. It was impossible, ridiculous, and yet the fact remained. She was falling in love with a ghost. She reminded herself that she had vowed never to fall in love again. Of course, she hadn't allowed for falling in love with a ghost, so maybe this didn't count, since nothing could ever come of it. No matter how much she might yearn for more, it was unthinkable. The most they could ever be was friends, since it was impossible for them to have any kind of physical relationship.

Rising, she showered and dressed, wondering where he was, what he was doing, if he had held her all through the night.

She caught the scent of coffee perking as she walked down the hall, and when she entered the kitchen, she saw Dalton sitting on the counter beside the stove. Seeing him caused a flurry of excitement in the pit of her stomach.

Dalton's gaze moved over Kathy in a long, slow glance, appreciating the way her blue jeans and soft yellow T-shirt clung to her every curve. There was something sexy, intimate almost, about the fact that her feet were bare. He had held her all through the night, his body aching with a need he couldn't satisfy, torturing himself with images of the two of them lying in her bed, bodies entwined beneath the sheets. He shifted uncomfortably on the counter as his body responded to his thoughts.

"Morning, darlin'."

The sound of his voice, the ease with which he called her darlin', filled Kathy's heart with sunshine.

"Good morning. Did you get a good night's . . . oh, I forgot. You don't sleep, do you?"

Dalton shook his head. "No, don't seem to need any. How about you? Did you sleep well?"

"Very."

Desire pulsed between them, vibrant and alive and hopeless.

Dalton poured her a cup of coffee. "Hope it's not too strong."

She took a sip, and shook her head. "Perfect. Thank you."

He smiled at her. "Sometimes I think I'd kill for a cup of coffee and a cigarette."

It was a perfectly innocent thing to say, but it reminded her again of all the reasons why she couldn't be in love with him. Not only was he a ghost, a man who had earned his living with a gun, but there was over a century between them that could not be breached or ignored. In her experience, men and women rarely viewed things the same. Even Wayne hadn't been able to see some things from her point of view, but she was certain that a woman from the twentieth century and a man from the nineteenth century would have even more differences to contend with. Like his reaction to her hanging the curtain rod, thinking it was a "man's" job.

Feeling suddenly depressed, Kathy turned away. She had an almost uncontrollable urge to go to Dalton, to throw her arms around his neck and kiss him until they were both breathless, but she didn't. Couldn't. Because she wanted so much more than kisses.

"Kathy?"

"What?" She forced a cheerful note into her voice, plastered a smile on her face, and turned around.

"Is everything all right?"

"Of course," she said brightly. "Why wouldn't it be?"

"I don't know." He looked at her and frowned.

"But something's bothering you. What is it?"

"Nothing."

"Kathy, don't lie to me."

"Nothing's wrong. Everything is perfect. Oh!" She slammed her coffee cup on the counter. "Everything is wrong! You shouldn't even be here!"

A muscle twitched in his jaw. "Then I'm gone."

"No! No, I don't want you to go. It's just that you don't belong here, in this time, and I . . ."

Tears of frustration burned her eyes and she turned away from him, not wanting him to know she was on the verge of crying.

Dalton stood up, his hands clenched at his sides. "What do you want from me?"

"I want the impossible," she murmured.

"Tell me."

She shook her head. How could she explain what she was feeling when she didn't understand it herself? She was falling in love with him. There was no rhyme or reason to it. It was simply a fact. She was drawn to him. His smile, his voice, the way she had felt when he held her last night, the vulnerability she sometimes saw in his eyes. She wanted to hold him and comfort him. She wanted to be held and comforted in return. It didn't make any sense, but she felt as if her whole life up until this point had been nothing but a dress rehearsal, a period of waiting for the star of the show to arrive so the performance could begin. Only the star had arrived a hundred and twenty-five years too late.

She felt guilty for loving Dalton.

She felt as though she were betraying Wayne and the love they had shared.

"Kathy . . ."

The uncertainty in his voice tugged at her heart. There was a breath of cool air at her back, and then his arms slid around her waist.

"Kathy." His voice was low and husky. "Don't shut me out, darlin'. Not now."

"I'm sorry." Tears trickled down her cheeks.

Dalton blew out a sigh. He knew she was trying not to cry, knew his presence had turned her life upside down. Knew he should just disappear, go back to the limbo in which he had lived before she arrived at the ranch. And knew he wouldn't do it. Knew he wouldn't leave her unless she asked him to.

Slowly, giving her plenty of chance to object, he drew her back against him and rested his chin on the top of her head. As she had the night before, she melted against him, and he thought again how right it felt to hold her, how perfectly she fit into his arms. She was soft and warm and alive, so alive. Every nerve in his body reacted to her nearness.

"Kathy," he said thickly. "Damn."

Gently, he put her away from him before his body betrayed the path his mind was wandering, before the intensity of what he was feeling undid him.

"Got any plans for today?" he asked.

She turned around and looked up at him, her heart pounding. "Not really. Why? What did you have in mind?"

"How about a ride down by the creek?"

She took a deep, calming breath. "Let me grab a bite to eat first, okay?"

"Sure," he said. And then, needing to put some distance between them. "I'll go saddle the mare."

A short time later, they were riding toward the stream. With Kathy sitting in front of him, her shapely behind cradled between his thighs, Dalton couldn't help wondering if riding double was such a good idea. She shifted her weight, and he tightened his arm around her waist. Maybe he should have walked.

"You didn't wear your boots," he remarked, hoping conversation would distract him.

"I know. I forgot." Kathy wriggled her toes. Her tennis shoes were about a hundred years old and as comfortable as a pair of house slippers.

Talking didn't help. A lock of her hair brushed against his cheek; when he took a deep breath, his nostrils filled with the scent of soap and shampoo and woman. Her breasts felt full and warm against his arm, reminding him that she was all female, and that he hadn't had a woman in over a hundred years. Damn.

He had never associated with a woman like Kathy before, not with the kind of life he'd led. If only he had met her when he was still alive, she might have saved him a lot of grief, might have been able to make him put up his gun and settle down. But then, if she had met him in his time, she wouldn't have had anything to do with him. Decent women didn't associate with half-breed gunfighters.

155

He reined the mare to a halt when they reached the hanging tree.

Kathy glanced over her shoulder. "Why are we stopping here?"

"I don't know." He rubbed his hand over his neck as he glanced up at the long branch that had once held a hanging rope.

A sudden stillness seemed to gather around them, as if time had stopped. As if the earth were holding her breath.

"Did they hang very many men here?" Kathy asked, her voice a whisper.

Dalton nodded. "Rustlers, mostly. Back in the early days, before there was any law to speak of in these parts, justice was right quick. There wasn't any need for a trial. A man caught branding a calf with a running iron had no defense, and justice was dispensed on the spot."

Kathy shivered. "That's awful."

"Yeah."

She stared up at the tree, remembering how she had imagined seeing a man hanging there, a man dressed all in black. With a shock, she realized that she had been seeing a glimpse of the past. Dalton's past.

She leaned against him. "I wish there was a way to clear your name. . . ."

His arm tightened around her waist. "I wish I could go back and do it all over again. . . ."

They spoke simultaneously, words trailing off as they kissed.

Kathy felt suddenly dizzy, as if the world were

spinning out of control. There was a low roaring in her ears, like the sound of distant thunder.

She screamed Dalton's name, and then everything went black.

Chapter Eleven

Awareness returned slowly. Feeling dizzy and disoriented, Kathy opened her eyes. "What happened?"

Dalton shook his head. "Beats the hell out of me."

Kathy glanced around, wishing the world would stop reeling. The sun was shining, there were no clouds in the sky, nothing to explain the sudden darkness that had engulfed her.

She looked over her shoulder when she heard Dalton swear. "What's wrong?"

Dalton pointed to the east. "The sun."

"What about it?"

"Before whatever happened happened, it was a little after ten."

Kathy glanced down at her watch. It was ten-fifteen. "Yeah. So?"

"So, I'd say that, judging by the sun, it's just a little after dawn."

"It can't be." She looked at her watch again, checking the second hand to make sure it was still running. She frowned as she glanced across the stream. "Look!" She pointed at a herd of cattle grazing in the distance. "Where did they come from?"

"I don't know."

"Maybe they strayed from Holcomb's ranch."

"I don't think so. He raises horses, not cattle."

Kathy turned and stared toward the house. A blue-gray column of smoke rose from the chimney. The paint, which had been dingy gray the last time she had seen it, was now a bright white, as if it had been freshly painted. The broken window on the second floor had been magically replaced. Flowers bloomed on both sides of the porch stairs. A dozen or so horses were penned in two large corrals near the barn. The barn itself looked new.

"I don't understand," she said, feeling faint. "What's going on?"

Dalton shook his head. "I'm afraid to say it out loud."

"Say what?"

"What I'm thinking. Come on, let's get the hell out of here."

Tugging on the reins, he turned the mare downstream, seeking the cover of the trees.

"Where are we going?"

"I'm not sure."

There were clumps of cattle everywhere, all carrying the brand of the Triple Bar C. The cement driveway was gone, and in its place was a wide, rutted lane. They passed a wooden arch that spanned the road. It was dark red, with the words "Triple Bar C" painted in white.

Kathy shook her head. What had happened to the driveway? Where had that sign come from? And all those cattle wearing the Conley brand . . .

"I've got a bad feeling about this," she murmured.

"Yeah."

When they reached the end of the narrow path that paralleled what should have been the driveway, Dalton turned the mare south.

Kathy felt a shiver of unease as she took in her surroundings. The paved highway was gone. Her mailbox was gone. There were no telephone poles. Acres of gently rolling grassland fell away as far as the eye could see.

Too stunned to speak, she held tight to Dalton's arm. The landscape looked familiar, but the landmarks—the gas station and the mini-mart a mile down the road, the sign advertising Saul's Crossing—were gone. There was nothing to see but grass and cattle and the endless blue vault of the sky.

"Dalton?"

He grunted softly.

"What do you think happened? Where are we?"

"You'll think I'm crazy."

"Right now I think *I'm* crazy."

"I think we've gone back in time."

"That's impossible," Kathy said, horrified to hear her own thoughts put into words.

"I know it is." He blew out a deep breath. He jerked his chin at the road. "See that?"

Kathy frowned. "See what? Our shadow?"

Dalton nodded. "Take a good look. This morning, down by the river, I didn't have a shadow." His gaze held hers. "I haven't cast a shadow or a reflection for a hundred and twenty-five years."

Kathy stared at him, speechless, as her mind tried to grasp what he was suggesting. He couldn't be serious.

"Take hold of my hand."

"What?"

"Give me your hand." He slipped his hand into hers. It was warm. Warm when it had always been cold.

Kathy shook her head. "This can't be happening."

"That's what I keep telling myself."

The enormity of the situation hit her all at once. Everything she had ever known was gone. The people she loved had not yet been born. And Dalton was alive, really alive.

Feeling suddenly light-headed, she swayed against him.

Dalton reined the mare to a halt and slipped his other arm around Kathy's waist. "You all right?"

"I don't know. What if it's true? What if we're really in the past? What does it mean?"

He shrugged. "Maybe it means I've got a chance to turn my life around. Keep a promise I made to my father." He grunted softly. "And stay the hell away from Lydia Conley."

"Well, that's great, for you. But what about me? I don't belong here."

His dark gaze met hers. "Maybe you do," he murmured. "Maybe you were meant to be mine, and this is Fate's way of putting things straight."

"You don't believe that?"

"I don't know what I believe." He gave her a squeeze, then clucked to the mare. Saul's Crossing was about fifteen miles ahead. Once they reached town, they would know for sure where, and when, they were.

She was bone weary, her thighs and back aching, her nose sunburned, by the time they reached Saul's Crossing. The trip, which would have taken no more than twenty minutes by car, had taken hours. But her discomfort was quickly forgotten when she caught her first glimpse of the town—along with any hope she had clung to that she was dreaming.

There was no doubt in her mind that she was looking at the town as it had been in the nineteenth century.

The paved roads were gone. The streetlights were gone. There wasn't a car in sight, just a dozen or so horses standing at the hitch rails, dozing or swishing their tails at flies. Red, white, and blue bunting was draped across the front of several of the buildings.

She heard Dalton swear under his breath.

"It's true," she murmured as they rode down the center of the street. "We really are in the past."

She stared at the wide dirt road, at the boardwalk, the rough-hewn wooden buildings. The Cattlemen's

Bank and Trust. The Square Deal Saloon. Saul Brown's General Store. Lawson's Furniture Emporium. Henderson's Livery.

Her fingers dug into Dalton's arm. "It isn't possible." She stared at the building that would, in a hundred years or so, become a Holiday Inn. The sign out front read:

MARTHA DUNN'S BOARDINGHOUSE
ROOMS TO LET BY THE DAY, WEEK, OR MONTH

"Looks damn possible to me," Dalton muttered.

He reined the mare to a halt in front of the newspaper office. Dismounting, he picked up a newspaper someone had left on a chair.

"July second," he muttered. "Eighteen seventy-three." He had died on the 28th. That didn't give him much time.

Kathy shook her head. "Eighteen seventy-three. I don't believe it."

Dalton blew out a sigh. "Well, you'd best get used to the idea."

He held up the newspaper so she could read it for herself. 1873. A hundred and twenty-five years in the past. She swayed in the saddle.

Dropping the paper, Dalton lifted her from the back of the horse and wrapped his arms around her. "You okay?"

"I don't know."

"Humph! Such goings on! And in public, too!"

Startled, Kathy leaned to one side to see a woman glaring at her. "I beg your pardon?"

163

The woman, covered in pink gingham from neck to toe and wearing a matching bonnet snugly tied under her chin, stared at Kathy in obvious disdain.

"Have you no shame?" she declared in a voice thick with indignation. "Wearing men's clothes, and carrying on like that in public? And in front of a child, too!" Clicking her tongue, the woman grabbed her daughter by the arm and hurried across the street.

Kathy stared after her, shocked by the woman's outburst.

"Old biddy," Dalton muttered.

"She seemed a little upset," Kathy remarked. "Good thing I wasn't wearing shorts."

"Good thing," Dalton agreed, "but I think she was more upset because I was holding you in my arms."

"Well, what's wrong with that?"

Dalton shrugged. "You heard her. It ain't seemly."

"What isn't?"

"Me holding you in my arms in public."

"But you weren't holding me! I mean, you were, but not like that . . ." Kathy's voice trailed off. In the 1990s, a decade filled with AIDS and R-rated movies, a hug on the street wouldn't have been noticed. But this was the nineteenth century, when intimacy was carried on behind closed doors.

Dalton raised one brow. "She probably thinks you're a fallen woman," he said with a roguish grin.

"Fallen woman!" Kathy sputtered. "That's just great. I haven't even been here a day yet and my reputation is ruined."

"Take it easy," Dalton said, laughing.

"Sure, easy for you to say."

"We need to find you some clothes," Dalton remarked.

"What? Oh." She looked down at her jeans and tennis shoes and then glanced across the street. No doubt the woman had been shocked by her attire, too. Women in this day and age probably didn't wear pants to town, if they wore them at all. "Well, I don't have any money to buy a dress, even if I was of a mind to."

"I've got some."

"You do?"

"Sure. I told you, being a gunfighter was a profitable line of work." He secured the mare's reins to the hitch rack. "Come on."

"Where are we going?"

"The bank."

She couldn't help staring at every building they passed. Some, like the Square Deal, looked familiar. Dalton grabbed her by the arm when she started to peer inside.

"Decent women don't go into saloons."

"I wasn't going in. I just wanted to look inside."

He shook his head. "Nope."

"Fine." She followed him down the street and into the bank, acutely aware of every curious glance that followed her.

Entering the bank, Dalton walked up to the teller's cage.

"Good afternoon, Mr. Crowkiller," the teller said, his voice cool but polite. "How can I help you?"

"I'd like to make a withdrawal."

Kathy glanced around while Dalton took care of

business. A wooden partition topped by a wire grate divided the bank. A man in an old-fashioned city suit and cravat sat behind a large desk, thumbing through a stack of papers. There were several posters tacked to one wall. On closer inspection, she saw they were wanted posters for bank robbers.

"Ready?"

She glanced over her shoulder to find Dalton standing behind her. "Yes, I guess so."

Leaving the bank, they went to the general store. It looked like something out of an old John Wayne movie, with shelves and counters stocked with all manner of canned goods, blankets, bolts of cloth, cooking utensils, boots, shoes, bonnets, and ready-made dresses.

"Pick out whatever you need," Dalton said.

"Where are you going?"

"I need a few things myself. Meet me up front when you're ready."

"Okay."

She wandered through the store, amazed at how much stuff was crammed on the shelves and counters. She glanced at the signs tacked to one wall: Peaberry Coffee, 13 cents: Corn, four cans for 25 cents; butter, 23 cents a pound; eggs, 9 cents a dozen; KC Baking Powder, 11 cents; Farmer Jones Syrup, 21 cents a gallon; Silver Leaf Pure Hog Lard, eight-pound bucket, 49 cents.

In the shoe department, she sat down and tried on a pair of half-boots. The clerk looked at her oddly. She guessed she couldn't blame him. He had probably never seen a woman in jeans and a T-shirt before, let alone one wearing Mickey Mouse socks.

Tucking her new shoes under one arm, she went through the dresses on the rack until she found a few that seemed to be the right size. She picked out two—a pretty blue gingham, with a round neck, puffed sleeves and a wide sash, and a lavender flowered print with a square neck. She was going to look as though she had just stepped out of the pages of Little House on the Prairie. She found petticoats, too, and a pair of white cotton stockings, complete with garters. She found a hairbrush and a package of pins, and a long white nightgown that was so stiff she wondered if she'd have to sleep standing up.

She looked for a toothbrush, but to no avail, and then wondered if they had even been invented yet. On her way to the front of the store, she picked up a bonnet made of white straw; then, with a shake of her head, she put it back on the shelf.

Dalton was waiting for her at the front counter. "Find everything you need?"

"Almost." She placed her things on the countertop. "Do you have enough money for all this?"

"Sure."

She noticed then that he was wearing a new hat, black, with a wide brim. And a gunbelt, complete with holster and gun.

He rested one hand on the gun butt and grinned at her. "I felt naked without it."

Kathy nodded. Some men looked drop-dead gorgeous in a cowboy hat, and he was one of them.

The clerk added up their purchases the old-fashioned way, with pencil and paper. Kathy noticed that Dalton's gun cost twelve dollars.

A short time later, the transaction was completed and their purchases were wrapped in brown paper tied with string. Dalton paid the bill, tucked the bundle under his arm, and they left the store.

"What now?" Kathy asked.

"I keep a room at the boardinghouse. You can change clothes there." Descending the stairs, he took up Taffy Girl's reins.

Kathy looked at him in feigned astonishment. "Go to your room, sir? You must be joking. Whatever will people think?"

He grinned at her. "They'll think you're a tart, and that I'm damn lucky. Come on."

She stifled the urge to stick her tongue out at him as they walked down the dusty street.

Martha's Boardinghouse was a big, two-story building surrounded by a neat white picket fence. A huge tree shaded the front porch. Flowers grew in neat rows along the walkway. Smoke curled from the chimney.

Dalton looped the mare's reins over the hitching post at the front gate. "Martha must be fixing dinner," he remarked as they climbed the porch stairs. "She's a mighty fine cook."

"What will she think about me?"

"I dunno. I'll tell her you're my cousin, visiting from New York."

"Chicago."

"What?"

"I'm originally from Chicago."

Dalton grunted as he opened the door for her and Kathy stepped inside.

"Is that you, Miss Canfield?"

"No, Mrs. Dunn, it's me."

"You're just in time for vittles, Mr. Crowkiller."

"I've brought a guest. My cousin from"—Dalton flashed Kathy a grin—"New York City."

"Your cousin." Martha came out of the kitchen, wiping her hands on a towel. "I didn't know you had any family."

Dalton smiled at his landlady. "Martha, this is my cousin, Katherine. Katherine, this is Mrs. Dunn."

"Pleased to meet you, ma'am," Kathy said.

"Why, I'm right pleased to meet you, Miss Katherine. My, aren't you a pretty thing," Martha said with a cheerful smile.

"Thank you," Kathy replied, thinking that Martha Dunn could pass for the Fairy Godmother from *Cinderella,* with her bright blue eyes and her gray hair gathered in a bun at her nape.

"My, my," Martha remarked as she took in Kathy's jeans and bright yellow T-shirt, "but they do dress strangely where you come from, don't they, dear?"

"I . . . that is . . ."

"Katherine had an unfortunate accident and had to borrow some clothes," Dalton interjected smoothly.

"Why, you poor thing." Martha patted Kathy's arm. "Will you be visiting long?"

"I'm not sure."

"Mr. Carmine has left town," Martha said. She smiled up at Dalton. It was easy to see that he had charmed the woman long since. "If your cousin needs a room, his is available."

"That'd be right nice," Dalton said.

"Why don't you show your cousin where it is? I've got biscuits in the oven. Don't be late for dinner," she called, hurrying back into the kitchen.

"She seems very nice," Kathy said.

"Yeah, she's a sweetheart. Come on, your room's down the hall—across from mine."

"She likes you, too," Kathy muttered.

"What?"

"I saw the way she looked at you."

"What the devil are you talking about? She's old enough to be my mother."

"Uh-huh."

Dalton muttered an oath as he opened the door to Kathy's room. "You should be comfortable in here."

"It's nice," Kathy said, stepping inside. A large window overlooked the main street. There was a big double bed covered by a calico quilt, a chest of drawers, and a commode. A pretty rag rug brightened the wooden floor; lacy white curtains billowed softly at the window. "Very nice."

"Yeah." He thrust the paper-wrapped bundle into her hands. "Why don't you change? I'll meet you in the dining room in twenty minutes."

Kathy glanced at her watch. "Okay."

Dalton left the room, closing the door behind him.

With a sigh, Kathy sat down on the edge of the bed, clutching the package to her breast. It was all so bizarre, so unreal, like a dream.

Only she wasn't dreaming.

Chapter Twelve

Kathy hardly recognized herself as she stared at her reflection in the oval mirror on the highboy. Dressed in crisp blue gingham, with her hair pinned back and no makeup, she looked just like one of the Little Women! Jo, she thought, or maybe Meg.

She glanced at her watch and then, realizing that her digital timepiece would likely raise a few eyebrows, she slipped it off and tucked it into a drawer, then left her room, long skirts swishing about her ankles. She had never felt so weighted down in her whole life.

She found Dalton in the dining room. He stood up when she entered, a slight smile on his face as he held out her chair.

"Such manners," Kathy murmured. "Who would have guessed?"

"I wasn't always a gunfighter," he retorted, his voice pitched for her ears alone.

She sat down. "No?"

"No, *cousin.* You forget, my mother was born and raised in Boston."

Kathy grinned at him. "Touché, Mr. Crowkiller."

Martha Dunn bustled into the room carrying a huge wooden tray. "Miss Canfield won't be joining us this afternoon," she remarked as she placed the tray in the center of the table, "but Mr. Petty should be down directly."

"How many boarders have you?" Kathy asked.

"Four including you, now that Mr. Carmine has left town. Poor man, he was called home due to the illness of his sister."

Kathy nodded sympathetically.

"Please, Miss Katherine, help yourself."

Martha lifted the cover on the tray, revealing several large bowls containing mashed potatoes, corn, and chunks of beef swimming in gravy.

"It looks good," Kathy said.

Martha beamed at her. "Oh, I forgot the biscuits."

"Don't believe a word about old Carmine," Dalton said. "He left town because he couldn't meet his gambling debts."

"Really?" Kathy asked.

"Really."

"Here we go." Martha placed a basket of biscuits on the table, then sat down at the head.

A few minutes later, a rather portly man dressed in a dark brown coat and striped pants entered the room.

"Mr. Petty," Martha said, smiling, "this is Miss

Katherine . . . oh, dear, I'm afraid I didn't get your last name.''

''Wagner,'' Dalton said.

''Of course. Miss Wagner, this is Mr. Hyrum Petty. He works at the bank.''

''Nice to meet you,'' Kathy said.

Petty bowed over her hand. ''The pleasure is all mine, Miss Wagner,'' he said gallantly.

''Thank you.''

Petty sat down across from Martha. He was a rotund man, with a fringe of dark brown hair, brown eyes, and a pencil-thin moustache. A ruby stickpin gleamed in his cravat.

The meal passed pleasantly enough. Petty dominated most of the conversation, talking about stocks and bonds and rumors that the railroad would soon be coming to town.

Dalton said very little. He concentrated on the food on his plate, savoring each bite. So many different tastes and textures! He had forgotten what food tasted like, it had been so long since he had eaten anything. When he'd told Kathy that Martha was a good cook, he had almost forgotten just what that meant. And the coffee. He took his black, savoring the rich aroma, the warmth, the slightly bitter taste. How many times had he longed for a cup of coffee in the last hundred and twenty-five years?

Martha served apple pie still warm from the oven for dessert, and Dalton thought maybe he'd gone to heaven after all.

When the meal was over, Petty bade them all farewell and left to go to the bank.

173

Kathy stood up as Martha began clearing the table. "Mrs. Dunn, can I help you with the dishes?"

"Well, isn't it sweet of you to offer!" Martha exclaimed. "But I can't let you do that. You just run along now and have a nice visit with your cousin. Supper is at six, Mr. Crowkiller. Don't be late."

Dalton winked at his landlady as he followed Kathy out of the dining room.

"Why did you tell them my name was Wagner?" Kathy asked.

Dalton lifted one brow. "Why do you think? The name Conley's pretty well known in these parts."

"Oh, yeah, right. I didn't think of that." She turned toward the parlor, then paused when Dalton didn't follow her. "Where are you going?" she asked, following him outside.

"I thought I'd take your horse over to the livery, then go over to the saloon."

"Oh."

He raised an eyebrow. "Something wrong?"

"What am I supposed to do while you're gone?"

Dalton shrugged. "Anything you like."

"Can't I go with you?"

"To the saloon?" He looked at her as if she had just suggested they stroll naked down main street.

"Why not? In my day, women frequent bars all the time."

"Maybe so, but this is *my* day," he reminded her, and then he blew out a breath. "Hell, it's your reputation," he said, taking up the mare's reins. "I guess you can come along, if you've a mind to."

Kathy couldn't help staring at her surroundings as

they walked down the street. It was like being on a Western movie set, seeing women in long dresses and bonnets and men wearing leather vests over long-sleeved cowboy shirts and Stetson hats. And guns. All the men wore guns. They passed a shopkeeper sweeping the boardwalk in front of his store. He nodded and smiled at Kathy. Further down, the sheriff was sitting in front of his office, his feet propped on the railing.

He stood up as they drew closer. "Crowkiller."

Dalton stopped. "Morning, sheriff," he said, his voice neutral.

The lawman grunted. "Burkhart came to see me this morning. Seems one of his new hands turned up dead last night. You wouldn't know anything about that, would you?"

Dalton shook his head. "Not a thing."

"Uh-huh. Where were you last night?"

Dalton hesitated. "I was out at the Conley place, playing poker with Russell." It was a lie, but he figured Conley would back him up.

The sheriff jerked his chin toward Kathy. "Who's this?"

"My cousin, Miss Katherine Wagner."

Kathy smiled brightly. "Pleased to meet you, sheriff."

The lawman tipped his hat. "Pleasure to make your acquaintance, ma'am."

"Anything else I can do for you, sheriff?"

"You haven't done anything yet," the Sheriff replied sourly. "Nice meeting you, Miss Wagner."

Kathy smiled at the lawman, then followed Dalton

down the street. "You never told me why you killed that man, just that it was personal between the two of you."

"He was a young gun, cocky, mouthy. At that age, you think you'll live forever. He was determined to prove he was the better man." Dalton shrugged as he turned to face her. "He was wrong."

Kathy gazed up at Dalton, wondering why she felt so disappointed. She had known from the beginning that he was a hired gun.

Dalton looked at her for a long moment, then started walking again.

Kathy trailed after him, a dozen questions hovering on the tip of her tongue, yet afraid to ask them for fear of what the answers might be.

When they reached the livery, a big, broad-shouldered man clad in a pair of loose canvas pants and a stained leather apron came out to meet them.

"Wot can I do for you, Mr. Crowkiller?" he asked.

"I'm looking to leave my cousin's horse here for a day or two."

The man nodded, his gaze running over Taffy Girl in a quick, assessing glance. "I vill take good care of her, don't you vorry." He patted the mare on the shoulder. "She's a fine beauty. If you vant to sell her, let me know."

"You'd have to talk to the lady about that," Dalton said. "The mare belongs to her."

"Ah." The man looked at Kathy and smiled. "Do you vant to sell her?"

"No, I'm afraid not."

"Vell, if you change your mind, you let me know, ya?"

"I will."

"He's got a good eye for horseflesh," Dalton remarked as they headed back toward the middle of town. "Are you sure you want to come with me?"

She wasn't sure at all, but she nodded, unwilling to go back to the boardinghouse and twiddle her thumbs.

The Square Deal was quiet this time of day. Kathy glanced around, taking it all in, noting that it looked pretty much the way saloons in cowboy movies always looked. There was sawdust on the floor, a long bar with a brass rail, tables covered in green baize, a picture of a voluptuous nude behind the bar. A man sat at a back table, playing solitaire. Two others were involved in a desultory game of poker. Two heavily painted women stood at the bar. They smiled at Dalton, the interest in their eyes fading when they saw Kathy.

Dalton went to the bar and ordered a whiskey, then looked at Kathy, a question in his eye.

Kathy hesitated. She had never been much of a drinker, a wine cooler now and then, a little champagne on New Year's. "I'd like a beer."

"Beer for the lady," Dalton said.

"She don't belong in here," the bartender said.

"Is that right? Well, she belongs with me, and I'm here."

"Yessir, Mr. Crowkiller," the bartender said quickly. "Whiskey and a beer, coming right up."

Dalton met Kathy's gaze in the mirror. "All right," he said, his voice low. "Spit it out."

"What do you mean?"

"You know damn well what I mean. You're upset about that kid I killed. It's written all over your face."

She shook her head, unable to put the question into words.

Dalton rested one foot on the rail. "It was a fair fight. He was looking for trouble. I told him to get the hell out of town, and he refused. He was slow and stupid, and now he's dead."

She was trying to think of a reply when the man who had been playing solitaire swaggered toward the bar.

"Well, now, who's this?" he drawled. " 'Bout time Carly got some new blood in this joint."

"Get lost, Sullivan. She's with me."

Sullivan grinned at Kathy. "You don't wanna be with him, do ya, honey? Come on, lemme buy you a drink."

"I said she's with me."

Dalton's words hung in the air. The bartender glanced from Sullivan to Dalton and moved to the far end of the bar. The two men playing poker paused in their game to see what all the ruckus was about.

"Sure, sure." Sullivan winked at Kathy. "Get rid of 'im and I'll show you a good time." He reached into his pocket and withdrew a gold coin, which he waved in front of her face. "I got money. Lots of money."

Kathy stared at the man, not knowing whether to laugh or be insulted.

Reaching forward, he dropped the coin down the front of her bodice, then grabbed her hand. "Come on, darlin'. Let's go find a room."

She was trying to pull her hand away when Dalton grabbed Sullivan by the shirtfront and slammed him up against the bar. "I said she's with me." He bit off each word. "You got that?"

Sullivan raised both hands. "Sorry. I didn't mean nothing."

Dalton glared at him a moment, then let him go. "Get the hell out of here."

Red-faced, Sullivan scrambled away from the bar and left the saloon.

The two poker players went back to their game.

The bartender placed a shot of whiskey and a glass of beer on the bar, then moved away.

Dalton picked up the whiskey. He downed it in a single swallow, then motioned for another.

Kathy sipped her beer, thinking maybe she should have stayed at the boardinghouse after all.

Dalton drained his glass and set it on the bar. "Let's go." He dropped a few coins on the bar and headed for the door.

Kathy pulled the gold piece from her bodice and put it on the bar, then followed him outside.

Dalton hesitated on the boardwalk a moment, then turned left and started walking, fast. It was all she could do to keep up with him.

Leaving the town behind, they came to a small pond surrounded by trees and shrubs. Dalton sat down on a log, arms resting on his thighs, hands dangling between his knees.

Kathy stared at him, wondering what he was thinking, wondering how she was going to get back home, to her own time, where she belonged.

She heard him swear, and then he glanced up at her. "I wish I knew what the hell we were doing here."

"Yeah, me, too." She sat down beside him.

"Do you think it's possible to change the past?"

"We already have," she said, and when he looked confused, she shrugged. "My being here has already changed the past, hasn't it?"

"I reckon so."

"Where were you on this date before?"

"Out at the Conley ranch being interrogated by the sheriff."

"Then we have altered the past," Kathy mused, "because he questioned you here, in town, instead."

"Yeah, I reckon."

"What else did you do?"

"There was a dance at the schoolhouse to celebrate the Fourth. I stayed in town that night, then spent the next three or four days harassing Burkhart and his men. After that, I went back to the ranch." Back to Lydia. For all his big words about not fooling around with another man's wife, he hadn't been able to stay away from her.

"Well, if you never go back to the ranch, you won't get caught in the barn with—You won't get caught, and Russell Conley won't have any reason to hang you."

"Yeah." Dalton massaged his throat, wondering if it could be that easy, wondering if he had truly been

180

given a second chance, or if he was fated to die on the morning of July 28th, if not at the end of a rope, then by some other means.

He slid a glance at Kathy. She was gazing into the distance, a bemused expression on her face. Looking at her made him forget everything but the way she had felt in his arms.

Moving closer, he slid his arm around her waist.

Kathy blinked at him. "What are you doing?"

"It's an experiment."

"What do you mean?"

"Trust me."

"Can I?"

"Sure you can," he murmured. "Trustworthy is my middle name."

She would have argued about that if he hadn't kissed her. Her eyelids fluttered down as a delicious warmth spread through her. His arm tightened around her, drawing her closer, dragging her into his lap. His tongue teased her lower lip and she moaned softly, lost in a maelstrom of wild emotions. She felt the heat of his hands penetrate her clothing, felt the tension building within him. He kissed her until she was breathless, and all the time she felt herself waiting, waiting for him to disappear. Her hands folded over his shoulders, feeling solid flesh and muscle as he turned her on his lap so that she was straddling his thighs.

He drew back a little, his dark eyes searching hers, and then, with a low groan, he kissed her again, his hands moving restlessly up and down the length of her back, his thumbs skimming the curves of her breasts.

She wrapped her arms around his neck, holding on for dear life as the world spun out of focus and she felt herself falling, drowning in a molten sea of desire. This was no ghost, no phantom, but a very real man, with a man's needs. She could feel the evidence of that desire in every taut line of his body, in the urgency of his kisses.

With a jolt, she realized that everything was different now. She could love him. She could make love to him, and he wouldn't disappear. The thought filled her with equal parts of fear and excitement, uncertainty and anticipation. She didn't belong in this world any more than he had belonged in hers, and yet, she didn't care.

It startled her to know that she wanted him desperately, wanted him more than she had ever wanted anything in her life.

"Kathy." His voice was harsh, ragged with longing. He lifted his head and glanced around, searching for a place a little more secluded, but there was none, and as much as he wanted her, he couldn't take her there, within sight of the town.

Arms locked around her waist, he stood up, carrying her with him, and headed for town. He had a room at Martha's, and that room had a bed, and a door, with a lock on it.

"Dalton!" Kathy gasped, "what are you doing?"

"Going where we can be alone."

"Put me down."

He shook his head, afraid if he let her go, she

would come to her senses and change her mind.

"People are staring at us," Kathy exclaimed. It was early afternoon and the street was filled with people.

"Let 'em."

She buried her face against his shoulder, wondering why she should care what a bunch of strangers thought anyway.

Dalton came to an abrupt halt. At the same time, a stillness fell over the town. Puzzled, Kathy lifted her head and glanced over her shoulder. There was a man standing a few yards away. Legs spread, hat tilted back, one hand resting on the butt of his gun.

"I been looking for you, Crowkiller," the man said.

"Have you?"

The man nodded.

Moving slowly, Dalton set Kathy on her feet and gave her a little shove. "Get out of here."

"What's going on?"

"I don't have time to explain. Just do as I say."

Heart pounding, she went to stand on the boardwalk. She remembered reading somewhere that the idea of two men facing each other in the middle of the street was a product of Western myth and had never happened. But it seemed about to happen now.

"You've found me," Dalton said. "Now what?"

"I aim to kill you."

"Is that right?"

The man nodded. "You killed a friend of mine last night."

"Did I? I wouldn't think a man as ugly as you would have any friends."

Both men were moving before Dalton finished speaking. For a moment, Kathy was sure Dalton was going to be killed. The other man reached for his weapon a fraction of a second sooner, but Dalton was moving, too, dropping to the ground, drawing his gun as he rolled quickly to the right. The other man fired a hair's breath sooner, only his target was no longer there.

The two gunshots sounded like one. She noticed, in a distant part of her mind, that real gunfire wasn't as loud as it was in the movies. Twin columns of blue-gray smoke drifted on the breeze. The other man reeled backward, his free hand grabbing at his chest before he fell.

Dalton stood up slowly, his gun tracking the man's every move.

There was a loud silence, and then the sound of footsteps as the sheriff came running down the street. People emerged from the shops along the boardwalk, all talking at once.

"Did you see that?"

"Damn! They was fast, both of 'em."

"Is he dead?"

Kathy stared at the man lying in the street, at the bright red blood that stained his shirtfront, and felt sick to her stomach. She had seen death before, but never like this, never seen anyone killed right before her eyes.

She swallowed the bile in her throat, and then she turned to look at Dalton. He was still standing in the street, his gun dangling at his side. Slowly, as though it weighed a hundred pounds, he lifted the revolver and slid it into his holster.

Descending the steps, Kathy ran to him. "Dalton? Dalton, are you all right?"

"Yeah."

"Okay, what's the story?" the sheriff demanded, pushing through the crowd that had gathered around the body of the dead man.

"He called me out," Dalton replied. He jerked a thumb toward the people milling around. "There are a dozen witnesses if you don't believe me."

"I'll get to 'em. In the meantime, I think you'd better come on down to the jail. I'll have to lock you up until the circuit judge can hear your case."

"Like hell."

The sheriff started to reach for his gun, only to back off, his face turning a sickly shade of white, when he found himself staring into the barrel of Dalton's Colt. "I'm not going to jail," Dalton said, his voice cold. "I'll be at the boardinghouse if you need me. You got that?"

"Y-yeah, I've got it." The sheriff squared his shoulders. "Don't leave town," he said loudly. He turned back to the crowd still gathered around the body. "All right," he bellowed, "move along."

"Did you know that man?" Kathy asked.

"Never seen him before."

"Does this kind of thing happen often?"

"Often enough." He took her arm and cut across the street, heading for Martha's Boardinghouse.

Kathy was aware of the looks thrown their way as

185

they passed by, expressions that ranged from respect to fear. She caught bits and pieces of hushed conversation.

"... hired killer ..."

"Works for Conley, I heard ..."

"Killed more'n two dozen men ..."

"... wonder who the woman is ..."

Dalton's fingers were like iron where they gripped her arm and didn't relax until they were walking up the path to the boardinghouse.

Inside the parlor, he took a deep breath, then blew it out in a long, shuddering sigh.

"Well, I guess that proves we can change the past," he muttered.

Kathy nodded, wondering what the repercussions, if any, would be.

He shook his head. "I'm sorry you had to see that." He regarded her a moment. "Are you all right?"

"I feel a little queasy."

"Maybe you should go lie down until supper time."

"Yes, I think I will." Some time alone was just what she needed, she mused, time to sort her feelings, time to remind herself that she did not belong in this place, in this century. Time to remind herself that, no matter how intoxicating his kisses, she could not be falling in love with this man, not now, not ever. She was never going to risk her heart again.

All of Martha Dunn's boarders were present at the supper table that night. Martha introduced Kathy to

Enid Canfield, who was the schoolteacher. She was a tall, buxom woman with light brown hair, which she wore in a severe bun, and pale blue eyes that were magnified behind thick spectacles. She sat as straight as a telephone pole.

"I don't wish to be rude," she said in a voice that sounded like a rusty hinge, "but . . ." She pressed a hand to her heart. "I believe in airing problems when they arise, and I . . . that is . . . well, I'm not sure I can keep a room here any longer."

Martha frowned, disturbed at the thought of losing one of her boarders. "Heavens, is it something I've done?"

"I believe I know what's bothering Miss Canfield," Petty said. "I heard Mr. Crowkiller was seen carrying his cousin across the street." Petty smiled. "Some folks might view that as unseemly, if you know what I mean."

Enid Canfield's cheeks turned bright pink. "That is exactly what I am referring to." She cleared her throat, obviously uncomfortable. "But that is not the only thing. Mr. Crowkiller shot a man this afternoon."

"I heard it was in self-defense," Petty remarked.

"Be that as it may, I must be careful in my associations."

Kathy glanced at Dalton. His face was impassive, but she could sense his anger boiling under the surface. "Please, Miss Canfield," she said, "you needn't be concerned about your reputation. I had twisted my ankle and Mr. Crowkiller came to my aid. As for the gunfight . . ." Kathy shrugged. "That was quite be-

yond my cousin's control. As Mr. Petty said, Dalton
was only defending himself.

"Perhaps I was too hasty in my judgment," Miss
Canfield replied.

"Of course you were," Petty said. "Let's eat."

Kathy sat down, and Dalton sat across from her.

Eager to change the subject, Martha piled Kathy's
plate high with chicken and dumplings and baking
powder biscuits. "You're too thin," she chided.
"Men like a woman they can hold onto. Isn't that
right, Mr. Petty?"

"Yes, indeed," Petty replied with what could only
be called a leer.

Kathy slid a glance at Dalton, who was hiding a
smile behind his hand.

"It's a lovely evening," Petty remarked. "Perhaps
we can go for a walk later."

Kathy looked over at Dalton, silently pleading for
him to save her.

"I'm afraid that won't be possible," Dalton said.
"My cousin is a recent widow. You understand."

Petty nodded. "Oh, to be sure, to be sure."

"I'm so sorry, dear," Martha murmured. "Dalton,
why didn't you tell me?"

Now it was Dalton's turn to seek help.

"I asked him not to mention it," Kathy interjected.

Martha nodded sympathetically. "Of course. I
know just how you feel. My Henry passed just a year
ago."

Kathy nodded.

"My condolences," Enid Canfield said.

"Thank you."

"Well," Martha said, rising. "I hope you all saved room for dessert. We've got apple cobbler."

"I think old Petty would like to get to know you better," Dalton mused.

"Oh, please, spare me," Kathy said with a groan. "He's old enough to be my father."

They were sitting out on the front porch. Everyone else in the boardinghouse had turned in for the night.

Kathy slid a glance at Dalton. His chair was tilted back on two legs; his feet, crossed at the ankles, were resting on the porch rail. His profile was sharp and clean in the yellow lamplight shining through the parlor window. He had a fine, straight nose, a strong, square jaw, high cheekbones, straight black brows. It all combined to create a face that was both arresting and incredibly handsome. Even the faint scar on his cheek did nothing to distract from his roguish good looks.

As though feeling her gaze, he turned toward her. "Something wrong?"

"Wrong?" she asked, bemused. "What could possibly be wrong except that I'm a hundred and twenty-five years in the past?"

He grunted softly. "Yeah, I guess that is a bit of a problem for you, isn't it?"

"Just a bit," she retorted.

"Still, there's not much waiting for you in your own time."

The fact that he was right filled her with a sudden sense of dismay. Of course, her family was there, but they were hundreds of miles away and, except for holidays, she didn't see them very often. She had left all her old friends behind when she moved to the ranch.

"Hey," Dalton said softly. "I didn't mean that the way it sounded."

"Maybe not, but it's true. There isn't anything waiting for me there. Probably no one will even realize that I'm gone until I don't show up at home for Christmas."

Feeling the sting of tears, she lowered her head so Dalton couldn't see. Even though there was no one waiting for her in her own time, she didn't want to be here. There were things she would miss, like all the modern conveniences that she took for granted—washers and dryers and microwaves, her car, her stereo, movies, TV, shopping centers, pizza, hot running water, toilet paper, toothpaste.

"Kathy?"

She looked up to find him standing beside her chair. Gently, he lifted her to her feet and drew her into his arms.

"Ah, Kathy."

Just her name, but he didn't have to say anything else. She knew what he wanted. She could see it in his eyes, feel her own need flowing through her.

Slowly, giving her plenty of time to refuse, Dalton lowered his head and claimed her lips with his.

A maelstrom of sensations and emotions flooded through her. She wanted him with an intensity that threatened to consume her, wanted him to lay her down on the porch and take her there, with her skirts up around her waist and his hands tunneling through her hair. The thought shocked her. She had never felt this way before, not even with Wayne. Guilt was like a knife plunging into her heart.

"I can't!" She put her hands against his chest and pushed him away. "Please, I can't."

"You want me," Dalton said, his voice gruff. "Dammit, I know you do. Why won't you admit it?"

"All right, I admit it." She shook her head. "But I can't."

"Why the hell not?"

"It's too soon."

Dalton frowned, and then sighed. "You're thinking of him, aren't you? Your husband?"

Kathy nodded, wondering when she had ever felt so miserable.

Dalton blew out a breath, then shoved his hands in his pockets. "I'm leaving tomorrow."

"Leaving?" Panic surged through her, obliterating everything else. "Why? Where are you going?"

"To find my father's people."

"The Sioux?"

"Yeah."

"Why?"

"I made a promise a long time ago. I mean to fulfill it."

She stared at him, unable to believe her ears. He was going to go off and leave her. What would she do without him? "How long will you be gone?"

"I don't know."

"But . . . you can't go."

"I think it's for the best."

"What do you mean?"

He scowled at her. "You're driving me crazy. I can't stop thinking about you, wanting you. I . . . shit!" He turned away from her and raked a hand through his hair. "It's better this way."

"Better?" Her voice came out in an anguished squeak. "You're going to go off and leave me here, alone?"

"Damn." What was he thinking of? He couldn't just ride out and leave her behind. Slowly, he turned to face her. "I need to find my people," he explained. "I made a promise to my father before he died, and now that I've been given another chance, I intend to keep it, if I can."

"There's more, isn't there? Something you aren't telling me."

He blew out a breath. "I'm afraid," he said quietly, so quietly she had to lean forward to hear him. "Afraid if I stay here, I'll wind up at the end of that damn rope again."

Kathy nodded. She didn't blame him for being afraid. "Can't I go with you? To the Sioux?"

He thought of what it would be like, to be with her day and night and not touch her, to look into her eyes and know she was thinking of her husband. He knew the hell he had lived in before had been a pale shadow of the hell he was about to endure.

"It won't be easy for you," he said, hoping to discourage her. "Most of my people don't speak English, or have much affection for the *wasichu*."

"*Wasi* . . ."

"*Wasichu*. The whites."

"Oh." She pondered that a moment, but knew

she'd still rather go with him than be left behind. "I don't want to stay here without you."

"Why don't you sleep on it?"

"Okay," she agreed, even though she knew she wouldn't change her mind. Maybe it was her imagination, but she couldn't shake the feeling that they had to stay together, that something awful would happen if he left her behind.

"I'm going for a walk."

Kathy nodded, her mind in turmoil as she watched him descend the stairs. She'd sleep on it, if she could sleep at all, but she didn't think she would be getting much sleep, not with the memory of Dalton's kiss still playing havoc with her senses.

As she feared, she didn't get much sleep that night. She tossed and turned until the wee small hours, reminding herself that she had vowed never to love again, that even if she decided to risk her heart a second time, it couldn't be with Dalton. He was a hired gun, a man from another century. They should never have met and sooner or later, Fate would step in to set things right. She would find her way to her own time, and Dalton Crowkiller would stay here, in his.

Rising, she put on her bra and panties, pulled on her petticoat, and slipped the dress over her head, wondering, as she did so, why it had taken women so long to wear jeans. She put on her stockings and boots, brushed her hair, wished again for a toothbrush.

Glancing in the mirror, she shook her head at her

reflection. "Morning, Miss Katherine," she muttered. "Time to go visit the outhouse."

When she saw Dalton at the breakfast table later, she could tell, from the dark shadows under his eyes, that he hadn't gotten much sleep either.

He offered her a wintry grin when she sat down at the table across from him.

Martha Dunn clucked at them like a mother hen as she filled their cups with coffee. "You've missed breakfast," she scolded. "Mr. Petty and Miss Canfield have already gone."

"That's all right," Dalton muttered. "I'm not hungry."

"Me, either," Kathy said.

Martha stood beside the table, her hands fisted on her hips, a frown on her face. "I have some blueberry muffins left," she said. "Still warm from the oven."

Dalton shook his head. "Not for me."

"I'd love one, if it's not too much trouble," Kathy said, the temptation of a fresh muffin too much to resist.

"No trouble at all," Martha said. She left the room, returning moments later with a fat blueberry muffin on a white china plate. "I'll just leave the coffee pot here," she said. She smiled from one to the other. "I've got laundry to do. Lordy, it just never seems to end."

Laundry. Kathy frowned as she imagined heating water on the stove, then washing her long gingham dress and petticoats on a scrub board in a wooden tub, wringing the heavy cloth out by hand, hanging everything up on a clothesline.

Dalton drained his cup and poured another. "So, what did you decide?"

"I don't want to stay here alone."

He nodded, a resigned expression on his face. "We'll need to go over to the mercantile and stock up on a few things. And then I'm gonna take a ride out to the Triple Bar C."

"Whatever for?"

"My horse is there."

"Oh. Is it safe for you to go there?"

"Safe?" Dalton shrugged. "I reckon so. I've been staying there for the last three months." He frowned. "Or I was." He muttered an oath. "You know what I mean. Damn, this time thing is confusing."

"Tell me about it."

She finished her muffin and drank another cup of coffee, heavily laced with sugar and real cream. It was stronger than she was used to, but delicious.

"Well," Dalton said, "let's go."

Careful not to touch each other, they left the boardinghouse and walked to the mercantile.

"Go buy whatever you think you might need," Dalton said. "I'm not sure how long we'll be gone, so you'd better buy another dress, and a hat." He frowned. "I guess you know what you'll need better than I do. I'll meet you up front when you're done."

With a nod, Kathy walked down the nearest aisle. If they were going to be riding across the plains, she didn't intend to do it mired down in yards of gingham and petticoats.

Going to the men's department, she picked out a pair of men's Levi's, two flannel shirts and a sheepskin jacket. She chose a gray hat with a wide brim. Going to the shoe department, she tried on several pairs of boots until she found a pair that felt right, shaking her head when she saw the price. Three dollars. The last pair she had bought had cost almost a hundred bucks. She wished she'd been wearing them when they were zapped through time.

Moving on, she picked up a bar of white naphtha soap priced at five cents a bar, a washcloth, and a length of toweling. She picked up a couple of large white handkerchiefs that were priced at twenty-five cents each. Kidskin gloves were a dollar and a half a pair. In passing, she noticed that three yards of ribbon sold for seventy-five cents, and that five yards of linen was only two-fifty.

Intrigued by the store itself, she wandered around for a few more minutes, amazed by the wide variety of items for sale: salt, spices, raisins, sugar, cheese, eggs, butter, salted meat and fish, tea, coffee, Arm and Hammer Soda, KC Baking Powder. A ten-pound bag of Matoma Rice was only sixty-five cents. Beer and whiskey, molasses and vinegar were dispensed through spigots from barrels. Pickles and crackers were also sold from barrels. She was startled to see cans of Van Camp's beans in tomato sauce on the shelf.

One counter held chamber pots, slop jars, spittoons, dish pans and wash basins, coffee grinders, flour sifters and bread pans, milk pails, coffee pots, foot warmers, frying pans and teakettles.

A showcase held knives of all sizes from tiny penknives to a huge Bowie knife in a leather sheath. And there were guns, of course, clearly marked: an Iver Johnson .32 caliber for a measly three dollars and forty cents, a Frontier Colt .45, a small lady's revolver.

With a start, she remembered that Dalton was waiting for her. Hurrying to the front of the store, she saw him standing with one hip canted against the front counter while a clerk rang up his purchases.

"Got everything?" he asked.

"I guess so."

She glanced at the jars of peanut brittle, taffy and fudge displayed near the cash register and asked the clerk to please add a piece of fudge to their order.

Dalton frowned when she placed the Levi's and shirts on the counter.

"I'm not riding in a dress," she explained, daring him to argue with her. "For one thing, it isn't practical."

"Suit yourself."

"What about dishes?"

"I got those." He gestured at two tin plates, a blue-speckled coffee pot and a couple of matching cups, knives, forks and spoons, a large frying pan and a dutch oven. "You ever cooked outdoors?"

"A little." She had gone camping in Yellowstone with Wayne and his folks one summer soon after they were married.

Dalton nodded, then turned to the clerk. "Pack all this stuff up for me. We'll pick it up first thing in the morning."

"Yes, sir."

Dalton paid for their supplies, then opened the door for Kathy. She walked out, turning toward the boardinghouse, only to come face to face with Lydia Conley.

Chapter Thirteen

Lydia Conley spared hardly a glance at Kathy as her gaze sought Dalton's. A slow smile spread across her face. It was the most blatantly sultry, provocative, predatory smile Kathy had ever seen.

"Good afternoon, Mr. Crowkiller," Lydia said. Her voice was soft and seductive, like warm silk sliding over cool satin sheets, as she offered him her hand.

Kathy glanced over her shoulder, curious to see Dalton's reaction to the woman who had been the cause of his death.

Dalton took Lydia's hand and quickly released it. "What brings you to town, Mrs. Conley?"

Kathy frowned, wondering if it was her imagination, or if he had stressed the word *Mrs*. Was it to remind Lydia that she was a married woman, she mused, or was it to remind himself that she was off limits?

Lydia lifted an elegant hand and let it fall. "I was bored, so I asked Whitey to bring me to town." She slid a glance at Kathy, the look in her eyes reminding Kathy of a mongoose eying a cobra. "Who is this?"

"My cousin, Katherine Wagner, from New York City. Kathy, this is Mrs. Conley."

Kathy nodded at the other woman. Lydia Conley was indeed beautiful. The pictures she had seen had not done the woman justice. She wore a blatantly expensive orange and brown taffeta dress that complemented her wavy auburn hair and deep brown eyes and emphasized her creamy white skin. A bonnet with matching orange and brown streamers was tilted at a jaunty angle over one eye. Expensive brown kidskin half-boots and a pair of white gloves completed her outfit.

Standing beside her, Kathy felt about as attractive as an old, worn-out shoe.

"Pleased to make your acquaintance, I'm sure," Lydia said, her voice perfectly modulated. "How long will you be visiting?"

"I'm not sure." Driven by some perverse urge, Kathy slid her arm through Dalton's. Smiling up at him, she batted her eyelashes. "Dalton is such fun to be around, I just may stay here forever."

Dalton frowned at her, as if to remind her that they were supposed to be cousins, but Kathy didn't care. Even without meeting Lydia's gaze, she could feel the other woman's animosity.

Lydia turned back to Dalton. "What brings you to

town?'' she asked, her full attention again focused on Dalton. ''Are you taking care of business for Russell?''

Dalton shook his head. ''No, ma'am. I've been taking care of my own business.'' Deciding it was useless to go on pretending they were cousins, Dalton placed his hand over Kathy's, the gesture flagrantly possessive. ''Why don't you do the same?''

Jealousy, disbelief, and indignation clashed in the depths of Lydia Conley's eyes. ''How dare you speak to me like that!'' she hissed, and lifting her skirts, she swept past them, as aloof as a queen among peasants.

''So,'' Kathy murmured, ''that's the infamous Lydia Conley.''

''That's her.''

''Did you love her?''

''No.'' Dalton glanced over his shoulder. Lydia was walking across the street, back rigid, skirts swaying. ''But I wanted her,'' he muttered. ''Heaven help me, I wanted her.''

Kathy withdrew her arm from Dalton's. She could understand why Lydia was jealous. Foolish as it was, she was feeling a touch of the green-eyed monster herself.

''Why don't you go on back to the boarding-house,'' Dalton said. ''I'm going out to the ranch to get my horse.''

''Do you really think that's wise? I think you should stay as far away from the Conleys as possible.''

Dalton watched Lydia go into the dressmaker's shop across the way. If he knew Lydia, she would be in there for at least an hour, more likely two. "I think now is just the right time."

"All right. I'll see you at Martha's later. Be careful."

With a nod, he headed for the livery.

Kathy stood there a moment, watching him walk away; then, with a sigh, she started walking toward the boardinghouse.

"How long have you known Dalton?"

"Excuse me?" Turning around, Kathy again found herself face to face with Lydia Conley.

"I am not a fool. If you two are cousins, then I am the Queen of England."

"I haven't known him very long," Kathy said, "not that it's any of your business."

"Are you in love with him?"

"Are you?"

"Of course not," Lydia said quickly, but her flushed cheeks betrayed her. "Does he love you?"

Kathy hesitated, sorely tempted to lie and say yes just to see Lydia's reaction. Instead, she said, "No. We're just friends. Good friends."

"Indeed?"

Kathy felt her cheeks grow hot as Lydia's gaze swept over her in a glance that said, more clearly than words, just what kind of "friends" Lydia thought they were.

"It's not like that at all," Kathy sputtered. "We never . . . oh! You're jealous, aren't you? Jealous to think he might have come to my bed when he turned you down flat."

Lydia's jaw dropped open in astonishment. "How

do you know that?'' Color flooded her cheeks. ''Did he dare to tell you that?''

Kathy covered her mouth with one hand as she realized what she had let slip. Afraid she might accidentally blurt out something else that she shouldn't know about, she turned and ran back to the boarding-house.

Dalton thought about Lydia on the ride out to the ranch. Seeing her had filled him with a dozen conflicting emotions. Chief among them had been anger and a soul-deep rage that she had let him die when she could have saved him. Damn her! He wondered if she would have spoken in his behalf if, instead of rebuffing her advances, he had taken her to bed. Damn and double damn, it had been all he could do to keep from wrapping his hands around her pretty little neck and giving her a taste of what gut-wrenching fear was like, what it felt like to gasp for breath.

Lydia. Her cool beauty paled when compared to Kathy's warm loveliness. Kathy, whose dark eyes were always filled with grief. Kathy, who turned to flame in his arms and set him on fire with longing. What was he going to do about Kathy?

He hadn't reached any decision when he arrived at the ranch.

The yard was empty this time of day. The hands were all out looking after the cattle, riding fence, checking the river, clearing away any debris that might be clogging the bend near the south pasture.

Old Carmen would be in the kitchen, cooking up something hot and spicy for dinner.

And Conley . . . there was no telling where he might be. Russell took an active hand in the running of the ranch and could be found out on the range as often as in his office.

Dalton reined the mare toward the barn. The big buckskin stud was his. He didn't need Conley's permission to take it.

Dismounting, he looped the mare's reins over a fence rail and went into the barn. The buckskin whickered softly as Dalton approached the stall near the back of the barn.

"Hey, boy." The stallion poked its nose over the door of the stall and nuzzled his chest, and Dalton scratched the horse between the ears. "Miss me?" At the sound of footsteps, he dropped his hand to his gun butt, but it was only Conley.

"Crowkiller," Russell said, "I've been looking for you. We need to talk."

"I've got nothing to say. I'm leavin'."

"Leaving? Where're you going?"

"Anywhere I damn well please. I'm through here. I just came back to get my horse."

Conley frowned. "You can't leave now. Burkhart's hired himself a new gun. I don't think this one's gonna scare as easy as the last one."

"That's no longer my problem. I'm leaving the ranch. Leaving town."

"The hell you are. We had a deal."

"I'm breakin' it."

Conley's face turned ugly. It was the same look

Dalton had seen the night Conley took a whip to him.

A muscle ticked in Conley's jaw. "Nobody walks out on me."

"Is that right?" Dalton took a step backward and turned so that he was facing Conley head on. In a movement that might have been casual, he rested his hand on the butt of his Colt.

Like all men in the West, Russell Conley went armed. But he wasn't a fast gun, and he wasn't stupid enough to draw against a man who was.

"When I pay for a job, I expect it to get done."

"You can pick up your money at the bank."

"You'll regret this," Conley warned.

"I got lots of regrets."

Conley fixed him with a hard look, then turned and stalked out of the barn.

Dalton slid a bridle over the stud's head, then led the horse out of the stall. He ran a brush over the horse, checked its feet, cinched the saddle in place. Swinging onto the stallion's back, he rode to the front of the barn, pausing a moment to let his eyes adjust to the glare of the sun.

The yard was empty. Taking up the mare's reins, he urged the stallion into a trot, eager to put the Conley family and the Triple Bar C behind him once and for all.

He left the horses at the livery, then walked over to the boardinghouse. He found Kathy sitting in the parlor, an untouched cup of tea in her hand.

She looked up when he entered the room. "Everything okay?"

"Fine, why?"

"I was worried about you."

"No need."

"I know you want to leave first thing in the morning," Kathy remarked, "but do you think we could leave Sunday, instead?"

"Why?"

"Mrs. Dunn said there's going to be a big celebration tomorrow, for the Fourth. She said there would be food and games and homemade ice cream. I just thought . . ." It was silly, might even be dangerous, but she wanted to stay. She had always wanted to see an old-fashioned Fourth of July celebration, and this might be her only chance.

"I don't think that's such a good idea."

"Me, either, but can we? Stay, I mean?"

He looked at her, at the excitement shining in her eyes, and knew he couldn't refuse. It was his fault she was here. The least he could do was try to make her happy. "I reckon we can stay, if you've got your heart set on it."

She smiled at him, and he felt a sudden tightness in his chest.

"Lydia thinks I'm your . . . your whore."

Laughter erupted from Dalton's throat. Grabbing a chair, he swung it around and straddled it, his arms folded over the back.

Kathy glared at him. "I don't think that's so funny."

"Sure it is."

"Would you tell me why?"

"She's a whore at heart, so she paints all women

with the same brush. Makes it easier to believe that she's no worse than any of the rest.''

''Well, maybe,'' Kathy allowed.

''Forget about her. What did you do while I was gone?''

''Nothing much. I was bored, so Mrs. Dunn showed me how to make bread.'' She had never realized what a long process was involved in turning out a single loaf of bread. How much easier to buy it, already packaged, off the shelf. ''We made pies, too. Apple.''

''My favorite.''

Kathy nodded. ''She made one, and I made one.''

''Be sure to tell me which one's hers,'' Dalton said with a wink.

''Oh, you!'' Kathy exclaimed, and grabbing the cushion from behind her back, she threw it at him.

Dalton ducked instinctively, and the cushion went sailing past his head. It landed on the table beside the sofa, knocking a large china figurine to the floor. There was a crash.

Kathy jumped to her feet, horrified by what she had done. ''Look what you made me do!''

''Me?'' Dalton stood up. ''I didn't tell you to throw that pillow at me.''

Kathy crossed the floor. ''Oh, no,'' she wailed. ''It's broken.'' She picked up the pieces. ''I feel awful.''

''Hide it. Maybe she won't miss it.''

''Dalton!''

He shrugged. ''It was ugly, anyway.''

Well, that was true, Kathy thought as she stared at

207

the now-headless figure of a ballerina in her hands. Feeling like a little girl who has just broken one of her mother's favorite knickknacks, Kathy squared her shoulders and went in search of Mrs. Dunn.

Dalton stared after her. It probably wasn't a good idea to stay here for the Fourth. As he recalled, Lydia had arranged for him to dance with her.

He blew out a deep breath. But he had Kathy with him this time. He would keep her close. With any luck, Kathy's presence would discourage Lydia.

If not . . . hell, he'd worry about that when the time came. Crossing to the window, he gazed into the distance. It was July, the time of year the Lakota called the Cherry Ripening Moon. The people would be busy hunting, raiding, gathering wild fruits and vegetables. It was the time of the Sun Dance . . .

He glanced over his shoulder as Kathy entered the room. "Got it all squared away?"

Kathy nodded. "Yes, she was very nice, said I shouldn't fret about it."

"Well, then?"

"I just know it had some special meaning for her."

"Well, there's no sense worrying about it. What's done is done, and you can't undo it." He looked back out the window, wondering if those words were true, wondering if, no matter what he did, he was destined to die at the end of a rope.

Kathy stood in front of the mirror, grinning. She had bathed in an old-fashioned hip tub with a bar of lavender soap, and now she was dressed in starched blue gingham, her hair neatly coiled at her nape. Mrs.

Thrill to the most sensual, adventure-filled Historical Romances on the market today...

FROM 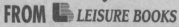 LEISURE BOOKS

As a home subscriber to Leisure Romance Book Club, you'll enjoy the best in today's BRAND-NEW Historical Romance fiction. For over twenty-five years, Leisure Books has brought you the award-winning, high-quality authors you know and love to read. Each Leisure Historical Romance will sweep you away to a world of high adventure...and intimate romance. Discover for yourself all the passion and excitement millions of readers thrill to each and every month.

Save $5.00 Each Time You Buy!

Each month, the Leisure Romance Book Club brings you four brand-new titles from Leisure Books, America's foremost publisher of Historical Romances. EACH PACKAGE WILL SAVE YOU $5.00 FROM THE BOOKSTORE PRICE! And you'll never miss a new title with our convenient home delivery service.

Here's how we do it. Each package will carry a FREE 10-DAY EXAMINATION privilege. At the end of that time, if you decide to keep your books, simply pay the low invoice price of $16.96, no shipping or handling charges added. HOME DELIVERY IS ALWAYS FREE. With today's top Historical Romance novels selling for $5.99 and higher, our price SAVES YOU $5.00 with each shipment.

AND YOUR FIRST FOUR-BOOK SHIPMENT IS TOTALLY FREE!

IT'S A BARGAIN YOU CAN'T BEAT! A Super $21.96 Value!

 LEISURE BOOKS   A Division of Dorchester Publishing Co., Inc.

Get Four Books Totally FREE – A $21.96 Value!

PLEASE RUSH
MY FOUR FREE
BOOKS TO ME
RIGHT AWAY!

Leisure Romance Book Club
P.O. Box 6613
Edison, NJ 08818-6613

AFFIX
STAMP
HERE

Dunn had lent her a white straw hat, insisting that a lady always wore a hat when she went out. Kathy shook her head. She looked as if she had just stepped out of the pages of a book about frontier life in the Old West.

She felt a thrill of excitement as Dalton knocked on the door. "Hey," he called, "you ready yet?"

"Yes." She spun away from the mirror and went to open the door. "How do I look?"

Pretty enough to eat, he thought. "You look fine." Until they came here, he had never seen her in a dress. He had to admit, he liked the way she looked in pants, but there was something about a woman in a dress that made him glad he was a man. "Let's go."

It looked as though most of the townspeople were gathered near the lake. Red, white and blue bunting was tacked to a bandstand. A rather stout woman was singing "I Dream of Jeanie With the Light Brown Hair," accompanied by a three-piece band. They were all slightly off key. Children and dogs ran everywhere. Women sat on blankets in the shade, babies sleeping beside them. Farther on, a man with a violin was playing "Little Brown Jug" to the delight of several little girls who stood around him, clapping their hands.

It was late afternoon, and all manner of contests and games were under way.

Dalton slid a glance at Kathy. Her eyes were shining with excitement. He didn't understand the attraction. It all seemed like foolishness—bobbing for apples, seeing who could make the biggest pig of himself by gobbling down a pie. He saw the blacksmith arm-wrestling with the preacher. A couple of kids were flying kites. Some young men were playing tug o'war over a mud puddle.

He thought about what Kathy had said about changing history. He was changing his, he mused. In his first life, or past life, or whatever the hell it was, he hadn't come to the picnic, only to the dance that evening.

A small carnival was set up near the lake. Kathy took his arm and dragged him over to where a man was trying to knock three milk bottles down with a ball. There were boos and catcalls when he failed.

"All right, who's next? How about you, little lady?" the barker asked, offering the ball to Kathy.

She shook her head and backed up. "No."

"Go on," Dalton said. "Give it a try."

"Three tries for ten cents," the man said.

"I don't have any money."

Dalton grinned as he slapped a dime on the counter. "You're covered."

She hit two bottles on the first try, one on the second, two on the third.

Dalton made a clucking sound when she missed again.

"Here," she said, thrusting the ball into his hand. "If you think it's so easy, you try it."

Dalton tossed the ball into the air a couple times, then drew back his arm and let it fly. All three bottles tumbled to the ground.

"A winner!" the barker exclaimed. "See, folks, nothing to it!" He handed Dalton a Kewpie doll. "Who's next? Step right up, folks."

Dalton handed the doll to Kathy with a wink. "See? Nothing to it."

She made a face at him. "Think you're so smart, don't you?"

"Never claimed to be smart," he retorted. "Just a damn good shot."

He turned as the sound of gunfire caught his attention. "Come on," he said, and taking her by the hand, he led her to where a dozen men were lined up, shooting at targets.

Gradually, the number of contestants dwindled to two. They were both amazing shots, Kathy thought, watching as the contestants repeatedly hit whatever targets were placed before them: bottles, cans, playing cards, bottles tossed in the air.

"The big fella is Woody Fryer," Dalton remarked. "He rides shotgun for the stage company. The other man is Johnny Palmer, one of Burkhart's fast guns. The guy in charge is Lars Hansen."

Kathy nodded. Fryer was big and blond; Palmer was of medium height, and so skinny he looked as if he might be suffering from anorexia. He had delicate-looking hands, thin lips and gray eyes that looked as hard and cold as stone.

After a time, Fryer missed a shot. With a good-natured grin, he holstered his gun and offered Palmer his hand. Palmer lifted one brow, but didn't take Fryer's hand.

"Guess that proves that Mr. Palmer is the best shot in town," Lars Hansen declared. "As such, Mr. Palmer is entitled to a month of free haircuts, courtesy of Vaughn's Barber Shop, and a champagne dinner at the hotel. Oh, and the prize money, of course. One hundred dollars.''

Palmer accepted the money with a slight nod, and the crowd began to disperse.

''Wait!'' Russell Conley plowed his way through the crowd. ''I'd like to propose a new contest.''

''Well, sure, Mr. Conley,'' Hansen said. ''What did you have in mind.''

''I'd like to see a match between Palmer and Crowkiller.''

Palmer glanced over at Dalton, then shook his head. ''I got nothing to prove.''

Conley ignored the gunman. ''What do you say, Burkhart? Your man against mine?''

Burkhart nodded. ''I'll put a hundred on Palmer.''

''Not very sure of him, are you?''

''Five hundred, then.''

''Done.''

Dalton scowled at Conley. ''Forget it.''

Russell dismissed his objection with a wave of his hand. ''I can't back down now.''

''I don't want any part of this.''

''I'll make it worth your while. Just be sure you win.''

Dalton glanced at Kathy; then, with a shake of his head, he went to stand beside Palmer.

Hansen and a couple of the other men quickly set up several rows of bottles, cans, and jars of various sizes.

Kathy stood to one side, while all around her, men were making side bets on the outcome of the match. She saw a movement out of the corner of her eye and noticed that Lydia Conley had joined the crowd. She wore a fitted pink jacket over a frilly white shirtwaist, and a full skirt that matched the jacket. A pink bonnet with white streamers shaded her face. She looked like a strawberry ice cream cone. Beautiful and cool.

Dalton and Palmer made quick work of the targets. Next, Hansen tossed bottles in the air, one at a time at first, then two, then three, but neither man missed.

"This isn't proving anything," Palmer said, holstering his gun. "All we're doin' is wastin' good ammo."

Dalton nodded. "He's right."

"Have 'em draw agin each other," someone called. "That'll prove who's faster."

"Good idea, Charlie."

"I have to agree," Burkhart said, grinning. "Although it's the first time Charlie ever had a good idea."

Laughter rippled through the crowd.

Kathy forgot about Lydia as she watched the sheriff step forward. Palmer and Dalton handed him their guns, and the lawman emptied both weapons.

"On three," Burkhart said.

Dalton and Palmer stood about six feet apart. Palmer looked tense. Eyes narrowed to mere slits, legs spread, he looked deadly, like a rattler poised to strike.

In comparison, Dalton looked almost relaxed.

"One. Two. Three."

It was close, almost too close to call, but Dalton's gun cleared leather a fraction of a second before Palmer's. It was a sobering thought to realize that such a minute amount of time could have made the difference between life and death had the shoot-out been for real.

Burkhart scowled. Conley laughed out loud as he slapped Dalton on the back. Palmer pushed his way through the crowd and headed for the saloon.

Kathy glanced over at Lydia. There was an odd look in the other woman's eyes, a look that sent a chill down Kathy's spine, the kind of look the Romans must have worn while watching the lions devour the Christians.

"Let's go."

She looked up to see Dalton standing beside her, loading his Colt. "Congratulations."

"Yeah." He shut the loading gate and slid the gun into his holster. "Let's get out of here."

They made their way through the crowd. Several of the men congratulated Dalton, but Kathy noticed that they were careful not to touch him.

They went to one of the long tables and picked up two glasses of punch. Dalton took a swallow and grimaced.

Muttering, "I need something stronger," he steered her away from the crowd to a small table where several men were gathered around another punch bowl.

"Good shootin', Crowkiller," one of the men said, and Kathy recognized him as the drunk from the Square Deal Saloon. "Can I get you something to drink?"

Dalton grunted. "Don't tell me you're selling liquor?"

"Well, I ain't givin' it away," Sullivan said with a grin. "Carly hired me."

"Must be a dream come true. You got any whiskey back there?"

"Sure thing." Sullivan reached under the table and withdrew a bottle. He poured a shot, and handed it to Dalton.

"Thanks." Dalton drained the glass in a single swallow, then wiped his mouth with the back of his hand. "Come on," he said to Kathy.

"Where are we going?"

"I don't know."

Side by side, they left the crowd behind. Kathy's head was reeling. The bloodless contest she had just seen was nothing like the real thing. But Palmer had been fast, faster than the man who had called Dalton out. In the books she'd read, a quick draw was always compared to greased lightning. Now she knew why.

"He was fast, wasn't he?"

Dalton grunted.

"Is he the fastest you've ever seen?"

"Yeah." Dalton took a deep breath, held it, then blew it out in a long slow sigh. "I wouldn't want to have to face him when it mattered."

"But you beat him."

"I beat him today with an empty gun. You saw how close it was."

"So, what do you want to do now?

"I want to make love to you."

"Oh. I . . . oh." She came to a halt, hardly aware that she had done so.

He looked at her, and shrugged. "You asked."

It was tempting, she thought, and tempting was putting it mildly. She had been attracted to him from the first, had wished for this very thing, wanted it, dreamed of it. Before, the fact that he was a ghost had prevented them from having any kind of physical relationship. Then, she had thought, if only he were real. . . . And now he was, and she was still reluctant, afraid to pursue the attraction she felt, afraid to trust her heart, to risk being hurt again. Afraid she might be sent back to the future without Dalton. He didn't belong in her time, and she didn't belong in his. Making love would only complicate things. She couldn't give him her body without giving him her heart, as well.

He blew out a breath. "Well, it was worth a shot."

"Dalton . . ."

"Forget it. Listen, will you be all right on your own for a little while?"

"I guess so. Why? What are you going to do?"

"I'll meet you at the dance later."

"All right, but where are you going?"

"I need a little time alone."

She nodded. "Sure, I understand."

Dalton caressed her cheek. "I doubt it," he muttered. "I'll meet you at the schoolhouse in about an hour, all right?"

"All right."

He could feel her gaze burning into his back as he headed for the Square Deal. He had an itch that needed scratching in the worst way. For a hundred and twenty-five years, that need had burned within him and he had been powerless to do anything about it. But he wasn't powerless anymore.

The saloon wasn't doing much business. Most everyone was over at the picnic, but his favorite dove was sitting at one of the tables, playing solitaire. She was a pretty girl, younger than she looked, with dyed red hair, blue eyes outlined with kohl and rouged cheeks.

She looked up, a slow smile spreading over her face when she saw him standing beside her.

"Hi, Chief," she purred. "Have you come for my scalp?"

It was the same thing she said every time he saw her. Usually, he just laughed. Today, it irritated him. Grabbing her by the hand, he pulled her to her feet.

"Hey!" she protested. "Careful with the merchandise."

"Sorry, Linette," he muttered. "I guess I'm in a hurry."

"Really?" She ran her fingertips over his chest. "Let's go then."

Taking his hand, she led him up the stairs, her hips swaying provocatively.

She glanced over her shoulder as she paused to open the door. He was her favorite customer, and they both knew it.

She let him go in ahead of her, then closed and locked the door.

Dalton removed his hat and tossed it on the bedpost, then sat on the edge of the mattress, waiting. It was a small room, but she kept it neat and clean. Her wrapper hung from a hook behind the door. A rag doll sat on a shelf, alongside a couple of bottles of cheap perfume.

Linette moved around the room, drawing the shades, unpinning her hair, removing her shoes. Slowly, so slowly, she began to undress.

"Dammit, hurry up!" he growled, and then, unable to wait a moment longer, he grabbed her around the waist and pulled her down on the bed beside him.

Chapter Fourteen

Kathy watched Dalton cross the street to the saloon. He might just be going in for a drink, but she knew, somehow, that whiskey was the last thing on his mind.

He had told her what he wanted, and she had refused. Could she really blame him for going elsewhere?

She hugged the Kewpie doll to her chest, wondering why she felt so betrayed. He was nothing to her. Nothing at all. Instead of fretting because he had gone to satisfy his lust elsewhere, she should be worrying about how to get back to her own time where she belonged. And yet . . .

Turning, she stared at the town. Strange as it seemed, she felt at home here. Or maybe she just felt at home because Dalton was here.

The thought irritated her. She didn't want to need him, or be in love with him. Or think about him. But she couldn't help it. All she could think about was Dalton lying in another woman's bed, another woman's arms. And the longer she thought about it, the madder she got. She knew she was being unreasonable. After all, he was a man, a man who hadn't had a woman in a very long time. She could hardly blame him for going elsewhere. But she did.

She had a sudden urge to march into the saloon and give him a piece of her mind, and before she quite realized what she was doing, she was across the street and inside the saloon.

The place was as quiet as a church. Dalton was nowhere to be seen. Two men were playing blackjack at a table in the back. A heavily painted woman clad in a low-cut, red satin dress, black fishnet stockings and black slippers sat on the edge of the bar, one leg swinging slowly back and forth.

Kathy's gaze moved toward the stairway. She was too late. Once his mind had been made up, he certainly hadn't wasted any time!

"Can I help you?"

She glanced over her shoulder at the bartender. "Did you say something?"

"You're becoming quite a regular in here," he remarked, his expression wry. "If you're looking for Crowkiller, he's upstairs. If you're looking for work, you'll have to talk to Carly, but he's not here now."

"Work?" Kathy gaped at the man, not knowing whether to laugh or be insulted. "No, no, I'm not."

"Well, like I said, Crowkiller's upstairs, but I

doubt if he'd want to be bothered just now.''

Kathy nodded, unable to believe she had actually come here. What had she hoped to prove? And what would she have done, what would she have said, if she had found Dalton, anyway? He didn't owe her any loyalty, or any explanations.

Cheeks flushed with embarrassment, she turned and headed for the door.

''Kathy? What the hell are you doing here?''

His voice, edged with surprise, stopped her in her tracks.

''I . . . nothing.''

He had descended the stairs and was coming up behind her. ''Kathy?''

Suddenly, it was all just too much. She couldn't face him, couldn't admit she had come here because she couldn't bear the thought of his being with another woman.

With a wordless cry, she pushed her way through the bat-wing doors and ran down the street toward the boardinghouse, wanting nothing more than to be alone. She had to think, had to find a way to return to her own time. Dalton was back where he belonged and right now, all she wanted was to go home.

She was breathless when she reached her room. Flinging open the door, she rushed inside, tossed the Kewpie doll on the dresser, then threw herself down on the bed and let the tears flow. She cried because Wayne was gone, because her whole world had turned upside down, because she was in love with a man she never should have met.

''Kathy.''

She sat up, startled. She had been so lost in her own misery, she hadn't been aware that he had followed her. "Go away. Go back to your . . . your floozy. Oh, just go away and leave me alone!"

But he didn't go away. Instead, he closed the door, tossed his hat onto the chair, then sat down on the edge of the bed and lifted her onto his lap.

"Let me go!" She struggled against him, hating him, hating herself for being jealous, for wanting the impossible.

"Kathy, nothing happened."

"Yeah, right."

"Well, it's true."

"Don't lie to me. I can smell her cheap perfume all over you." She put her hands against his chest and pushed. "Let me go!"

"Dammit, nothing happened!"

"I don't believe you." She tried to twist out of his grasp, but his arms held her tight. "Let me go."

"You're jealous, aren't you?" he asked with a knowing grin.

"Jealous! Don't be ridiculous."

"Why are you so mad then?"

"I'm not mad!"

He lifted one brow. "No?"

"Of course not. Now let me go."

"I don't think so."

"Why not?"

He ran one hand down her back. "I kind of like you right where you are."

Some of her anger evaporated as she became aware of how good his arms felt around her. She risked a look at his face, saw that his dark eyes were smoldering. She could feel the evidence of his desire. Either he was telling the truth and nothing had happened at the saloon, or he was ready again in a remarkably short time. Of course, since he hadn't had a woman in a hundred and twenty-five years, that was entirely possible. "Let me go."

"You want me," Dalton said quietly. "Admit it."

"Pretty full of yourself, aren't you, cowboy?"

"Am I? Tell me you don't want me as much as I want you." His arms tightened around her, crushing her breasts against his chest. "Tell me you've never thought about it, wondered what it would be like between us."

Her gaze slid away from his. As much as she wanted to deny it, she couldn't. It seemed she hadn't thought of anything else since they'd met.

Dalton put his finger under her chin and tilted her face up, forcing her to look at him, and then he kissed her.

Kathy struggled against him for all of three seconds before she surrendered to the need that burned hot and deep within her. What was the use in fighting it? She wanted him, wanted him with every fiber of her being. Right or wrong—and she knew it was wrong—she wanted him.

He kissed her as he lowered her to the mattress and stretched out beside her, drawing her body up against his, one hand sliding slowly, seductively, over her back and down her thigh. She returned his kisses fervently, her tongue dueling with his in a mating dance as old as time, her hands needy and restless as they skimmed over his broad back and shoulders, delved beneath his shirt to caress his back.

"Hey," he murmured, "that's not fair."

"All's fair in love and war," she replied, a hint of a smile in her voice.

"Really?" His hands made short work of the long row of buttons down her back. Gently, he eased her dress down over her shoulders, only to frown when he saw her bra. "What the devil?" he muttered.

Kathy grinned at his look of surprise. She seemed to recall that women in this time wore corsets, corset covers and a chemise, in addition to drawers and about a hundred petticoats. She hadn't seen the need for all those undergarments. Her bra, panties, and a petticoat were more than enough.

"Like this," she said. Unhooking her bra, she flung it aside, then wriggled out of her dress and underpants and dumped them on the floor.

Dalton's gaze devoured her. "Beautiful," he murmured. "So beautiful. You've been driving me crazy since the first time I saw you."

Kathy frowned. "Did you watch me take a bath one night right after I moved in?"

He hesitated a moment. "Maybe."

"I thought I saw you in the doorway."

"Okay, I watched, but I didn't really see anything but bubbles."

"A ghost *and* a Peeping Tom," Kathy murmured with a rueful shake of her head.

His lips nibbled her ear. "You taste so good."

"Do I?" The words were a gasp as his tongue slid along the curve of her neck.

"Sweet," he said. "Sweeter than molasses in summer."

She felt the fire building deep within her. Needing to touch him, to feel him against her, she tugged his shirt from his trousers and tossed it aside, then fumbled with his belt buckle.

"Careful," he warned.

"Why? Got a tiger in your tank?"

Dalton frowned, and she laughed softly. "It's an old TV commercial."

With a grunt, he sat up and removed his gunbelt. Hooking it over the bedpost, he shucked his boots and trousers, then drew her into his arms again.

"You won't disappear on me this time, will you?"

"I hope not."

"Then kiss me," she whispered. "Kiss me, kiss me, kiss me."

"My pleasure," he replied, his voice low and husky.

She pressed herself against him, loving the heat of his skin against hers, the solid feel of his body, the taste of his kisses, the touch of his hand in her hair, the sound of his voice whispering that he wanted her, needed her, that she was beautiful.

He told her everything but the three words she wanted to hear.

"What is it?" He drew back, his gaze searching her face. "What's wrong?"

"I can't do this."

Dalton swore a short, pithy oath.

"I'm sorry, it's too soon." It was a lie, but she couldn't tell Dalton the truth, couldn't tell him that making love to him without the words made her feel like one of Carly's crib girls.

Dalton sat up, his back toward her.

Kathy grabbed a corner of the bedspread and drew it over her. "I think maybe I'll stay here while you go visit your people."

"No."

"Why not? You said you thought I should stay here."

"I've changed my mind." He wasn't about to leave her behind. She was too pretty, too vulnerable, and there were too many men who would try to take advantage of her. *And you want to be the first one.* He ignored the taunting voice of his conscience.

"You can't make me go with you," Kathy said.

"Can't I? What are you going to do here, alone?"

"Whatever I want," she retorted. "I'll . . . I'll get a job."

"Yeah? Doing what?"

"I don't know." There probably wasn't much call for a computer programmer in Saul's Crossing, but she was a college graduate. There had to be something she could do, even if it was waiting tables in the hotel restaurant.

"Well, forget it, you're going with me."

"No."

"I don't think we should separate."

"Why not?" she asked, even though, in her heart, she felt the same way.

He shrugged. "We came here together. I think we should stay together."

Kathy didn't argue. Even though she knew it would

be better for her peace of mind if she stayed here, she was certain Dalton was right, certain she would never get home again if they separated. There had to be a reason why they had been sent back through time together; it seemed logical that they would have to be together to travel forward again.

"Maybe you're right," she remarked sullenly.

"I'm always right," he muttered. Rising, he began to dress.

Kathy knew she should look away, but she didn't. He was tall and lean and gorgeous, well-muscled without being bulky. Her gaze was drawn to the spider web of scars on his back. When he'd been a ghost, the marks had looked fresh; now they appeared old and faded. She wondered why they hadn't disappeared, since they had returned to a point in time before the beating.

The sight of his scars made her sick to her stomach, not because of how they looked, but because of how he had gotten them. How had he endured the pain of such a beating? How could one man do that to another?

"Did it hurt terribly?" she asked quietly.

"Did what hurt?"

"The whipping Conley gave you?"

"Damn right it hurt. Burned like hellfire."

"It was a terrible thing for him to do."

Dalton grunted. Terrible didn't begin to describe it. Yet, as painful as it had been, the worst part had been the humiliation of having Lydia there, watching. It had taken every ounce of his self-control to keep from crying out. He had wanted to scream, to beg for

227

mercy, to curse Lydia. Instead, he'd ground his teeth together until his jaw ached.

"Why don't you get dressed and we'll go to the dance?" he suggested. He didn't really feel much like dancing, but it would give him a good excuse to hold Kathy in his arms again. "I'll wait for you out on the porch."

"All right."

Grabbing his hat and gunbelt, he left the room.

The sun was setting when they left the boardinghouse. The western sky was ablaze in a riot of crimson and gold and lavender. Kathy stared at the heavenly display, a sense of awe rising up within her. Never had she seen such a glorious sunset. The sky seemed to stretch away into forever, making her think of eternity, of distant planets and galaxies, and worlds without end.

She heard the sound of music as they neared the schoolhouse. Kathy smiled as the strains of "Silver Threads Among the Gold" drifted toward them.

Dalton paused in the doorway, and Kathy glanced around the room. The desks had been removed to make room for dancing. A couple of long wooden tables covered with white linen cloths had been set up against the far wall. Two of the town ladies stood behind the tables, dispensing cake, cookies, pie, and apple cider. Several couples, including some kids, were dancing. A small knot of women stood in one corner, chatting amiably; a group of men were gathered near the punch bowl. Pictures titled "What the

Fourth of July Means to Me'' were tacked to one wall.

Dalton tugged gently on Kathy's arm. "Do you wanna dance?"

"Sure."

"Mind your toes," he warned with a smile, and taking her by the hand, he led her onto the dance floor, then swept her into his arms.

For a moment, she was transported back to the ranch, to the afternoon when Dalton had waltzed her around the living room. He had been a ghost then, but there had been nothing the least bit ghost-like about the attracton that had flowed, hot and sweet, between them.

Dalton looked into Kathy's eyes, recalling the last time they had danced together, wondering if she was remembering that day, too.

She smiled up at him as he twirled her around the floor.

She was like a feather in his arms, Dalton mused, and spun her faster and faster, until she was laughing out loud. He loved the sound of her laughter, the way her eyes glowed with merriment.

They were both breathless when the music ended. Feeling young and carefree, Dalton hugged her close. He was about to ask her if she wanted to get something to eat when he felt a sudden chill slither down his spine. Glancing over his shoulder, he saw Lydia glaring at him from across the room.

Some perverse demon rose within him, made him lower his head, and claim Kathy's lips with his. He could almost hear Lydia's hiss of outrage, feel her hatred arrowing into his back.

"Dalton . . ." Kathy turned her head to the side, embarrassed that he had kissed her so intimately in a public place.

"Sorry. Come on," he said, placing her hand on his arm, "let's go get something to drink."

The lady behind the table smiled as she handed them each a cup of apple cider.

Kathy murmured her thanks, then followed Dalton to a clear space against the wall. The band was playing a waltz. She tried not to stare as Russell and Lydia swept past. Russell was smiling; Lydia was as stiff as a mannequin. Kathy didn't miss the look Lydia gave Dalton, though she had trouble deciphering it. Hatred? Jealousy?

When the waltz ended, Kathy was surprised to see Russell and Lydia heading in their direction. She heard Dalton swear.

"Well, having a good time?" Russell asked. His gaze moved over Kathy in a long, assessing glance. "Who's this pretty little filly?"

"My cousin, Katherine Wagner."

Russell offered his hand. "Pleased to make your acquaintance, Miss Wagner. Mind if I have the next dance?"

Kathy looked up at Dalton uncertainly, and he shrugged, as if to say, "It's up to you."

"I promise not to step on your toes," Russell said, and taking her by the hand, he led her out onto the floor.

"Cousin, indeed," Lydia said, her voice low and

angry as she watched Russell waltz Kathy around the floor. "You must take me for a fool. What is she to you?"

"A friend?"

"Is she good in bed?"

"I don't know."

"Liar."

"Dammit, Lydia, mind your tongue."

"Dance with me."

"I'd as soon dance with a snake."

"Dance with me."

Afraid she'd make a scene if he refused again, Dalton led her onto the dance floor and took her in his arms.

"You dance divinely," Lydia remarked. "Most big men don't, you know. Russell is as clumsy as an old bull."

"I'll be sure to tell him that."

A soft laugh escaped her lips. "He would not believe you," she replied smugly. "He loves me, you know. If I told him the sky was green, he would believe me."

"I know." It was one of the reasons he hadn't tried harder to proclaim his innocence at the hanging. Conley thought the sun rose and set in Lydia's eyes. He would never have believed her capable of betraying him, much less of lying about what had actually happened in the barn that night.

Dalton glanced over Lydia's shoulder to where Conley was dancing with Kathy. It irked him to see her in another man's arms. She laughed at something Conley said, and Dalton's heart turned over. He had never been in love before. Was that what he was feeling now? Another of Fate's dirty tricks, no doubt, for him to find love when it was too late.

"Dalton."

"What?"

Lydia glanced up at him, a seductive smile playing over her pouting pink lips. "Let us take a walk outside. I feel the need for some fresh air."

He shook his head, relieved that the music had ended. "Your husband is coming to claim you, Mrs. Conley," he said. "He can take you outside."

Anger flared in Lydia's eyes, but before she could say anything, Conley was there.

Dalton nodded at his former employer, grabbed Kathy by the arm and steered her off the dance floor and out of the building.

"Hey, take it easy," Kathy exclaimed. "Where's the fire?"

"In Lydia's eyes," Dalton muttered.

"What?"

"Never mind."

Kathy laughed. "She's really on the make for you, isn't she?"

"On the make?"

"Hot for your bod?"

Dalton came to an abrupt halt. "What the hell are you talking about?"

She laughed again. "Lydia has the hots for you."

"Hots? Oh, yeah," he said, comprehension dawning at last. "I don't know why, unless it's because I keep saying no. I don't think she's used to that."

Kathy's gaze moved over Dalton. Tall and lean,

dark and handsome. Sexier than Tom Cruise and Brad Pitt rolled into one. "I'm sure that's not the only reason," she murmured under her breath.

"What?"

"Nothing."

A slow smile spread over Dalton's face. "What other reason could there be?"

"I thought you didn't hear what I said."

He shrugged. "What reason, Kathy?"

She lifted her hand in a vague gesture. "You're a very handsome man, but I'm sure you already know that."

"Am I?"

"Well," she hedged, her cheeks growing warm beneath his probing gaze, "some women might think so."

"Some women?" He was close, too close. "Are you one of them?"

"Me?" she squeaked.

He took a step toward her, and she backed up, only to find there was no place to go. He had very neatly backed her up against a tree.

"Who do you think?" he drawled softly.

She couldn't think at all, not with him standing so close. She couldn't see his face clearly in the dark, but she could feel the heat of him. She could feel the intensity of his gaze, feel the warmth of his breath on her face.

"Kathy . . ."

He leaned toward her. She stared up at him for a moment and then, helpless to resist, she lifted her face for his kiss. This was what she wanted, what she had

233

wanted since she first saw him. Why fight it any longer? The only regrets she had in life were the things she hadn't done.

His mouth was warm and firm and gentle, asking, not demanding. With a sigh, she melted against him, felt his arms circle her waist, felt the hard length of his body mold itself to hers as he drew her close, closer. Her breath quickened. Fire raced through her veins.

"Kathy," he whispered, his voice almost a groan. "Don't kiss me like that unless you mean it."

"I do."

"Tell me you want me as much as I want you."

"How can you doubt it?"

"If you change your mind this time, I think it'll kill me all over again," he muttered wryly, and sweeping her into his arms, he carried her away from the schoolhouse.

"Where are we going?"

"You'll see."

She wrapped her arms around his neck and closed her eyes, not really caring where they were going. Her hand delved beneath the hair at his nape to stroke his neck. Eyes still closed, she kissed his cheek, nibbled on the lobe of his ear. She laughed when she heard him mutter an oath, and then he was setting her on her feet.

She opened her eyes to find they were in a sheltered glade on the far side of the lake. Lacy ferns and shrubs grew all around them. Moonlight shimmered in ribbons of silver on the face of the water. "It's beautiful."

"You are," he said, his voice thick.

"Thank you."

"Kathy . . ."

Just her name, yet she heard a hundred and twenty-five years of loneliness, of yearning, in his voice.

He slid his knuckles over her cheek. His thumb traced the outline of her lips, and then he kissed her.

Magic. It could only be magic, the rush of emotion that swelled up within her heart and soul. He was so gentle, so tender, she knew somehow that he was as awed by what was happening between them as she was.

Their clothing disappeared, and then he lowered her to the ground, his shirt spread beneath her.

"Kathy, tell me if I hurt you."

"You won't."

"I might." His grin was bittersweet. "It's been a long time since I made love to a woman."

She smiled, her fingers tracing the muscles corded in his arms.

"I'm afraid . . ."

"Don't be," she whispered.

Cupping his face in her hands, she kissed him, her hips lifting in silent invitation.

Wayne had been her first and only lover. She had never been able to imagine making love to anyone else, had always thought she would feel awkward with another man, but there was no awkwardness between them. They melded together perfectly, and she had the feeling that she had been searching for Dalton Crowkiller all her life, that she had been born a hun-

dred and twenty-five years too late and this was Fate's
way of bringing them together.

His hands were eager as they touched and caressed
her, his voice thick as he whispered in her ear, telling
her she was beautiful, desirable, that he had never felt
like this before. And she believed him, believed every
kiss, every caress, every word. It felt too right to be
wrong.

She was on fire for him, as eager as he, her body
trembling, her hands curious and impatient. She
gasped his name as his body convulsed and she clung
to him, her legs wrapped around his waist, her nails
raking his back.

And it was like the first time, filled with wonder
and awe.

And fireworks.

She opened her eyes, blinking as a shower of col-
ored lights filled the air. And then she grinned. Of
course there were fireworks. It was the Fourth of July.

She slept with her head pillowed on his shoulder,
one arm draped over his chest. Watching her, Dalton
felt something tighten inside him. He didn't know
what had just happened between them, but it had
never happened to him before. He felt as though he'd
been reborn. It was as scary as hell.

He loved her. He knew it as surely as he knew the
sun would rise in the east, and yet, as much as he
wanted to, he hadn't been able to say the words. He
hoped she knew. Women were good about that kind

of thing. Hell, they usually knew what a man was feeling before he did.

"I hope you know," he whispered, and prayed that he would find the courage to tell her before it was too late.

Chapter Fifteen

Kathy woke to the touch of Dalton nibbling at her ear lobe. "Hmmm," she murmured.

"Wake up, sleepyhead."

"Don't want to." She snuggled against him, shivering a little.

"Come on, we can't stay out here forever."

"Why not?"

He laughed softly. "I'd like to, darlin', believe me, but I think we'd better get dressed before the sun gets any higher. Pretty as you look with nothing on, I'd hate for anyone else to come by and see what I'm seein'."

Kathy's eyelids flew open. "Oh!" she exclaimed, startled by the discovery that it was daylight and she was lying naked in his arms. "I can't believe you didn't wake me up last night."

Dalton shrugged. He would have, but he hadn't wanted to let her go. Instead, he had covered the two of them with her skirts, then held her all through the night, watching her sleep.

She couldn't believe she had spent the night on the hard ground. She hadn't slept so soundly in months, not since . . . She thrust the thought from her mind. She couldn't think of Wayne, not now.

She started to sit up, but Dalton's hand stayed her. "How about a good-morning kiss?"

Happiness welled up inside her. He had held her all night, and now he wanted to kiss her good morning. The thought made her ridiculously happy. Leaning forward, she kissed him lightly.

"Hey," he chided softly, "I know you can do better than that."

"I thought you were in a hurry."

"Not that big a hurry," he replied, and slipping one hand behind her head, he kissed her, long and hard, as though he were staking a claim. And maybe he was.

She was breathless when he took his lips from hers, breathless and yearning for more. But there was no time for that now. She heard a clock chiming in the distance. It was eight o'clock. People would be out and about.

"Turn your back," she said.

"What? Why?"

"Please." She knew she was being silly. They had made love, but it had been dark then. She wasn't ready to get dressed in front of him, not yet.

He frowned at her. "You can't be shy, not after

239

last night.'' He knew every inch of her, he mused, every delicious curve.

''Please, Dalton.''

With a shrug, he turned his back to her. Her skirt slid off his shoulders, and her gaze was drawn to the broad expanse of his back, to the network of scars that marred his bronze flesh. She couldn't begin to imagine the pain he had suffered, couldn't believe that Lydia Conley had remained silent while her husband whipped Dalton. What kind of woman was she, to watch such brutality and say nothing?

''You dressed yet?''

His voice spurred her to action. Gathering her underwear and clothing together, she stood up and dressed, glancing over her shoulder at Dalton from time to time to make sure he wasn't looking. It was silly to feel so shy, but she couldn't help it. She had never been promiscuous. Wayne was the only man she had ever been intimate with, the only one who had seen her naked in the light of day, and that only after they were married.

''All right, I'm done.'' She smoothed her skirts as best she could. Her dress was badly wrinkled, making her wish it was made of a polyester blend instead of cotton.

She could hear Dalton dressing behind her and she was sorely tempted to turn around. She had explored his hard, lean body the night before; now, she yearned to know if it looked as good as it felt. But she had asked for privacy; surely he deserved the same.

Dalton buckled his gunbelt in place and reached for his hat. ''All right, you can turn around now.''

She smiled at him, then blushed when her stomach growled.

"Yeah, me too," he said. "Come on, let's go get some breakfast."

He took her hand and they walked back to town. The stores were just opening. She couldn't help thinking that Main Street looked like one of the streets at Knott's Berry Farm—the wooden boardwalk, the hand-lettered signs, the old-fashioned clothing and hats on display in the front window of the general store.

A sign outside the stage office announced that the noon stage would be late due to "Injun trouble."

"I still can't believe I'm here," she murmured.

"Yeah, I can't believe it myself."

"What did it feel like for you, when we woke up here?"

"I don't know how to describe it," Dalton replied. "One minute I was—I don't know—light as a feather, and the next, I felt heavy, sort of weighted down. I'll tell you one thing, having a body sure beats being a ghost."

"I'll bet."

Dalton lifted his head and sniffed the air. "Bless her heart, Martha's fryin' bacon. Come on!"

Hyrum Petty and Enid Canfield were already seated at the table when they entered the dining room.

Hyrum's brows rose as he looked at them; Enid sniffed, as though she smelled something bad.

Kathy looked at Dalton, and flushed hotly. There was a leaf in his hair, and his clothing was as rumpled as hers. She hadn't given much thought to how they

241

must look; now she realized they probably looked as though they had spent the night doing exactly what they had been doing.

Kathy tugged her hand free. "I need to freshen up."

"You look fine," Dalton said.

She shook her head.

"Well, there you are," Martha Dunn exclaimed as she bustled into the room. "Just in time for breakfast." She beamed at Dalton. "I made all your favorites. Bacon and eggs and buckwheat cakes. Oh, and some nice fried potatoes. Sit down—eat it while it's hot."

Dalton looked at Kathy, then held out a chair. Head high, she sat down and spread her napkin in her lap.

He sat beside her. As unobtrusively as possible, she plucked the leaf from his hair and slipped it into her skirt pocket.

Kathy ate quickly, eager to make her escape. She could well imagine what Hyrum and Enid were thinking. She and Dalton were supposed to be cousins, for goodness sake!

Blotting her lips with her napkin, she placed it on the table and stood up. "Thank you, Mrs. Dunn, that was delicious."

"You're welcome, dear." Martha frowned. "Would you like me to fetch you some hot water?" she asked tactfully.

"Yes, please," Kathy said, and fled the room, her cheeks flaming.

Moments after she reached her room, there was a knock at the door.

"Kathy?"

"What?"

"You all right in there?"

"I'm fine."

"I want to leave this morning. How soon can you be ready to go?"

"I don't know. An hour?"

"Fine. I'll be back then."

"Okay."

"Kathy?"

"What?"

"I . . . never mind. An hour."

Kathy glanced over her shoulder, feeling a sudden uneasiness as she saw nothing but miles and miles of unbroken prairie behind her. They had lost sight of Saul's Crossing about an hour ago, and now there was nothing but grass and blue sky as far as the eye could see. It was unsettling somehow. Back home, there was a McDonald's or a mini-mart or a gas station on every corner. Back home, she'd had a cell phone in her car in case she ran into trouble. Out here, there was nothing. She couldn't imagine why anyone had ever left the comfort and security of life in the East to brave the dangers of the West, with its poisonous snakes and wild animals, deserts and mountains and rivers to cross, outlaws and Indians waiting to rob and plunder. Had it been up to her, the West would never have been settled.

She urged her horse closer to Dalton's, reassured by his presence. He would protect her. She refused to dwell on what would happen to her if something happened to him.

It felt good to be wearing her jeans and T-shirt again. She couldn't imagine spending long hours in the saddle hampered by a voluminous skirt and petticoats. She wore a long-sleeved cotton shirt over her T-shirt to protect her skin from the hot prairie sun. She was glad Dalton had reminded her to buy a hat, knowing that without it her face would have been burned to a crisp. She was glad, too, for the gloves Dalton had thoughtfully provided. They were made of butter-soft leather. Her new boots weren't as comfortable as the ones she had left at home, but she figured they'd be all right once she got them broken in.

She looked over at Dalton. He was wearing black pants, a dark gray shirt, a blue kerchief, scuffed black boots without spurs, and a hat. There was a rifle in the saddle scabbard; his saddlebags and hers bulged with supplies. There was a bedroll fastened behind the cantle of her saddle.

He met her look with a grin. "You all right?"

Kathy nodded. "All this space"—she made a broad gesture with her hand, encompassing the land around them—"it's a little . . . I don't know, intimidating, I guess."

"Yeah, well, it's a big country."

"How long will it take us to find your people?"

"I don't know. A few days, a few weeks."

"How long has it been since you were there?"

He thought for a moment. "Thirteen years," he said, and then grinned. "More, if you count the hundred and twenty-five years that I've been dead.''

"Is your mother still alive?"

"Yeah."

"When was the last time you saw her?"

"About a year before I died."

"Were you . . . I mean, are you close?"

He shrugged. "Close enough to keep in touch. Of course, she wasn't pleased with my line of work, and every time I went back to see her, she'd start in on how I should give it all up and get married, and settle down." He grinned. "You know how mothers are. She wants some grandchildren."

"What about you? Do you want kids?"

"Yeah. I've always wanted a family. Guess I just never found anyone I wanted to settle down with." His gaze moved over her face, intense, penetrating. "Until now."

Kathy stared at him. Was he proposing? "I . . . I don't know what to say."

"You don't have to say anything. I know I'm not good enough for you."

"Don't be silly."

"It's true. You'd be a fool to think we could have a life together, and I'd be a bigger fool to offer you one."

"So, I'm just a one-night stand, is that it?"

"A what?"

"One. Night. Stand. Just good for a quick roll in the hay. Wham, bam, thank you, ma'am."

Dalton scowled at her. "Of course not! You know it was more than that."

"Do I?"

245

Dalton jerked on the reins. Startled, the stallion reared, forelegs pawing the air.

Kathy gasped, certain Dalton would be thrown and killed. Before she quite realized how it had happened, his horse was beside hers and he was lifting her from her saddle to his.

"Don't ever think that!" he said. "You hear me? Dammit, Kathy, I don't ever want you to think that again." He took a deep breath, blew it out in a long sigh, and then slid one finger down her cheek. "You know it was more than that, don't you? Don't you?" he repeated when she didn't answer right away.

"If you say so."

"I do."

"All right." She poked him in the chest with her forefinger. "And I don't ever want to hear you say you're not good enough for me. And don't scowl at me like that."

"You're talking crazy, girl. I'm a half-breed, a hired gun. Hell, I don't know what you're thinking."

"I'm thinking there must be some reason why I could see you when no one else could, some reason why we're here, together."

"Yeah? And what might that reason be?"

"You'll laugh."

"I doubt it."

"I think we're meant to be together, and that this is Fate's way of putting things right."

He lifted one brow.

"Don't you dare laugh," she warned.

"No, ma'am. I wouldn't think of it."

"But you don't believe it?"

246

"I don't know." He dragged a hand over his jaw. It was preposterous, unbelievable, yet it was the only explanation that made any kind of sense at all. "So, does that mean you're here to stay?"

"I don't know. But I think we were meant to be together. Your time, my time, maybe it doesn't matter as long as we're together."

"And is that what you want? To be here, with me?"

"Yes. If you want me."

His arm tightened around her waist. "You know I do."

Happiness spread through her, warm and sweet. With a sigh, she rested her head on his shoulder. This was where she wanted to be, now and always.

Dalton rested his chin on the top of her head, more content than he'd ever been in his life. Maybe she was right. Maybe they *were* fated to be together. A one-night stand. He grinned at the thought. She would never be that. She wasn't like Linette. She wasn't some cheap crib girl to be had for a night, services bought and paid for. Kathy was a lady. And a lady meant forever.

Only he couldn't count on forever. Couldn't even count on tomorrow. But she was here, now, and he wanted her more than his next breath.

He kissed her again, light and quick, as the stallion moved restlessly beneath him.

"I think your horse is trying to tell us something," Kathy said.

"I reckon."

"We can pick up where we left off later."

"You are a bold one," Dalton remarked.

"Are you complaining?"

"No, ma'am, just thinking how lucky I am." He kissed her again, then deposited her, very gently, on Taffy Girl's back. "Later," he said.

It was near dark when Dalton drew his horse to a halt. They had ridden about fifteen miles. Had he been alone, he could have covered twice that distance, but Kathy wasn't used to long hours in the saddle, so they had stopped often so she could rest. Watching her dismount, he knew fifteen miles had been about ten too many.

"You all right?" He swung out of the saddle and took the mare's reins.

"Fine, but I may never walk, or sit, again."

With a grin, Dalton removed her bedroll from behind the cantle and spread it on the ground. "Come here and sit down while I look after the horses."

With a groan, Kathy did as bidden. Every muscle in her body screamed in protest. She hadn't realized how sore she was until she dismounted. She had expected her fanny and legs to ache, but so did her back and shoulders.

After pulling off her gloves, she removed her hat, tugged off her boots and wiggled her toes. They were the only things that didn't seem to hurt.

She watched Dalton unsaddle the horses and rub them down, then tether them to a couple of trees so they could graze.

It was pretty out here. The setting sun painted the sky with broad splashes of red and gold. A quiet breeze ruffled the tall grass. She could hear the faint gurgle of water from somewhere nearby. She had never realized the world was so big. Mile after mile after mile of seemingly endless prairie spread out all around them. There were no buildings or power poles rising toward the sky, no smoke, no smog to pollute the air. Nothing marred the stillness of the evening. She had never heard such complete quiet.

When Dalton finished caring for the horses, he built a fire, put the coffee pot on, opened a couple of cans and dumped the contents into a pot, which he placed on a corner of the coals.

And then he was kneeling beside her. "Lie down on your belly."

She looked at him a moment, then did as he asked. She groaned as he began to massage her back and shoulders, his big hands gentle. Gradually, his hands moved lower, massaging her thighs, her calves, her ankles, even her feet.

With a little moan of pleasure, she fell asleep.

Chapter Sixteen

Dalton heard the change in Kathy's breathing, knew the moment sleep claimed her, and yet he continued to stroke her back, her shoulders, her nape. He liked touching her. It grounded him somehow, made it all seem real.

His fingers slid up into her hair. Soft and silky, it fell over his hand, his forearm, as he lightly massaged her scalp. It was hard to believe he was here, back in his own time. He grinned wryly. Back in his own skin. He was acutely aware of the world around him— of the sights and scents of the night, of the woman sleeping beside him, of the fragile bond between this world and the next.

His gaze moved over Kathy's face. She was in love with him. That in itself was a miracle. Lydia had wanted him, but she had never loved him. He wondered if she had ever loved anyone but herself.

But Kathy . . . He sat back on his haunches and watched her sleep. She loved him, and he was very much afraid he was in love with her. The mere idea scared the hell out of him. What did he know about love? He had never been in love before, never had the time for it, never felt the need. Until now. He was sorely afraid he would fail her in some way, that he would hurt her.

He contemplated waking her for dinner, and then decided to let her sleep. She'd had a long day; no doubt she was more in need of rest than food just now, he thought as he covered her with a blanket.

He ate quickly, gathered the dirty dishes, washed them in the stream. Returning to their camp, he added fuel to the fire, then watered the horses and tethered them close by for the night. He stood for a moment, stroking the stallion's neck, recalling the nights he had gone raiding the Crow horse herd with his Lakota brothers, the summer buffalo hunts, the sacred ceremonies held in the shadow of the Black Hills.

It was full dark now. Removing his hat and boots, he slid under the blanket and drew Kathy into his arms. She made a little sleepy sound of contentment as she snuggled up against him. Damn, he thought, but he could get used to this right quick.

Lying there, he knew a sense of peace that he had not known since leaving the Lakota. Mother Earth was solid and comforting beneath him. Old Father Wi shone brightly in the heavens, surrounded by the Star people. From far off, he heard the faint, melancholy howl of a wolf. The evening breeze carried the scent of sage and grass and damp earth. One of the horses stamped its foot.

He took a deep breath, and his nostrils filled with the scent of woman.

He was smiling when he fell asleep.

It was still dark when Kathy woke. She stared up at the sky, trying to judge the time the way Dalton did. It felt like early, early morning.

Dalton stirred beside her and she drew back a little so she could see his face. How could she have fallen in love so hard, so fast? She had known Wayne for months before caring turned to affection, before affection deepened to love, yet it seemed as though she had loved Dalton from the first moment she saw him.

She stared up at the sky, thinking about the ranch, wondering if she would ever see it again, wondering what her family would think if she never returned. There were always accounts of people who disappeared without a trace, never to be heard from again. She grinned into the darkness. Maybe they had all been zapped into the past.

Her gaze drifted over Dalton's face again. She wouldn't mind staying here, in his time, so long as he was with her. If only there was some way to know what the future held. Everything was so tentative. What if, in spite of all they could do, Dalton was fated to die on the 28th of July? What if he cheated the rope and they got married and then she was suddenly zapped back to her own time without him?

She never should have fallen in love with him, never should have made love to him. It had only complicated things, made her want him more than ever. She couldn't let it happen again. Good Lord, what if she got pregnant? What if she was pregnant even now? That would really complicate matters.

"Hey."

With a start, she realized he was awake.

He smiled up at her. "What's wrong?"

"Nothing, why?"

He glanced at the sky. "It's only about five o'clock."

"Well, go back to sleep then."

"I can think of better things to do."

"Can you?"

He slid his arm around her shoulders and drew her up against him, his gaze suddenly hot.

"It's later," he murmured.

His touch, the desire that blazed in his dark eyes, wiped every doubt from her mind. She might have only a moment with this man, she might have years. No one ever really knew what the future held. Maybe she would wake up in her own bed and find it had all been a dream. But he was here now, watching her, wanting her. Waiting.

She threw her arms around him and kissed him fiercely, determined not to waste a single minute of whatever time they might have.

They made love passionately, wildly, and she wondered, in a distant part of her mind, if Dalton's thoughts had been running along lines similar to her own, if he, too, was aware that Fate could separate them at any time.

"Kathy, Kathy . . ." His voice was low, husky with

desire; his hands trailed fire, his lips scorched her flesh, burning a path to her soul.

She clung to him, tighter, tighter, lifting her hips to embrace him more fully. She was chasing rainbows, flying, higher, higher, until she toppled over the brink into ecstacy. And he was there beside her all the way, his heart pounding wildly, his breathing as uneven as hers as they soared skyward, then slowly, slowly, drifted back to earth.

She opened her eyes to see his face hovering over hers, and behind him, the sun rising in a bright blaze of color, and she knew she would remember this moment as long as she lived.

The days that followed were like none Kathy had ever known. The countryside was beautiful—gently rolling hills that stretched away as far as the eye could see, a sky that was a brilliant sapphire blue, streams that ran clear and cold. Occasional stands of timber broke the monotony of the grassland.

Riding became easier. It no longer took all her concentration just to stay in the saddle. Racing across the prairie gave her a sense of exhilaration unlike any she had ever known, a sense of freedom and excitement. She felt a bond forming with Taffy Girl. She liked the way the mare nuzzled her shoulder, the way Taffy Girl sometimes used her back to scratch her forehead. She enjoyed brushing the mare down at night. It was soothing somehow.

And there was Dalton. She never tired of looking at him, of listening to the stories he told her about growing up with the Lakota, of pony raids and war parties, of summers camped along the Little Big Horn and winters spent in the shelter of the Black Hills.

But, best of all, she liked the nights she spent in his arms under the prairie moon. She had never known such happiness, such contentment. He was unlike any man she had ever known. He was ever aware of her wants, her needs, her desires. He seemed to know when she wanted gentleness, and when she wanted passion, when she needed to be held and reassured, and when she wanted to be the aggressor. She tried not to wonder where he had learned so much about women, tried not to think of all the women he had known before her, tried to be grateful he was such a skilled lover. Instead, she felt a deep and abiding jealousy for every other woman he had ever known, touched, desired. That, in itself, was unusual. She had never been given to jealousy until now. She was forever watching him, thinking of him, wanting him.

As she wanted him now. They had paused beside a slow-moving stream to rest the horses. Dalton was kneeling beside the stream. He had removed his shirt and the sun caressed his back and shoulders as he splashed water over his face and chest.

Impulsively, she moved up behind him. Sliding her arms around his waist, she began to rain little kisses over his back, her heart aching anew as she touched his scars. She wished she could wipe them away, wipe away all the pain he had ever known. She wanted to hold him and comfort him, to erase the memory of every bad thing that had ever happened to him, wipe out the memory of every other woman . . .

''Hey,'' Dalton exclaimed softly.

"Hey, yourself." She ran her tongue over his back; he tasted of sun-warmed flesh and perspiration.

Before she quite knew how it happened, Kathy found herself flat on her back, his hips straddling hers, her hands imprisoned in his. She stared up into Dalton's eyes. Eyes that were deep and black, filled with amusement—and unmistakable desire.

"My turn," he said, his voice a low growl.

Kathy giggled as he dragged his tongue across her cheek.

He scowled at her. "What's so funny?" he asked with mock severity.

"Nothing," she said. "I'm just happy."

His gaze searched her face. "Are you?"

"Yes." She slipped one hand from his and stroked his cheek. "Happier than I've ever been in my whole life."

He didn't say anything, but he looked as if he didn't believe her.

"It's true, Dalton."

"No more ghosts between us?" he asked, and she knew he wasn't referring to himself, but to Wayne.

"No more ghosts."

He murmured, "Ah, Kathy," as he gathered her into his arms. And then he was kissing her, his mouth urgent, demanding.

His hands were hot as they slid under her T-shirt, drifting over her skin. She felt the calluses on his palms, shivered with delight as he stroked her back, brushed his knuckles across her breasts.

Her own hands were needy as they slid over his chest, his shoulders, down his arms, reveling in the heat of him, the touch of him, the reality of him. There was nothing ghost-like about him now. He was solid, vibrant, alive—so alive. His desire aroused her own and she peeled off her T-shirt and bra, wanting to be next to him, to feel his skin next to hers.

The grass was cool beneath her back, the sun was hot against her face, but they were noticed only in passing. Dalton was the center of her world, the air she breathed. She drew him in, embraced him, enveloped him, until they seemed to be one flesh, one heart, one soul. She thought of a line from a Dracula movie, something about crossing oceans of time. That was what she had done, she mused, crossed oceans of time, to be here, in this place, with this man.

She gasped as warmth exploded through her, filling her, completing her. And then, like a leaf falling from a tree, she drifted down, down, spent, satiated, totally, completely, at peace.

It took them the better part of two weeks to find the summer camp of the Lakota.

Kathy could only stare at the village sprawled alongside a winding river, at the tipis with their smoke-blackened tops, at the vast horse herd that grazed on the sun-bleached grass, the dogs sleeping in the sun. It looked like a scene from *Dances With Wolves.*

And yet, for all that it was beautiful and peaceful, she felt a shiver of apprehension. These were real, honest-to-goodness *Indians,* not Hollywood extras hired by Kevin Costner. Honest-to-goodness real Indians, who made war on the settlers moving West, who took the scalps of white women. Indians who would, in only a few years, kill Custer and all his men. What was she doing here?

"Kathy?"

She looked at Dalton, and knew, from his expression, that her fear was visible in her eyes.

"They won't hurt you."

"Won't they?"

He shook his head. "We're not savages, at least not in the way you're thinking. You'll like my people, if you give them a chance."

"Maybe, but will they like me?"

"I'm sure of it."

"You won't leave me alone while we're here, will you?"

"Of course not."

"You promise?"

"I promise."

She took a deep breath. Dalton would protect her. "Ready?"

She nodded, her heart beating double-time as they rode down a gentle incline toward the village. Dogs began barking as they drew nearer; several armed warriors rode out to meet them. Other warriors who had been out of sight, standing guard, rode up behind them, neatly boxing them in.

Dalton reined his horse to a halt when they reached the edge of the village. *"Hau, kola."*

Several of the warriors gathered around Dalton, all speaking at once.

Though Kathy couldn't understand what they were saying, it was easy to see, from their gestures and expressions, that they were beginning to recognize him. She could imagine them asking him where he had been, why he had been gone for so long, who the white woman was.

She smiled tentatively at the women and children who stared at her. The Lakota were a handsome people, she thought, with their long black hair, dark eyes, and dusky skin. The women wore ankle-length tunics, many with intricately beaded yokes. Most wore belts of some kind. She was surprised to see that the belts held knives. The little girls wore dresses. The little boys and most of the men wore only clouts and moccasins.

She glanced over her shoulder when she heard her name, felt a little shiver of apprehension when she saw that all the men gathered around Dalton were staring at her. And then Dalton was swinging out of the saddle, lifting her to the ground.

"Is everything all right?" she asked.

Dalton nodded. "I told them you were my woman, and that we wished to stay here for a while. My cousin, Okute, has two wives. His second wife, Yellow Grass Woman, has agreed to let us live in her lodge while we're here."

"He has two wives?"

"Yellow Grass Woman is his first wife's sister. Her husband was killed by the Crow. It is Okute's duty to look after her."

"Oh. What did they say when you told them I was your woman?"

Dalton grinned. "They said I was a lucky man."

"I'll bet."

"Honest." His eyes caressed her. "Any man would consider himself lucky to have you in his lodge."

"Thank you."

"Come on, I want to introduce you to my cousin."

Dalton's cousin was tall and lean. He had two faint white scars on his chest; another, longer scar ran down the length of his left arm. He smiled at her when Dalton introduced them.

"*Hou, hankasi,*" he said solemnly. "*Tanyan yahi yelo.*"

Kathy looked at Dalton. "What did he say?"

"He bids you welcome."

"Tell him thank you."

"You tell him. The Lakota word for thank you is *pilamaya.*"

"*Pila-may-a,*" Kathy said.

Okute grinned at her. "*Waste, hankasi.* I am happy to meet you."

Kathy stared at him. "You speak English!"

"*Han.* But only a . . ." He looked at Dalton. "*Cikala.*"

"Little," Dalton said.

"Little," Okute repeated.

"And only when it suits him," Dalton said with a wry grin. "This is his first wife, Dancing Cloud, and this is her sister, Yellow Grass Woman."

Kathy smiled at the two women. Both were of medium height, with long black braids and dark brown eyes. They returned Kathy's smile, then giggled behind their hands.

"Do they speak English?"

"About as much as Okute," Dalton said.

One by one, men and women came forward to welcome Dalton. Kathy tried to remember them all, but it was impossible. She had thought they would look at her with distrust or hatred, but they all welcomed her kindly, save for one woman, whose dark eyes blazed with loathing.

"Don't pay any attention to the woman of Black Otter," Dalton said as the woman turned away.

"Why does she hate me so?"

"She hates all whites. They killed her husband and her only son fifteen years ago, and she still carries the bitterness inside her."

Kathy watched the crowd disperse, the people going back to doing whatever they had been doing before their arrival. "I guess she has good reason to hate me."

Dalton snorted. "Why? You didn't do it."

"Well, that's true, but I guess it's just human nature. People in my time are the same. I had a friend who hated all Italians because one of them beat up her brother in high school."

"I guess prejudice is everywhere," Dalton mused.

"Human nature," Kathy said again. "In my time, they've passed laws against it, but they don't work all that well."

"You gonna be okay here?" he asked, squeezing her hand.

Kathy nodded. "I guess so."

She glanced around the village, at the conical lodges, the people in buckskins and feathers, the vast horse herd grazing in the distance. There were dogs everywhere. Children stopped their games to stare at her with large, dark eyes.

She took a deep breath and caught the aroma of roasting meat, the acrid smell of a cook fire, a scent Dalton told her was sage and sweet grass.

She saw a woman scraping a hide, another shaking out a big woolly robe, a man holding a sleeping child, a little girl playing with a rag doll.

"Kathy?"

"I'll be fine."

"Come on, I'll show you where we'll be staying. Yellow Grass Woman should be moved out by now."

"I feel bad, putting her out of her home."

"She won't mind."

"Are you sure?"

"Yeah. And it won't be for long. In a few days, we'll have a lodge of our own."

"We will?"

Dalton nodded. "Okute's wives will do some trading and when they've got enough hides, they'll build us a lodge."

"Oh."

"Okute's women are giving a feast in our honor in two day's time."

Kathy grinned at him. "Sort of a welcome home for the prodigal son, I guess."

"Yeah, something like that," Dalton said. He stopped in front of a large tipi. "This is it."

He let go of her hand, and she ducked and stepped inside. The interior of the lodge was far bigger than Kathy had expected. It was, she decided, about the size of her bedroom back home, only round instead of square. There was a fire pit near the center of the floor. Backrests made of wood and covered with furs were arranged on either side of the fire. Pots and pans were stacked on the left side of the doorway; buckskin packs were piled on the right. There was a pile of furs and blankets along the back wall of the lodge.

"It's nice," she said, glancing around. And far cleaner and roomier than she would have expected.

"Yeah." He closed the door flap, which had been open on their arrival. "Come here."

"Why?"

"Why do you think?"

She grinned at him. "I don't know. Tell me."

He lifted one brow. "All right. See that bed back there? I want to lay you down on it, and then I want to undress you. And then I want to touch you, and taste you, and—"

"I think I get the idea," Kathy murmured, her blood heating as she imagined the two of them entwined on the soft furs.

"Smart girl," he said with a teasing grin. He drew her into his arms, his hands skimming over her back, her breasts.

"I always got A's in school," she said, suddenly breathless.

His hands delved beneath her shirt, caressing her back. "I never went to school," he replied, his voice husky. "Why don't you teach me what I missed."

"All right. We'll start with the alphabet. A is for Awesome," she said as he nibbled her ear lobe. "As in, that feels awesome."

"Does it?" He ran his tongue over her breast. "What is B for?"

"Body." She tugged at his shirt, drew it over his head, and tossed it aside. "I love your body." She measured the width of his shoulders, kneaded the muscles in his arms.

"What about C?"

"C is for Cuddle." She pressed herself against him. "I love to cuddle with you."

Dalton laughed softly as he nuzzled her neck. "What about D?"

"D is for Don't, as in don't stop."

He smiled down at her. "Don't worry."

"E is for Enough," Kathy said.

"As in I can't get enough of you?" Dalton asked.

"Exactly."

"And F?" He lifted her into his arms and carried her to the bed.

"F is for Forever," she whispered.

"Ohinyan," Dalton said, his voice low and husky. "What?"

"It's Lakota. It means forever." Kneeling, he placed her on the furry buffalo robes, then cupped her face in his hands. "I will love you forever, Katherine Conley," he vowed, and kissed her.

She slipped her arms around his neck, drawing him down beside her, clinging to him, as he kissed her again and again, his hands and lips and words wrapping her in a warm cocoon.

They discarded their clothing, then came together again, want turning to need, and need turning quickly into desperation.

She clung to him, the only solid thing in a world spinning wildly out of control.

"Ohinyan," Dalton murmured, and with one last thrust, he carried them both over the edge of desperation to ecstasy. "I will love you forever."

Chapter Seventeen

"Why did you want to come back here?" Kathy asked. "I know you said you made a promise to your father. But what did you promise him?"

They were sitting on the bank of the river, their bare feet dangling in the cool water.

"It was just before my father was killed," Dalton replied. "I'd never sought a vision. I'm not sure why. I think maybe I was afraid I didn't deserve one."

"Why not?"

"Because I was a half-breed. My white blood didn't matter to the Lakota. No one ever looked down on me because of it, or made me feel I was different, but—"

"But you felt you were, didn't you? Different, I mean?"

"Yeah. A couple of days before my father went to

battle, he took me aside and told me it was his strong
wish that I seek a vision. He said I would never have
any direction in my life, any balance, until I did. I
promised him that I would do as he asked.'' Dalton
blew out a sigh of regret. ''But then he was killed
and my mother decided to go back to Boston. I never
forgot that promise, though.''

''What do you have to do to get a vision?''

''You have to prepare yourself, spiritually. And
then pick a secluded place, usually up in the hills
somewhere.''

Kathy nodded. It made perfect sense. In the Bible,
it seemed the prophets always went looking for inspiration on a mountaintop.

''Does someone go with you?''

''No.''

''How long will it take?''

''I'll probably be gone about four days.''

''Four days! What will I do while you're gone?''

''Okute and his wives will look after you. Don't
worry.''

She wanted to protest, to remind him that he had
promised not to leave her here, alone with people she
hardly knew, but she didn't. She could see that this
was important to Dalton, that it was something he felt
he had to do. And four days wasn't all that long.

''How soon will you be going?''

''Not for a few days. I need to talk to the shaman
and arrange for a sweat.''

''A sweat?''

''Sweat lodge. It's a way of purifying yourself.''

''Oh. Do all Indian men seek visions?''

Dalton nodded.

"And do they all have them?"

"I don't know. I never knew anyone who didn't, but—" He shrugged. "I don't know." He slipped his arm around her shoulders and drew her close. "I'm glad you're here, with me," he said gruffly.

Warmth spread through Kathy at his words. She knew how difficult it was for him to express his affection and cherished his words all the more because of it.

"Come on," he said, "let's go for a swim."

"A swim? Here?" Kathy glanced around. It was early, but she could see a few women outside, stirring the coals of their cook fires. Dogs were prowling the camp, looking for scraps. Three men stood outside a lodge.

"Sure, come on," Dalton said, rising. "No one will bother us."

"But anyone could come down and see us . . ."

But he was already undressing, stripping off his shirt, then his pants. He held out his hand. "Come on."

Feeling horribly shy, she took off her shirt and jeans, but left on her panties and bra, rationalizing that in her day and age girls often wore far less at the beach.

Dalton lifted one brow, but said nothing.

"Fine!" Kathy muttered, and with a sigh of exasperation, she removed her bra and panties and plunged into the river, shrieking as the cold water closed over her.

With a grin, Dalton dived in after her.

"It's freezing!" Kathy exclaimed.

"Feels great," Dalton said. "Come on."

He swam away from her with long, even strokes. Kathy watched him for a moment, then swam after him, thinking that all those hours she had spent swimming at the Y had finally paid off. She quickly caught up with him and they swam upstream for about fifteen minutes, then turned and swam back to where they had left their clothing.

She had to admit that the cold water was invigorating once she got used to it. She had never gone swimming in the nude before. It was wonderfully exhilarating to feel the water moving over her bare skin.

She shrieked when she felt something slither past her leg.

"It's just a fish," Dalton said.

"Are you sure?" Treading water now, she glanced around, visions of man-eating sharks and electric eels flashing through her mind even though she knew neither of them were likely to be found in a river. Snakes were a very real possibility, though.

"I'm sure."

Moments later, they stepped out of the water. Kathy used her T-shirt to dry off, pulled on her panties, bra and jeans, then shrugged into her damp shirt. She scowled at Dalton. He stood fully nude, letting the warmth of the sun bake him dry, apparently not caring that anyone who happened by would see him.

Her stomach growled loudly, reminding her that she hadn't eaten since the night before.

"Hungry?" Dalton asked.

"Very."

He nodded. He hadn't realized just how much he had missed food, how much pleasure there was in the simple act of eating. He dressed quickly, then took Kathy by the hand. "Come on, let's go see what we can rustle up for breakfast."

Kathy felt as though everyone was staring at her as they made their way toward the lodge. And maybe they were. And who could blame them? The Indians probably didn't see a lot of white women, especially women wearing pants.

She wondered what they thought of her. Wondered if they assumed that she and Dalton were married. She didn't know much about Indians except what she'd seen in movies, and she was pretty sure Hollywood's view of Indians was badly skewed. One thing she was pretty sure of was that Lakota men and women probably didn't live together unless they were married.

She felt a twinge of conscience as she ducked into the lodge. She had never believed in sex outside of marriage. She didn't believe in casual affairs. She never had. And with the very real threat of AIDS, it seemed stupid to sleep around. She'd had a few friends who claimed they were careful, but nothing was one hundred percent safe, and no matter how wonderful sex was, it wasn't worth dying for.

She slid a glance at Dalton. No doubt she was safe enough with him, she mused, since he had been a ghost, and celibate, for over a hundred years. She couldn't believe how quickly he had stirred her desire, how easily she had surrendered to him. She and

Wayne had indulged in some pretty heavy petting before they were married, but they had never gone all the way. She had said no, and Wayne had respected her wishes.

"Kathy?"

"Hmmm?"

"Dancing Cloud left us something to eat." He handed her a bowl.

"Thanks."

She sat down, and Dalton sat beside her. The stew was warm and savory and filling.

There was a rap on the lodge flap.

"*Tima hiyuwo,*" Dalton called, and Dancing Cloud and her sister stepped into the lodge, both bearing folded bundles in their hands.

They spoke to Dalton, placed the bundles on the floor, smiled at Kathy, and left the lodge.

"What was that all about?" Kathy asked.

"They brought us a change of clothes. Yellow Grass Woman said she would be pleased if you would wear her gift at the feast."

Kathy glanced dubiously at the pile on the floor, trying to imagine herself in a dress similar to what the Indian women wore.

"Ever wear buckskin?"

Kathy made a face at him. "What do you think?"

"I think you'll like it."

"Can't I just wear the dress I brought with me?"

"Sure, if you want."

"I guess it would hurt Yellow Grass Woman's feelings if I refused."

"Yeah."

"Okay, I'll wear it."

"Thanks, darlin'."

She would have worn a potato sack to have him look at her like that.

The next two days passed swiftly. As Dalton had predicted, Yellow Grass Woman and Dancing Cloud soon collected enough hides to erect a new lodge. It was not so large as Yellow Grass Woman's, and the hides, unpainted and without decoration of any kind, looked rather plain when compared to the surrounding tipis, many of which were elaborately painted.

Dalton grinned at Kathy when she remarked on it. "Well," he drawled, "The paintings on Blue Fox's lodge depict his exploits in battle. The painting on Okute's lodge represents the time he stole one hundred ponies from the Crow. I guess I could always draw one of my gunfights on ours."

With a laugh, Kathy punched him on the shoulder.

They had laughed a lot in the last two days. She had put her fears for the future aside and now, for the first time in her life, she felt completely free. She had no responsibilities, no pressing appointments, nothing to worry about. They made love far into the night, slept late, swam in the river, walked along the shore.

Dalton taught her a few Lakota words and sentences that he thought she would find useful.

Toniktuka he? How are you?

Iyuskinyan wancinyankelo. I am happy to meet you.

Ake u wo. Come again.

Pilamaya. Thank you.

Sunkawakan. Horse.

She watched the women, amazed by the amount of work they did each day—caring for their children, scraping hides, preparing meals, mending their clothes or making new ones, gathering wood and water. Nothing they did was quick or easy, and she thought how spoiled women of the future were, with refrigerators and freezers and microwave ovens, and how lucky she had been to be born in a time of ease and luxury. It gave her a new appreciation for all the conveniences she had taken for granted. And, even more than the luxuries, she was grateful to have been born in a time when babies were delivered in hospitals, when there were vaccinations for childhood diseases. True, AIDS was a plague to be reckoned with in the twentieth century, but Dalton told her that whole tribes had been wiped out by measles and smallpox and cholera.

The Lakota made her feel welcome, accepting her as one of them because she was Dalton's woman.

She sighed as she watched him walk toward her. She was Dalton's woman, and that was all she ever wanted to be.

Kathy smoothed the dress over her hips, wishing she had a mirror so she could see how she looked. It was made of antelope skin, tanned a creamy white, and softer than velvet against her skin. Rows of tiny blue, red and yellow beads adorned the bodice and the point of each shoulder. She had found a pair of moccasins wrapped inside the dress. They were a sur-

prisingly good fit, and more comfortable than she
would have imagined.

She turned, feeling nervous, as Dalton stepped into
the lodge. What would he think?

He stood just inside the doorway, his gaze moving
over her from head to foot and back up again. Never,
he thought, never had he seen anything so lovely. The
dress, while not snug, still managed to show every
curve. Her hair fell over her shoulders, a dark contrast
to the creamy color of the buckskin.

Kathy tugged at her skirt. "Well?"

"You look beautiful, darlin'. Prettiest thing I've
ever seen."

"Really?"

"Really."

"Thank you." She smiled, warmed by his words,
and the look in his eyes. "You look mighty fine yourself," she remarked, and felt her heart skip a beat as
she took a good look at Dalton.

He was wearing a clout, a buckskin vest, and moccasins. The left side of the vest was painted with a
sunburst, the right side depicted a man on horseback.
Long fringe dangled from the bottom hem. It was a
lovely garment, one that emphasized his broad shoulders and muscular arms. His legs were long and
straight and well-muscled. He wore a beaded head-
band; there was a feather braided into his long, inky-
black hair. He looked primal, virile, sexy as hell.

He cocked his head to one side. "What?"

"Nothing."

"Tell me."

"You look so . . . so . . ."

"So what?"

She shrugged. "Indian."

"Is that good?"

"Very."

He blew out a breath between his teeth. He hadn't realized, until this minute, how much her acceptance of this part of his heritage meant to him. "Are you ready?"

"I guess so." She bit down on her lower lip. "I'm a little scared."

"Don't be." He crossed the distance between them and took her in his arms. "I'm glad you're here."

"Me, too." With a sigh, she rested her head against his chest. She stood there, content, for a moment and then, summoning all her courage, she blurted, "Are you ever going to make an honest woman out of me?"

Dalton's head jerked up. "What?"

"I'm proposing to you."

"You are?"

"Geez, you're dense."

"Well, where I come from," he said with a grin, "the woman usually waits for the man to do the asking."

"I'm tired of waiting."

"Shouldn't I be down on one knee, or something?"

"You should be, but it isn't necessary."

"Kathy . . ." His gaze moved over her face. She was so lovely, and she deserved so much more than he would ever be able to give her.

"Yes, I'll marry you."

"I haven't asked you yet," he said with a growl.

"Well, hurry up so we can kiss."

"Will you marry me, Katherine Conley?"

She frowned, as if she was thinking it over.

"Change your mind already?" he asked dryly.

"No, I just want to savor the moment. You already know my answer . . ."

He kissed her then, kissed her fiercely, passionately, afraid he would wake up and find it was nothing but a dream and that he was still drifting through time and space, caught between heaven and earth, empty and alone.

Kathy pressed herself against Dalton, heat spiraling through her. Never in all her life had she been kissed like this, with such feeling, such a sense of forever.

"I don't know how much time we've got. Maybe it's crazy to even think about, but I want you to be my woman."

"I want that, too. More than anything."

"Say it again," Dalton growled. "Say you'll marry me as soon as possible."

"Yes, oh yes."

"You're sure?"

"More sure than I've ever been of anything in my life."

His gaze searched hers, dark and penetrating. "I'll try to make you happy."

"You already make me happy."

"I love you."

She felt the sting of tears and closed her eyes. What was there about those three simple words that had the power, in a matter of moments, to change one's whole life?

"Ah, Kathy," he said, his voice gruff.

"I love you, Dalton. *Ohin . . .*"

"*Ohinyan.*"

"*Ohinyan.*" She smiled up at him. "Forever."

His gaze met hers, the expression in his eyes far more eloquent than words. And Kathy knew, in her heart, that no matter what ceremony they might later have, she would never be more fully his woman than she was at that moment.

The feast was like nothing Kathy had ever imagined. It seemed everyone in the village had turned out to welcome Dalton home. She could tell the Indians had dressed in their finest clothes. The scent of roasting meat filled the air, and everytime she turned around, someone was offering her something to eat.

Several fires held the night at bay. There was drumming, and singing. Several men and women came forward to offer them gifts: a red wool blanket, a buffalo robe, a bow and a quiver of arrows for Dalton, a sewing kit for Kathy, a cook pot.

After everyone had eaten, there was dancing. Kathy watched it all with a growing sense of excitement. She was seeing things that no one had seen for over a hundred years, actually participating in a way of life that was forever gone. She wasn't sure exactly what she had expected. Her knowledge of Indians and the Indian way of life had been sketchy at best, limited to a few books she had read and movies she had seen. It had always bothered her, the way Hollywood portrayed Indians, especially the fact that the Indians had never been played by Indians until recent years. She had always thought it ludicrous to cast Rock Hudson and Victor Mature as Indian heroes. The only white man cast in the role whom she had ever found believable was Jeff Chandler as Cochise. The movie *Broken Arrow* had always been one of her favorites. But this . . .

She looked around the camp, at the tipis outlined against the night sky, at the dark land that fell away as far as the eye could see, at the stars scattered overhead. So many stars.

She watched the people, noting that the elderly were treated with love and respect. She recalled Dalton saying that his whole family had had a hand in raising him, and she thought how wonderful that must have been, to be surrounded by one's whole family. She heard two dogs fighting over a bone, the sound of a young girl's laughter, the sleepy cry of a child.

She listened to the drumming and the singing and the sound of laughter, and then she looked at Dalton, so handsome, sitting beside her, and knew she could be content here for the rest of her life. Her gaze lingered on his profile, so sharp and clean, so handsome. The light of the fire cast rosy highlights on the dark bronze of his skin. He seemed to be all Indian now, as if here, in the land where he was born, he had somehow shed the white half of himself.

An old man approached them. He nodded politely to Kathy, then spoke to Dalton.

Dalton stood up. "I'll be back in a few minutes, okay?"

"Okay." She watched him follow the old man away from the circle, then turned her attention to the dancing. It was for unmarried men and women, and she smiled as she watched the shy looks that passed between one couple in particular as they danced back and forth. It was easy to see they were very much in love.

Dalton returned a few minutes later, taking his place beside her.

"What was that all about?" she asked.

"I'll tell you later," he said, and then, seeing the look of concern in her eyes, he smiled reassuringly. "It's nothing to worry about."

There was a dance for the women only, and one for the men. Kathy saw Okute walk into the dance circle.

Kathy bumped Dalton's shoulder with her own. "Why don't you dance?"

"Me? I haven't danced in years."

"Oh."

She was about to say he should go do it if he wanted when Okute walked up. He smiled down at Dalton, then jerked his head toward the dance circle. "Come, *tahunsa,* join us."

Dalton looked at Kathy, then rose to his feet and followed his cousin into the dance circle.

The drumming began, the beat slow and regular. At first, Dalton appeared hesitant, but his self-confidence seemed to return as the drumming grew faster. He danced with sensuous grace, his movements well defined and strong. She felt her heart pound in her breast as she watched him. He was all Indian now, a warrior, one with the land, one with his people, and she wondered if he would have become a great leader if his mother hadn't left the Lakota.

She couldn't take her eyes off him. The drums beat even faster; the steps of the dance grew more intricate. She took a deep breath and inhaled the scents of fire and sage and dust and sweat. But mostly she was aware of Dalton . . . who was now wholly the Lakota warrior known as Crowkiller. His skin, sheened with perspiration, glistened like burnished bronze.

He was breathing hard when the dancing ended and he came back to sit beside her. He looked at her, and she knew he was wondering what she thought, if she would think the ways of his people were foolish, if she thought less of him now.

"You were magnificent," Kathy whispered.

His eyes glowed at her praise. "You think so?"

Kathy nodded. "Oh, yes."

Out of the corner of her eye, she saw the young couple she had watched earlier run off together in the dark, and she imagined them standing in the moonlight, holding hands and sneaking kisses, and suddenly she wanted to be standing in the moonlight with Dalton, wanted to feel his arms around her, his mouth on hers.

Impulsively, she placed her hand on his knee.

Dalton turned at Kathy's touch. He started to ask her what she wanted, but there was no need. The look smoldering in the depths of her eyes said it all.

Taking her by the hand, he lifted her to her feet and they walked away from the dancing into the moon-dappled shadows, until the fire and the drumming were far behind them.

There was no need for words. When they found a secluded spot near the river, he drew her into his arms and kissed her, and the touch of his lips on hers was like putting a spark to dry grass.

As if it were the first time, as if it might be the last time, they clung to each other, driven by the need to express their love for one another in the most primal, elemental way.

He whispered to her, unconsciously speaking in the language of his youth, telling her how much he loved her, how beautiful she was, how desperately he needed her. And though she could not understand the words, she understood the meaning behind them.

He worshiped her with his hands and his lips, silently thanking the Great Spirit for sending her to him, for giving him this woman, this moment, for letting him return to his father's people.

They undressed each other with a tenderness that bordered on reverence, their hands trembling with the force of their need, bodies aching to be one. Kathy sank down to the ground, drawing him with her. The grass was cool beneath her heated flesh, but she spared it hardly a thought as Dalton settled between her thighs. She felt the brush of his hair against her breasts, the whisper of a summer breeze against her cheek.

Moaning his name, she lifted her hips to welcome him, sighed with pleasure as his heat filled her, and knew she would always remember this moment, with the moon bright overhead and the sound of a Lakota drum beating in the background—and Dalton in her arms, loving her, kissing her, giving her his heart, his soul, his very life.

Later, lying in his arms blissfully content, she looked at him and grinned. "Was it good for you?"

"What?"

"Nothing." Laughter bubbled up inside her.

Dalton frowned at her. "What the hell are you talking about?"

"Nothing. It's a line from a movie or a joke or something. Who was that man you talked to? What did he want?"

"His name is Star Chaser. He's the shaman. Medicine man." His hand slid up her belly to cup her breast. "He's arranged a sweat for the day after tomorrow."

"Oh." She knew how much he wanted this, but even though she knew she had nothing to fear, she couldn't help being a little apprehensive at the thought of spending four days in the village without him. There were, after all, only a handful of women who spoke English, and even though she had been accepted and made welcome, she was still a stranger.

"The dance is breaking up," Dalton remarked.

"It is? We'd better get dressed."

He held her down when she started to get up. "Don't go."

"But what if someone comes by?"

"Nobody's gonna be coming down here at this time of night."

"Really? *We're* here."

282

Dalton chuckled. "True enough." Rolling onto his side, he kissed the curve of her neck. One hand moved slowly up and down the inside of her thigh. "Do you really want to go back?"

"Hmmm, did you say something?"

"Nothing important," Dalton replied with a grin.

With a sigh, she surrendered to his kisses, oblivious to everything but the touch of his hands. They made love and slept and made love again.

Weary and sated, they slept in each other's arms, oblivious to the passage of time as the sun chased the moon and stars from the sky.

Chapter Eighteen

The dome-shaped sweat lodge was made of willow poles covered with robes which were arranged in such a way that the lodge was airtight. Dalton, stripped naked, sat near the back.

Near the center of the lodge was a small pit, called *iniowaspe,* which would hold the heated stones. The floor of the lodge was covered with a layer of sage. The dirt that had been removed from the pit was piled into a small mound called *hanbelachia,* or the vision hill. Between the vision hill and the pit, the earth was cleared to form a small path known as the smoothed trail. The *iniowaspe,* the *hanbelachia,* and the smoothed trail were a symbolic representation of the vision quest. Small bundles of tobacco were attached to sticks and placed to the west of the hill as an offering. The sacred pipe was placed on the hill, with the stem facing east. The lodge door also faced the east.

Star Chaser spoke to Okute, who would pass the heated stones into the lodge. A moment later, Okute passed four stones into the lodge. Star Chaser placed the stones in the pit, picked up the pipe, and held it aloft.

"All my relatives, living and deceased." He took a puff, then passed the pipe to Dalton, who took a puff and passed the pipe back to the medicine man. They did this four times.

When that was done, Star Chaser passed the pipe out to Okute for refilling. Then, lifting a spoon made from the horn of a mountain sheep, Star Chaser dipped it into a paunch of cold water and flicked water over the hot stones. Great clouds of steam rose in the air, filling the lodge.

The heat seemed suffocating. Dalton gasped for breath as Star Chaser began to sing a sacred song.

Four times they smoked the pipe.

Four times, Star Chaser sprinkled cold water upon the hot rocks.

Four times the medicine man sang the sacred song.

Dalton sat back, his eyes closed, emptying his mind of all thought, all memory. Sweat poured from his body. Steam filled the lodge, and with it rose the scent of sage.

Mindless, weightless, he was drifting again, a spirit without a body, heart and mind and soul seeking unity, a sense of oneness with the Great Mystery of life. Only those who were pure in body and spirit could expect to find communion with *Wakan Tanka*.

Lost in time and space, he prayed for courage, for guidance and forgiveness.

Once, he thought he heard the scree of an eagle.

Once, he thought he heard Kathy's voice, weeping softly.

Once, in the clouds of steam that filled the lodge, he thought he saw his father's face.

When he could endure the suffocating heat no longer, Dalton ducked out of the lodge and plunged into the stream. The water felt like winter ice against his heated flesh, but when he stepped out of the water, he felt renewed, reborn.

Dalton planned to leave the village late that night. He had told Kathy he wanted to reach the place he had chosen before dawn the next day. Now, lying in bed, she watched him as he dressed in clout and moccasins. She loved to look at him, to watch the sensuous play of muscles in his arms and back.

He had been quiet when he returned from the sweat lodge. He had eaten little at dinner, gone early to bed. They had not made love. She seemed to recall reading somewhere that warriors thought intercourse before battle weakened them; perhaps it also applied to men yearning for a vision.

When he was ready to leave, he knelt beside her. "I'll only be gone a few days," he said. It would take him a day to travel to the hill and back. He would spend no more than two days waiting for his vision. A shaman on a holy quest might spend as many as ten days in vision seeking, but for a personal quest, two days was considered sufficient.

"Should I wish you good luck?"

"You could pray for me while I'm gone."

"I will."

He smiled down at her. No one had ever prayed for him, at least not that he knew of.

"I'll miss you," she whispered. "Be careful."

"I'll miss you, too. Okute and his wives will look after you. If you need anything, let them know, okay? Don't be afraid to ask for their help."

Blinking back her tears, she nodded.

"I have to do this," Dalton said.

"I know. I'll be fine."

He nodded. "I know you will." Leaning down, he kissed her. Her lips were warm and soft and he was sorely tempted to strip off his clout and crawl back under the covers. Instead, he kissed her once more, then stood up. "Good-bye, darlin'."

"Bye."

Taking up a small pouch of tobacco, he left the lodge.

For a moment, he stood outside, breathing in the cool night air. His stallion whinnied softly as he secured the pouch to the saddle horn, then took up the reins and vaulted onto the horse's back.

Leaning forward, Dalton scratched the stud's neck. "Wanna run, boy?" he asked as he touched his heels to the buckskin's flanks. "Me, too. Come on," he said, "let's go."

The big buckskin needed no urging. He crowhopped once, then, neck stretched and ears laid back, he lined out in a dead run.

"Eeiiiiiiyaha!" A soft shout rose in Dalton's throat

as he leaned over the stallion's neck and lost himself in the sheer joy of racing over the moonlit prairie. The buckskin was one of the fastest horses he had ever owned. He'd won the horse from a Texas cowboy in a poker game in Galveston five years before.

That was a night he would never forget. There had been four men in the game besides himself—a flat-faced muleskinner who smelled worse than his team, a drummer who hailed from Kansas City, a greenhorn from Philadelphia, and the Texas brushpopper.

The Texan had been sure of his hand but short on funds. In desperation, he had wagered the buckskin against Dalton's raise of a hundred dollars. Dalton didn't think he would ever forget the look of excitement on the cowboy's face when he turned over his cards, displaying a full house, jacks over tens. But it hadn't been good enough.

One by one, Dalton had turned over his own cards to reveal a royal flush. For a moment, he had thought the cowboy was going to start bawling.

Dalton reached forward, patting the stallion's neck. The big horse was the best thing he'd ever won on the turn of a card.

It was almost dawn when he reached the summit known as Eagle Feather Ridge. Dalton reined the stud to a halt when they reached the foot of the hill.

He sat there a moment, looking up, and then, feeling the urge to climb to the top of the hill on foot, he dismounted. Holding the reins in one hand, he began to walk. It wasn't a particularly steep hill, but he was out of breath when he reached the top.

He had timed it perfectly. The lightening sky signaled the birth of a new day.

Dropping the stallion's reins, Dalton made a slow circle, his gaze sweeping the land below. It stretched away as far as the eye could see, miles and miles of rolling grassland broken by an occasional stand of timber or a cluster of rocks.

He stripped off his clout and moccasins; then, kneeling on the ground, he drew a circle in the dirt. Rising to his feet, he opened the tobacco pouch, chanting the words given to him by the shaman as he offered a pinch of tobacco to the four winds, to the sky above, to Mother Earth.

A soft summer wind stirred the dust, lifting the tobacco into the air and carrying it away.

It was a solemn thing, to seek a vision, to seek power. His friend, Black Horse, had sought a vision, and dreamed of Thunder. Those who dreamed of Thunder must be Heyoka. Heyokas were expected to act strange, always to play the clown. They wore foolish clothes, lived in ragged lodges, slept without blankets in the winter, and covered themselves with heavy robes in the summer. Those who refused to live the life of Heyoka risked angering the Thunder gods, thereby risking death by lightning.

Lifting his arms over his head, Dalton gazed up at the rising sun, the words he now uttered coming from his own heart, his own soul. His own need. Naked and alone, he prayed for strength, for help, for guidance. His throat thickened, and the words came harder as he asked for forgiveness for the lives he had taken, for blood, both human and animal, that he had shed. He prayed for wisdom, and courage.

The sun climbed higher, grew hotter. Sweat beaded on his brow, trickled down his back, his chest. His legs grew weary, his arms heavy. He was plagued by thirst. And still he stood there, gazing at the sun, humbled by his own weakness, by a growing sense of nothingness. Hours passed. His voice grew hoarse, his pleas more desperate.

His thoughts wandered, so that the past and the present and the years he had lived between one world and the next ran together, the sum total of his life blending together, until all his hopes, all his fears, all his dreams, stood beside him on the top of the world. Good and evil warred within him, fighting over his soul, drawing him in two directions. The faces of the men he had killed rose up before him, their eyes burning with hate and accusation. And there was Lydia, beckoning him with seductive smiles and pretty lies. He recalled the lessons he had been taught in childhood, to be reverent of the earth, to honor the old ones, to defend the weak and the helpless, to speak only the truth.

With a groan, he sank to his knees, the burden of his guilt too heavy to bear. He had turned his back on his people, on all he had been taught.

He stared at the sky, surprised to see that night had fallen. Ignoring the cramping of his empty belly, the thirst that plagued him, he curled up on the hard ground and closed his eyes, afraid that he had waited too long to seek the blessing of the spirits, afraid that there was no redemption, no hope of starting over, for one such as he.

He shivered as a cold wind blew across the top of the hill, clinging to the hope that all could not be lost. Surely, if he were beyond redemption, he would not have been given a second chance. *Kathy* . . .

Whispering her name, he fell asleep, and sleeping, began to dream of a dark red light that pulsed with energy and called to him with soft words, promising him pleasure beyond his wildest dreams, and he followed the siren call of the red glow that was lust and desire and power and the embodiment of earthly pleasure, and as he followed, he felt himself grow heavy, bound with chains that slowly led him away from the Life Path of the Lakota . . . and then, when he was in the depths of despair, a pale white light appeared to him, and she was hope and goodness, and he reached out for her, but the chains held him captive, and he could not reach the warmth of that white light, could not escape the shackles of greed and lust that bound him. The red light pulsed and glowed and the chain around his neck became a rope and he felt himself falling, falling, plunging into a darkness beyond black, helpless to save himself. . . .

He woke with a start, the sound of his own voice echoing in his ears . . . Kathy!

"Kathy." He whispered her name, and the demons fled.

Kathy sat inside the lodge, a blanket draped over her shoulders. It had been a long day. Time and again she had gone outside to stare at the distant hills. Dalton was up there somewhere, praying for a vision. She knew little of visions except for those she had read about in the Bible. Pharaoh had dreamed, and Joseph had interpreted the dream for him. Moses had seen God in a burning bush. Saul had seen a vision on the road to Tarsus. To her recollection, none of them had gone seeking a vision.

Of course, if one had faith enough, anything was possible.

Okute had tried to explain it to her, telling her that the Lakota believed that a man, or woman, received power from *Wakan Tanka,* the Great Mystery, whose spirit was in all and through all. The eagle, the hawk, the buffalo, the deer, the swallow, the elk, all possessed a certain power. When a man sought a vision, his spirit guide would come to him and endow him with power.

She had thanked him for explaining it to her, though she didn't fully understand it.

The lodge seemed huge, empty. The fire burned low, casting shadows on the lodge skins. Remembering her promise to pray for him, she closed her eyes.

Please keep him safe. Please grant his wish. Please bring him home to me. . . .

Home . . . she was back at the ranch, sitting on the front porch. Cattle grazed in the distance. There were corrals filled with mares and foals. Three children played tag in the front yard. And Dalton was there, smiling at her.

The scene changed abruptly, and she was standing at the foot of the hanging tree, staring up at a body dangling from the end of a rope. She shook her head, not wanting to see its face, heard a scream echo in-side her mind as the body slowly revolved and she saw Dalton's face, swollen and discolored, heard the sound of a woman's insane laughter. . . .

She woke with a start, and the images faded.

Knowing she would not sleep again that night, she threw some wood on the fire. It hadn't been a vision, just a bad dream, nothing more.

She told herself that, over and over, as the night turned to day, and then, utterly weary, she crawled into bed. Just before she fell asleep, she thought she heard the high-pitched cry of an eagle.

He woke with the dawn. Shivering from the cold, his belly empty, his throat dry, he rose to his feet and sang his dawn song to *Wakan Tanka,* the Great Spirit, who was the center of all life. The words, filled with joy and wonder, spoke of how the earth and the sky were all part of the circle of life, and how man, through following the Life Path, learned to be a part of it.

When the last notes of the song faded away, he again offered tobacco to the earth and the sky and the four directions. Standing atop the hill, he watched the sun climb over the edge of the world, watched as long fingers of pure light painted the sky with bold strokes of red and orange and gold.

And then, from out of the west, he saw an eagle flying toward him. With a gentle flapping of wings, the eagle landed on the edge of the circle, its sharp black eyes fixed upon Dalton.

293

"What is it you want?" the eagle asked. "Why do you stand here like this?"

"I have come seeking guidance," Dalton replied. "And to fulfill a promise I made long ago."

The eagle cocked his head to one side and regarded Dalton out of fathomless black eyes. "You have lost your way, son of Night Caller. You have strayed from the true path."

"I have come to find my way back."

"No," the eagle said, and his voice was a low rumble, like distant thunder. "You have lived two lives already, and now you seek a third, but your destiny does not lie with the People. The one who once guided your steps is now in need of help only you can give."

"I don't understand."

The eagle flapped mighty wings. "Follow your heart, Crowkiller. It will lead you back to the true path."

"Wait!"

But the eagle was already gone. Great wings outspread, the bird rose up into the heavens and disappeared into the rising sun.

Dalton stood there for what might have been minutes or hours. Confused, he sat down on the ground. He had been certain he had been sent to the past to fulfill the promise he had made to his father, but if the eagle spoke the truth, that was not the reason he was here at all.

One who had once guided his steps . . .

His father? Dalton shook his head. His father was no longer in need of help.

His mother?

What could she possibly need from him?

With a shake of his head, he pulled on his clout and moccasins. It was time to go back to the village. He would seek out Star Chaser and they would make a sweat, and then he would tell the shaman what the eagle had said. Perhaps Star Chaser would know the answer to the riddle.

Filled with a sense of peace, he again made an offering of tobacco to the earth and the sky and the four winds, and then he murmured a fervent prayer of thanksgiving to *Wakan Tanka*.

Moments later, he was riding toward the village.

Chapter Nineteen

Lost in thought, he didn't see them until it was too late.

They rose up out of a fold in the ground, a dozen Crow warriors. Judging by their paint and the carcasses draped over the pack horses, they had been hunting. For a moment suspended in time, the Crow warriors stared at Dalton, and then, with a high-pitched cry, eight of them charged toward him, leaving the other four with the pack horses.

Dalton muttered an oath as he slammed his heels into the stallion's sides. Neck stretched, ears flat, the buckskin lined out in a dead run.

The sound of the stallion's hooves and the thunder of the pursuing horsemen echoed the rapid pounding of Dalton's heart as he raced for home, and knew, with a cold and clear certainty, that he would never make it.

Bullets whizzed past his head. An arrow buried itself in his right thigh. He felt the sting of a bullet graze his left shoulder, a bright burst of pain as another bullet tore through his left side.

He bent low over the stallion's neck, his heels drumming into the horse's flanks, his only thought to get home, to Kathy.

A thick gray haze spread before him, a darkness, an emptiness that was all too familiar. Dalton risked a glance over his shoulder, wondering if death might not be preferable to a return to that thick gray haze, to that life between this world and the next that was not life at all.

Behind him, the Crow warriors reined their horses to a halt, unwilling to enter the eerie grayness that was not night, not clouds, not fog.

Dalton counted the days in his mind as he urged the stallion into the roiling gray mist. Had he the strength, he might have laughed. It was July 28th, and instead of dying at the end of a rope, he was going to die from a wound inflicted by the Crow.

Hokahey! The war cry rose up in his mind. It was a good day to die.

He rode steadily into the thick gray nothingness that seemed to stretch endlessly before him. In returning to the past, they had altered the future, he mused ruefully, but it seemed his destiny could not be changed and he was, indeed, fated to die on July 28th.

His last thought before darkness claimed him was that they wouldn't have to change the date on his tombstone.

Blackness hovered around him, and in the center of that blackness he saw the crimson glow of Satan's inferno, felt the fires of hell burning through him, long fingers of flame that seared his back and thigh and shoulder.

He had not expected this kind of pain in hell. An anguish of spirit, yes, an eternity of regret, but not this constant throbbing agony that pounded through him with every breath. His body felt heavy, his mind drugged, sluggish.

The acrid scent of smoke stung his nostrils. Hellfire, he thought, but instead of the stink of brimstone he caught the scent of white sage and sweet grass. As from far, far away he heard the soft sound of chanting. The music wound around him, whispering peace, and then he felt a sharp pain in his back. The scent of blood filled his nostrils; he felt it run warm and thick down his sides.

Demon hands clutched him in the darkness, holding him down so that he couldn't move. Heat, like the devil's own breath, hovered over his back, growing closer, hotter. He screamed as a searing tongue of flame licked his tortured flesh. And then, mercifully, the blackness of eternity swallowed him up again.

He was floating again, lost in an unforgiving hell of pain and thirst and unquenchable fire that made him long for the days when he had drifted through a

298

cold gray fog, blissfully unaware of light or darkness or pain.

In the distance, he heard voices, saw a beautiful white light beckoning to him, and he turned toward it. He knew in the deepest part of his soul that he would find some measure of peace there, a release from the pain that tormented his body, perhaps even forgiveness. But it would mean leaving Kathy behind. Kathy, with the promise of forever in her eyes.

He whispered for water and an angel appeared beside him, an angel with a cloud of auburn hair and worried brown eyes. An angel with Kathy's face. Her memory would haunt him through eternity, he thought bleakly, and cursed Satan for letting him remember the softness of her touch.

She lifted his head and offered him water, one sip, then two, when he could have drained a river.

He heard murmured voices, words that made no sense, cried out as the devil's breath seared his skin once more, giving rise to excruciating pain that pitched him again into the blackness of infinity.

Aeons passed, days and years of darkness and pain, pain and darkness, and an occasional glimpse of his angel's face. But it was only an illusion. Kathy was alive and well, walking among the living. Her face, her voice urging him to drink, to eat—it was all a lie, and he burrowed deeper into the darkness, away from the pain and the memories.

Memories of holding her in his arms, of seeing her smile, hearing her laugh, dreaming dreams that could never come true. Regret ate at his soul like acid, and

he wanted to die. . . . He would have laughed had he
been able. He had died twice already.

"Dalton! Dalton! Damn you, wake up."

Kathy's voice again, only he knew it wasn't Kathy's voice, couldn't be Kathy's voice.

"Dalton! Don't you dare die on me! Do you hear
me? I need you. You can't die and leave me here
alone. Please, Dalton."

The voice grew thick, he heard the sound of crying,
felt wetness, like cool rain, upon his fevered face.

"Please, Dalton. I love you. Please don't leave me.
Please, please, come back to me."

He struggled toward the sound of her voice, ignoring the pain that grew ever sharper as he swam upward through thick layers of blackness.

"Kathy . . ."

"I'm here. I'm here."

"No . . . not possible . . ."

"Dalton!" A hand on his shoulder, shaking him.
"Dalton." Her voice reaching out to him, guiding
him away from the abyss of eternity.

"Kathy?"

Her hand clasping his, tighter, tighter. It was an
effort to open his eyes, and he blinked and blinked
again, and she was there, beside him, her eyes red
and swollen, her cheeks damp with tears.

"Oh, Dalton," she sobbed, "thank God!" And
laying her head on his shoulder, she began to cry.

"Hey." He lifted his hand and patted her back.
"Don't cry, darlin'."

"I can't help it," she wailed. "I thought I had lost
you."

He frowned, trying to remember what had happened, but he could recall nothing after he rode into the mist.

"No." His fingers delved into the wealth of her hair. "You're never gonna lose me, darlin'. I promise." He smiled at her and then, overcome with weariness, he closed his eyes and slept.

When he woke again, Kathy told him how Okute had found him, lying unconscious on the far side of the river. The stallion had stayed beside him.

"And the mist," Dalton asked. "Was it still there?"

"Mist? I don't know. Okute didn't say anything about a mist."

"It was strange," Dalton said. "I thought I had died again. It was the right day for it, you know. The 28th of July."

A cold shiver snaked its way down Kathy's spine. "But you didn't die. Did you find what you went looking for?"

Dalton nodded. "Yes. I found the vision I sought, and I have fulfilled the promise I made to my father."

She stroked his hand, a dozen questions chasing themselves through her mind, like a dog chasing its tail. She wanted to ask him if he planned to spend the rest of his life here, with the Lakota, if he still wanted to marry her, what he had seen in his vision, but she asked none of them. There would be time for questions later, when he was well again.

"Rest now," she said, but he was already asleep.

*   *   *

He felt a little better when he woke again. Kathy was there beside him with a bowl of thin soup to ease his hunger and a cup of cool, sweet water to quench his thirst.

He looked amused when she told him she was going to bathe him.

"I haven't had a woman give me a bath since I was in short pants," he remarked, the ghost of his old roguish grin playing over his lips.

"Well, then, this will be a new experience for both of us," Kathy retorted, "cause I've never given a man a bath."

"Well," he drawled, "I don't know about you, but I'm looking forward to it."

She made a face at him as she washed his right arm, then his left, being careful not to get his wounded shoulder wet. She dried his arms, then carefully moved the cloth over his chest, avoiding the bandage wrapped around his middle.

She could feel Dalton's gaze on her as she slid the cloth over his belly. Although they had made love numerous times, she was still a little shy and she felt her cheeks grow hot as she washed that part of him that made him a man.

Her touch aroused the expected response, and he chuckled softly when she turned her back to him.

"Hmm, that feels mighty good," he remarked, unable to keep from teasing her. "But I think maybe you missed a spot."

"I don't think so."

"Are you sure?"

"I'm sure." Her cheeks were on fire as she washed and dried his legs.

"Kathy?"

"What?"

"There's no need for you to be embarrassed."

"I know."

He reached for her arm, wincing as the movement sent slivers of pain through his shoulder and side. "Come here."

He drew her down beside him, his right arm wrapping around her shoulders.

"Dalton . . ."

"I just want to hold you close for a little while."

She drew the blanket over him, then snuggled against him, glad to be in his arms again. She had come so close to losing him. It had made her realize how deeply she cared for him, how empty her life would be without him. She had prayed fervently, selfishly, for his recovery, unable to bear the thought of again losing someone she loved. And she did love Dalton, desperately.

She heard his breathing slow and knew he had fallen asleep again. But that was good. Rest was the best thing for him now.

Content to be near him, she closed her eyes and offered a silent prayer of thanks that he was going to be all right.

During the next week, Star Chaser came several times each day to examine Dalton's wounds. Okute and his wives came to visit, as did others whose names and faces Dalton remembered from long ago. The People were generous. They brought blankets and food; Yellow Grass Woman made Dalton a long-sleeved buckskin shirt; Dancing Cloud made him a pair of leggings.

Kathy was touched by their generosity, by their willingness to share what they had.

Dalton was not a good patient, and grew worse with each passing day. He didn't like staying in bed, didn't like being weak and helpless. He insisted that he felt fine, that he wanted to get up.

Now, exasperated after arguing with him for the last eight days, Kathy's temper snapped.

"Go ahead, then," she said irritably. "Get up. But don't expect any sympathy from me when you fall flat on your face."

Jaw clenched, he tried to stand up, only to be overcome with a wave of dizziness.

"All right," he muttered. "You win."

She tried not to gloat as she made him comfortable. "You were badly hurt, Dalton. You lost a lot of blood. You almost died. It's going to take time to get your strength back."

"Time," he repeated. Once, he had taken it for granted, but no more. Every day, every hour, was precious, and he didn't want to waste any of them lying in bed, as weak as a newborn kitten. He had a sudden inexplicable urge to see his mother, to make sure she was all right.

"Kathy, I've been thinking. How would you feel about going to Boston?"

"Boston?"

"Yeah. I don't know how long I'll be here, how

long *we'll* be here. I want to go see my mother, in case I don't get another chance.''

She had forgotten, for the moment, how temporary their presence in the past might be. At his words, she felt a tremor of unease. She didn't belong here, in this time. What if they were separated? What would she do if she was sent back to the future without him?

''Sure,'' she said, not meeting his eyes, ''whatever you want.''

He took her hand in his. ''I thought, while we were there, we could get married.''

''Oh, Dalton . . .'' Joy and happiness misted in her eyes.

''I take it you don't mind, then.''

''No, I don't mind. I just thought you'd probably want to stay here.''

He was quiet a moment, his expression thoughtful. ''Kathy, what will happen to my people?''

''I'm not sure. I never paid much attention to history when I was in school. I know there were a lot of battles fought, but the only one I remember is the battle against Custer at the Little Big Horn. The Indians won that one, but it was all downhill after that. Eventually, they were all sent to reservations.''

''There's got to be something I can do to make the future better for them.''

''I don't know what it would be. Maybe you could warn Okute, tell him to take his people away from here before it's too late, but I don't know where they could go. And even if you could change the future, I don't know if you should.''

''We've already changed it.''

"I know, but I don't think we've tampered with anything that has historical implications. I mean, we haven't killed anyone who might have saved the world, or anything like that."

Dalton nodded, his expression thoughtful.

"Get some rest, okay?"

He nodded again, but sleep was a long time coming.

Chapter Twenty

Kathy bolted upright, not certain what it was that had awakened her. And then she heard it again, a sound like Fourth of July firecrackers.

Dalton stirred beside her. A moment later, he was struggling to his feet.

"Where are you going?"

"We're being attacked."

"Attacked!" Kathy exclaimed.

"That's gunfire."

Kathy scrambled to her feet, her heart pounding wildly. "But who? Why?"

"I don't know." He dressed quickly. "Stay here."

"You're not going out there?"

"Damn right." He picked up his gunbelt, checked to make sure the Colt was loaded.

"Dalton, don't go."

"What do you want me to do, Kathy? Hide in here while my people are fighting for their lives?"

"But you haven't recovered from your wounds yet." It had been three weeks since he had been attacked by the Crow, and though he had regained a good deal of his strength, he was still not fully recovered.

"I'll be all right." He slid one arm around her waist and kissed her, hard. "I love you." He picked up his rifle and thrust it into her hand. "Use it if you have to," he said, and then he was gone.

She put the rifle down long enough to pull on her tunic and moccasins. Whether the Indians won or lost, she intended to be fully dressed when the battle was over.

She stared at the rifle with distaste; then, with a sigh, she picked it up and walked to the doorway.

The sound of gunfire had increased. She heard a woman scream, the frightened cry of a child. The ground seemed to shake as the cavalry rode through the village. She caught the scent of smoke and dust.

Lifting the flap, she peered outside. It was like a scene from every old Western she had ever seen. Women ran everywhere, seeking shelter for themselves and their children. Men in blue uniforms rode through the village, firing at anything that moved. A thick layer of dust and gunsmoke hung in the air, burning her nostrils, stinging her eyes.

She gasped as she saw Okute and a soldier struggling over a knife. They fell to the ground, rolling back and forth. Okute grabbed a rock and struck the soldier over the head and the man fell back, unconscious. Okute took a deep breath, then stood up and started to hurry toward his lodge, which was in flames. It was then that Kathy saw a soldier aiming his gun at Okute's back.

Hardly aware of what she was doing, Kathy lifted her rifle, aimed and fired. The recoil practically knocked her off her feet. When the smoke cleared, the soldier lay sprawled on the ground, blood oozing from a hole in his back. Okute paused to glance over his shoulder and his gaze met Kathy's. He smiled at her, then turned and disappeared into the swirling dust.

Kathy stared at the body lying in front of her lodge. She had killed a man. She looked at the other bodies lying in the dirt, horror washing through her. These were people she had talked with, laughed with, people who had brought food and blankets.

She had killed a man. She thought of all the spiders she had carried outside because she couldn't bear to kill them, the fish she had caught and thrown back, the baby bird she had saved from a cat. She despised the thought of taking a life, yet she had killed a man.

Feeling sick to her stomach, she dropped the rifle. ''Dalton.'' She whispered his name, praying that he was all right. She needed him, needed his arms around her, needed to hear his voice telling her she had done the right thing.

The battle seemed to go on for hours, but it was over in far less time. There was a sudden, ominous silence, the sound of a bugle, a voice giving orders.

As the dust settled, she saw the cavalry herding a small group of men and women toward the center of the village. Eyes straining, she searched for Dalton, but he was not among them. Neither were Okute or his wives.

With a cry, she bolted from the lodge, and into the arms of a tall man in Army blue.

"Whoa, there, ma'am," he said, his hands gripping her arms to steady her. "No need to be afraid. It's over."

She stared at him blankly.

He smiled reassuringly. "It's all right now," he said. "We've come to take you home."

"Home?"

"Yes, ma'am."

"Dalton . . . my . . . my husband. I have to find him."

"I'll help you, ma'am."

"Thank you."

Side by side, they walked through the village. There were bodies everywhere. Soldiers moved among the dead, covering their comrades with blankets. She saw other soldiers looting the lodges, taking blankets and weapons and furs. In the distance, she saw several soldiers rounding up the horse herd.

She saw a soldier bending over a body, removing the eagle feather from the warrior's hair. The warrior moved, and the soldier plunged a knife into his back.

She turned away, retching. And then she saw Dalton. He was lying near a dead trooper. With a cry, she ran toward him. Dropping to her knees, she ran her hands over him, relieved that, except for a shallow gash along his left temple, he seemed unhurt.

She shrieked as rough hands caught her and hauled

her to her feet. "What are you doing?" she cried. "Let me go."

The soldier looked at her, astonished. "You're a white woman."

"Yes, and this is my husband."

"Husband?" he asked, his voice filled with scorn.

"Yes, my husband. We—we were captured by the Indians. Please, he needs help."

"I'll see what I can do, ma'am."

She noticed that his voice was respectful, now that he had ascertained that she was not an Indian. But there was no time to worry about prejudice now. Ripping the kerchief from the dead soldier, she pressed it to Dalton's head to stop the bleeding.

"Dalton? Dalton!"

Slowly, his eyelids fluttered open. "Kathy?"

"Yes. Don't talk. Just rest."

"Star Chaser. I must see him."

Kathy shook her head. "He's . . . he was killed."

With a groan, Dalton closed his eyes.

"Dalton? Dalton!"

He took a deep breath and opened his eyes.

"Are you all right?" he asked.

"Yes, I'm fine. The soldiers think we're married, that we're prisoners."

Dalton nodded. Had he been alone, he would have taken his place with his people, met whatever Fate had in store for them, but he had Kathy to think of now. He couldn't leave her.

A short time later, the Army doctor arrived. He quickly examined Dalton's injuries, washed and bandaged his head wound, pronounced him lucky to be alive, and admonished him to rest until they were ready to leave.

The soldier who had assisted Kathy returned with a canteen. He offered her and Dalton a drink, informing them that they would be pulling out within the hour.

Kathy stared at the small group of Indians huddled together, then looked at Dalton. "Are they the only ones left?"

"I don't know. Have you seen Okute or Yellow Grass Woman and her sister?"

Kathy shook her head. At the mention of Okute's name, the horror of what she had done returned.

Dalton frowned as Kathy's face paled. "What's wrong?"

"Oh, Dalton, I killed a man."

"What?"

She nodded, her eyes filling with tears. "Okute . . . and a soldier . . . they were, they were fighting and . . . and . . . I shot him."

Ignoring the dizziness that swept through him, Dalton sat up and cradled Kathy in his arms. "It's all right, darlin'," he murmured. "You saved my cousin's life. Look."

She glanced over her shoulder to see the soldiers herding a small group of people toward the prisoners. She was relieved to see Okute and his wives were among them.

She had saved his life, but she had taken the life of a man who might have lived if she hadn't interfered. And what of the life she had saved? What if Okute had been meant to die? What if changing the past meant she could never return to her own time?

She felt sick to her stomach; her head began to throb.

"Kathy, you did what you had to do." Dalton stroked her hair. "Try not to think about it."

"I can't help it. I feel awful."

"Yeah, I know." He rocked her in his arms. It was never easy, taking a life.

"How did you live with the guilt?"

"It was me or them." He brushed a kiss over her cheek. "I'm grateful to you for what you did."

She clung to that thought. She had saved Okute's life. He was part of Dalton's family and therefore, part of hers, as well. She thought of the kindness of Yellow Grass Woman and Dancing Cloud, and knew she would have felt worse if she had let Okute be killed.

Dalton's arms tightened around her. "Damn!"

"What's wrong?"

"They're burning the village."

Sniffing back her tears, Kathy looked over Dalton's shoulder. Thick black smoke choked the air, causing the horses to stir restlessly. A high keening wail rose from the women as they watched their homes burn. The men stared straight ahead, their faces impassive. The children huddled against their mothers, their dark eyes wide and scared.

A short while later, a freckle-faced private approached them leading two horses. "We're ready to pull out." He looked at Dalton. "Can you ride, mister, or do you need a litter?"

"I can ride."

"My horse," Kathy said. "Where's Taffy Girl?"

"I couldn't say, ma'am," the soldier replied.

"I want my own horse."

"I'm afraid the herd's already moved out," the soldier said apologetically. "I'm sure you'll be able to look for your horse when we make camp for the night."

"But . . ."

"Let it go, darlin'," Dalton said quietly. He helped Kathy to her feet, held the horse's bridle while she mounted, then handed her the reins.

Taking up the reins of the second horse, Dalton took a deep breath, then climbed slowly into the saddle. Though the wounds he had received from the Crow were almost healed, his head throbbed and he ached from head to foot, but as he looked out over the village, his own discomfort seemed minor. The bodies of men and women he had known since childhood lay sprawled on the ground, eyes blank and staring. He felt a surge of anger as he thought of them being left unburied, prey to wolves and vultures.

When a warrior was killed, custom demanded that he be buried in his finest attire, with an eagle feather in his hair and his face painted. His weapons and his flute were placed alongside his body, and then his body was wrapped in a robe. His loved ones would slash their flesh and cut their hair to show their grief.

He drew his gaze from the carnage as the order to mount was given and the cavalry moved out, herding the captured Indians ahead of them.

Dalton watched them with a sharp sense of guilt. He should not be riding with the enemy, but with his people. He caught Okute's eye. There was no accusation in his cousin's expression, only understanding.

They rode all that day, stopping only briefly to rest the horses and allow both solders and prisoners time to relieve themselves.

At dusk, the soldiers made camp near a shallow waterhole. The prisoners were kept in a tight group, under heavy guard.

"Can we go look for Taffy Girl now?" Kathy asked.

"Sure, come on."

No one stopped them as they walked through the camp toward the horse herd. Dalton whistled softly, and a few minutes later, his stallion trotted up. Taffy Girl followed close behind.

"Is she all right?" Kathy asked.

Dalton ran an expert eye over both horses, then nodded. "She's fine. They both are."

Kathy ran her hands over Taffy Girl's neck, surprised at how quickly she had become attached to the mare. Maybe it was because, except for a couple of goldfish and a cat, she had never had any pets to speak of. Or maybe it was because Dalton had chosen the horse for her.

"Let's go back to camp," Dalton said.

"All right. Are you okay?"

"Fine. Just a little tired."

The Army doctor fell into step beside them a few minutes later. "I need to check those wounds," he said.

"I'm fine."

"Maybe, but I need to take a look just the same. My tent's over here."

Kathy stood near the doorway while the doctor examined Dalton's injuries. "Everything seems to be healing up just fine," the doctor said. "How do you feel? Any dizziness, blurred vision?"

"No."

With a nod, the doctor spread a thick coat of salve on the wound in Dalton's temple, then applied a fresh bandage. "Like I said, you're a lucky man."

"Yeah. Thanks, doc."

"Here." The sawbones plucked a shirt from his saddlebags and handed it to Dalton.

"Thanks."

"Sure. I'll see if I can't find you a pair of boots."

"Obliged, doc."

"Just take care of yourself."

Dalton and Kathy spread their bedrolls apart from everyone else. One of the soldiers brought them a plate of jerky and hardtack and dried apples, and two tin cups of strong black coffee.

Kathy grimaced at the rough fare. Even the Indians ate better than this.

"What will happen to them?" she asked. "To Okute, and the others?"

"They'll be taken to the reservation."

"That won't be so bad, will it?"

Dalton looked at her, his eyes hot with suppressed anger. "I suppose that depends on what you call bad."

He took a bite of jerky and chewed it thoughtfully. He had never lived on the reservation, but he had heard stories from those who had. There was never enough food or blankets. Forbidden to have weapons, the men could not hunt. Imprisoned, lacking the means to provide for their families, the warriors grew bitter, despondent. Many took to drinking heavily in an effort to forget.

"Well, it doesn't really matter," he remarked. "They won't stay there for long."

Kathy regarded him over the rim of her cup. "What do you mean?"

"Okute will take his people and leave as soon as they can."

"But where will they go? There's nothing left of the village."

"They'll find those who survived and go north, to Crazy Horse. He'll take them in."

Kathy put her cup down and slipped her hand into his. "And what are we going to do?"

"We're going to Boston."

Dalton remained awake long after Kathy had fallen asleep. He could hear his people whispering in the distance, heard the soft sound of a lullaby as one of the women tried to calm a fretful child.

Staring up at the stars, he wondered what the future held for his people, for Kathy, for himself. The day when he was to have died had come and gone, giving him a second chance at life. No more gunfighting, he thought, no more living on the edge. It was time to make his dreams of building a ranch come true. He had the land; he had a stake. He glanced at Kathy sleeping beside him. Soon, he would have a wife and,

God willing, children. It was a scary thought. He hadn't been responsible for anyone but himself in years.

Kathy stirred beside him, tossing restlessly. She moaned softly, then began to whimper, "No, no, I didn't mean it."

"Kathy? Kathy, wake up."

"I'm sorry," she sobbed, "so sorry."

He shook her shoulder gently. "Kathy, darlin', wake up."

She woke with a start, her eyes wide and frightened, her face pale in the moonlight. She stared at him for a moment, then began to cry.

"Come here, darlin'," Dalton said, gathering her in his arms.

She clung to him. He could feel her trembling as the last vestiges of her nightmare faded away.

"Shhh," he murmured. "Shhh, it's all right now. It's over."

"It was awful," she said, sniffing. "I saw him everywhere I looked, that man I killed. His blood was on my hands, and I couldn't wash it away. I scrubbed and I scrubbed, and it wouldn't go away."

He held her closer, one hand stroking her back.

She blinked at him, the horror of her nightmare fading. "Have you ever had any bad dreams?"

"Oh, yeah, usually after I've had too much to drink."

"I want to go home." She looked up at him, her dark eyes luminous with unshed tears. "Do you think it's possible for us to go back?"

"I don't know. But I don't belong in your world,

318

darlin', and you sure as hell don't belong in mine."

"Dalton . . ." She held him tightly, as if he might suddenly disappear. "I'm so afraid of losing you."

"I know." His lips brushed her cheek. He was scared, too—scared of losing her, scared of finding himself back in Kathy's time, trapped between worlds in a thick gray mist, not dead, not alive.

He glanced around, wishing they were alone. As weak as he was, as sore as he was, he had a desperate urge to make love to her, an incomprehensible feeling that he needed to possess her, to brand her as his before it was too late.

But this was not the place, and as sleep claimed him, he wondered if he would ever make love to her again.

Chapter Twenty-one

Because of the wounded, they were forced to travel slowly. Hours in the saddle left Dalton feeling sore and utterly exhausted, and he sometimes wondered if he wouldn't be better off walking.

His strength returned gradually. His wounds ached less. By the time they reached the fort a little over a week later, he was feeling pretty good, though his wounds were still tender to the touch.

They reached the fort late in the afternoon. Kathy stared at the clump of wooden buildings and corrals, at the flag hanging limply in the hot sun. This was a fort? Where were the high walls, the big gates, the sentries patrolling the catwalks?

The notes of a bugle rose in the air and a bunch of men in Army blue streamed out of the buildings and assembled in a group.

Kathy and Dalton were escorted to a squat wooden building, which proved to be the hospital, and taken into a back room.

A tall, thin man wearing a white coat over his uniform came in a few minutes later.

"I'm Doctor Blankenship, the post surgeon," he said. He gestured at Dalton. "Climb up on that table, son, and let me have a look at your wounds."

Dalton stripped off his shirt and sat on the table. Kathy stood beside him.

"Mrs. Nash is seeing about quarters for you," the doctor remarked as he examined Dalton's injuries. To Kathy's untrained eye, they seemed to be healing nicely, though he would have more scars.

The doctor applied a fresh dressing to the wound in Dalton's temple. "Try to keep this dry," he said. "The colonel's striker will be here soon to show you to your quarters. Oh," he said as the hospital door opened and a tall, clean-shaven young man entered the room. "Here he is now."

A short time later, Dalton stood in front of a small mirror, scraping away a three-week growth of beard.

Kathy luxuriated in a tub of hot water, her gaze lingering on Dalton. The bandages on his shoulder and swathed around his middle looked very white against the dark bronze of his skin.

They would be traveling light when they went to Boston, she mused. They had lost everything in the raid except the clothes they'd been wearing. She grinned as she imagined meeting Dalton's mother. No doubt the woman would be shocked when her future daughter-in-law showed up in a doeskin tunic and beaded moccasins.

"What are you grinning at?" Dalton asked.

"I was just thinking about meeting your mother."

"Yeah?"

Kathy glanced pointedly at his clout. "We aren't exactly dressed for Boston society."

Dalton grunted softly. "I'm sure we can get a change of clothes at the subtler's."

"I hope so." Reaching for a towel, she rose from the tub, aware of Dalton's hungry gaze. "Not here," she said, shaking her head.

"Why not?" he asked with a roguish smile. "We're alone."

"No, Dalton. Anyone might walk in. And you're not fully recovered yet."

She was right, dammit. As much as he wanted her, he wasn't sure he was up to it. Still, he was willing to give it a try.

Crossing the floor, he tugged on a corner of the towel.

"Dalton, you're incorrigible!"

"If that means I'm hard as a rock, you're right." He drew her into his arms, eliciting a small shriek when the towel fell away. Lowering his head, he nuzzled the warm curve of her neck.

With a sigh, Kathy melted against him, all her arguments lost in the wonder of his kiss, in the feel of his skin against her bare breasts. She pressed against him, wanting to be closer.

She twisted out of his arms and dived for the towel as someone knocked on the door.

"Yeah?" Dalton called. "Who is it?"

"Private Stuart, sir. Colonel Nash has invited you to dine with him this evening."

"Tell the colonel we appreciate the offer," Dalton replied, "but we don't have anything suitable to wear."

"The colonel's striker is taking care of that. He should be here in just a few minutes. Dinner is at seven. Sharp."

"We'll be there."

"Yes, sir. Very good, sir."

Dalton blew out a breath. "Well, what do you think of that?"

"I can't have dinner with the colonel," Kathy wailed. "Look at me! My hair's a mess. I don't have any makeup. I—"

"You look fine."

Kathy grimaced. "Yeah, right."

Crossing the floor, he took her in his arms. "Hey, stop worrying."

"I can't help it. It's what I'm good at."

"I can think of something else you're good at."

"Honestly, Dalton, don't you ever think of anything else?"

He lifted one brow in wry amusement. "How can I, when you smell so good, and all you're wearing is a towel?"

She drew a deep breath and let it out in a long, shuddering sigh as she ran her hands over his shoulders. His skin was warm and firm beneath her fingertips, and suddenly her thoughts were running parallel with his. "Later, okay?"

"Definitely okay," he replied.

*   *   *

Kathy slipped into the dress that had been provided for her, wondering if she would ever get used to all the undergarments nineteenth-century women were compelled to wear. The dress itself was pretty enough. A dark green plaid, it had a round neck, long fitted sleeves, and a full skirt.

She glanced over at Dalton, who looked quite handsome in a white shirt, buff-colored trousers, and brown boots.

"Ready?" he asked.

"I guess so."

"Let's go get this over with, then," he muttered.

The colonel's wife met them at the door. She was a tiny woman, with merry blue eyes and skin lined by years of living on the plains.

"Come in, come in." She beamed at Kathy. "You can't imagine how glad I am to see you. We get so few visitors here."

She ushered them into the parlor. "The colonel will be here in a moment. Please, sit down."

"Thank you, Mrs. Nash," Kathy said. She sat down on a high-backed sofa, and Dalton sat beside her.

The colonel's quarters were larger than Kathy had expected. White lace curtains covered the windows. A carpet, obviously imported, covered the floor in the parlor. There were sepia-toned photographs of a stern-faced young man and a pretty young woman on the mantle. Kathy assumed they were the Nashes' children.

"We don't stand on ceremony here, my dear. You must call me Verna," the colonel's wife said. She sat down on the chair beside the sofa, her back ramrod stiff, her hands folded in her lap.

"Thank you. I'm Kathy, and this is my husband, Joe Dalton." Earlier, they had decided to continue with the charade that they were married. They had also decided it would be easier all around not to mention Dalton's Lakota name, or to mention his connection with the Lakota.

Verna smiled at Kathy, her expression sympathetic. "Nash tells me you were captured by the Sioux. That must have been dreadful."

Kathy glanced at Dalton. "Well, not really. They treated us very well."

Verna Nash sat back in her chair, clearly disbelieving. She looked at Dalton. "Doctor Blankenship tells me you were wounded in the battle."

"Yes, ma'am."

Verna studied him closely for a moment. It was obvious to Kathy that the colonel's wife was wondering if Dalton had Indian blood, but was too polite to ask.

"Where are you from, Mr. Dalton?"

"Boston."

"Really?"

"Yes, but I haven't been back there for quite some time."

They were saved from more questions by the appearance of the colonel. Verna made introductions, and then they went in to dinner.

The colonel and Dalton discussed the "Indian problem" over dinner. According to the colonel, there would never be peace in the West until the tribes were subdued.

"But surely there's room enough for everyone," Kathy remarked.

Verna and the colonel looked at her as if she had suggested sharing space with Satan and his angels. After a long, silent moment, Verna reached across the table and patted Kathy on the hand. "Of course, we all wish that were possible, my dear, but the Indians are savages, you know. Why, the tales I could tell you!" She pressed a hand to her heart. "They're brutal creatures, you know, capable of terrible atrocities."

Kathy looked at Dalton. His jaw was clenched tight. "Would you excuse us, please? I'm very tired." She smiled apologetically at Verna Nash. "We've had a long journey, and Joe is not fully recovered from his wounds."

"Of course, dear," Verna said. She glanced over at her husband. "We understand, don't we, Nash?"

"Indeed."

The colonel and his wife walked them to the door.

"If you need anything," Nash said, "just tell my striker."

"Thank you," Kathy said. She laid her hand on Dalton's arm. It was rock hard beneath her fingertips.

"I hope you'll be comfortable," Verna said. "Do come visit us again before you leave."

"Yes, we will, thank you," Kathy said. "Good night."

She followed Dalton down the stairs. Anger flowed off him in waves.

"Savages!" he muttered. "Atrocities!" He loosed a string of obscenities that burned her ears.

"Dalton, wait."

He swung around to face her, his eyes dark with fury. "Old biddy. I could tell her stories that would curl her hair."

"Dalton . . ."

He swore again. "I'll wager that husband of hers has committed some atrocities of his own!"

"Dalton, calm down."

"I am calm."

"Yeah, right."

"I feel like a damned traitor."

Kathy bit down on her lower lip. It was her fault he felt that way. He knew she was afraid of being left here alone, knew she was afraid she couldn't get back to her own time if they were separated. "I'm sorry."

The anger drained out of Dalton. With a sigh, he drew Kathy into his arms. He could have kicked himself. He knew what she was thinking, knew she was blaming herself.

She pressed herself against him. "I'm scared."

"Don't be."

"I can't help it. I feel like time is running out for us."

Dalton's arms tightened around her, the gesture more eloquent than words, and she knew he had felt it, too—that sense that their days together were growing short.

She looked up at him. "If you could choose, would you stay here, or go back to my time?"

"I don't know." He brushed his knuckles over her

cheek. Neither decision appealed to him. He didn't want to stay here without Kathy, but at least here, he was alive. He didn't think he could bear to go back to her time, to be caught between two worlds again, to see her and yet not be part of her world, to hold her, but not be able to possess her. Talk about hell. He would be damned either way.

He looked into her eyes and saw his own fears, his own desire, mirrored there. Sweeping her into his arms, he carried her swiftly down the row of ugly wooden bungalows to the one at the end. He took the steps two at a time, eager to be alone with her, to possess her, to brand her as his for now and always.

He didn't bother to light the lamp. Carrying her into the bedroom, he lowered her to the bed. There was an urgency between them that hadn't been there before. Kathy clutched at him, her fingers digging into his back, assuring herself that he was there, that he was real. Her senses seemed more alive than ever before, and she was acutely aware of the coarse cotton sheet beneath her back, the distant sound of a soldier calling the hour, the alien scents of lamp oil and the land itself. But mostly she was aware of Dalton, of his hands exploring, caressing, arousing her until she was wild with need, until she cried his name, desperate for the fulfillment only he could give her.

Only later, lying in utter contentment in the circle of his arms, did she remember that he was still recovering from his wounds.

She traced meaningless patterns on his chest, her fingers brushing against the bandage wrapped around his middle. "Are you all right?"

He made a soft sound in his throat. "Never better."

"I love you, Dalton."

His arm tightened around her shoulders. The words didn't come easy to him, but he said them, never meaning them more. "And I love you, darlin', more than you can imagine."

She clung to his words as if they were a talisman that could bind them together, shield them from unseen forces that might tear them apart.

Dalton held Kathy close until she fell asleep, and then he slid out of bed. Dressing quickly, he buckled on his gunbelt and left the bungalow. Outside, he waited a moment, listening, and then he made his way through the shadows to the storehouse where the Lakota were being held.

Two soldiers stood guard, one on either side of the door. They were leaning against the building, apparently dozing on their feet.

Dalton stood in the shadows, watching, for several minutes and then, on cat-quiet feet, he went around the building and came up alongside the guard on the right. Clamping his hand over the man's mouth, he struck him a quick blow over the head, then slowly lowered him to the ground. Going around the back of the building, he came up alongside the second guard. He rendered him unconscious in the same way, then searched the guard's pockets until he found the key. He relieved both men of their weapons, then unlocked the door to the storehouse.

"Okute?"

"Hau."

"Get your people together. Hurry."

Okute did not waste time asking questions. In less than five minutes, the Lakota were ready to leave.

"Here," Dalton said, handing Okute the soldier's handguns.

"Pilamaya."

"Go quickly," Dalton said.

"Come with us, *tahunsa.*"

Slowly, Dalton shook his head. "No. My destiny lies along another path. Travel in safety, my brother."

The two men embraced, and then, like shadows on the wind, the Lakota drifted out of the storehouse and disappeared into the darkness.

Dalton blew out a long, low sigh. With luck, Okute and his people would be long gone by morning.

He dragged the two guards into the storehouse, closed and locked the door, and threw the key into a clump of brush. Keeping to the shadows, he made his way back to the bungalow.

Kathy was awake when he entered the bedroom. "Dalton! Where were you? I was so afraid."

He sat down on the edge of the bed, and she threw her arms around him.

"I freed Okute and the others."

"You did?"

"Yeah. With any luck at all, they'll get away."

"Maybe the Army won't go after them."

"Maybe."

He kissed her cheek, undressed, and slid into bed beside her.

"I hope they get away," Kathy murmured as she snuggled up against him.

"Yeah." He turned on his side and drew her into

his arms. He had done all he could. The rest was up to Okute.

She woke to the sound of a bugle. For a moment, she couldn't remember where she was, and then she felt Dalton's arm lying over her waist, felt his warmth at her back. She wondered if Okute and his people had managed to get away, and what the future held for them, and for herself and Dalton.

He stirred, his hand creeping up her belly to cup her breast, and she forgot everything else. He pressed kisses to her back and shoulders, then rose on one elbow and began raining kisses over her neck and cheek.

A soft sound of pleasure rose in Kathy's throat as she rolled onto her back and wrapped her arms around his neck.

"What a wonderful way to wake up," she murmured as his weight settled over her.

Dalton smiled, pleased by her quick response to his touch. Lowering his head, he drank deeply from her lips.

There was a shout from outside, followed by the sound of running feet, and more shouts.

Five minutes later, there was a hard knock on the door.

Dalton blew out a sigh as he rolled out of bed and pulled on his trousers.

A red-faced corporal stood at the door. "Colonel Nash would like to see you immediately."

"What about?"

"He didn't say, sir, just told me to get you, right quick."

Dalton nodded. "I'll be there as soon as I get dressed."

"Yes, sir."

Dalton shut the door. He knew what the colonel wanted.

Returning to the bedroom, he reached for his shirt.

"Who was that?" Kathy asked.

"The colonel wants to see me."

"Why?"

Dalton slanted a wry glance in her direction. "Why do you think?"

"Oh." Kathy sat up, the sheet tucked under her arms. "They can't prove you did it, can they?"

"I don't think so."

"What if they can?"

"They'll probably lock me up."

"Dalton!"

"Don't worry. They can't prove anything unless somebody saw me."

"I'm coming with you."

"All right."

Twenty minutes later, Dalton and Kathy were in the colonel's office. They were not invited to sit down.

Dalton stood at ease, one hand resting idly on the butt of his gun. "Something I can do for you, Colonel Nash?"

"Someone turned the captives loose last night."

"Really?"

"You wouldn't know anything about it, would you?"

Dalton shook his head. "No, should I?"

Nash regarded him through narrowed eyes. "You tell me. You came in with them."

"That's right."

Nash's gaze moved to Kathy. "What about you?"

"Me?" Kathy squeaked. "Surely you don't think I had anything to do with it?"

"I don't know." The colonel slammed his hand flat on the desk. "I want some answers."

"Fact is, neither one of us heard anything," Dalton said. He slid an arm around Kathy's waist and drew her close. "My wife and I are newlyweds, and last night was the first real chance we've had to be alone since we were captured by the Sioux, if you take my meaning."

Kathy blushed.

A tide of pale red washed up the colonel's neck. "I see." He shuffled through the papers on his desk. "That will be all."

Taking Kathy by the hand, Dalton led her out of the colonel's office.

Outside, Kathy punched him on the arm. "Stinker."

Dalton grinned at her. "I had to think of something, quick."

"Do you think Okute will get away?"

"I'd say there was a good chance." He looked over to where a bunch of soldiers were getting ready to ride out. "They've got a good start. And I think we should get started ourselves."

*   *   *

They left the fort an hour later, headed for Johnson's Landing, which was the nearest town. From there, they would take a stage to Ash Grove, and then catch the train to Boston.

It was a beautiful day for a ride. Taffy Girl pranced and tossed her head; Dalton's big buckskin stallion pulled on the reins, obviously eager to run.

"What do you say?" Dalton asked. "Shall we let them go?"

"I don't know," Kathy said dubiously.

"Just a slow gallop, then," Dalton suggested, and she knew he was as eager as the horses to go thundering over the grassland.

"All right," she said.

Dalton touched his heels to his horse's flanks and the buckskin shot forward. Taffy Girl immediately took off after the stallion. With a shriek, Kathy grabbed for the saddle horn.

Dalton drew back a little on the reins, slowing the stallion to an easy lope.

It was exhilarating, riding across the plains, with only miles of green grass and blue sky as far as the eye could see. After a few minutes, Kathy released the saddle horn and let herself enjoy the ride, the feel of the breeze in her hair, the warmth of the sun on her face.

She loved horseback riding, loved the sense of freedom it gave her, the bond she felt with her horse. It gave her an odd sense of power, to be in control of such a large animal.

She watched Dalton. She never tired of looking at

him, never grew weary of thinking about him. A look, a touch, and her insides turned to mush. It was like being a teenager again, madly in love, certain no one else had ever felt the way she felt, certain that the love they shared was a love like no other.

That, at least, was true. Surely she and Dalton shared a love like no other. It was a sobering thought, reminding her that they could be separated at any moment. But surely Fate would not have brought them together only to tear them apart. She couldn't bear the thought of going back to her own time without him. What would she do without Dalton? He had become the most important thing in her life, her reason for going on. He had given her hope and love, pulled her out of the well of despair she had been floundering in ever since Wayne's death. She couldn't go on without him, wouldn't want to go on without him.

They rode for several hours, then stopped alongside a shallow stream to rest and water the horses.

Kathy sat with her back against a rock, her thoughts drifting, while Dalton watered the horses, then tethered them to a bush so they could graze.

"Something wrong?" he asked, dropping down beside her.

"No."

"Come on, something's bothering you. What is it?"

"I don't know how to explain it. I feel like Fate's manipulating us in some way."

"What do you mean?"

Kathy blew out a sigh. "I don't know. It's like the village was attacked so that we'd have to leave. And now we're going to Boston, and..." she shrugged. "I don't know. I guess I'm just scared."

"Scared?" He frowned at her. "Of what?"

"The future. I feel like time is getting away from us, that we're not going to be together much longer."

Her words made his gut clench. He knew exactly what she meant. He remembered standing near the stream back at the Triple Bar C, remembered thinking of the promises he had made to his parents. Was that why he had been given a second chance, to fulfill those promises?

"You feel it, too, don't you?" Kathy asked.

"Yeah." He'd made a promise to himself, too, he mused, thinking of the land he owned in Wyoming. He'd always wanted to build a ranch there. Would Fate grant him time enough for that, as well?

Dalton slid his arm around Kathy's waist and drew her up against him. "I'll never leave you—you know that, don't you?"

"But what if it isn't up to you?"

"I don't know, darlin'. I guess we'll just have to play the cards we're dealt."

With a sigh, Kathy rested her head on his shoulder. He was right. There was no point in worrying about things over which they had no control.

They reached Johnson's Landing at dusk. It was a large town, prosperous by the look of it. They saw several Army mounts tethered in front of the saloon.

After leaving their horses at the livery, they walked down the boardwalk to the hotel. Dalton asked for a room with a bath and in a remarkably short time,

Kathy was happily immersed in a tub of hot water.

"You look as happy as a flea on a long-haired dog," Dalton mused.

"I am." She regarded him through half-closed eyes as he began to undress, felt a thrill of anticipation uncurl deep inside her when she realized he meant to get into the tub with her.

Her heart was pounding as he slid into the tub behind her, his body cradling hers. His hands cupped her breasts, and she felt his lips move in her hair.

"I begin to see why you like baths so much," he drawled.

Kathy laughed softly. "Do you?"

"Oh, yeah." She shivered with pleasure as he slid one hand over her belly. "Like that, do you?" he asked.

"Hmmm, very much."

"And this?" His hands caressed her thighs.

Her breath quickened as his hands moved over her. "Dalton . . ."

"What?" he asked, his voice almost a growl. "Tell me what you want."

"I want you. Inside me. Now."

She didn't have to tell him twice. In one fluid movement, he picked her up and stepped out of the tub. Dripping water over the floor, he carried her to the bed, placed her on it, and lowered himself over her. He whispered love words to her, his voice husky with desire, and she embraced him with her whole heart and soul, praying, fervently, that his seed might take root within her, that she might have a child to love when Dalton was gone.

Later, they bathed again, then went to the hotel dining room for dinner. Still later, they walked to the stage station to check the schedule. There was a stage leaving for the East first thing in the morning. Fate was with them, Kathy mused—or perhaps against them, depending on what awaited them in Boston.

Chapter Twenty-two

It took two days by stage to reach Ash Grove. Kathy felt bad, seeing Taffy Girl and the buckskin tethered by long leads to the back of the coach even though Dalton assured her the horses would be fine.

When they reached Ash Grove, they secured a room in the hotel, bathed, and went to dinner. After dinner, they took a walk through the town, then went back to the hotel where they made love, then fell asleep in each other's arms.

They boarded the train at noon the next day. Taffy Girl had gone up the wooden ramp into the stock car without protest; Dalton's stallion had balked and refused to enter the car until Dalton blindfolded him.

She had expected the train ride to be an improvement over the bouncy, cramped stagecoach, and it was. Even so, trains in the nineteenth century were nothing like what she was used to. It was noisy. It was smelly. Soot and ashes and sparks floated through the windows. The man in front of them puffed on a cheap cigar that smelled even worse than the train.

The woman across the aisle was traveling with four children, and couldn't control any of them. They ran up and down the aisle, playing cowboys and Indians, until Dalton caught the oldest one by the arm and threatened to scalp him if they didn't settle down.

She had never liked flying, but she thought, in this instance, she would gladly have taken a plane.

With a sigh, Kathy turned away from the window and looked at Dalton. "Maybe we should have wired your mother that we were coming."

He shrugged. "Maybe."

"Does she still work for that family you told me about?"

"The Worthinghams? Yeah, as far as I know. She and her husband live in a cottage behind the big house. It's a nice place, big enough for the two of them."

"Did your mother ever have any more children?"

"No."

"I hope she'll like me."

Dalton put his arms around her shoulders and gave her a squeeze. "She's gonna love you. I just hope . . ."

"What?"

"I hope she's all right."

"Why wouldn't she be?"

"I don't know. I've just had this feeling . . ." He shook his head. "I hope I'm not too late."

* * *

Kathy was glad when they reached Boston. She was tired of the noise and the smoke and more than ready for a long, hot bath and a good night's sleep.

Kathy waited at the depot while Dalton went to collect their horses.

Their first stop was the livery stable. After making sure both horses were settled in clean stalls with fresh hay and water, they went to the bank where Dalton kept an account. He withdrew several hundred dollars and they went shopping for a new wardrobe.

"You first," Dalton said.

The sign outside the dressmaker's shop read *Madame Tulare, Modiste.*

Kathy was enchanted by the lovely gowns inside. No gingham frocks here, but gowns of silk and satin, bombazine and velvet. Dalton told her to buy whatever she liked. She ordered several dresses, which the seamstress promised to have ready by the end of the week. There were several ready-made dresses to choose from and Kathy picked a pretty russet silk that brought out the red highlights in her hair. It had fitted sleeves, a square neckline, and a slim skirt that was gathered to form a modest bustle in the back. She felt like a queen. She also bought a pair of half-boots made of kidskin. Dalton declared she looked good enough to eat.

They went to the tailor shop next. Kathy waited for Dalton in the front of the shop. Sitting near the front window, she watched the traffic in the street. Boston was a busy place, filled with people in a hurry. Well-dressed women paraded along the sidewalk, their faces shaded by dainty parasols. She saw men in dapper suits, and girls, obviously servants, who were running errands.

She hardly recognized Dalton when he appeared. He was clad in a pair of black trousers, a white linen shirt and wine-colored cravat, and a black jacket that emphasized his broad shoulders and swarthy good looks.

"Wow," she said, wiggling her eyebrows in her best Groucho Marx imitation. "Wow, wow, wow."

One corner of his mouth lifted in a wry grin. "Quit that."

"Dalton, you look so pretty, like the groom on the top of a wedding cake."

"Are you trying to remind me that I asked you to marry me?"

"No, but now that you mention it . . ."

"I haven't forgotten." He tucked her arm through his. "Come on, let's go get a hotel room, and then go out to the estate. We can spend the day in the cottage." He smiled at Kathy, his eyes alight with anticipation. "I can't wait to see the look on my mother's face when she comes in tonight and finds us there."

A hired hack conveyed them to the Worthingham estate. Kathy stared at the place in open-mouthed awe. It was huge. Made of glistening white stone, it looked like a storybook castle. Tall trees and hedges surrounded the house. There was a huge fountain in the front yard.

Alighting from the hack, they walked along a wide pathway toward the rear of the house. The backyard was as impressive as the front, with more trees, more hedges, another fountain. There were stables off to the left. A peacock sat in the shade of a large gazebo, preening its feathers.

The cottage where Dalton's mother lived was to the right of the main house. It was a pretty little place, white with yellow trim. Colorful flowers bordered the walkway that led to the house. A thin plume of blue-gray smoke rose from the chimney.

Dalton felt a rush of unease. No one should be in the cottage in the middle of the day.

"What's wrong?" Kathy asked.

"Probably nothing," he said, but the sense of fore-boding increased as he opened the door. "Ma?"

"Dalton? Is that you?"

"Yeah." He took Kathy by the hand and led her down a narrow hallway and into a large bedroom lo-cated in the rear of the house.

He paused in the doorway. Peeking around him, Kathy saw a small woman propped up in a big four-poster bed. Her hair was brown, just turning gray. Her face was pale, making her dark eyes seem huge. And she was thin, so thin.

"Dalton!" The woman put down the book she had been reading and held out her arms.

Dalton crossed the floor in two long strides. Drop-ping to his knees beside the bed, he drew his mother into his arms.

"What brings you here this time of year?" his mother asked. She looked at Kathy over her son's shoulder. "And who is this lovely young woman?"

"Ma, this is Kathy. Kathy, this is my mother."

Kathy smiled. "I'm pleased to meet you, Mrs.—"
Her voice trailed off as she realized she didn't know
her future mother-in-law's last name.

"Call me Julianna, dear." She looked at Dalton.
"You've never brought a woman home before."

"She's special, Ma," Dalton said. "We're getting
married."

"Married! That's wonderful."

"Ma, what's wrong? Why are you in bed?"

A shadow passed over Julianna's eyes. "I'm fine.
Just feeling a little under the weather today. Dalton,
it's so good to see you." She patted the bed. "Come,
sit beside me, Kathy, and let us get acquainted. Dalton, why don't you go find us something to drink?"

Rising to his feet, he kissed his mother on the
cheek, then left the room.

"My dear," Julianna said, taking one of Kathy's
hands in hers, "I am so happy to meet you. How soon
are you planning to be married?"

"I'm not sure."

Julianna patted Kathy's hand. "I hope you'll make
it soon."

"Me, too."

"I always dreamed of having a daughter," Julianna
said. "We tried several times, but . . ." She sighed.
"I could never carry another child after Dalton."

"I'm sorry. He's a wonderful man."

"Do you love him very much?"

"Oh, yes."

"How long will you be staying in Boston?"

"I don't know."

A rattle of china heralded Dalton's return. He entered the room carrying a bottle of brandy and three glasses.

"Brandy?" Julianna asked.

Dalton shrugged. "I thought a toast was in order."

"Of course," his mother said. "For the bride and groom. Dalton, I can't tell you how happy I am."

He poured brandy for his mother and Kathy, and then a glass for himself.

Julianna lifted her glass. "To the bride and groom," she said. "May you have a long and happy life together, and make me a grandmother as soon as possible."

"I'll do my best," Dalton said with a wry grin. "Is Murray up at the house?"

"Yes."

"I think I'll go up and let him know we're here."

Julianna smiled. "You do that. It will give me a chance to get acquainted with Kathy."

Dalton brushed a kiss across Kathy's cheek. "I'll be back soon."

He found Murray in the kitchen, sharing a cup of coffee with the cook.

"Dalton!" Murray exclaimed. "What are you doing here?"

"Just felt like I needed to come home," Dalton said.

"I'm glad you did."

"I'll leave you two alone," Mrs. Sheffield said. "It's good to see you again, Dalton."

"It's good to see you, too. Any chance of getting one of your apple pies while I'm here?"

"I think that can be arranged," Mrs. Sheffield said.

Dalton sat down at the table across from Murray. "What's wrong with my mother?"

Murray sat back in his chair, looking suddenly old and tired. "She's dying."

"Dying?"

Murray nodded.

"But why? What's wrong?"

"It's her heart."

"Her heart?"

"She's always had a weak heart. Didn't you know?"

Dalton shook his head. "No."

"It's true. She never told me, either, until she couldn't hide it anymore. You know how badly she wanted children. We tried several times, but she miscarried them all. The last one was just a few months ago. I came home a few days after she lost the last one and found her lying on the floor, unconscious."

"A few months ago! She's forty-eight years old."

Murray seemed to shrink in his chair. "I know. I'm glad you're here. She's been praying you'd come home before . . ." Murray choked on the words. "I'm glad you're here," he said again.

"Yeah." Dalton stared out the kitchen window. He'd known something was wrong.

"I'm sorry, Dalton. When I found out about her heart, we stopped—ah, being intimate. But then one night we went to a party, and we both had a little too much to drink, and I . . ." A slow flush climbed up Murray's neck. "I never meant for it to happen, but I'm not made of stone."

"How much time does she have?"

Murray shrugged. "A few weeks, maybe a month. Who knows?" He looked up, his eyes filled with anguish. "You'll stay until . . ."

"Yeah."

"I'm sorry, Dalton. It's all my fault. I would have written if I'd known where you were."

Dalton nodded. He couldn't believe she was dying. His mother had always been so full of life. When they lived with the Lakota, she had always made the best of things. Even when times were hard and food was scarce, she hadn't gotten discouraged. *Things will get better,* she'd say, and they always did. Even though he hadn't spent a lot of time with her in the last few years, he had always known she was there if he needed her. He wished now that he had made the time to visit more often, that he'd been the kind of son she deserved. He knew she was appalled by what he did for a living, knew she would have preferred him to stay in Boston and settle down, but she had never said or done anything to make him feel bad, never acted as though she was ashamed of him, or of what he did.

More regrets. His life was full of them.

Contemplating her son's wedding seemed to infuse Julianna with new life. She insisted on accompanying Kathy to the dressmakers, oohed and aahed as they pored over the different styles, and proclaimed Kathy's choice the perfect one. Kathy had remarked that it seemed foolish to spend money on a fancy dress when there wouldn't be anyone at the ceremony except the two of them and Dalton's family, but he had insisted. *We're only gonna do this once,* he had said, *so let's do it right.*

Now, a week later, Julianna's eyes were bright as she watched Kathy try on her gown.

"You're going to be a beautiful bride," she murmured with a sigh. "Dalton is a lucky man."

"Thank you."

"You never told me how you two met."

"Didn't Dalton tell you?"

"No. You know how men are."

Kathy smiled. Stalling for time, she asked the dressmaker if the hemline shouldn't be just a little shorter. She paid scant attention to the woman's reply as she cast about for an answer to Julianna's question. Finally, she opted for the truth.

"I met him at my ranch."

"Oh? You're from out West then?"

"Yes, Montana."

A melancholy smile passed over Julianna's lips. "It's beautiful country, isn't it? I suppose Dalton told you we lived with the Indians for many years."

"Yes." At the dressmaker's request, Kathy made a half-turn.

"Dalton's father was quite a handsome man. Dalton looks just like him. It was a hard life, but very satisfying in many ways. Dalton always said he'd go back someday, but he never did."

Kathy nodded. Dalton had decided they shouldn't say anything to his mother about their recent stay with the Lakota for fear that hearing what had happened would upset her.

"I often wonder what happened to Okute and Star

Chaser and to Yellow Grass Woman.'' She laughed self-consciously. ''Listen to me, rambling on like an old woman.''

Kathy smiled and said nothing, but, for a moment, she had been transported back to the day of the massacre.

The dressmaker finished pinning the hem and stood up. ''All done,'' she said with a smile. ''It'll be ready tomorrow afternoon.''

''Thank you.''

Kathy quickly changed clothes and they left the shop. ''Julianna, are you all right?'' she asked.

''Fine. Don't worry about me.''

She didn't look fine, though, Kathy thought as they walked across the street to where Dalton was waiting for them. He seemed worried as he helped his mother into the carriage they had borrowed from the Worthinghams.

''So,'' he asked. ''How'd it go?''

''Fine,'' Kathy said.

''Wait until you see her,'' Julianna said. ''You're going to fall in love with her all over again.''

''That shouldn't be too hard,'' Dalton murmured as he handed Kathy into the carriage, then took the seat across from her. ''I talked to the minister. He said Saturday afternoon will be fine.''

Kathy smiled. In two days, she would be Mrs. Dalton Crowkiller.

''Kathy was telling me she has a ranch in Montana,'' Julianna remarked.

Dalton nodded. ''That's right.''

"Are you going to live there after you're married?"

"I don't know." Dalton and Kathy exchanged glances. "I think maybe we'll be staying here."

"In Boston? But you've never liked it here."

Dalton shrugged. "We'll be all right."

Julianna's eyes filled with tears. "You're staying for me, aren't you? You don't have to."

"Ma," Dalton said with a wry grin, "have you ever known me to do anything I didn't want to do?"

Julianna laughed through her tears. "No, I guess not." She looked over at Kathy. "He can be a very stubborn man."

"And very persuasive," Kathy said. "He made me buy a horse."

"Tell me you're sorry," Dalton said.

"You know I'm not."

"Well, what are you complaining about then?"

"I'm not complaining," Kathy said.

Julianna laughed softly. "Children, children," she chided softly.

"Sorry, Ma."

When they reached the cottage, Julianna went into the bedroom, saying she thought she would rest for a while.

"I like your mother," Kathy said.

"I knew you would. I think maybe she's one of the reasons I was sent back here."

"Really? Why?"

"I'm not sure." He stared out the window. A memory tugged at the back of his mind, distant and just out of reach.

UNDER A PRAIRIE MOON

Murray came home a short time later. He brought dinner with him, and they spent a quiet evening together, with Dalton and his mother reminiscing about their early days in Boston.

About ten, Dalton and Kathy took their leave and went back to the hotel.

The following afternoon, Julianna accompanied Kathy when she went for the final fitting on her wedding dress.

"I hope you don't mind," Julianna said, "but I've invited the Worthinghams to the wedding, and a few of my friends."

"No, I don't mind."

"I'm glad. I know I should have asked you first."

Kathy smiled at Dalton's mother. "It's all right, really. I don't mind."

They went to a small cafe for lunch, then returned to the cottage. Dalton was there, waiting for them.

"Well," Julianna said, "tomorrow's the big day."

Dalton looked at Kathy and grinned. "You haven't changed your mind, have you?"

"Not a chance."

Julianna beamed at them. "You two are made for each other, I can tell."

"I think so, too," Kathy agreed.

Dalton nodded. "You could say Fate brought us together."

"Yes," Kathy said, "you could indeed."

On Saturday morning, Kathy woke with a fluttery stomach. Today was her wedding day. She rolled onto her side, her heart swelling with love as she gazed at

Dalton, sleeping beside her. She had never expected to fall in love again, to marry again. Was she making a mistake? She had no idea how long she and Dalton would be allowed to stay together, and yet, did any couple ever know how many days or years they would have together? She had thought she would spend the rest of her life with Wayne, but Life had had other plans. She only knew that she wanted to be Dalton's wife, to have his children, to grow old at his side, God willing.

"Hey, bride," Dalton murmured. "Today's the day."

"Did you think I'd forget?"

"I'm more afraid that you'll change your mind."

"Why would I do that?"

"I can think of a lot of reasons, darlin'."

"Really?" She sat up, looking worried. "Are you having second thoughts?"

"Not me. Hell, you're the best thing that ever happened to me, but . . ."

"But what?"

"You know."

Lifting one hand, she caressed his beard-roughened cheek. "We can't do anything about that."

"I love you, darlin'."

"And I love you." Kathy's eyes widened as a distant clock chimed the hour. "Dalton, it's ten o'clock!"

"So?"

"So we're supposed to be at the church in two hours."

He looked puzzled. "We've got plenty of time. It's just across the street."

Kathy let out a sigh of exasperation. Men! "Dalton, I have to take a bath and go over to your mom's and get dressed and ..." Sitting up, she ran a hand through her hair. What she wouldn't give for a blow-dryer or some hot rollers.

Dalton let out a sigh of his own as Kathy bounded out of bed and started getting dressed. He could be ready in ten minutes, he thought, and wondered why it took women so long.

Twenty minutes later, he dropped Kathy off at the cottage.

"See you at the church at noon." He pulled her into his arms and kissed her. "Don't be late."

"Don't you be late," Julianna warned. "Murray, you be sure he's there on time."

"Don't worry your pretty little head," Murray replied. "I'll have him at the church at high noon, and sober, too."

Julianna gave her husband a playful slap on the arm. "You just be certain that he's not the only one who's sober. Now, go along with you." Julianna closed the door, then turned and smiled at Kathy. "Men," she said with a grin.

Dalton stood at the altar, feeling slightly uncomfortable at momentarily being the center of attention. There were about twenty people in the church. He recognized most of them. They knew who he was, and what he did for a living. Murray stood beside him, relaxed, as always. In all the years Dalton had known the man, he had never seen him flustered. Julianna was sitting in the front pew. Dalton smiled at his mother, and she winked at him.

And then Kathy was walking down the aisle toward him and Dalton forgot everything else. Beautiful was the only word to describe her. Or maybe angelic. She wore a dress of white silk. A veil covered her face.

Stepping forward to meet her, Dalton took her hand in his and squeezed it. Then they turned to face the minister.

Kathy slid a glance at Dalton. Tall, dark and handsome, she thought.

He caught her gaze and mouthed the words, *I love you,* and she repeated them back to him.

His voice sounded a little shaky as he promised to love her so long as he lived.

Tears of happiness welled in her eyes as he slipped a wide gold band over her finger. The minister pronounced them man and wife, and then Dalton lifted her veil and kissed her.

Kathy's eyelids fluttered down as his mouth slanted over hers. She had expected a quick peck, but Dalton's arms closed around her and he held her tight, his kiss deep and possessive and more binding on her heart than any words they had said.

The people in the church were standing on their feet, smiling, when they walked up the aisle.

The Worthinghams hosted a party for them following the ceremony. It did Dalton good to see his mother being waited on for a change. She looked so frail. He'd had more substance when he was a ghost than she did now, he thought, and knew that, in spite of her cheerful facade, she didn't have much time left.

The party broke up around five. Dalton and Kathy thanked the Worthinghams for the lovely party. Dalton was surprised when Lawrence Worthingham took him aside and handed him an envelope.

"The bridal suite has been reserved for you tonight. Order anything you want. It's all been taken care of."

Dalton stared at the man. "I don't know what to say."

Worthingham made a dismissive gesture. "You don't have to say anything. It's the least we can do for Julianna's only son. After all these years, she's part of the family."

"Thank you," Dalton said.

Worthingham cleared his throat. "And don't worry about . . . about . . . we've made arrangements for . . . you know."

"Thank you," Dalton said, his voice thick.

Worthingham nodded, squeezed Dalton's shoulder, and left the room.

There was a carriage waiting for them when they left the house.

Kathy looked at the elegant coach, at the two white horses, at the footman clad in the Worthingham livery, and grinned at Dalton. "I feel like Cinderella."

"Who?"

"A princess in a fairy tale."

"I'll bet she wasn't as pretty as you, darlin'."

"The prince wasn't as pretty as you, either," Kathy replied. She rested her head on Dalton's shoulder as the coach pulled away from the house. "This is real, isn't it? I'm not going to wake up and find it's all been a dream?''

''I had a lot of dreams in the last hundred and twenty-five years,'' Dalton replied. ''None of them were like this.''

When they reached the hotel, the footman opened the door and Dalton stepped out of the carriage; then, lifting Kathy into his arms, he carried her into the hotel.

There were several people gathered in the lobby. They all stopped what they were doing as Dalton walked toward the desk.

The clerk grinned from ear to ear as Dalton entered the lobby. ''Room 203, sir,'' he said.

With a nod, Dalton carried Kathy up the stairs.

Cries of congratulations and applause followed them up the stairs.

Kathy was laughing when they reached their room. There was a large bouquet of flowers on the table beside the bed, along with a chilled bottle of champagne and two glasses.

Dalton put Kathy on her feet, then closed and locked the door. ''Alone at last,'' he murmured.

''At last,'' Kathy echoed. She looked up at her handsome husband, a grin hovering on her lips. ''So,'' she asked with mock innocence, ''what do you want to do now?''

''What do you think?'' Dalton growled.

Kathy shrugged. Crossing the floor, she sat down on the edge of the bed and crossed her legs. ''Take a nap? I'm kind of tired.''

"I can think of better uses for that bed than sleeping," Dalton said.

"Really?" Kathy looked up at him and batted her eyelashes. "Like what?"

"Like this," Dalton said, bending over her.

It was magic, she thought, the way one touch of his lips, one stroke of his hand, made her forget everything but how much she wanted him, needed him. Loved him.

She caressed his cheek, delved under his hair to caress the back of his neck.

"Barber wanted to give me a haircut today," he said, his breath warm against her ear. "And I don't mean just a trim."

"No! Dalton, don't ever cut it. I love your hair just the way it is."

"Do you?"

She ran both hands through his hair, loving the feel of it against her skin. His hands were moving, too, unfastening the hooks at the back of her gown, sliding the material over her shoulders, peeling off her chemise.

"What happened to that sexy underwear you had?" He ran his tongue over her bare shoulder.

"I couldn't very well let your mother see it . . . oh, Dalton. . . ."

"Like that, do you?"

"Hmmmm."

"And this?"

He kissed and caressed her out of her gown and undergarments, then fell back on the bed, quiescent and smiling, while she undressed him.

"Married," Kathy murmured. "I can't believe it."

"You're not sorry?" He rose over her, a study in bronze flesh and long black hair.

"No! No, don't even think that." She smiled up at him. "Mrs. Kathy Crowkiller. Sounds nice, don't you think?"

"Kathy . . ." Her name was a groan of desire, a prayer of thanksgiving, as she arched upward, her body taking his and making it a part of her own.

There was no past then, no future, only the wonder of the present and the desire that flamed between them, hot and fierce. Mingled with that desire was a raw, aching need that could be satisfied but never quenched.

Later, lying close together, they toasted each other with champagne, then made love again, and yet again, and Kathy prayed as she had never prayed before, prayed that when the night was over, she would be pregnant with Dalton's child.

Chapter Twenty-three

Julianna had suggested that Kathy and Dalton go to New York City for their honeymoon. Dalton had talked to Kathy about it, and they had decided to stay in Boston.

"There's plenty here to see and do," Kathy explained to Dalton's mother the next day. "I've never been to Boston before, you know."

"This was Dalton's idea, wasn't it?" Julianna said. "He's staying because of me. Well, I won't hear of it."

"Are you trying to get rid of us?" Kathy asked.

"Of course not," Julianna replied quickly, "but it's your honeymoon. I don't want you to feel you're missing anything because of me."

"Don't be silly! We both want to stay," Kathy said. And it was true. She'd always hoped to go to

Boston someday. There were a lot of historical sites she wanted to see, like the Old North Church where the signal, "one if by land and two if by sea," had been given to Paul Revere. "After all, who knows when we'll get back here to see you again?"

A shadow passed through Julianna's eyes, and was gone. "Where is Dalton?"

"He's outside, talking to Murray about stocks and bonds, of all things."

Julianna laughed softly. "Murray's always wanted to indulge in the stock market, but he's never had the nerve. Maybe after I'm . . ."

Kathy looked out the window, wishing she could think of something comforting to say to Julianna.

"Kathy, would you send Dalton in to me, please?"

"Sure." Kathy patted the older woman's hand. "I'll see you later."

A few minutes later, Dalton knocked on his mother's bedroom door. "Ma, you wanted to see me?"

"Come in, Dally."

Dally. No one but his mother had ever dared call him that, and it had been years since she had done so. He entered the room and closed the door behind him.

"Something wrong, Ma?" he asked.

"No, nothing."

Dalton sat down on the edge of the bed. "Something's troubling you," he said. "You might as well tell me what it is."

"I never could hide anything from you, could I?"

"No." He looked at her, really looked at her, and

felt a sudden heaviness in his heart. She looked so tiny, so frail, lying there in the big four-poster bed. Her skin was pale; there were dark shadows under her eyes, hollows in her cheeks. "Ma, I . . ."

"I'm glad you're here, Dally. I prayed you'd come home, that I'd get to see you again before . . ."

Feeling as though he were the adult and his mother the child, he drew her into his arms. "Shh, don't talk like that. You're gonna be fine. Just fine."

She shook her head. "You sound like Murray. He won't talk about it, either."

"Ma . . ."

"I need someone to talk to, Dally."

Dalton blew out a deep breath. "You can talk to me, Ma. You know that."

She looked up at him, her eyes like dark bruises in her face, and then she sagged against him, her face buried against his chest.

"Oh, Dally," she whispered. "I'm so afraid." Her hands clutched at his back. "I've always been afraid of dying, not just of the pain, but of what lies beyond."

"Ma . . ."

"I know, it's silly. Everyone dies, and there's nothing we can do about it. I've always believed in God, but death scares me so." She looked up at him, her eyes dark with fear. "I'm afraid there's nothing after this life, Dally, nothing beyond the grave. I want to believe there is, but I can't, I just can't." She buried her face against his shoulder, her slender body racked with sobs.

Knowing it was probably inappropriate, Dalton

lifted his mother in his arms, then crossed the room and sat down in the rocking chair beside the window.

"Dally, what are you doing?"

"I'm gonna tell you something, Ma," he said as he settled her in his lap. "You're not gonna believe it, and I won't blame you, but it's true."

"What?" She stared at him, her eyes wide with interest.

"Ma, I died."

"Dalton, don't make fun of me."

"I'm not. I was hanged."

"Dally."

"July 28th, Ma. I died that day."

"So, what are you telling me—that you're not really here? That you're a ghost?"

"I was." As quickly and clearly as he could, he told her everything that had happened from the time he followed Lydia Conley into the barn that fateful night.

"You can ask Kathy if you don't believe me," Dalton finished. "I know it's hard to believe, but it's all true, every word. I wasn't sure why we were sent back here. I thought maybe it was so I could fulfill a promise I made to my father, but now I think you're the reason. Maybe I was given a second chance at life to make your passing easier." Dalton rubbed a hand over the back of his neck. "Hell, Ma, I won't blame you if you don't believe me, but it's true. Every word. I swear it."

Julianna stared at him for a long while, and then she shook her head. "It isn't possible."

"That's what I thought."

"You were a ghost for a hundred and twenty-five years?"

Dalton nodded.

"But you never went to heaven?"

"No. But I know it's there, waiting for you, as surely as I know anything."

She stared at him, wanting to believe. Needing to believe. "How do you know?"

Dalton clenched one hand. He had never told anyone what he was about to tell his mother, not even Kathy. Until now, he had always thought maybe he had dreamed the whole thing. Now he wasn't so sure.

"It was right after I died," he said slowly. "I was floating above my body and I realized I wasn't alone. I looked around, and I saw a man in the distance, and I knew it was my father. I called his name, but he didn't seem to hear me, so I walked toward him, and as I drew closer, I saw that he was looking out over a deep green valley. There were Lakota lodges there, and more buffalo than I'd ever seen in my life. And horses grazing alongside a wide river. I recognized an old sorrel mare I'd ridden when I was a boy. You remember the one I mean?"

Julianna nodded. "Go on."

"I saw people, too, and they all looked happy and peaceful. And then my father turned toward me. He looked surprised to see me. He told me he was waiting for you, that you would be there soon. He said when I saw you again I should tell you that he missed you, and that the child you lost before I was born was there, waiting for you, too. And then he told me I wasn't supposed to be there yet, that I still had much to learn.

"I started to ask him what he meant, but . . ." Dalton shook his head. "I don't know how to describe what happened next. It was like a thick fog fell between us, and when it cleared, I was standing alone by the hanging tree."

Dalton stared out the window. If you discounted the hundred and twenty-five years he'd been a ghost, it had only been a few weeks since he'd died.

"That's incredible," Julianna murmured.

"I know."

"And you actually saw Night Caller there?"

"Yeah."

"And he was waiting for me." She smiled softly.

Dalton nodded. "I didn't know you'd lost a child before I was born."

"Your father is the only one who knew. I was six months pregnant when the Crow attacked our village. I lost the baby that night. It was a little girl. We never told anyone.

"Thank you, Dally." She smiled at him, a wonderful radiant smile. "I'm not afraid anymore."

"I'll miss you, Ma."

"And I'll miss you, Dally. But don't grieve for me when I'm gone. Go on with your life, and be happy. Have lots of children." She blew out a long, slow sigh. "I think I'd like to lie down for a little while now."

With a nod, Dalton carried her to bed, and tucked her in. "Sweet dreams, Ma."

"Thank you, Dally, for telling me."

Dalton nodded.

"Dally, are you still earning your living hiring out your gun?"

"No, Ma. Not anymore."

She smiled then, and for a moment she looked young again, the way she had when he was a little boy.

"See ya later, Ma."

She nodded, her eyelids fluttering down, a faint smile lingering on her lips.

When Murray went to look in on her an hour later, she was gone.

Chapter Twenty-four

Dalton stood alone beside his mother's grave. He had endured the words of the preacher, the condolences of his mother's friends, Murray's quiet tears, Kathy's quiet compassion. Now he wanted only to be alone with his memories.

"I'll miss you, Ma," he whispered, and wished he could cry. Maybe tears would dissolve the painful lump in his throat and ease the ache in his chest. It hurt to know he would never see her in this life again, and perhaps not in the next. Heaven knew he didn't deserve the same reward as his mother. He had rarely done a kind or unselfish thing in his whole life. Not like Julianna. Among the Lakota, her generous spirit had been loved and revered. Even here, in Boston, where she had been a servant, she had enriched the lives of others. He knew she'd gone to visit the hospitals on her days off, taking treats to the old and infirm, telling stories to the orphan kids. As long as he could remember, people had been drawn to her, and now she was gone.

He thought about the vision he'd had, of his father standing on the edge of a deep green valley. As from far away, he seemed to hear the scree of an eagle. But there were no eagles here, in the city.

And then, looking beyond this life, he saw his father turn away from the valley, saw him smile as he held out his hand. And his mother was there, her smile serene as she placed her hand in that of her husband. Side by side, they walked back to the valley and disappeared through the mists of time. . . .

Dalton drew in a deep breath and let it out in a long, slow sigh. All this time, he'd thought he had been sent back to fulfill the vow he'd made to his father, but that hadn't been the reason at all. It was to quiet his mother's fear of death, to see her safely along the path of spirits into the next world.

He knew it with a sureness deep inside himself and knew, in that same instant, that his time in this place was almost gone.

Kathy stood up as Dalton entered the room. She knew, before he said a word, that something was very wrong.

"Dalton, are you all right?"

"Yeah, fine."

Crossing the floor, he drew her gently into his arms and held her close.

"I'm sorry about your mother. I wish I'd had time to get to know her better."

He nodded. "She was fond of you, too."

Kathy rested her cheek on his chest. "So, what are we going to do now?"

"I need to take you back to Saul's Crossing."

A whisper of coldness slid down Kathy's spine. "Take me back?"

Dalton blew out a deep sigh. "Yes."

"I thought maybe you'd want to stay here for a while, to be with Murray."

"Murray will be fine. He's gonna quit his job and go stay with his sister in South Carolina."

"Oh." Her hands moved restlessly up and down Dalton's back. "What aren't you telling me?"

He drew her over to the sofa and pulled her down beside him. "All this time, I thought we'd come back here so I'd have a chance to fulfill the promise I made to my father, and because we were meant to be together, and this was the only way."

"Go on."

"But I know now it was because of my mother. She'd been praying that she'd get to see me again before she died."

"Well, that seems perfectly natural. I mean, you're her son."

"I know. But the reason she needed to see me was because I was the only one who could ease her fears about dying. That last day, I told her that I'd been dead, that I'd seen my father waiting for her on the other side."

"You saw your father? You never told me that."

"I was never sure if it really happened until I talked to my mother and saw how afraid she was. And then I knew why I was here."

"But why am I here?"

"I don't know. But . . ."

"What?"

"I think my time is about over."

Kathy grabbed his arm. "No!"

"If you're going to get back to your own time, we have to get you back to Saul's Crossing, back to the hanging tree."

"I don't want to leave you."

"I know." He wrapped his arms around her and held her tightly. "I don't want to leave you, either, darlin'. You're the best thing that ever happened to me. But I can't shake this feeling."

They bade farewell to Murray and the Worthinghams two days later. Kathy blinked back her tears as she waved good-bye to Murray from the train window. Ever since the funeral, the feeling had grown stronger in her that she had been caught up in a tide of time and events and that she no longer had control over her own life, her own destiny.

She sat at the window and watched the city disappear from sight. Taffy Girl and the stallion were in the stock car. Dalton had decided to take the train as far as possible, then take a stage the rest of the way.

She placed her hand over her belly, wondering if she was really pregnant, or if she was just imagining it because she wanted so badly for it to be true. She hadn't said anything to Dalton. He had enough on his mind as it was, and she didn't know if her news, coming now, would make him feel better or worse.

She tried to remember when she'd had her last period, but she had been irregular since Wayne passed away.

A son, she thought, with Dalton's tawny skin and black hair and dark eyes. A baby, created out of their love for one another.

She thought of little else on the long trip back to Montana.

They arrived in Saul's Crossing just before dusk. Kathy felt a sense of unease as they left the horses at the livery and made their way to Martha's Boardinghouse. Something bad was in the air. She had never been so certain of anything in her life.

Martha welcomed them with a smile that quickly turned to a frown when she saw the way Dalton looked at Kathy. Her sharp eyes noticed Kathy's wedding ring and her frowned deepened.

"It's all right," Dalton said. "She isn't my cousin."

"No? Why the subterfuge?"

"It's a long story," Dalton said. "Maybe I'll tell it to you sometime."

"Well, I wish you would," Martha replied. "I'm sure it's a dilly."

Dalton looked at Kathy and grinned. "It is that," he said.

Martha shook her head as she glanced from one to the other. "My, my," she said, and then she chuckled. "I declare, I can't wait to see Mr. Petty's face when he hears this." She patted Kathy on the shoulder. "He had quite a crush on you, you know."

Not knowing what to say, Kathy smiled, then shrugged.

Martha wished them well, declaring they would have to have a wedding celebration at supper that night. "A cake," she said, "I'll have to bake a cake."

"We'd like to rest a while and then freshen up," Dalton said. "Think we could get some hot water in about . . ." He looked at Kathy, his eyes hot. "Say, in about an hour?"

"Of course." Martha beamed at them, then bustled off toward the kitchen, muttering something about needing more eggs.

Dalton looked at Kathy, a faint smile on his lips. "Your room or mine?"

"It doesn't matter."

"Yours," he decided, and then he winked at her. "It's got a bigger bed."

They had spent the day bouncing around in a stagecoach and she'd been thinking of a bath and a nap, but the look in Dalton's eyes made her forget how tired she was, made her forget everything but how much she loved him.

Dalton closed the door, then drew Kathy into his arms, aware that this might be their last night together. He had never been more conscious of time passing, knowing that every second brought them that much closer to parting.

He had thought of little else on the journey from Boston. The feeling that their time together was almost over had grown stronger with every passing mile.

And now, holding her in his arms, he was overcome with a desperate need to bury himself within her, to imprint her memory deep in his mind so that he might cherish it through the long years of eternity. Even hell would not be so bad, if he could remember Kathy's face, her smile, the sound of her laughter, the way she always melted against him, as if she wanted to be a part of him. And she was a part of him, he thought, the best part.

With a groan, he carried her to the bed and stretched out beside her, his hands and lips moving over her, memorizing every inch of her face, the touch of her, the taste of her. He buried his face in her hair and took a deep breath, filling his nostrils with her scent.

His desperation telegraphed itself to Kathy, and she clung to him, driven by the need to hold him close, to absorb his very essence.

She took him deep inside her body, inside her heart, her soul, felt the world fall away until there were only the two of them, clinging together. She whispered that she loved him over and over again, the fervent words inadequate to express the feelings of her heart.

She felt a wetness on her cheeks and knew she was crying, and when she opened her eyes, she saw that there were tears in Dalton's eyes, too.

"*Ohinyan, wastelakapi,*" he murmured. Forever, beloved.

* * *

372

Martha had, indeed, planned a celebration. She had set the table with her best Sunday china and prepared all of Dalton's favorites—steak and fried potatoes and baked beans. She served wine with dinner, and then offered everyone cake and champagne.

Hyrum Petty had sighed with regret when he learned of their marriage, and then slapped Dalton on the arm. "You're a lucky man," he declared. "A right lucky man."

Dalton had looked at Kathy and nodded. "Yes," he had replied soberly. "I am."

Enid Canfield wished them a long and happy life together.

Kathy looked at Dalton and prayed it would be so.

Later, they went for a walk on the outskirts of town.

"We'll ride out to the hanging tree tomorrow morning," Dalton said.

"So soon? Maybe if we never go back there, everything will be all right." But even as she said the words, she had the feeling that she was being inexplicably drawn back to the Triple Bar C, that no matter how she tried to avoid it, her time in the past was coming to an end.

They stopped in the shadows, reaching for each other. Kathy stood in the circle of Dalton's arms, wondering why she had been transported into the past, why she had met Dalton in the first place, if they weren't meant to be together.

"Maybe we aren't going to be separated," Kathy said, voicing the hope in her heart. "Maybe we need to go back to the ranch for some other reason."

"Maybe."

"Maybe whatever force sent us here will send us both back to the future."

"Maybe."

"But you don't think so."

"I don't know, darlin'." He rested his chin on top of her head and closed his eyes, knowing he would rather face the hanging rope again than lose Kathy. And yet he knew, knew in the deepest part of his soul, that they were going to be parted, that she was destined to go back to her own world where she belonged, and that his soul would at last complete the journey it had started a hundred and twenty-five years ago, to spend the rest of eternity in whatever heaven or hell awaited him.

"I love you," Kathy said. "I'll love you as long as I live."

"Kathy, ah, Kathy, darlin' . . ."

"I know."

Hand in hand, they walked back to the boarding-house. They made love again, then held each other close all through the night. And Kathy prayed again, prayed fervently that she was pregnant, that she would have Dalton's child to love when he was gone.

In the morning, they made love again. Kathy clung to Dalton, cherishing what she knew would be their last moments together. Each word was filled with bit-tersweet sorrow, each touch a renewal of the love that burned in her heart.

They left the boardinghouse a short time later. Ka-thy was wearing the green plaid dress she had bought in Boston. She had packed her buckskin dress and moccasins in her saddlebags.

Walking down the dusty street beside Dalton, she felt like a condemned man on his way to the gallows.

A short time later, they were riding out toward the Conley Ranch.

They reached the hanging tree a little before eleven.

Dalton dismounted and tethered his stallion to a bush. He patted the horse's neck, then vaulted up onto Taffy Girl's back. His arm slid around Kathy's waist and he drew her back against him, silently praying for a miracle that would allow them to stay together.

Kathy leaned against him. This was where she belonged, she thought. Here, in his arms, always. Several minutes passed.

"I don't feel anything," she said. She felt a faint stirring of hope. Maybe she would be allowed to stay here, with Dalton.

"Me, either."

She looked at him over her shoulder. "I don't want to leave you."

"I don't want you to go."

"I wish . . ."

". . . that we could be together always . . ."

They spoke the words as on a single breath, the words muffled as their lips met.

Kathy moaned, "no, no," as a familiar dizziness overcame her.

She screamed Dalton's name as the world grew dark, spinning her into a churning vortex. There was a dull roaring in her ears, a sound like distant thunder.

As from far away, she heard Dalton's voice, a hoarse whisper filled with anguish and despair.

Kathy, Kathy, remember me . . .

She cried his name again, and then everything went black.

Chapter Twenty-five

He was gone when she opened her eyes. Heavy-hearted, she urged Taffy Girl toward the house, hoping, praying, that somehow he would be waiting for her there.

"Let him be a ghost again," she begged. "Please. I don't care if he's real or not, just don't take him away from me."

She rode to the barn, dismounted, and led the mare inside, hoping against hope that Dalton would be there. But the barn was empty.

She brushed Taffy Girl, forked her some fresh hay, filled the water barrel.

Please . . .

She started at every sound, real or imagined, always hoping that he would be there, that she would look over her shoulder and find him smiling his roguish smile, one black brow cocked in wry amusement.

Carrying the saddle to the back of the barn, she draped it over the rack, then opened the pouch where she had packed the buckskin dress and moccasins. They were gone.

Refusing to relinquish her hope, she went to the house. Everything was as she had left it. There were several messages on her answering machine from her mother, several more from John, one from her father, another from her brother. She listened to them, hardly hearing the words, not caring that they had been worried about her. She wondered fleetingly how long she had been gone, but didn't care enough to find out. She felt dead inside, cold, empty, lifeless.

Slowly, she went from room to room. *Please be here.*

She stood in her bedroom, remembering the night she had held a gun on him and threatened to call the police, remembering how frightened she had been.

Please . . . She went into the bathroom. Standing in the doorway, she remembered hanging the curtain rod and slipping on the edge of the tub, and how good it had felt to be in his arms when he caught her.

She wandered into the kitchen, recalling the nights she had sat at the table, listening as Dalton told her the story of his life, remembering the day he had followed her into Saul's Crossing, the day they had gone over to the Holcomb ranch to buy Taffy Girl, the day they had ridden down to the hanging tree . . .

The hanging tree! Of course. If he was anywhere, he would be there.

Leaving the house, she ran down the path, her heart pounding.

Breathless, she placed her hands on the rough bark of the trunk, praying that she would feel that brush of cool air that meant Dalton was near.

Please!

She stood there for a long while, hardly aware of the tears that washed down her cheeks.

"Dalton, come back to me. Please come back to me."

She stared up at the tree, waiting, wishing, but nothing happened. The sun was warm on her face; the air was still.

"He was real," she said. "I know he was. I couldn't have made it all up. I couldn't have."

He had been real. He had told her the story of his life. They had traveled into the past. She hadn't dreamed it. She couldn't have. There had to be a way to prove it had happened.

The diary! She ran back to the house and up the stairs. In the bedroom, she jerked open the dresser drawer and grabbed Lydia's diary, quickly flipping through the pages to July 4th.

She quickly skimmed the first few sentences, until she came to the passage about the dance that night.

. . . a repeat of the one held in the spring. At last, when I had given up all hope, Dalton arrived with the woman claiming to be his cousin. Cousin, indeed! The little whore. Could not believe it when Russell asked her to dance, but I didn't care, as it left me alone with Dalton.

Kathy blew out a sigh. She hadn't imagined it then. It had happened, all of it, just as she remembered.

With a sigh, she began reading again, hoping to find a clue as to what had happened to Dalton.

Asked Dalton who she really is, but he said she was just a friend. He must think I'm a fool, if he expects me to believe that. Wanting to be alone with him, I tried to get him to take me outside, but he refused, and then, all too soon, Russell was there.

How my heart burned when I saw the way Dalton smiled at that woman. He had no qualms about taking her outside. I watched for him the rest of the night, but they never returned to the dance.

July 5th.
This morning, I learned that Dalton is no longer working for Russell.

July 10th.
Russell went to town today. Tonight, at dinner, he mentioned that Dalton and that woman had left town together the day after the dance.

August 15th.
Dalton has still not returned, nor does anyone seem to know of his whereabouts.

August 30th.
The impossible has happened. I am in the fam-

ily way . . . Russell will never let me go now. . . .

Putting the diary aside, Kathy switched on her computer and pulled up the web page that had sketched Dalton's life.

Crowkiller, Dalton (1844–?). Born in Dakota Territory, Crowkiller gained notoriety when he killed Hager Whittaker in a gunfight in Virginia City.

Crowkiller is believed to have gunned down more than two dozen men in cold blood. Nothing is known of his death. There is speculation that he retired from gunfighting and changed his name, but there are no known facts to substantiate this theory.

Kathy read the short article three times. It was true. They had traveled into the past and changed history. Lydia didn't go insane. Dalton wasn't hanged.

What had happened to him? Had he stayed in the past when she was swept back into the future, or had his soul finally found the rest it had been denied for the last hundred and twenty-five years? There had to be a way to find out. Tomorrow, she would go into town and go to the library. Perhaps she could find something there. She had to know.

Suddenly weary, she went downstairs and curled up on the sofa. Maybe, if she was lucky, she would dream of Dalton.

Chapter Twenty-six

At first, he thought he was dreaming. His body felt lighter than air, and for a moment, he thought he was in the nether world between heaven and hell again, that he was destined to spend eternity in a formless gray cloud. Not a bad thing, he thought, and knew he would count himself lucky if he could just be a ghost again, with Kathy again.

Gradually, the gray haze thinned, then disappeared. The colors he saw were brighter, clearer; the sky was an incredible shade of blue.

And then he saw the lodges spread across the floor of the valley, and he knew where he was.

A man appeared in the distance, a tall man clad in white buckskins. A woman stood beside him, all pain and fear gone from her eyes, a radiant smile on her face.

There was no need for words. A thought willed him to his mother's side, and he felt tears sting his eyes as he embraced her, and then his father.

"Dally," his mother said, her voice tremulous. "Oh, Dally."

"Hi, Ma."

She smiled at him, alive and radiant. And then her smile faded. "You can't stay here, Dally."

Dalton laughed a short, bitter laugh. "Is heaven throwing me out again?"

"You have not yet lived out your span of years," his father explained. "You have a long life ahead of you."

Dalton shook his head. "I don't want to go back. There's nothing waiting for me there."

"Kathy is waiting for you," Julianna said quietly.

His heart clenched at the sound of her name. "Kathy?"

"Of course. The two of you are fated to be together. She carries your child."

A bright flame of hope caught fire in Dalton's heart. "You mean I can go back, to her time?"

"If that is your wish."

He nodded, unable to speak past the lump in his throat. Kathy. To be with her again, to hold her, to love her. "What do I have to do?"

"Nothing," his father said. "All that was needed was for you to decide where you wished to spend the remainder of your life."

"Have a care, Dally," his mother urged. "Few are given a second chance at life. Make the most of it."

"I will."

She hugged him again, hard. "Be happy."

Her words echoed in his ears . . . *be happy . . . be happy* . . . echoed and faded and he found himself drifting, falling, spiraling through a familiar gray mist.

When awareness returned, the sun was just climbing over the horizon, and he was standing beneath the hanging tree.

Chapter Twenty-seven

She was dreaming, she thought, a glorious dream from which she hoped she would never awake.

Dalton's voice was whispering in her ear. *Ohinyan, wastelakapi. Ohinyan . . . Ohinyan . . .*

She felt his lips brush her cheek, felt the bed sag as he stretched out beside her, and it was so real, so real. She squeezed her eyes shut, hardly daring to breathe for fear she would awake and find it all a dream.

"Kathy?"

His voice, filled with tenderness and the sound of unshed tears. It sounded so real.

"Kathy, darlin', wake up."

"No."

"Please?"

"No." She shook her head. "If I wake up, you'll be gone."

"I'll never leave you again, darlin', I swear it."

Afraid to believe, desperate to believe, she slowly opened her eyes to find him bending over her, his hair falling forward over his shoulders, his dark eyes glowing with love.

"Dalton! Is it really you?" She touched his cheek, ran her hands over his chest. His skin was warm, vital, alive beneath her fingertips.

"I missed you," he said.

She nodded. "How? How is it possible for you to be here? What happened to you? Where did you go?"

He laughed softly as he sat up and drew her into his arms. "You remember that valley I told you about, the one I thought I'd dreamed?"

Kathy nodded.

"I went there again. My mother was there, with my father. They told me my time wasn't up yet, that I had a long life ahead of me." His gaze held hers. "Ma said you were pregnant. Is it true?"

"I think so."

"Why didn't you tell me before?"

"Well, I'm not a hundred percent sure, and . . ." She shrugged. "You seemed so certain we were going to be separated—I thought it would make it harder if you knew."

"Yeah, I reckon it would have."

"I still can't believe you're here."

"Believe it, darlin'. I'm here, and I'm never gonna leave you again."

"As if I'd ever let you go." She hugged him

tightly. "I guess you were right. We really were fated to be together."

"Together," he repeated. *"Ohinyan, wastelak-api."*

"Ohinyan," she murmured.

"I love you, Kathy Crowkiller," he said softly, fervently. "More than life itself."

"Show me," she whispered.

And he did, every day for the rest of their lives.

Epilogue

The Triple Bar C
Spring, five years later

"Hurry, Mom."

"I'm coming," Kathy said. "I hope we're not too late." Lifting the hem of her nightgown, she hurried after her oldest daughter. Julianna was four, and the spitting image of her father.

As they neared the barn door, she could hear Dalton's voice.

"Easy, girl," he said, his voice low and soothing. "Easy, now, Mama. One more push."

Kathy peered over the side of the stall. Taffy Girl lay stretched out on her side. "How's she doing?"

"Fine." Dalton stroked the mare's neck.

"Does it hurt?" Julianna asked.

"A little," Dalton said. "Look, here it comes."

The mare gave a mighty heave and the foal slipped out of the birth canal onto a pile of fresh, sweet-smelling straw.

There was a flurry of activity as the mare nosed the baby, inhaling her offspring's scent, then lurched to her feet. Dalton peeled away the last of the membrane from the foal, then dried the foal off with a soft cotton towel.

"It's a filly," he said.

Julianna clapped her hands. "I'm gonna name her Buttermilk."

Dalton smiled at Kathy. "You're crying."

"I can't help it," Kathy said, wiping her eyes. "It's so incredibly beautiful."

Dalton looked at his daughter and nodded. He had been there when Julianna was born. Never, in all his life, had he seen anything to compare with the miracle of watching his daughter come into the world. And then, two years later, his son had been born. And now Kathy was pregnant again.

They stood there for the next hour, watching the filly struggle to stand up. Only when she was steady on her feet and nursing did they leave the barn.

Dalton lifted Julianna in one arm and draped his other arm around Kathy's shoulders. He was a lucky man, he mused as they walked toward the house. He had a beautiful, loving wife, two healthy children and another on the way, the ranch he had always dreamed of.

It was another miracle, he thought, that he had

found his greatest blessings here, on land he had once cursed.

He carried Julianna up to bed and tucked her in, then went to check on his son. David, named for Kathy's father, was asleep, his arm wrapped around his favorite stuffed dinosaur. Dalton stood at his son's bedside for a moment, then padded quietly out of the room and down the stairs.

He found Kathy standing on the porch, watching the sun rise. Easing up behind her, he slid his arms around her waist. She leaned back against him, and he placed his hands over the softly rounded swell of her stomach, silently thanking God for giving him a second chance at life, for giving him this woman who filled his arms and his life.

She had finished writing the story of his past. One day, when their children were old enough, he would let them read it.

It was a hell of a story, he thought, one that would have ended very differently if it wasn't for the woman in his arms.

The rising sun rose over the ranch like a benediction, bathing the land and its buildings in a warm golden glow, and as Dalton Crowkiller followed his wife into the house, he knew he couldn't have been richer if the land was sprinkled with gold dust and the driveway paved with silver, because Kathy was the true treasure of his life, worth far more than any wealth the world had to offer.

Hi all:

Hope you're all having a wonderful summer, and that you enjoyed *Under a Prairie Moon.* Some books are special, and this is one of them. Dalton Crowkiller burrowed deep into my heart and hasn't let go.

I was saddened last year to learn of the death of Eddie Little Sky. Eddie used to dance at Disneyland many years ago. He was an "older" man, tall, dark and handsome, and sexy as all get-out, surely one of the best looking men I've ever seen. I watched him dance, and I fell in love with Eddie and with Indians, and my respect and affection for both remains to this day. When I started writing, it was Eddie I saw in my mind, and I modeled Dancer and Shadow and Dalton and all my other Indian heroes after him.

On a happier note, my thanks to all of you who have written to me via E-mail or snail mail this past year. I enjoy your letters. Thank you for your kind words and support.

God bless you all.

Madeline

BESTSELLING AUTHOR OF
THE PANTHER AND THE PEARL

He rides from out of the Turkish wilderness atop a magnificent charger. Dark and mysterious, Malik Bey sweeps Boston-bred Amelia Ryder into an exotic world of sultans and revolutionaries, magnificent palaces and desert camps. Amy wants to hate her virile abductor, to escape his heated glances forever. But with his suave manners and seductive charm, the hard-bodied rebel is no mere thief out to steal the proper young beauty's virtue. And as hot days melt into sultry nights, Amy grows ever closer to surrendering to unending bliss in Malik's fiery embrace.

_4015-8 $5.99 US/$6.99 CAN

MIDNIGHT FIRE

MADELINE BAKER

**"Lovers of Indian Romance have a special place on
their bookshelves for Madeline Baker!"**
—*Romantic Times*

A half-breed who has no use for a frightened girl fleeing an
unwanted wedding, Morgan thinks he wants only the money
Carolyn Chandler offers him to guide her across the plains,
but halfway between Galveston and Ogallala, where the
burning prairie meets the endless night sky, he makes her
his woman. There in the vast wilderness, Morgan swears
to change his life path, to fulfill the challenge of his vision
quest—anything to keep Carolyn's love.

_4056-5 $5.99 US/$6.99 CAN

A WANTED MAN.
AN INNOCENT WOMAN.
A WANTON LOVE!

Renegade Heart
Madeline Baker

When beautiful Rachel Halloran took Logan Tyree into her home, he was unconscious. A renegade Indian with a bullet wound in his side and a price on his head, he needed her help. But to Rachel he was nothing but trouble, a man whose dark sensuality made her long for forbidden pleasures; to her father he was the answer to a prayer, a gunslinger whose legendary skill could rid the ranch of a powerful enemy.

But Logan Tyree would answer to no man—and to no woman. If John Halloran wanted his services, he would have to pay dearly for them. And if Rachel wanted his loving, she would have to give up her innocence, her reputation, her very heart and soul.

_4085-9 $5.99 US/$6.99 CAN

APACHE RUNAWAY

MADELINE BAKER

RECKLESS LOVE

MADELINE BAKER

"Madeline Baker's Indian romances should not be missed!"
—*Romantic Times*

Joshua Berdeen is the cavalry soldier who has traveled the country in search of lovely Hannah Kincaid. Josh offers her a life of ease in New York City and all the finer things.

Two Hawks Flying is the Cheyenne warrior who has branded Hannah's body with his searing desire. Outlawed by the civilized world, he can offer her only the burning ecstasy of his love. But she wants no soft words of courtship when his hard lips take her to the edge of rapture...and beyond.

_3869-2 $5.99 US/$7.99 CAN